Legacy

SHERIDAN ANNE

A DARK SECRET SOCIETY REVERSE HAREM

Sheridan Anne

Legacy: Empire (Book 2)

First Published in 2023

Anne, Sheridan

Legacy: Empire #1

Cover Design: Sheridan Anne
Photographer: Tatyaby
Editing: Fox Proof Editing
Formatting: Sheridan Anne
Alpha Team: Holly Swain-Harvey & Kat Uluave

To my high school boyfriends,

You're all assholes. Fuck you.

And yes, your junk smelled weird—I'm looking at you, Michael! There's a reason I never went near it. I mean, clean that shit up! Is basic personal hygiene really so hard to achieve?

God, that feels good to finally get that off my chest!

Oh, and no, this doesn't include the one high school asshole I married. He's okay, I guess!

CHAPTER 1

Oakley

Zade DeVil is a raging cunt.

If he ever felt the overwhelming need to eat my ass, I wouldn't hesitate to let out a little fart right into that motherfucker's face. And I hope the asshole gets pink eye. Actually, he deserves a shitload more than a bad case of pink eye. He deserves a life of misery for what his bullshit Empire has put me through. He deserves to share in my fate—his heart torn right out of his fucking chest.

I'm. His. Sacrifice. A pawn used in Empire's sick fucking games.

If I had known this was the shit waiting for me in Faders Bay, I never would have returned. But something tells me that no matter where I was in the world, he would have found me. Zade won't rest until it's my heart served up on a fucking platter.

Since the moment I got here, Zade and his crew of loyal assholes have done everything in their power to haunt me. They stalked me through the streets, watched me as I worked, and didn't allow me out of their sight for one fucking second. I'd understand it if they were the overbearing jealous boyfriend types, always needing to keep tabs on their girl, but that's not it at all.

I'm their target. Their fucking game. Zade's one-way ticket to claiming the power of Empire—a society which should rightfully be mine.

They made me into a fool. I was their puppet with strings welded to my body like cast iron cuffs. They led me right into their trap, and I followed them blindly.

Never again.

I clench my jaw as I grip the small piece of paper, rolling the weathered note between my fingers. It's a stark reminder of Empire's brutal betrayal.

I've memorized every fucking word.

One cannot flourish in the power of Empire without first giving his soul.
A sacrifice to be made, an innocent life to be lost.
In sixty suns and sixty moons, he shall sacrifice an innocent in the hour before dawn.
Her still beating heart carved from her body, he shall offer it to the sacred fortress.

For this is his offering to his Empire. This is his sacred ritual to bind him in blood.

Like I said, Zade DeVil is a raging cunt.

What kind of fucked-up bullshit is this anyway? Who just decides they're gonna find a girl and tear her heart out of her chest so they can offer it up to their people for power? I mean, fuck. I've heard of some messed-up culty shit over the years, but it's always in movies or on true crime documentaries, not in real life. And it especially does not happen to me. I'm supposed to graduate college and make a life for myself.

Instead, I'm sitting here in Empire's darkened prison cell, across from a man who I thought was dead.

My father.

Matthias Quinn.

The man was killed when I was eight years old in the line of duty. He was a fireman, and up until an hour ago, I thought this was all true.

Empire took him away from me. I was told my father was dead, and I was sent to live with my aunt in Missouri as the ghost of my father haunted me. I grieved for him. Cried for the father I'd lost, and I fought my way out of the darkness in the hope of trying to have some kind of semblance of a real life. He was my best friend, and I was the apple of his eye. All of it was taken in an instant.

If I'd known he was down here in the putrid cells of Empire this whole time . . . fuck. Twelve years stolen from him, and all for what? Being the bastard child of the DeVil legacy, the real heir of Empire?

This world is callous and cruel. A place where broken souls come to die.

Fuck, if this is what this place does to its sole living blood heir, then I don't want anything to do with it. Though, I suppose what I want doesn't matter. The second Zade gets his hands on me, I'm all but dead. My only hope is that whoever locked me up in this cell has enough of a brain not to utter a single word to Zade. Only one question remains now; would I rather die quickly by Zade's hand or rot in this cell until my dying day?

Fuck those options.

I'm not ready to lay down and die here, and I'm definitely not going to let Zade get his hands on me without a fight. I'll do whatever I have to in order to save myself, even if it means killing the bastard who wants me dead.

My ass quickly grows numb on the cold concrete, and I drop my head into my hands, trying to figure out how the hell this became my life. One minute, I thought I was getting railed within an inch of my life by the intriguing stranger I met outside of my apartment complex, and the next thing I know, I'm wrapped up in this bullshit.

And it all started with Dalton fucking Eros and his ginormous pierced cock. I shouldn't have fallen for it, but the second he ordered me onto my knees and told me he was my god, I was putty in his wicked hands.

I think his betrayal hurts the most. It's not as though I was expecting anything to come from our strange little infatuation, but at least the others never pretended to be anything they weren't. He deceived me, allowed me to think he was there to protect me. Fuck him and his huge cock.

Hell, fuck them all. Sawyer and Easton too. All four of them deceived me in the worst way and offered me protection for the sole purpose of saving me for Zade to slaughter me himself. I suppose this is what I get for being such a whore for good dick.

"You're thinking too much," a voice across the basement says.

A shiver sails down my spine, still unable to believe he's really here. I lift my head from my hands and meet my father's haunted stare, hating every bit of this. I used to dream of being reunited with my father, back when I stood awkwardly to the side at the daddy-daughter dances in school. But this isn't what I had in mind. I pictured him coming back to me unscathed, loving me and spoiling me as he always had, but this . . . I never wanted this. To learn he's been down here this whole time suffering has my heart shattering into a million pieces.

I can't lie though, if I have to be down in these cells, then I'm glad I have someone on my side. There's not a lot of people in this world I can trust, but my father . . . All he ever wanted was what's best for me.

"Oh, I'm sorry," I mutter, unsure why I'm giving him such an attitude when I should be trying to figure out how the hell to get us both out of here. "I wasn't aware there was much else for me to do down here."

My father scoffs. "Twelve years later and you're still a brat." His voice is gruff, but I hear a distinct happiness in his tone, something he's surely missed over the years. "Trust me, O, I wasted years fuming about the people who put me in here. It does you no good. Think about the good times, the people you love. Otherwise, you're left with nothing but a cold bitterness, and it makes for a very lonely life."

Letting out a sigh, I scramble across my cell, pressing my body against the bars to be as close to my father as possible. I grip the cold metal as a soft tear tracks down my dirty face and drops to my collarbone. "I can't let it go," I tell him. "They're not even the ones who put me in here, but what they did . . . what they want with me . . . I'm never going to be free from them. They'll hunt me down and they won't stop until I'm dead."

My father creeps closer, moving right up against the bars, his weathered blue eyes staring into mine. "Since the day you were born, you've had a target on your back. Your days are numbered here, Oakley, just as mine are," he tells me. "As long as my blood runs through your veins, you'll never be free."

I grip the bars tighter, my chest sinking under the weight of undeniable hopelessness. "But I didn't ask for this," I cry. "I don't understand. It's not like I'm breaking down doors and demanding to rule over this shit and challenging anyone for power. I just . . . I don't want anything to do with it."

"I know," my father says. "I gave everything I had to try and shield you from the dark side of this world, but Empire has a way of punishing those who do not embrace their values."

I scoff. "Don't try to sugarcoat it. Empire punishes those who are a threat to their bullshit."

My father shakes his head, and there's a slight hesitation flashing in his eyes. "While this is true, there is so much more depth to Empire than you could ever understand, my sweet girl. Yes, we are callous and cruel at the best of times, but there are reasons for everything we do."

"We?" I question, disgust pulsing through my veins. "After everything, after they took you away from me and let you rot down here in this cell for twelve years, after offering me up on a silver fucking platter for Zade DeVil's twisted ritual, you still consider yourself one of them?"

"I . . . what do you mean Zade's ritual?" he questions, his whole body stiffening as his piercing eyes seem to hold me captive. "The leadership ritual?"

"Yes," I say. "I don't know much about it. Just that your people gave him my name and all of a sudden, I'm as good as dead. I was happy living my life before any of this."

"How is this possible?" he questions, barely taking note of a damn word I'm saying. "For Zade to be partaking in this ritual, it must mean—"

"That Lawson DeVil is dead," a cold voice says from deeper in the cells.

My head whips to the right as I peer into the darkness, my heart racing with fear. I thought we were alone in here, thought it was just us left to rot in Empire's twisted cells.

Movement catches my attention, and I watch with bated breath as a familiar face steps out of the darkness, moving right up against the bars of his cell. My eyes widen, my heart leaping right out of my chest, remembering the vile plans this man had for me.

Nikolai Thorne stares right back at me, not a hint of regret in his eyes. I'd stupidly come to Empire, seeking answers to the questions his very son refused to give me, when he decided to take it into his own hands to slaughter me. Hell, as much as I want to pulverize Zade, if he hadn't come when he did, I would have been long gone.

I've been so wrapped up in my own fears that I didn't even give it a second to think there could be others down here. I should have known. I was there when Zade had Sawyer's father locked up with the intention to face The Circle with a private trial, something Sawyer had referred to as a death sentence.

"Fuck," my father continues, completely unaware of the way my world has begun folding in on itself. I can't be locked up with this man. I can't face him every day with the memories of what he was going to do to me. Though, I suppose it could be worse. It's not as though he was being violent. He was actually quite a gentleman about it.

My father pushes off the bars and paces the length of his small cell, shaking his head as he clenches his jaw, his hands balling into tight fists. "When?"

"When what?" Nikolai questions, sounding bored of the conversation. "When was Lawson slaughtered like cattle, or when will his son rise in his wake?"

My father grips the bars again, rage burning in his eyes. "Both."

Nikolai sighs. "Lawson was killed a little over a month ago. Zade made the sacred vows over the flames of his father's remains, and now—"

"Sixty suns and sixty moons."

"Wait—what?" I cut in, horror rocking through my body. "Sacred vows over his father's remains? What the fuck are you talking about?

What kind of messed-up, culty bullshit is this?"

Nikolai sends me a sharp glare, and I'm promptly ignored again. "What's this got anything to do with my daughter?" my father roars, his deep rumble echoing down the long line of cold cells.

"What do you think?" Nikolai questions, his voice like a wicked taunt in the night. "She's his sacrifice. The innocent life that must be lost."

My father falls away, shaking his head in horror. "No," he breathes. "You can't do that. The Circle can't do that. She's my heir, the only real blood heir of Empire. To kill her would be to betray the blood."

I scoff. "Yeah, well, something tells me that Nikolai doesn't give a shit about betraying the blood."

"You watch your mouth, girl," Nikolai spits. "You don't know anything about my loyalties or just how far I would go to protect them. It did not please me to hurt you. I do not get off on violence like others within my rank. However, if there were a chance that I could have taken the leadership for myself, nothing would have held me back."

My father locks his sharp stare back on me. "What the hell are you talking about?"

"The asshole tried to kill me himself, sputtering some shit about if I were to die, Zade wouldn't be able to complete his ritual, and without any other heir to step up in his place, he'd be able to campaign for power. How do you think the asshole ended up in here?"

My father lets out a barking laugh. "You?" he spits at Nikolai. "You thought my people would have followed you? What a fucking joke."

"Your people?" Nikolai throws right back at him. "They were never your people. You were never fit to lead. You might have the blood in your veins, but that was never enough. You would have burned Empire to the ground. We had no choice but to get rid of you, for the sake of our people."

"That's a load of shit, and you know it," he spits. "Tell me, just how easily was Lawson DeVil able to manipulate you? The blood never even ran through his veins and yet you were at his beck and call, ready to betray everything our fathers fought for. It's greedy motherfuckers like you who will burn Empire to the ground. Just look around you, Nikolai. The only blood heirs Empire has left are rotting in cells while those frauds are out there trying to work out how to steal the power for themselves."

A smirk pulls at the corner of Nikolai's lips. "If only it were that easy," he says. "But unfortunately for you, no one knows you exist. I can't betray the blood when there's no record of a blood heir ever being born. As far as I'm concerned, Lawson DeVil was the rightful leader, and on paper, I was a faithful servant."

My father lets out a heavy breath, shaking his head. After all, he knows Nikolai is right. My father's existence was the best kept secret Empire has ever had, something men like Lawson DeVil and Nikolai Thorne would have gone to extreme lengths to keep buried. And now, I suppose that means Zade, too.

"Tell me how I can save her," he says, begging.

Nikolai's soft laugh is like a knife right through my chest. "You know just as well as I do, Matthias, you can't save her. This is her fate.

Zade DeVil will find her, and when the time comes, he will carve her heart right out of her chest and offer it as his sacrifice."

A chill sails down my spine, and I stumble back a step, wishing there were something I could do. Anything that could save me from the horrors of Zade's knife.

"Please, Nikolai. What if this was your son, your daughter?" Dad pushes. "Surely you couldn't sit back and accept it?"

"You're right, I wouldn't just sit back. I would tell them to hold their head high with pride," he says. "Giving one's life for such a cause is admirable. You should be honored that your daughter is seen to hold such value within our ranks."

"Value?" my father splutters. "She should be seen as your fucking queen. She is the blood heir. The power belongs to her and her alone. The Circle members are betraying the blood. You must do something. Right this wrong, Nikolai."

He laughs and holds his arms out wide. "What do you think I can do?" he spits. "Look at me, Matthias. I am rotting down here with you, waiting on a private trial. My word is weightless, my pull is none. I am a traitor to my people. There is nothing I can do to change this. Your only choice is to accept it with grace."

"I won't do that."

"Then there is nothing more I can offer you."

My father lets out a heavy breath and looks back at me with sorrow in his eyes. "I've failed you, O. I failed you as a child. I wasn't strong enough to withstand Empire's rule, and now I've failed you again. I don't know how to save you."

A tear falls down my cheek, and I hastily wipe it away, hating to see my father falling apart like this. I know I never really got a chance to get to know him, but I always pictured him as a strong warrior, always ready to protect his little girl. It kills me to see him like this now. "I don't need you to save me, Dad. I can save myself."

He shakes his head. "I admire this strong woman you've grown into, Oakley. You're so fierce and determined, but there's no standing against Empire. Don't be foolish. Zade DeVil will come looking for you. He will take you out of here, and in the hour before dawn, he will slaughter you. He will take your heart in his hand and tear it right out of your chest while he listens to your agonized screams. All you can hope for is that he does it quickly."

I shake my head. "It's not going to happen," I tell him. "Even if it means taking Empire for myself. I won't give up my life for anyone."

"I'm so sorry, my sweet, sweet little girl. Had I had the chance to raise you, perhaps you would be able to see this clearly. I could have prepared you, and we could have fought together. We would have ruled together."

"I promise you, Father," I tell him, feeling my determination coming back to me. "You haven't failed me. If anything, I've failed you. I should have come looking, and I should have saved you from this hell a long time ago. I'm not going to let you die down here. I'm going to break free, and I'm taking you with me."

CHAPTER 2

Zade

Cross moves through my penthouse, his towel slung over his shoulder and his snake weaving through his fingers as he attempts to annihilate everything in my kitchen. He's just finished a workout, and I can't help but stare at the portrait of Oakley inked on his back. As much as the girl infuriates me, there's no denying she's a fucking phenomenal artist. The way she captured Venom weaving in and out of her eyes is the most beautiful yet haunting thing I've ever seen. It looks like the snake is quite literally plunging through Cross' skin.

He turns and braces himself against the counter, his gaze shifting to the dining table where Oakley left her lunch, the silver tray scattered across the table while her Diet Coke has been left barely touched.

"Where's she at?" Cross asks, nodding toward the table.

I shrug my shoulders. After sentencing my best friend's father to death last night, I really couldn't give a shit where she is. Trailing her every move and listening to the constant flow of bitching ain't doing it for me today. Especially not after Sawyer and Dalton took off last night and still haven't returned.

"Don't know," I tell him. "Probably sulking in her room, trying to figure out just how many cocks she can take on."

Cross rolls his eyes. "Low fucking blow, man," he says before chugging a whole bottle of water and slamming it back down on the counter. "Don't be salty because she doesn't wanna fuck you too."

I scoff, unable to believe these assholes. They know the fucking deal, and if they're stupid enough to get involved with a dead girl, then that's on them. "Really? You think I'm jealous because she doesn't want to ride my cock? I'll be carving her fucking heart out of her chest in twenty-nine days. If you want to go and get attached to a fucking ghost, then that's on you, man."

"Chill, bro," he laughs, a rare smirk stretching across his lips as he watches Venom weave through his fingers. "It's a tight pussy, and a fucking sweet one at that. She fucks like a greedy whore. Like she'll die without feeling my cock stretching her tight little cunt. Ain't nobody getting attached."

"Not getting attached?" I question, raising a brow. "Then why the fuck did you carve a cross into her skin? Sounds like some jealous boyfriend bullshit to me. What's up with that, huh? Can't handle that she likes to fuck Dalton and Sawyer too? Your cock not enough for her?"

Cross lifts his dark gaze to mine and the confidence in his stare almost has me wondering exactly what I've been missing out on . . . almost. "Don't do that, man. Don't make me be that bastard who boasts about just how fucking hard she came on my dick. I know you can hear her scream at night. That's not a fucking nightmare, man. It's me."

Rolling my eyes, I push up off the couch and grab the melted ice pack off my coffee table before striding to the kitchen. After shoving it back into the freezer, I look back at Cross, nodding toward his bandaged shoulder. "How's it going?" I ask, both of us knowing damn well he shouldn't have been working out while still healing from being shot in Oakley's room only a few nights ago.

Cross turns just enough so I can't see his wound, trying to hit me with the *out of sight, out of mind* bullshit. "It's fine," he mutters, more than ready to pretend there's not a damn thing wrong with him. He gives me a pointed stare. "I think you've got bigger problems of your own to be wasting time worrying about mine."

I clench my jaw and fix him with a hard stare, but he stares right back. He's probably the only motherfucker I know who isn't the least bit intimidated by me. "It's fine," I throw back at him, knowing damn well he's not about to back down. "Sawyer will come around. He just needs time to cool down."

"He beat the shit out of you, man. And you just stood there and took it," he reminds me as though I wasn't right there feeling the sting of every fucking blow. "It's not fine. This move pushes him into The

Circle. You're killing his dad and condemning him to a life of servitude to Empire. He's going to need a shitload more than just some time to cool down."

"You don't think I fucking know that?" I throw back at him. "What choice did I have? I should have put a bullet right between his fucking eyes the second I found him, but I didn't. I gave him a chance to go to trial, and at the very least, a chance for Sawyer to say goodbye to his old man. Or hell, should I have just let him take out Oakley?"

Cross scoffs and drags his hand down his face, slowly shaking his head. "I mean, life would be a shitload easier if someone just took her out already."

I can't help but laugh. That's the furthest thing from what we need right now, but goddamn, he's right. Not having Oakley Quinn messing with my days would make life a fucking breeze. Though, if someone happened to get to her before I did, I'd lose everything. All of what we're doing would have been for nothing. I won't risk it. Oakley must die by my hand on the night of the sixtieth moon, whether she likes it or not. She will be my sacrifice, and I will claim her heart like no other.

I'm just about to tell him just how fucking right he is when guilt flashes in his eyes, leaving just as quickly as it had come. "Right," I mutter. "If you really believe that, then be my guest. Go ahead and take her out."

Cross clenches his jaw, his stare hardening with hesitation and unease. "You're full of shit," he mutters, striding past me to put this conversation to bed.

I watch as he walks away, heading off in the direction of Oakley's room, probably needing her to stroke his ego back to health. When he disappears around the corner, I glance toward the dining table and press my lips into a hard line. It fucking irks me when people leave their discarded food on the table. How fucking hard is it to put it away?

Knowing damn well Oakley would have left it here just to get under my skin and that she's not about to come out here and clean it up, I stride over to grab the silver tray and find myself peering down at it. My brows furrowed as I take it all in.

Something isn't right.

Her Diet Coke is untouched, which is unheard of with Oakley. She sucks that shit back like it's an elixir of life. But what really gets me is the clean plate. It looks as though it's still fresh out of the dishwasher. Not a single crumb with the knife and fork still perfectly laying on either side of the plate.

Unease rocks through me when Cross appears from around the corner, that same unease flashing in his dark stare. "She's not in her room."

"She never had lunch," I rumble, my gaze shifting around my penthouse, checking for any hint or clue as to where she could be.

We snap into action.

"I'll check the roof," he says, already slamming his hand over the call button for the elevator as my hand flies under the table and grips the gun from its hiding position. The feel of the cool metal in my hand is like a fucking lifeline, sending power blasting through my veins, not that I need it. I could end someone's life with as little as a flick of my wrist. However, there's no denying a simple bullet makes my life a shitload easier.

My heart races as I fly through my home, checking behind every door and going as far as barging into her private bathroom, but she's nowhere to be found.

I check my bar, my room, Dalton's, and Sawyer's room, and even make sure she isn't lying dead on my floor after some emergency we missed. But again, I come up blank.

I clench my jaw, frustration burning through me. Where the fuck could she have gone? Oakley gets on my nerves, and she's slipped out of my hold on occasion, but more times than not, I knew where she was. When she followed us into the tunnels of Empire, I listened to every fucking step she took as they softly echoed through the long tunnel, making sure she was still breathing. There's only been one time where she's managed to get away, and when she did, she almost ended up a victim to Nikolai's blade.

She's a lamb—a sacrificial lamb—but a lamb all the same. No matter how strong she thinks she is or how well she believes she could handle Empire's wrath, she'll never make it on her own. She'll be dead in seconds.

The only question is whether she slipped out on her own, if she saw her shot and took it, or if some asshole came into my home, into my territory, and took her from me.

Anger burns through my veins, rage claiming my every thought. Oakley Quinn is a lot of things. She's frustrating and unpredictable, but she's not fucking stupid. There have been more than enough attempts on her life for her to know the only protection she'll ever have is here with me and the boys. If only she knew what I really wanted with her, then she'd be out of here in the blink of an eye. But there's nowhere she could go where I wouldn't find her. Once I have her back, there will be hell to pay. Though, I don't believe that's what's happened here.

She's been taken from me. My sacrifice, my one shot at rising in power, taken from me.

Whoever did this will feel the full extent of my wrath. No one steals from me without paying with their lives, and if I find her with her heart already dead and cold . . . well, shit. All hell will break loose.

Storming out into my living room and through my kitchen, I tear open the door of my butler's pantry, walking into the space I have converted into my weapons room. I start loading up, checking guns, and making sure every fucking one of my blades sparkle.

As I shove ammunition into a bag, Cross comes flying around the corner, instantly scanning over the selection of weapons, and knowing damn well it's go time. "She wasn't on the roof," he tells me. "She wouldn't just walk out the door, not after everything. Someone's taken her, right from under our fucking noses."

"My thoughts exactly," I say. "We'll start with surveillance and go from there."

He nods and we file out of the butler's pantry, ready to rain hell over these motherfuckers.

Venom rests securely in Cross' hand as I slam mine against the call button for the elevator, my other hand already on my phone. The elevator arrives within seconds, and as we step in, I put the phone to my ear. Dalton answers on the second ring. "Yo, what's up?"

"Is she with you?"

"What?"

Frustration eats at me. "Oakley. Have you fucking got her?"

"FUCK," he roars. "We haven't seen her. We're on our way."

Dalton ends the call, and despite the bullshit between me and Sawyer, they'll have my fucking back. Dalton's got a hard on for Oakley. The second he saw her, it was over for him, and despite his promises not to get attached, the fucker couldn't help himself. Even knowing I'll be ending her life in twenty-nine days, he's still falling for her. Without a doubt in my mind, he'll be here to find her. The only question is, why? Because he can't stand the thought of her slipping through our fingers and me losing my shot at completing my ritual, or because he can't fucking breathe when she's not around?

When I take her life, it's going to destroy him. I just hope he can learn to move past it, because no matter what, I will take my position on Empire's throne, whether I belong there or not.

Reaching the lobby, Cross and I step off the elevator and move out into the vast ground level of the DeVil Hotel. People pour in through the doors, some making their way to the bar while others check in at reception, all of them oblivious to the fresh hell weighing down on my shoulders.

Moving through the reception area, we push out into the back *employees only* section of my hotel, passing Benny, my eyes and ears around here. He clocks me immediately, his sharp gaze locking on mine just as quickly as I'd stepped into the corridor.

"What do you need?" he questions, knowing my hotel better than

I know it myself. He falls in beside us, waiting for instructions.

"Full sweep of the whole hotel and surrounding areas," I tell him. "Oakley's gone missing. Anything you can find—I want to know about it."

He pauses and I glance back at him, his face ghostly pale. "Missing, sir?" he asks, his eyes widening.

I move back, stepping right up to him. "You've got one fucking second to tell me what you know."

He swallows hard, and I can see the fear flashing in his eyes. Benny has been my personal bellboy since the day the hotel opened, and one simply does not hold a position like that for so long without knowing a thing or two about his boss. Over the years, I've trained him, molded him into the perfect watchman. If anything went down in my hotel, he'd know. So it has me wondering why the fuck I haven't heard about it yet.

His hands start to shake at his sides, but he holds his head up high. "I'm sorry, Zade," he says, his voice breaking with fear. "I received a call in the lobby. I was instructed to deliver a note and not to tell a soul, otherwise they'd take my baby. I didn't . . . I'm sorry. I should have come to you, but it was her over my child's life. I couldn't take the risk."

My jaw clenches as Cross steps away, needing a moment to compose himself. "It's okay," I say, knowing damn well if he didn't come through that child would be long gone. "Is your kid safe?"

"Yes, sir. I checked in with my wife. They're okay. Shaken, but okay."

"Did she say who it was? What they looked like?"

He shakes his head. "Nothing helpful. Just that they would take the baby if I didn't cooperate. There was a black SUV with no plates, dark window tint, and they were wearing suits. She said they looked important, but she couldn't recall any features that could help identify who they were. Dark hair, dark eyes. Medium build."

I nod and continue walking. "You're with me," I throw over my shoulder as I step up to the security control room of my hotel and quickly hash in the code.

Cross and Benny follow me in as we come face to face with my security team. "What can we do for you, boss?" my head of security questions.

I look over the multiple screens, all showcasing different areas of my hotel. "I need the footage from my front door over the last hour."

"Yes, sir," he says, nodding to one of his guys. "Is there anything in particular we're looking for?"

"Oakley. The girl who's been staying with me. She's disappeared."

"Yes, sir. Right away," he says with a nod, turning around to help his guy. They bring up the footage as I hear Benny on the phone, putting through the order of a full sweep with only minor details, knowing the reason for Oakley being here is privileged information. But whether we find something on the footage or not, my team will get it done and put forward anything they can find.

"Alright, here it is," my head of security says, pressing play on the footage.

Stepping in closer to the screens with Cross still right beside me, we watch closely as he speeds it up, waiting for something to happen. It takes only a second before we see Benny approach the door with what was supposed to be Oakley's lunch. She opens the door a moment later and they have a short conversation.

Oakley looks concerned while Benny looks as though he's about to throw up, but the door is quickly closed and Benny soon disappears out of the frame. The footage is sped up again, and I wait with bated breath, positive someone is about to break through my door while I was too fucking lost in my thoughts, too caught up with grief over what I'd done to Sawyer to even notice.

But then the door opens again and Oakley pushes out into the hallway. She looks left and right as she clutches onto a small piece of paper.

"She ran," Cross breathes in astonishment. "She fucking ran. After everything."

"She wouldn't have run unless she found out something she wasn't supposed to know," I say, meeting Cross's hard stare, knowing damn well that if Oakley has learned what I really want with her, this just became a shitload harder. Fear for her rattles his stare. Oakley is a fucking force to be reckoned with and she has the determination of a pit bull. If she knows, all of our lives are about to be turned upside down. Oakley won't stop until she gets what she wants. Hell, if she feels her back is up against the wall and there's no way out, she's the type to end it herself, just so I wouldn't get the satisfaction.

I glance at Benny, who looks like he's about to shit his pants. "What was on that note?"

He shakes his head. "I . . . I'm sorry, I do not know. I was instructed not to open the tray."

"FUCK," I spit, nodding back to the screen and watching as she races through the hallway and slips into the fire escape. "Follow her. Where does she come out?"

My security team gets to work, and I hover over the back of their chairs, my gaze locked on the screen as my heart thumps erratically. My fingers dig into the leather of their chairs, and I clench my jaw, certain it's over. I've never felt so fucking antsy in my life, not even before stepping into my father's home to slit his throat. But this . . . this makes me feel sick.

We follow Oakley right down to the lobby and watch as she breaks out of the fire escape and manically looks around. She looks petrified, like everything she's ever known was a lie. I suppose it is.

She hurries out to the road, and I watch as she stops to consider her next move. Joe, one of my only trusted mentors within Empire, doubling as my valet, steps into her side and relief begins pulsing through my veins.

"No, this isn't right," Benny says, shaking his head as he leans closer toward the screens, getting a better look. "Joe called in sick this morning. Dante was working valet today."

My brows furrow, and just as I'm about to start defending Joe, start telling Benny that he's got it wrong, Joe strikes out, a needle plunging into the base of Oakley's throat. My eyes widen, my chest sinking with betrayal as I watch Oakley collapse into his arms. He shoves her into the backseat of a black car before slamming the door behind her.

The car takes off, much further than the reach of my security cameras, and I step back, my hands flying up to my temples. "FUCK," I roar, my sudden outburst making Venom stand up from Cross' hand as though preparing for an attack. She'd be right. There'll be a fucking attack alright.

Betrayal burns through me as Cross turns to face me, his jaw clenched. "She could be anywhere."

I shake my head, my mind a mess of fucked-up thoughts. "No, it's fucking over. If Joe's working for someone, it's because they want Empire, just like Nikolai did. They take her out and my claim is done. She'll be fucking dead within seconds."

Cross closes his eyes, knowing damn well it's true. "No. I won't believe she's dead until I see a fucking body," he says. "This ain't over yet."

I couldn't agree more.

Shoving my hand against the door, my plan is already set in stone. Benny and Cross follow me out, and I nod toward Benny. "Finish your sweep. I don't want to hear from you until you know exactly how that note got inside my hotel."

Benny nods and turns to the left while Cross sticks right with me. "Hope you're fucking ready, man," I warn him. "Heads are about to roll."

CHAPTER 3

Oakley

"I hate that you've been dragged into this," my father tells me, gripping the cold, rusted bars and staring at me as though he still can't believe I'm right here in front of him. "If I knew they would hunt you like they did me, I never would have—"

"Never would have what? Had me?" I ask, my eyes widening.

"Still not capable of allowing someone to finish a sentence, I see," he laughs. I roll my eyes as I sit cross-legged on my bed, wondering how many before me have laid on these very sheets, slept on this very pillow. "What I was going to say is that I never would have introduced you to Empire. I would have hidden you away, but you were born before I knew what blood ran through my veins. I had no way of shielding you."

"It's okay," I tell him, hating that we're spending what little time we have left under a cloud of darkness, just waiting for the storm.

"It's not okay," he says, giving me a hard stare.

Letting out a heavy sigh, I drop my head into my hands, knowing just how right he is. "What are we supposed to do?"

"The only thing we can do—tell me about your life, how you were raised, and by who. I want to know it all. If we only have limited days left on this earth, then I want to know all there is to know about you, Oakley."

I glance up at him, giving him a sad smile. "You've been down here for twelve years. I highly doubt your days are limited . . . just mine."

Dad scoffs. "Zade DeVil will find you. Believe it or not, he's coming for you, and he won't leave a single stone unturned in trying to find you. So if he'll go to all that effort to find his sacrifice, don't you think he'll put a bullet between my eyes when he realizes I'm right here? If he's anything like his father, there's not a damn thing he wouldn't do to claim power. Even if it means eliminating every fucking threat that comes his way."

I shake my head. "He thinks you're dead. If you could find a way out of here, you could be a free man. Disappear and live your life."

Nikolai lets out a frustrated sigh from his cell, his elbows braced against his knees, looking as though he's deep in thought. "No one breaks out of here, child. If there were a way, don't you think the desperate men in these cells would have tried? Surely if there were a way for your father to have broken free to get to his only daughter, he would have."

My head drops, knowing he's right, and I can't help but feel for Nikolai, knowing he's got Sawyer and his daughter at home. "I'm really not your biggest fan," I tell him. "But for what it's worth, Sawyer was a mess when he found out you'd been put in here. He beat the shit out of Zade and then took off to tell his mom and sister. I know I've only known him for a few weeks, but I've never seen such a broken man. The thought of losing you was eating him alive."

Nikolai is silent for a moment before I hear a heavy sigh from deep within his cell. "Sawyer will be alright. He's a strong man, raised to lead. He'll fall into his position within The Circle and he'll enforce the much-needed change Empire has neglected over the years. He'll be good for our people."

A sad smile lingers on my lips. "From what I understood, Sawyer wasn't thrilled about becoming part of The Circle."

"No, he's not," Nikolai says, almost as though fondly remembering the million arguments they've surely had over the years about it. "However, he has learned to put duty before selfish needs and desires. He'll do the right thing."

I arch my brows, not sure I truly believe that. After all, Sawyer was more than happy to double team me with his friends until I screamed, and something tells me that goes directly against this whole *putting duty first* thing.

"Nikolai," I say, getting up off my bed and latching onto the bars. "Can you tell me exactly what's going to happen at this ritual thing?"

"No," my father breathes. "You don't want to know about this shit. All you're going to do is dwell on it. It's going to sit in your mind and eat at you."

"I want to know," I tell him. "I can't stand the thought of going into this unprepared. I need to know what's going to happen. What they'll do to me. If I'll get anything to dull the pain of it or if Zade is just going to go for it. The more I can mentally prepare for this, the more at ease I'll be. I'm already scared enough, the last thing I want is to be unprepared."

"Are you sure?" Nikolai asks. "What will happen in our sacred fortress will not be pretty. I'm not sure it is something anyone could possibly prepare for."

"I want to know," I repeat.

"Very well," Nikolai says. "On the night of the sixtieth moon, you will be brought to our fortress dressed in white, symbolizing the innocence of your youth and your sacrifice. We will circle you, among those who have ruled before. Then in the hour before dawn, you will offer yourself to Zade. Your bare chest will be exposed, and as the flames roar around our fortress, Zade will plunge his knife into your chest. From here it will be quick. Your bones will be broken to make way for his hands, and as your heart still beats, he will tear it from your body and offer it as his sacrifice."

Silent tears stream down my face, the fear locking around my throat and making it impossible to breathe. "How quickly will I die?"

Nikolai shrugs his shoulders. "I am not sure, child. I have only witnessed this sacrifice once before. She passed out from the pain as her rib cage was cracked open, so she didn't feel it as Lawson tore her heart from her chest. She bled out quickly. However, I can't guarantee that you will have the same response. You may pass out and go quietly, or you may feel every excruciating second of it."

My father curses, and as I look up, I realize just how tightly he's gripping the bars. His knuckles are white, matching his ghostly complexion, but I do what I can to try and ignore it. I know if I don't get these answers now, I might never have the strength to ask again. "What will happen to my body after the ritual?"

"You will be buried in Empire's tomb, among those who have also offered their lives as a sacrifice."

I scoff. "You're confused. I'm not offering anything. It's being stolen from me."

"However you wish to word it is your business," Nikolai tells me, a bite in his tone, clearly not fond of Empire's culty bullshit practices being called out. "The ritual is considered sacred and therefore not widely spoken of among our people. They know their leader must make a sacrifice, but many will never know what that is. Due to this, you will have a closed burial with only those closest to you welcome."

"You mean, you won't be sharing with the world what your people are going to do to an innocent life, and then you're going to bury me away where no one will ever find me."

"Empire is a powerful society," Nikolai tells me. "If we made careless decisions such as leaving heartless bodies out for the world to see, we would have crumbled years ago. We have learned to protect ourselves and do what's necessary to keep the authorities from sniffing around."

Clenching my jaw, I try to take a calming breath and see it from his side. I get it, I honestly do. If Empire was careless with this bullshit, someone would have busted this operation wide open years ago, and these assholes would already be rotting in cells. Or better yet, dead. But there's no denying the idea of my body being discarded in some unmarked grave, hidden away for the rest of eternity, doesn't sit well with me. Hell, I downright won't accept it.

"Okay," I say, moving on, knowing this isn't a fight that's worth having with Nikolai. After all, if Sawyer is right, he'll face the private trial with The Circle and be dead within days. This is something I'll have to talk to Zade about. "What about my heart? After it's torn from my body, what will Zade do with it?"

Nikolai forces a smile across his face and meets my stare through the bars. "Your heart will remain on a pedestal in our sacred fortress during Zade's reign. It will be perfectly preserved, and then burned with Zade's body when he ultimately passes."

Tears stream down my face, falling from my jaw and dropping to my collarbone as overwhelming grief claims me. "There's gotta be a loophole. Something in the archives that will save her," my father's broken tone cuts through the silence.

Nikolai laughs and the sound is filled with pity. "There once was, until Julius DeVil, your real father, stamped it out. He sacrificed his sister only days before the loophole was discovered. He believed that if he had to go through it, that every heir beneath him must do the same."

"Fuck."

My thoughts exactly.

My father meets my stare through the bars with wide, pleading eyes. "You have to promise me, Oakley. If you get out of here, run and never look back. Forget me, forget Empire, and just run."

I swallow hard and nod, feeling the weight of the world resting on my shoulders. "I will," I lie, knowing with every fiber of my being that I will never stop fighting for my freedom, and never stop fighting for his.

Wiping my dirty hands over my face, I try to find some composure. "What happens if he doesn't follow through with the ritual?"

"That will never happen," my father says. "Zade will never allow Empire to slip through his fingers like that. He will find you and hold onto you until your beating heart is in the palm of his hand. The only way for that to not happen is if you were to die before the sixtieth moon."

Nikolai meets my stare. "If no heir rises to power, Empire will crumble. It would turn into a bloodbath as people try to claw their way to the top. What I did to you would be nothing but child's play, and do not be fooled, once they start digging, they will find your name and both you and Zade will be seen as the biggest threat this world has ever seen. There is nowhere you will be safe. So you must ask yourself, is the loss of just one life, your life, not better than the loss of hundreds?"

My father rattles the bars of his cell, his face pressed right up against them. "Don't put that shit into her head. Why should she care about those hundreds of lives who've never once cared about hers? Lives that have only ever willed for her death? Oakley will not be manipulated by your bullshit, and it sure as fuck isn't her responsibility to take on the burden of all that spilled blood if Zade weren't to spill hers."

Nikolai scoffs, shaking his head. "If Zade doesn't complete his ritual, then God be with us all."

The weight of his words sit heavily in the cells as I fumble back to my bed, drop my ass onto the hard mattress, and curl up against the wall with my knees pressed to my chest. I drop my chin to my knees and try to breathe, focusing on calming my racing nerves, but it doesn't do nearly enough to ease me.

The idea of being slaughtered, of having a man who swore to protect me physically breaking my bones and shoving his hand deep inside my chest to claim my heart makes me sick. I'd give anything to trade places with someone, to fall at Zade's feet and beg for my life. There's nothing I wouldn't do to save myself. I'm not finished here yet. I've barely had a chance to live. To get married and raise children of my own. I mean, it's not something I've really ever thought about, but the idea of never getting to do it makes me crave a life I've never even considered.

"O," my father's soft tone rings through the cells. I look up and find his haunted stare on mine, and without a word passing between us, I know he knows what's circling my mind. "Tell me about your life. Where did you go to school? Which boys broke your heart? Where'd you end up after I was taken?"

A sad smile settles onto my face, appreciating his efforts to distract me. Despite not being in the mood to share all the ins and outs of my life, I know he needs this. Besides, I don't know when I might ever get another chance to speak with my father. Everything could all be stripped away from me in the blink of an eye.

Swallowing over the lump in my throat, I prepare to tell him every facet of my life over the past twelve years, racking my brain and trying to remember all those little things kids usually try to forget. "I was eight when you were kill—*taken,*" I say, still not used to the idea of him being alive, right here in front of my face. "There was a funeral for you, and I remember seeing some of the firemen there that worked with you, but I didn't recognize any of their faces."

"I'm sorry, Oakley. That must have been really hard."

"It was," I agree. "Everyone was offering me condolences and talking at me. No one actually asked me how I was doing. It was always *Poor Oakley* and *I'm sorry for your loss* but never actually *How are you feeling?* I couldn't understand that."

"It's death," Nikolai throws in. "People don't know how to act around others who are grieving. They overthink it and end up missing the most basic things."

I nod, agreeing with his statement. "Anyway, after the funeral, I met with social services and they placed me with Aunt Liv, and I was living with her in Missouri."

"Aunt Liv?" my father asks. "Who's that? I don't recall her name."

My brows furrow as I stare at my father. "What are you talking about? Aunt Liv? Olivia? Mom's sister? She's looked after me for twelve years."

"Honey," he says cautiously. "Your mom never had a sister. She was an only child."

I shake my head. "No, that's not right. She would tell me stories about them growing up together."

My father presses his lips into a hard line and slowly shakes his head. "I'm sorry, Oakley, but no. I met your mom when we were barely fourteen. There was no sister."

Nikolai clears his throat and cringes. "Yeah, I can shed a little bit of light on that one," he says, sounding awkward. "You were one of the two remaining blood heirs of Empire. Lawson wasn't just about to let you slip away. He wanted to keep tabs on you."

My brows furrow, so many questions coming from his statement, plus a shitload of betrayal from Liv. I thought she really loved me. She was there at my darkest moment and shed just a little bit of light over my life. For so long I thought of her as my guardian angel, but she was nothing but a pawn, a player in Empire's wicked game. Something I'll be talking to her about, assuming I get the chance. For now, I have other things that I need to wrap my head around. "Why didn't Lawson just kill me then? Why lock my father in here? Why spare our lives at all?"

"All good questions," Nikolai commends. "I've been asking myself the same for a very long time. At least, I always wondered why he spared you. To be honest, I thought your father was dead. Imagine my surprise when Zade DeVil locks me in here and I find the real blood heir a few cells down."

I scoff. "Has any of my life been real?"

Nikolai pulls a face and my eyes widen as I wait for him to continue.

"College," he says. "Your grades were terrible. I personally pulled some strings with Faders Bay University to get you transferred back here. Plus your apartment that you share with . . . Cara, is it? The previous tenants just happened to find the will to move out on short notice and the apartment opened right up for you both to slot straight in. There are many instances during your life where Empire has looked out for you, and despite everything, it is Lawson's doing that ensured you had such a fulfilled life."

"Fulfilled?" I question. "I lost my father and grew up away from home, only to come back to four assholes stalking me, and a fucked-up secret society insisting they want my heart torn out of my chest and put up on a pedestal. My life hasn't been fulfilling, it's been a wreck."

"Well, that's on you. Lawson ensured you had the tools at hand to build yourself a great life, and if you didn't seize the opportunity and enjoy the twelve years of freedom you received, then that's on you."

I clench my jaw, more than ready to break through these damn bars and tear his fucking heart out of his chest, only it won't be going on a pedestal. I'd turn the emotionless thing into minced meat.

"O," my father says, trying to draw my attention back to him, but a loud clanging sounds through the cells and my head whips around, listening to the sound of heavy boots against old, rickety stairs. My heart pounds, certain that this must be the asshole who put me in here coming to finish the job.

As if sensing the fear pounding through my veins, my father lets out a broken sigh. "It's okay, it's just Harrison bringing dinner. I know you don't feel it, but you're safer down here than you ever were out there."

As if on cue, a big, burly man walks through the cells, stopping every now and then to deliver a tray of food. As he gets closer, I recognize him as the man Zade had called last night after Nikolai's callous attempt to kill me.

He stops at my father's cell door, barely sparing him a glance before sliding a tray through a small gap in the bars and giving it a shove, hard enough to send the food flying through the cell and slamming into the side wall, spilling it everywhere. I gasp, watching as he continues walking, but what kills me is the way my father just accepts it and allows the prison guard to treat him like shit.

Harrison stops by my cell and glances at me with a furrowed brow, clearly having no idea who I am. "What's your name, girl?" he says, shoving the tray of food between the bars, though thankfully, he doesn't throw it at me.

"Oakley."

"Why are you here?"

"Good fucking question," I tell him. "Pretty sure whoever put me here is using Empire's prison system as a place to hide me in the hopes no one is stupid enough to come down here looking."

His gaze narrows further, clearly having no idea what's going on. "Right," he says with a firm nod. "Sounds like it's none of my business. I'm Harrison, and these cells are my domain. Don't fuck with me, and we won't have any problems. Got it?"

I nod, my heart racing. "Got it."

Without another word, he continues on his way, stopping by

Nikolai's cell next. "Hey, old man. How're ya holding up?"

"Not gonna lie. It's been a rough twenty-four hours," Nikolai says, taking the tray from Harrison's hands. "Look, I need you to do something for me."

"No," Harrison says, shaking his head. "No, you know I can't be doing you any favors down here. That's not how it works."

"Come on, Harrison. I just need to see my son. We've been friends for a long time—"

"Nik, I can't. The Circle—"

"I am The Circle," Nikolai says. "I have not been sentenced yet, and until The Circle votes at my trial, I remain an active member. If I request for my son to visit me in these cells, then you are bound by your vows to Empire to oblige my request. However, out of respect for our friendship, I am willing to make it worth your time."

Harrison scoffs. "You couldn't pay me enou—"

"How does a hundred grand sound?" Nikolai continues.

Harrison's eyes widen. "A hundred grand?" he questions. "You want to pay me a hundred grand to get your son down here?"

"Down here and returned safely back to the main floor."

Harrison rubs a hand through his hair. "I don't know, Nik. I know you're good for it, but you're a dead man, and it's not as though you can walk out of here and go and get it for me."

"The cash is in my safe under my office desk. I'll give you the code once Sawyer is out of here, or if you'd like it directly deposited into your account, Sawyer has full authority to make the transaction. What's it gonna be? I know those twins of yours are close to starting school, and your wife is putting on the pressure to enroll them in private school. Those fees are going to burn a hole through your pocket. It's bad enough with one, let alone two. Plus, I know Georgia wanted to start horse riding lessons."

"I don't know, Nik. It's risky. If The Circle finds out—"

"They won't. Besides, are you forgetting the moment I'm executed, my son will inherit my place in The Circle? If you do this, Sawyer will remember it, and I don't need to remind you how well it pays to have connections in high places. He'll protect you."

"Fuck," Harrison mutters. "Why do I feel like I'm going to regret this?"

Nikolai grins. "Just keep your mind on the money, and no one has to find out."

Harrison lets out a heavy breath and shakes his head, clearly torn with his decision. "Alright, old man. You've got yourself a deal." He continues down the line, delivering trays of food to my brand-new neighbors, but all that matters to me is that Sawyer is coming down here. If memory serves, that big bastard owes me a favor.

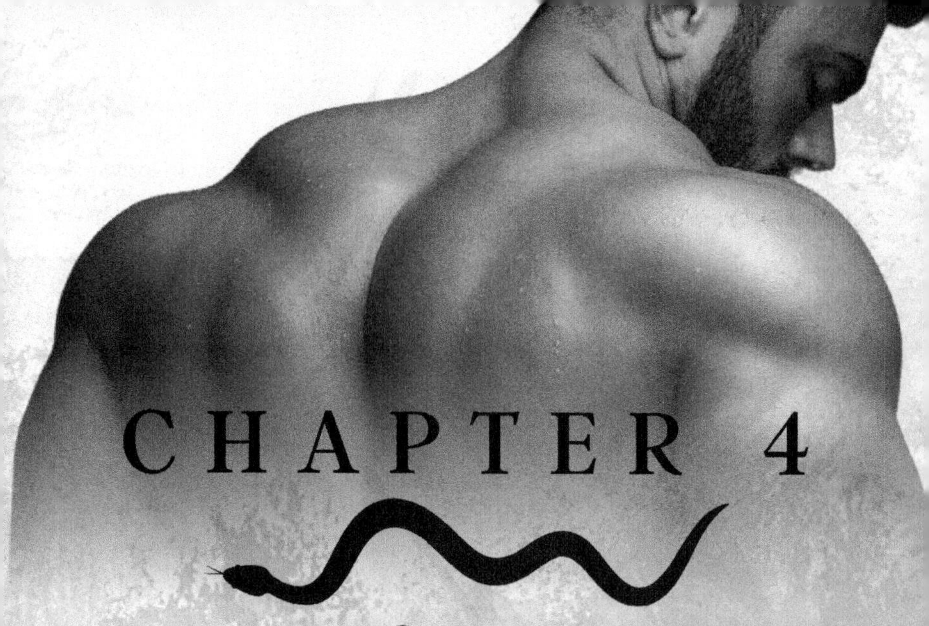

CHAPTER 4

Cross

"Really?" I ask, looking up at Joe's small home. "This is it?"

Dalton shrugs. "Apparently. This is the address listed on all his files, but I don't know. After all the years I've known him, he's never once invited me to his place. It doesn't exactly scream Joe," he mutters, his brows furrowed as he takes in the property. "What about you guys? Been here before?"

Sawyer shakes his head. "No. Never," he says, absentmindedly rubbing his split and bruised knuckles from beating the shit out of Zade last night. "He's usually so put together with his expensive suits and all the cars. This doesn't feel right. Almost like a trap."

Zade runs a hand over his beaten face, probably thinking the same thing, and I can't help but notice the wicked satisfaction burning in Sawyer's stare, taking in the damage he inflicted on Zade. Despite this place not feeling right, with Oakley still missing and no confirmation of her death, there's no way in hell we're about to walk away without checking it first. Our only priority is to find her while she's still breathing.

"Come on," he murmurs, starting up the driveway. We fan out, each of us heading to a separate entrance of the property, covering all our bases, and making sure no one inside this house has an opportunity to run.

I make my way around the back of the property, Dalton coming with me and stopping by what must be the kitchen window. He starts feeling around the frame, more than capable of getting inside without having to smash through it. Knowing that he's good, I keep walking around to the back door.

Unease blasts through my chest as I slip a pin into the rusted lock, unable to shake the feeling that this is all wrong. Joe has been a trusted mentor for years. He grew up with Zade's father. Hell, all of our fathers. He watched over us as we learned the ropes and became the men we are today. Seeing him out on the street with Oakley on the security footage was like a knife right through the back. He knows who she is to us and what her value is to Zade. Taking her away like that was one of the biggest betrayals Empire has ever seen.

Quickly working the lock, I slip inside the old home and am immediately hit in the face with a foul stench. I hold back a gag as I close the door behind me, making sure to lock it before gripping the front of my shirt and pulling it up to cover my nose and mouth. I've broken into enough homes to know that, nine out of ten times, I don't want to be inhaling that shit.

I do a sweep of the back rooms until I find both Sawyer and Dalton in the hallway, leaving only the front bedroom and the living room unchecked. Zade should have met up with us by now. The only reason why he wouldn't is if he's found something.

Meeting both Dalton and Sawyer's stare, we each nod and continue toward the front of the house. Sawyer quickly checks the bedroom before we all step through to the living room, finding Joe already beaten and bruised, strapped down against a hardback chair with a gun in hand.

My brow arches, and I glance across the room toward Zade, leaning against the dining table. He's watching Joe as if he's wondering what the fuck to do with him, not even remotely threatened by the gun. We stride deeper into the living room, evenly spacing ourselves.

Oakley was taken a little over six hours ago, and it's clear whoever Joe was working for had a message for him. I just wish I knew what that was.

My gaze settles on the gun, wondering why they'd leave him like this, and it occurs to me that they've left him with just enough room to turn the gun on himself. They knew damn well that we would come for him. It's almost sweet, giving him an out like that. But it's not going to be that easy. No one gets to betray us and simply take their lives before paying the price.

Make no mistake, Joe will die tonight. But not before we get exactly what we need.

Zade steps forward, looking at Joe with such deep disappointment that it almost makes me feel like I've been sent to the principal's office too. Joe watches Zade's every step with a sharp stare, his hand shaking on the arm rest, the gun gripped tight between his fingers.

"You knew we were coming," Zade comments.

"How could I not?" Joe spits. "I've worked at that hotel for years. I know where every single one of those security cameras are. Though I have to admit, I'm surprised it took you so long to find me."

Zade shakes his head. "Why now?" he questions. "You were a trusted adviser to my father for twenty years, a mentor to me. Why betray the blood?"

Joe scoffs and winces with pain. "Betray the blood? You're one to talk, DeVil. You were never the blood. I was protecting the blood by getting that girl away from you. The moment I realized who she was, I had to get her out of there."

Dalton narrows his stare and steps forward, itching to get in on the action. The fucker lives for the pain and gets off on giving it back. "You're lying, Joe. You've always been so easy to read. Someone put you up to this. You didn't figure it out on your own."

Joe sends a scathing glare to Dalton. "You don't know what the fuck you're talking about, boy."

I laugh as Venom makes her way over my knuckles. "As entertaining as this is, I'm bored. Let's get some things straight. Your life will not be saved, and I know you understand that, so why bother with the theatrics? We were trained by the best this world has to offer, so understand this now—there is no point in lying to us."

Joe swallows, his gaze flicking between the four of us, but I continue, ready to find Oakley and have this bullshit done with. "Look at the state of you, Joe. That's the face of someone who just pissed off some very important people."

"Just put a fucking bullet between my eyes. I'm not saying a fucking word."

"Go ahead. The gun is in your hand."

Joe freezes, and it's abundantly clear that he doesn't have the balls to turn the gun on himself, something each one of us would have been more than capable of if it meant protecting our loyalties. Though none of us would be dumb enough to put ourselves in this position.

Sawyer scoffs. "Let me guess, you were approached by someone within Empire's ranks, presumably one of The Circle members. They told you what blood really runs through Oakley's veins, and you thought all those years of loyal servitude to the DeVil name was a waste. You wanted to right those wrongs and save Oakley from our clutches. Only that's not what you were tasked with, is it? You were ordered to end her life, but you didn't have the balls to do it."

"She's dead. Forget about the girl," Joe spits, turning his gaze to Zade. "Your reign is over before it even begins."

Zade shakes his head. "But she's not though, is she? You forget just how well I know you, Joe. You don't have what it takes to end an innocent life. That's why you've never been promoted within the ranks of Empire. You're weak. Disposable. You hold no value, and my father knew it."

Joe's hand itches on the gun, but Zade continues toward him, knowing just how right he is. Joe can't pull that trigger. Zade pulls his own gun, not fucking around as he presses it right to Joe's temple.

Joe falters, his eyes widening with fear, knowing just how callous Zade can be. If he doesn't get what he wants, he will do exactly what Joe can't. Hell, the fucker's just lucky that Zade isn't in the mood to play games tonight. We could have dragged this out for hours, but instead, Zade is willing to end him with a single bullet out of respect for the years of mentorship. "Where is she, Joe?"

"I told you, she's dead," he says. "I slit her throat. Pressed my blade up against her creamy skin and ended her life in seconds. She didn't even scream, just begged me to end it before you could get your hands on her."

Zade scoffs, not believing him for one second. "Did it get you hard like it does for me?" he questions, pressing the gun harder to his temple.

"Empire can do so much better than the likes of you."

"No," Zade says. "They can't. I am exactly what Empire needs, and that throne is my birthright. Understand me, Joe. I will take it whether I have Oakley's heart or not, even if I have to burn it to the ground to get there."

"It's not your birthright," Joe rumbles, flinching away from the gun. "It never was."

"Perhaps," he says with a slight shrug. "It's a shame you won't be around to tell anybody though. Now, let's get down to it. Tell me where she is, and I'll let you die quickly. Refuse me, and I will ensure that you bleed out for hours. It will be cold and painful. Not the way I was hoping to do this. But I suppose I don't have anywhere else I need to be. No thanks to you."

Joe scoffs, a cocky smirk settling over his face, as if finally coming to terms with his fate and accepting what will be. Sawyer inches to the right, knowing damn well he's in the line of fire and will get splattered from head to toe with Joe's brains. "I'm not telling you shit, kid. You can't have her. I've hidden her so deep, not even you or your precious Circle will find her. Accept it, Zade. You're done, and when the time is right, Oakley is going to rise as the new head of Empire. Right where she should have always been."

A pang of guilt fires through my chest, realizing that all along, Joe has had Oakley's best interests at heart—or at least, had Empire's interests at heart. I'm sure Oakley would never want anything to do with Empire, but as he mentioned, it's her birthright. If nature had run its course without Lawson's intervention, her father would have ruled over us, and she would have claimed power upon his death. But as it is, Joe betrayed the DeVil legacy, and despite his intentions of trying to keep the pure Empire blood in power, he directly stepped against Zade. It will cost him his life—no matter what.

"Come on, Joe. You know damn well I'm not done until I say I'm done, and I'm only just getting started. Last chance, old man. Tell me where the girl is and I will make this quick."

"Fuck you, Zade."

"Wrong answer."

BANG!

The bullet plunges through Joe's chest and he cries out in agony as I suck in a breath through my teeth, knowing just how fucking bad that must hurt. Judging by where Zade's standing, the angle of the bullet, and the way Joe gasps for air, Zade's punctured Joe's lung—a slow, painful way to go.

Joe struggles against his binds as Zade moves back to his position across the room, more than ready to stand here all night and wait it out. "Don't fight against it, Joe," he says. "You're only making it worse."

Joe rasps in agony as I let out a heavy sigh and check my watch. It's only eight in the evening. This could be a long night.

Taking a seat on Joe's couch, I let Venom explore, but she stays close, not one to get too far away. The silence is too heavy, and I glance up at Joe. "Yo, what's that smell out the back? Have you got someone rotting back there? It was fucking putrid."

Joe glances at me and spits at my feet, and I roll my eyes. This bullshit is always the same with assholes trying to act tough when they know they're backed into a corner. I prefer it when they're screaming.

Dalton makes his way through the living room, looking at all of Joe's possessions and making sure to step right over the growing puddle of blood spreading across the floor. "I thought you had a wife and kids," he questions, noticing the lack of photo frames and girly shit. There's no woman's touch here, and it's definitely not somewhere anyone would want to raise a family. "You betray her too? Or is she what stinks out back?"

Joe grunts and fights against his binds once again, and I glance at Zade, wondering just how long he's going to make us sit here. I'm fucking starving, and I still haven't had a chance to shower after my workout earlier. I go to ask when Sawyer's phone cuts through the room, and all eyes fall to him.

He shoves his hand deep into his pocket and grabs his phone, glancing down at the screen with furrowed brows.

"Who is it?" Dalton asks from across the room.

"Harrison," Sawyer says, his sharp, venomous stare locking onto Zade. "I wonder what he could possibly want." Zade doesn't respond, just continues to take Sawyer's hits every time they come rolling in. Sawyer doesn't wait for an answer before he accepts Harrison's call. "Hey, man. Everything cool with Dad?"

There's a short pause while all eyes fall on Sawyer, and even Joe can't help but be curious.

"Look man, not tonight," Sawyer says into the phone, his tone conflicted. "I've got some shit going down that I need to be here for. What about tomorrow?"

Silence again, yet with each passing second, I can almost sense the way Sawyer's heart races. "Shit. Yeah, alright. I'll see what I can do."

Sawyer ends the call and glances at Zade before focusing on me. "I'm out, man. Dad's struck a deal with Harrison to get me in tonight. It's now or never."

"Yeah, man," I say, scooping Venom off the couch and standing. I step into Sawyer and clap him on the back. Neither of us like grand shows of affection, but he's about to say goodbye to his father, and despite the bullshit between him and Zade, I'm not about to let him walk out of here without reminding him that we've got his back. "We'll wait up if you need to throw back a few drinks."

"Yeah, no doubt," he says, before nodding toward Dalton and slipping out through the front door.

I glance back at Zade, finding his stare heavy with guilt and self-loathing, and suddenly, he's not so keen to spend his night waiting for this asshole to bleed out. He turns his gun on Joe again, his eyes darkening with the ghosts of his own insecurities. "When you get to hell, ask my father how he likes me now."

Without a second of hesitation, Zade pulls the trigger, sending the bullet directly between Joe's eyes.

CHAPTER 5

Sawyer

Empire's prison system is one of the most fucked-up places I've been. It's cold and stale and not somewhere I'd ever want to find myself. Now that Zade's claiming power, and I'm stepping up into The Circle, it's not something I should have to worry about. Though, it wasn't something I thought my father would have to worry about either, but here we are.

Harrison walks ahead of me, leading me down through the twisting tunnels, each of his heavy footsteps echoing around us. It's damp and smells like mold and rot, but nothing like the foul smell I endured in Joe's home. My curiosity wasn't great enough to go searching for it, but either way, I don't know how people live like that. Even Empire's deadliest assassins have to practice good hygiene.

"How is he?" I ask at his back, wishing I could be anywhere but here. This wasn't my plan. I was supposed to have another thirty or so years with my father, thirty years before I would be forced to step up into The Circle. But this is Empire, and nothing is guaranteed in this world.

"Considering everything, I'd say he's doing alright," Harrison tells me, a longtime friend of my father's. "He's torn up. I know what he did was wrong, but he wasn't expecting it to end like this. You know how much he loves your mom and sister."

I press my lips into a hard line, not missing the fact that he skipped right over me. It's no secret my father and I have struggled to get along over the years, but he's still my old man. Seeing him facing the firing squad isn't going to be easy. Deep down in his shallow heart, I know he cares for me, despite his need to deny it. To him, I'm nothing more than an heir to follow on his family name and maintain our position within Empire's ranks. Had I not been born, he would have kept trying until he'd produced a son.

"Yeah, Mom and Cara aren't taking it so well either," I tell him, wincing at the memory of breaking the news to them last night. It was the hardest thing I've ever done. It fucking gutted me having to break their hearts like that. "I'm sure you'll have Mom breaking down your door soon enough. She won't let him go without a fight."

"I know," Harrison says fondly. "But it's not my call. I just hold the keys."

"Yeah, I know," I mutter, letting out a heavy sigh as I continue following him down a set of rickety, old stairs, deeper into the darkness below. It's chilling, and as I hear clanging coming from the cells at the bottom, a shiver sails down my spine.

I'm not one to shy away from this shit. Hell, the things I've done and the people I've killed would have put me in these cells a million times over, but there's no denying just how fucked up this place is.

My phone buzzes in my pocket, and I consider letting it ring out, when the fleeting thought of Oakley crosses my mind. I haven't got the same kind of attachment to her that Dalton and Cross do, not that Cross is willing to admit it, but the thought of her being taken and hidden away hasn't sat right with me. Hell, none of it is sitting right with me, but I wouldn't dare admit that out loud. I know things aren't great between me and Zade right now, but it would kill him to learn I haven't got his back. Don't get me wrong, I want him to succeed. I want him to rise in power, I just wish there were a different way. Now that I've gotten to know Oakley just a bit . . . fuck. This isn't what I want for her. I feel like there's still so much to learn, so much more to explore with her.

Fuck. I sound like a pansy-ass bitch.

Zade warned us not to get attached, and there was a good fucking reason for that.

Considering there's no way my father will escape his trial, he'll be executed within days, meaning I'll be the one standing in his place as Zade completes his ritual. I'll be right there watching over her as my best friend plunges his knife into her chest and breaks her fucking bones. I'll watch her blood rush over her body and splatter against the ground as Zade digs his hands into her open chest and takes her beating heart right into the palms of his hands.

Her screams. Her cries. Her agony.

I'll be made to witness every fucking second.

Bile rises in my throat, and I push the thought aside as I pull my phone out of my pocket, surprised I have enough cell service to still receive texts. Though I'm sure as I hit the cells at the bottom, that service will quickly fade away.

Lighting up my screen, I find a text from my sister, and for a moment, I consider swiping away the notification and waiting to check it until I'm through here, but I wouldn't put anything past Cara. It wouldn't surprise me if she's already found out about my meeting with Dad and wanted me to pass along a message. She's just that good.

She's not as deep in the world of Empire as I am. She never really wanted anything to do with it. But that doesn't mean that she doesn't have all the right contacts in all the right places.

Opening her text, I quickly scan over it, preparing myself to be absolutely gutted by whatever message she wants me to tell Dad.

Cara - Hey asshole, where the fuck is Oakley? I know you've done something with her. She hasn't been home in days. But seriously, if you guys aren't planning on having me watch her at the apartment anymore, do I really need to stay here? This place gives me the ick. Do you have any idea how many college booty calls have probably happened within these walls? Plus, there's a strange smell coming from the shower drain and it makes me wanna hurl!

Relief surges through me at not having to deal with her wild emotions, and that can only mean that she's got no idea where I am right now.

I quickly hash out a response as the clanging sound from deep within the cells gets louder.

Sawyer - Mind ya business. And yes, you're staying at that apartment until Zade's completed his ritual. I'll get someone in to look at your pipes.

I hit send before immediately regretting my choice of words.

Cara - I wouldn't mind if Zade wanted to check out my pipes. I know he's got the right tools for the job.

Fuck me. If she knew what Zade had done to our family, that he's responsible for sending our father to his execution, she'd never speak to him again. Fuck, I don't even know if I'll ever speak to the asshole again. At least, not how I used to. There's too much damage. I understand why he did it. My father was foolish to make a move against Oakley, but I thought my friendship with Zade meant more than that. He's always said that he was loyal to his cause, and it's my fault that I chose to underestimate just how far he'd go. Hell, the asshole is his father reborn.

Sawyer - Don't you have your own friends you can fuck? Quit fucking mine.

My phone beeps with another response, but when Harrison steps up to a big metal gate, I slip my phone away. He jams an old key into the lock and gives it a hard turn, and the heavy clanging that follows is almost deafening.

Harrison opens the gate up wide before stepping back and looking at me, a darkness in his eyes that has me reaching for my gun. "After you," he says, waving me through.

My grip on the gun in the back of my pants eases as Harrison's familiar smirk calms my nerves. I've known him my entire life, and though he gets off on the power trip of locking people up down here, I don't think he's dumb enough to risk trying to keep me prisoner—not with Zade knowing exactly where I am and who I'm with. Harrison is the typical Empire lackey, normal enough on the outside, but once you get past his suburban dad persona, he's as messed up as the rest of us.

I walk through the gate and down another set of rickety stairs that lead to the main cells. There are so many cells down here that it's like a maze, so easy to get lost if you don't know where you're going.

It's broken up into two sections—people who will violently slaughter a man, use his skin as a blanket and his teeth as a necklace, and then the people who probably have no fucking idea why they've been shoved down here.

Old oil lanterns light the narrow corridor, and as I start to pass some of the cells, I expect some crazy asshole to jump out at me like they do in the movies. "How far is he?" I ask, glancing back at him to see the distorted shadows from the lanterns spread across his face.

"Just up ahead," he tells me. "Around the corner."

I keep going, listening to the continuous clanging that's

accompanied by a constant drip that must be driving the prisoners insane. Hell, I wouldn't be surprised if Harrison was responsible for leaving a tap on just to remind these fuckers who's the boss down here.

Moving around the corner, Harrison steps in closer and indicates to a cell to my left. "Your father is in there."

I nod, my gut twisting with unease, not knowing what the fuck I'm going to do. How am I supposed to say goodbye to the man who raised me? To the man who gave me my name and ensured I had a life worth living?

My footsteps echo through the darkened hall, and just as I approach his cell, something jumps at me from the right. "Sawyer?" A gasping, familiar voice breaks through the silence as the person slams into the bars beside me. My head whips around, my hand on my gun ready to fuck someone up, but the wide-eyed, terrified blonde staring back at me tears me to shreds.

"Oakley?" I rush out, my eyes widening as I throw myself up against her cell, my hands coming down on hers around the thick, metal bars. My split knuckles instantly open, blood trailing down my hands, but all that matters is her. "What the fuck are you doing here?"

Harrison jabs me in the ribs. "Move it along. You're here for your father, nothing else."

I shake my head, panic pulsing through my veins as her big, blue eyes fill with tears. She's filthy, dirt smeared across her face and body. "Get me out of here, Sawyer," she begs, the words breaking over a lump in her throat. "Please, I can't—"

"Move it along," Harrison utters, a dark warning in his tone.

My feet are planted to the ground, unable to move. "Fuck, I—" I whip my head around to Harrison. "Release her now."

"Over my dead fucking body," he mutters, trying to push me along. "I do not interfere with Empire business. I just uphold it. If she's down here, there's a reason for it. Now, move it along."

"Sawyer?" I hear my father from up ahead. "Son, is that you?"

FUCK!

Harrison jabs me hard enough to have me step away from Oakley, and I realize there's not a damn thing I can do about it right now. I let him push me away, but I can't tear my eyes off her. Seeing her so broken kills me.

"Sawyer?" she cries, and the pure agony in her tone is enough for me to know that I will not rest until I have her back safe in my arms. Oakley holds my stare, her eyes so wide and filled with fear. I nod, letting her know I won't give up on her. Hell, I know Zade sure as fuck won't. Even if it means breaking Empire law just to get her back. He'll fucking do it in a heartbeat, and I know damn well Cross and Dalton will too.

Harrison keeps pushing me until I'm standing right in front of my father's cell, but I find it hard to even look at him. My full attention is still locked on Oakley, already putting together a plan to get her out of here.

I need to call the boys. We need to do this tonight.

"Sawyer." My father's stern tone cuts through my panic. "Forget the girl. Look at me."

My head whips around out of pure habit. Even locked behind

bars, when my father speaks, I act. That's just how it's always been, what he raised me to do as his perfect little puppet. Only now I'm a grown man with a mind of my own. "Father," I say, my gaze shifting over him, making sure he hasn't been harmed down here.

"Son," he says, gripping the bars as that familiar sternness fades away, leaving a shell of a man who's had to come to terms with the fact he's only days away from his execution. He glances at Harrison who remains a few feet away, giving us only a fraction of the privacy we need. When a man is in prison, his rights disappear right along with his freedom. "Listen to me," he starts. "What I did . . . I need you to be a man now. I'm going to be executed, no matter what happens at my trial. If by some miracle they grant me freedom, you and I both know Zade won't allow me to walk away. It's time for you to step up, to take the reins and be the man of our family. I know you can handle this, but your mother and sister will be devastated. They're going to need you."

"I know," I say with a nod, hating how formal he's being about this. How fucking hard is it to tell your son you love him and mean it? "I've already told them what's happened. Mom isn't taking it well. She feels like this was somehow her fault, that she shouldn't have pushed you so hard."

He clenches his jaw and glances away for just a moment, trying to compose himself. "Understand me now, boy. My decision to hurt that girl had nothing to do with your mother. Do not allow her to shoulder any guilt for my actions," he says before forcing himself to calm down. "And your sister?"

Unease blasts through my chest and I discreetly look back toward

Oakley's cell, making sure she can't overhear our conversation. After all, the topic of my sister's identity isn't something that's been shared with her yet and I'm not in the mood to have to deal with that bullshit tonight.

"Shock, maybe," I tell him, my mind reeling as to why my mother would possibly feel as though any of this could be her fault. "She didn't want to talk about it. Just went to her room and didn't come out, but she was just sending me texts as though nothing's happened."

"She'll do that. She'll pretend nothing's happening and won't allow herself to grieve until after the fact. That's when you need to be there for her. Don't try to force her to talk about it beforehand."

"I know how to handle her, Father. She's my twin sister."

He presses his lips into a hard line and lets out a heavy breath before meeting my stare. I have to force myself to keep looking, knowing that whatever he's brought me here to say still hasn't been said. "Don't fail me, Sawyer. You need to take your position within The Circle. The moment I'm gone, you'll be sworn in with an initiation to follow."

"I know, Father. We've been over this a million times."

"You're young. They won't respect you. You're going to have to fight for your value within their ranks. Make it known that you're heading to the top and don't back down until you're there. Those men . . . they're bad news. They will try and manipulate you, try to take your vote. You can't allow that to happen."

"I know how to handle a bunch of old bastards," I tell him. "I'll be fine."

"I know you will," he insists, gripping the bars tighter. "I trust you to excel, you always have in every aspect of your life. Just as you were raised to do. It's them I do not trust. They are not the upstanding men they portray themselves to be. They each hold dark secrets, just as I do."

My brows furrow. "What are you talking about?"

"It's all in my office desk," he tells me. "You must go home and burn it all. Every last document you can find. The second I'm gone, others will be prying for information, anything to push you out. You must not let them do that."

I nod as I hear Oakley's soft whimpers reverberating down the corridor. "Okay. I will."

I glance back at her, those big eyes still on me, and my heart races just a little bit faster, my father's secrets and desperation the furthest thing from my mind. I need to get her out of here.

"Hear me, son," he demands, reaching through the bars and gripping my chin, forcing me to hold his stare. "Do not fail me. If Zade fails his attempt to claim power, you take it for yourself. You claw your way to the top. Do not let this great Empire crumble. The Thorne legacy must rise."

"It will," I lie, knowing with every piece of my being that if Empire were to crumble around me, I'd be the first to fan the flames and help it burn to ashes. Just because I'm loyal to this world, doesn't mean I have to like who they are, what they stand for, or help it remain in power.

"Son," he says, his demeanor shifting as he releases my chin and grips the bars again, his eyes softening. My whole body stiffens, knowing this is what I really came here for. "I've never told you that I'm proud of you. You've grown into an impeccable young man. I didn't expect for this to happen so soon, but I've trained you in my image, and I know you will succeed. You're exactly what Empire needs."

I nod, not knowing how to respond to that. Hell, I even start feeling like shit knowing the second my father is dead and buried, I won't hesitate to betray him. The need to tell him that I love him sits on the end of my tongue, but he's created such a fractured relationship between us that even now, knowing this could be the very last time I speak to him, the words still won't fly free.

"That's enough," Harrison says, inching closer and gripping my elbow. "Time to go."

Clenching my jaw, I keep my eyes on my father. "They're going to be okay," I promise him, not needing to clarify who I'm referring to. "I won't let them fall."

"I know, son," he says, a slight panic in his tone. "Continue to make me proud."

"I will."

Harrison gives me a hard tug, and I fall away from my father, knowing there was so much I wasn't able to share with him, so much I wish I could have told him. As I'm dragged away, that same desperation pulses through my veins.

My father steps back away from the bars into the darkness of his cell, and I stare after him, hating how much this fucking hurts. I stumble back another few steps until I'm passing Oakley's cell and she reaches out to me, her fingers brushing over my arm.

Turning to face her, she sees the devastation in my eyes. "It's going to be okay," she promises me. "You're strong, Sawyer. You can get through this."

I swallow hard and grip onto her cell before Harrison can pull me away. "He's going to die," I tell her. "I can't save him."

"No, you can't," she confirms, not wanting to sugarcoat it. She moves in closer, her hands clutching onto mine as though they're her only lifeline. "I know you're hurting, Sawyer, but I need your head in the game. I need you to get me out of here."

"I know," I tell her, knowing at some point Harrison is going to drag me away, and when that happens, it's going to destroy something deep in my chest. Walking away from her right now feels so damn wrong. How can I call myself a man if I leave her rotting away in here? "I promise, we're coming for you."

A laugh sounds from the cell behind me before a man's voice breaks the trembling silence. "You know damn well you shouldn't be making her promises you can't keep," the strange man says. "No one leaves these cells."

I go to look back over my shoulder, but Oakley grips my chin and forces my stare back to hers. "Are you a man of your word?" she asks in desperation, tears welling in her beautiful, blue eyes.

She knows me well enough to know that I am, at least when it counts, and I nod. I need to put her heart at ease.

"Do you remember our basketball game?" she questions as Harrison tries to pull me away, but I grip onto the bars tighter, refusing to move, the look in her eye almost bringing me to my knees. "You each owe me a favor, and I'm calling it in. Save me, Sawyer."

"We will," I promise her, letting her see the conviction in my stare. "Be ready. This goes down tonight."

She nods and with that, Harrison pulls me away. "Come on, lover boy," he rumbles, sick of my shit. He drags me away, not allowing me another second to put her at ease. As wrong as it feels walking away, I know I have to. In order to get her out of here, I have to get back to the boys.

Harrison all but drags me back up the rickety stairs and shoves me through the heavy metal gate, slamming it behind me to find my own way back. I whip around, clutching onto the gate and leveling him with a hard stare. "That girl is important. She means a great deal to a lot of people. You take care of her. If anything happens before I can get her out of here, I'm coming for your throat."

Harrison smirks as though welcoming the fight, and slinks away into the darkness without another word. Not wasting a damn second, I turn abruptly and fly back up the long, twisting corridor with my phone in hand.

It barely rings before Zade's voice cuts through the line. "What is it?"

"Oakley," I tell him. "I've found her."

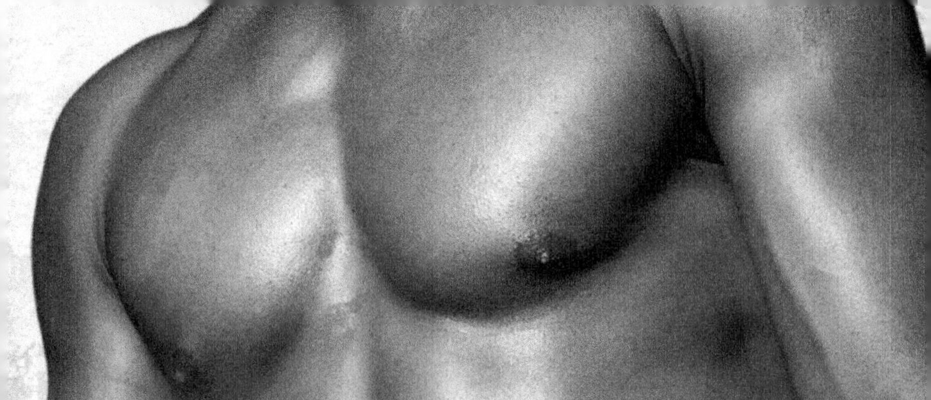

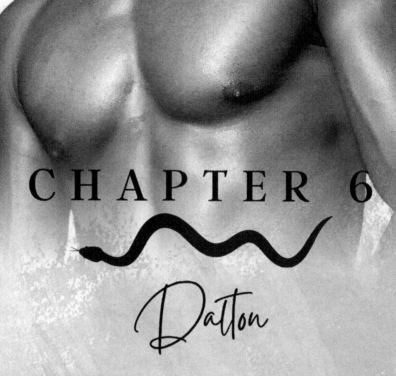

CHAPTER 6

Dalton

"FUCK," Zade roars, pacing back and forth through his penthouse, his hands pressed firmly at his temples. He stops and turns to face Sawyer. "How the fuck are we supposed to get her out of there?"

Sawyer shakes his head as the image of my girl in that fucking cell eats me alive. I've gotta give it to Joe. Considering he wanted her kept hidden, he chose the best fucking place to put her. Only he couldn't have known Nikolai was put down there barely twenty-four hours beforehand. Nobody knew, and he sure as fuck wouldn't have known that Sawyer would walk those damp corridors and find her. Hell, if it weren't for Nikolai trying to kill her the other night, we never would have found her. We never would have even considered looking in those cells.

"I don't fucking know," Sawyer says. "But I promised her we would do this tonight, and I'm not about to break that promise. Besides, she called in her favor. We have to do this."

"Favor?" Zade grunts. "The fuck are you talking about?"

Cross scoffs, almost amused. "The basketball game. We cut her a deal, remember? She and Dalton won, and now each of us owes her a favor."

I shake my head. "Fucking waste of her favors," I mutter as Cross strides across the room and puts Venom into her enclosure, knowing damn well what we're about to do isn't somewhere he should be bringing her. "We would have gone after her anyway."

"Too fucking right," Zade says. "Now that we know where she is, she's not slipping out of my fingers again. We go tonight. Whatever we have to do, we do it. I'm not forfeiting my claim because we can't figure out how to break some bitch out of a prison cell. I hope she's fucking ready."

"She's ready," Sawyer says. "She might fucking hate us, but she'll tolerate us if it means getting out of there."

"Good," Zade says, his eyes hardening, knowing just how fucking dangerous breaking into the prison system is. If we were to get caught, it's our heads. The Circle won't excuse this shit, not even for the sake of retrieving Zade's sacrifice. "Let's do this."

We file out of his penthouse and into the elevator, pressing the button for the private underground parking garage. The elevator quickly plunges to the bottom and then we're pouring out into the sea of Zade's luxury cars, a collector's wet dream. Despite the array of cars we can choose from, we head straight for the black Escalade and pile in, peeling out of the private underground garage, and flying toward Zade's storage locker.

The car ride is silent, each of us deep in thought.

Zade's fingers curl around the steering wheel, his knuckles turning white as Sawyer looks like he's going to be sick. I can only imagine the conversation he had with his father, let alone what else he must have seen down there.

Cross though, his knee is bouncing, anxious about this stupid shit we're about to do. He's usually the calm one, the one who has his shit together. But without Venom curled around his hand, his security blanket is stripped away. Don't get me started on their fucked-up relationship. I'll never understand it, but for some reason, that snake calms him and helps him escape the monsters living inside his mind.

We pull up at the secure storage locker, and Zade enters the code into the keypad, each of us watching as the massive metal door slides back, granting us entry. As we walk inside, a thrill sails through my body. I fucking love coming in here. It's the best kind of grown-up playground.

The whole room is decked out with weapons. Every type of gun under the sun resides here, along with knives, tranquilizers, grenades, and swords. Hell, there are even spears, cannons, crossbows, and sniper rifles. But my absolute favorite, the one thing that really gets me hard, is the motherfucking tank that stares back at me. Something tells me we won't be needing that bad boy today, which is unfortunate. I can't wait to drive that thing, and when the time comes, I'm going to be as happy as a pig rolling around in his own fucking shit.

We grab some bags and start filling them with everything we might need, and I make sure to add a few extra grenades. I doubt we'll run into many people, but there are bound to be a few walls we'll need to break through. Cross backs the Escalade into the storage locker, and I toss in a pair of industrial bolt cutters while Sawyer grabs the Jaws of Life, hoping like fuck that's all we'll need to bend the bars of her cells. Oakley is small. All it'd take is a slight bend in the bars for her to slip through them, but the question is just how hard is it going to be to make that happen?

To be on the safe side, Zade places an industrial-sized grinder in the back, making sure we have every fucking base covered.

I meet everyone's eyes. We've gone headfirst into much worse situations, but nothing that has such high risks. "We good?" I question, hoping like fuck we haven't missed anything. "Because once we're in there, we're not coming out without her. There are no second chances."

Cross nods. "We're good. Let's fucking do this."

CHAPTER 7

Oakley

My hands shake as I pace my small cell, the constant drip somehow even louder through the night. I lost track of time long ago, but if I had to guess, I'd say Sawyer's been gone for at least three or four hours. When he said he'd come back for me, I knew he would keep his word. The only question is how is it all going to go down? The boys don't do anything the easy way. They get off on the idea of death, and anything or anyone who stands in their way will suffer at their hands.

I've never felt anxiety like this before. Just the idea of seeing Zade in the flesh eats at me, and I know without a doubt that this isn't a rescue mission to him. He doesn't care what happens to me as long as my heart continues to beat. No, this is nothing but a mere stepping stone that'll take him closer to the top, closer to my death.

"Quit pacing, O," my father says, not able to sleep when he knows what's coming. "They'll come when everything is ready. They can't just storm in here guns blazing. They must be discreet. In and out without anyone the wiser, which means any of the main entrances are out. If they're taking their time, it means they're being cautious."

"I know," I groan. "But I don't have the patience for this."

My father laughs, and there's no mistaking the fondness in his tone. "Some things never change," he murmurs to himself. "You're still the same kid I've always remembered."

I roll my eyes, not exactly feeling the stroll down memory lane right now. My body is too on edge for any of that. I start to pace again when a loud clunking sounds from the top of the stairs. My body stiffens as my heart races.

My father looks at me, a fond smile across his face. "It's go time," he tells me. "Remember, once you're out, run. Run, my little girl. Run as far as you can."

I swallow hard and nod, hoping that one day he might forgive me.

I'm not running anywhere. I'm staying and fighting until the end.

I won't be sacrificed. I'll be crowned queen of this fucked-up empire, and then I'm going to burn it to the ground. I'm gonna save my father's life and then I'm gonna save my own.

"I don't want to leave you behind," I tell him, my heart breaking at the thought of being away from him after only just getting him back.

"You must, Oakley," he says, clutching the bars of his cell and fixing me with a hard stare, making sure I truly hear him. "Zade can't find out I'm alive. If he does, he will not hesitate to end my life. Do you understand me?"

Nodding my head, I let out a heavy breath, feeling as though I'm about to break.

It's almost bittersweet. Knowing he's alive and here, but also having to leave him again. I don't know how to feel about it. I want to celebrate, but the thought of leaving him behind is crippling me.

More loud clanging comes from high over the cells, and I keep my stare locked down the long hall, my heart racing with anxiety and fear. When it comes to these guys, there's no telling how this shit is going to go down. All I know is that I need to be prepared for the worst.

The eerie glow of the oil lanterns lights the way, sending long, flickering shadows across the corridor. There's the faint sound of a heavy metal door swinging open, the old hinges squealing in protest, before I hear the sound of feet scuffling across the floor.

"Where is she?" I hear a familiar whispered tone cutting through the deadly silence, sending my blood cold.

Zade.

"Bottom of the stairs. Turn right. Maybe fifty yards along," Sawyer responds.

Clutching the bars, I try to calm my racing heart, but it's no use. I won't be able to breathe properly until I'm out of here. My only saving grace is the fact that Zade won't kill me until the sixtieth moon. It means I have time to formulate a plan. But there's no doubt he'll make me pay for trying to escape him in the first place.

They're like ghosts in the dark, moving silently through the prison until I hear them on the rickety stairs. If I weren't trying to listen to every little whisper, I would have missed it. When Harrison comes down those stairs, it sounds like a herd of elephants, but these four guys . . . they're stealthy, deadly assassins.

They hit the bottom of the stairs and there's nothing but silence.

I shove my face right up against the bars, listening intently for anything that might clue me into their whereabouts, but there's nothing. Not a damn sound. Maybe they've stopped or have run into trouble. Perhaps Harrison is there and they're trying to figure out a way past him . . . or they're working out how best to kill him like the fucking sickos they are.

I continue staring into the darkened hallway, seeing nothing when I hear a strange gurgling sound, followed by a loud thump of something dropping to the ground. My eyes widen, realizing I've heard that sound before—the night I followed the boys into this very place and watched as Zade slit a man's throat.

Bile rises in my throat, and just as I'm about to gag, the shadows across the corridor begin to shift. I suck in a breath, my whole body shaking when I see them, the four demons living rent-free in my nightmares.

Sawyer. Dalton. Easton. Zade.

They can all rot in hell. But not until after they've busted my ass out of here.

"Where?" Zade questions again.

Sawyer's face comes into view, his dark stare filled with determination. "Little further. She's on the right."

Relief pounds through my chest as they storm toward me, each of them holding heavy tools. But I'm not going to lie. I'm surprised to see Zade and Sawyer working together. How could they possibly come back from that? The fight they had . . . the way Sawyer broke. I could have sworn their friendship was over.

One by one, their sharp gazes come to mine. I look up at Sawyer as he clutches the bars of my cell, those callous green eyes locking onto mine. "You came back," I breathe.

"I told you I would," he says, his gaze jumping around the darkened cells. Zade's laser-like stare hits my face, but I refuse to look at him. I'm not prepared to see evil staring back at me. Just as quickly as Sawyer appeared, he's gone again, flying down the corridor to check on his father.

Before I even get a chance to follow his movements, Easton is right there, his dark gaze sailing over my body from head to toe. "You good?" he questions, not allowing even a shred of emotion into his deep tone.

I nod, watching as he shoves something between the bars to try and pry them apart, his strong tattooed arms working overtime, bulging and flexing with every movement. "Just get me out of here," I insist, stepping away and focusing on the tool in his hands. It kinda looks like something firemen use to pry metal apart when trying to free victims from car crashes. I think they call it the Jaws of Life. Knowing my luck, the bars will probably snap and knock me out cold, though they won't kill me. After all, only Zade can do that.

A hand flies through the bars and grips my chin, and I look up to find Dalton, his stare filled with nothing but undeniable hurt. "You ran," he mutters as I shuffle in closer to him, desperate to feel his hands on mine, even if it's through the bars.

I scoff, my chest aching with his betrayal. I fix him with a hard stare, not capable of sitting back and allowing him to try and guilt me over my decision to leave Zade's penthouse. "Can you blame me?" I question, gripping the weathered note and holding it up to his face. "I know what you assholes really want with me. How you're holding me hostage in that big fucking apartment just so you can all get off while Bossman tears my heart out of my chest for some sick ritual. Anyone in their right mind would have run, Dalton. Hell, if you were in my shoes, you would have tried to run too. So don't look at me like I've offended you in some horrendous way. I'm the one who's been wronged here."

Dalton swallows hard, and I watch as his Adam's apple bobs up and down, regret shining so brightly in his eyes. "I'm sorry, Firefly," he murmurs. "It wasn't my place to say anything. This is bigger than me."

I scoff again and tear my chin out of his grip as Zade and Easton work on the bars, their muscles bulging as they try to bend them just enough for me to slip through. "You really want to start feeding me that shit?" I question, more than ready to put these assholes in their place. "You told me you were going to protect me, but you've done nothing but lie to me since the second I met you. Up on that roof, setting me up to be kidnapped by your asshole friends, and now this. That's two strikes, Dalton. You don't want to learn what happens at three."

"Really?" Zade grunts, pausing his efforts for just a moment to fix me with a hard stare, and I can't help but take note of how much worse he looks now that the bruising has started to really come out. "Right now? You want to start this shit right now?"

I meet his callous, cruel stare and a chill sweeps through my body. "The fucking audacity!" I say. "You haven't got a leg to stand on, Zade. If it weren't for you, I wouldn't be in this mess."

"You fucking ran," he spits. "That's on you."

"Really?" I scoff. "You want to put this on me? Why don't you look in the mirror? You promised me protection, yet somehow I was able to be lured out of your apartment right under your fucking nose, which tells me the great Zade DeVil failed. *You* allowed me to slip away. *You* lost me, and that's on you."

Zade clenches his jaw. He knows I'm right, yet he's too fucking stubborn to admit it.

The bars start to bend, and Zade looks away, focusing on what he needs to do as Sawyer returns to Easton's side and grips the weird tool, lending his strength.

My heart races, the anticipation of getting out of here burning through my veins. Something flashes in my periphery, and just as my gaze snaps around, Harrison's face comes into view. His arm whips out, a gun held tightly in his hand. My eyes widen with fear as I see Harrison's gaze locked on the back of Dalton's head. "WATCH OUT!"

I drop to the ground just as Dalton whips around, his foot already striking out. He kicks Harrison in the gut and he flies back against my father's cell as his shot goes wide, the bullet ricocheting off the bar in front of my face.

A scream tears from my throat, but before the sound echoes down the corridors of the prison, my father's arms dive through the bars of his cell and lock around Harrison's throat. He keeps him pinned against the door of his cell as Zade steps up in front of him.

Harrison fights against my father's hold as Easton, Dalton, and Sawyer work their asses off to keep bending the bars, certain that more guards are going to hear the commotion. My gaze flicks between the boys and Zade, my heart racing.

"I . . . I have a family," Harrison says, clawing at my father's arms. Despite not getting a chance to know my father over the past twelve years, I know without a doubt that he will endure any kind of pain Harrison deals if it means I will be free of this prison.

Zade scoffs while curiously glancing at my father, probably wondering why this strange man is helping him. Hopefully he puts it down to wanting revenge on his captor. "And I have Empire to claim," Zade tells Harrison as he snaps his fist out, and Harrison goes down like a sack of shit.

My eyes widen in fear. "Is . . . is he—"

"No," Easton says with a grunt as he pulls against the bars, bending them bit by bit. "Just knocked out, but he won't be down for long. We need to get you out of here."

Shit.

Zade returns, his gaze sailing over me before glancing at the bars. "That should be enough," he says, indicating for me to try to squeeze through. The boys step away, removing the Jaws of Life, and as I step up to the slight bend in the bar, Sawyer glances back down the corridor toward his father's cell, then back to Harrison, knowing our time is quickly running out.

I don't doubt the boys have left a trail of destruction on their way down here, and it won't be long until someone calls for help.

Gripping the bars, I duck down to the widest part and take a shaky breath before craning my neck to try and find the right angle. I slowly push, feeling the bars at both sides of my head, but it's just wide enough to squeeze through.

"Twist your shoulders," Easton says, reaching out and gripping my hand to help me through. "You're gonna have to go sideways."

My first shoulder slips through the bars, and I have to squeeze through one tit at a time before I'm able to get the second shoulder out. In order to create just a little bit of stability, I have no choice but to shove a leg through next. My ass gets stuck, and Easton curls his arm around my waist to pull me the rest of the way out. The second I have both feet on the ground, I let out a shaky breath.

"Good?" Easton mutters.

I nod, my gaze shifting to my father as a pang of guilt tears through my chest. "Love you, kid," he mouths, making my eyes well with tears.

"Love you," I mouth right back.

"Come on," Zade says, abandoning the tools on the ground by my cell. "We gotta bounce."

I turn on my heel, ready to haul ass out of here when Sawyer shakes his head and doubles back to his father's cell. "I'm not leaving without him," he says. "The trial is a fucking death sentence."

"Sawyer," Zade warns.

"No," Sawyer spits, spinning back around to fix Zade with a hard stare. "I'm doing this with or without you."

"The hell you are, boy," Nikolai's voice rumbles through the cells, forcing Sawyer to whip back around to face his father.

"The fuck are you talking about?" Sawyer demands. "Don't be such an old fucking fool. The Circle won't forgive your crimes, Dad. You'll be executed."

"I deserve to be," Nikolai says. "I betrayed the blood in a moment of weakness. I am right where I deserve to be. There is nowhere out there where I will be free. I need to pay for what I have done. Now get out of here before it's too late. If you're caught down here, we lose it all. Nothing is more important than ensuring your position in The Circle. Without that, we have nothing."

"But Mom and—"

"GO," Nikolai roars. "Look after our family and be the change Empire needs. Now, son."

Sawyer swallows hard, indecision flashing in his eyes.

"Come on, man," Dalton says just as Nikolai steps back into the darkness of his cell. "Your father has made his decision. It's time to go."

My gut clenches, and I turn back to face my father as Sawyer catches up with us, pain deep in his eyes. "I'm coming back for you," I tell my father, my voice low, though I feel curious stares on my back.

Anger settles in his features. "Don't you dare," he tells me. "I told you to run. You promised me that you'd run."

I shake my head. "No," I tell him, just as Zade's hand closes around my arm and pulls me away. "I promised nothing."

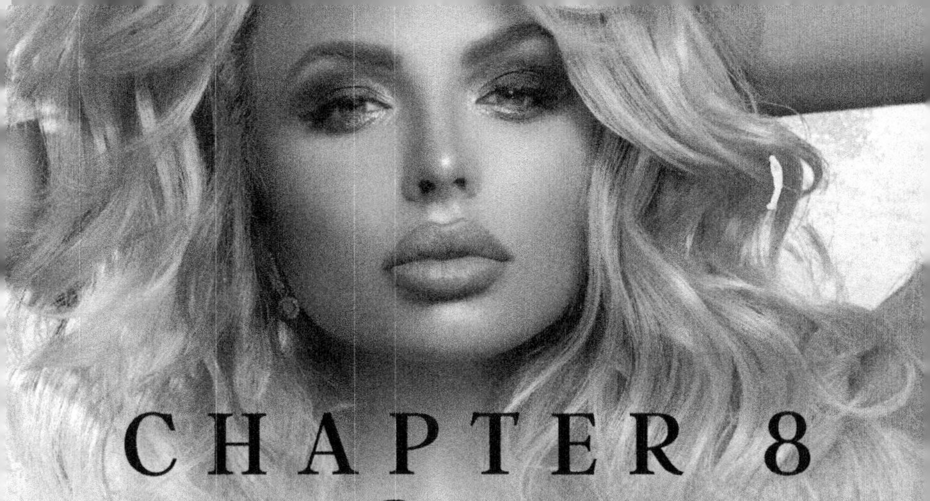

CHAPTER 8

Oakley

We race through the eerie corridors of Empire's prison, passing plenty of dead bodies along the way. Blood pools at the bottom of the rickety stairs, and as I race for the exit, it splashes up against my legs. I try not to think about it. My only focus is on putting one foot in front of the other.

I don't look down, don't look at the faces of the men who were brutally murdered in order for Zade to get me out of Empire's prison. These men might have had families, wives, and children. A life, hopes, and dreams, and in a matter of seconds, they were slaughtered like cattle.

The boys are much faster than me, and Zade clutches onto me like his only lifeline, all but dragging me along. I feel one of the guys behind me, his hand against my lower back, forcing me to move quicker, but we're running so fast that I can't risk looking back to see who it is. My guess would be Dalton. He's always been the one to show he cares for me, to have my back, despite being the one who likes to stab a knife right through it.

We fly up the stairs as they almost crumble beneath our weight, but the boys press on, Zade's hand clutching me even tighter. Sawyer reaches the top first and shoves through an old, metal gate, so similar to all the other ones deep in this twisted fortress. Only this one seems heavier, sturdier even. Designed specifically to keep assholes like Zade and his crew out . . . or in.

The gate creaks and whines, and it's clear it has been here longer than any of us have been alive. I can barely take a second to ponder the specifics of the old gate before we're already flying through it and darting up the long tunnel ahead, the creaking still echoing throughout the corridors behind us.

The old lanterns become further apart until they stop completely, leaving us in the eeriness of the long tunnels, so fucking dark I can't even make out the bold, intricate tattoos that wind up Zade's arms. There's nothing to keep us company except the sound of my heavy panting and my feet against the cobblestones. The boys don't make a sound, and if it weren't for Dalton's hand on my back and Zade's death grip on my hand, I could almost believe I was alone.

We run as my lungs scream for sweet relief, and the further we go, the more I trip over my feet, my aching muscles barely able to hold me up anymore. I struggle to see in front of me, blindly trusting Zade to lead me out of here. We turn a corner, and I stumble in the dark as an arm drags me to the left while my body attempts to continue straight ahead. No sooner have we raced around the corner, Zade wrenches back on my hand, bringing me to a violent halt.

He presses his back up against the wall of the dark tunnel, pulling me in hard against his chest, his hand braced over my mouth, muffling the sound of my heavy panting. "We're not alone," he murmurs in my ear as the boys fall in beside us. I feel Sawyer's arm brush against mine, so fucking close.

Craning my neck to peer into the darkness ahead, I see nothing. My brows furrow, trying to figure out what the hell they've all sensed in these tunnels, but I come up blank. Apart from the heavy thumping of my pulse in my ears, I hear nothing. Not even the faintest echo of footfalls or a whispered breath.

"Wha—" I start, but Zade's hand clamps tighter over my mouth, keeping me silent.

I feel him against me, his lips right by my ear. "Don't say a fucking word."

A chill sweeps through my body and goosebumps rise on my skin. I have no fucking idea if they're from our impending doom or from the way Zade's breath brushes across the sensitive skin just below my ear.

As the seconds tick by, my eyes begin to adjust, and I find Easton directly in front of me, his gaze intently locked on mine as Sawyer stands to my right, and Dalton to my left.

Easton watches me and the longer his intense stare remains on mine, the harder it becomes to breathe. There's something about this man, so raw and powerful, it terrifies me. And yet, it has me wanting to peel back the layers and figure out what kind of brokenness I'll find beneath.

As he watches me, I can't help but think about the cross engraved on my thigh, his mark left on my body. His possessiveness stamped right there for the world to see. He wanted to claim me, wanted to let Sawyer and Dalton know that he wasn't going to back down.

Easton is so different from Dalton and Sawyer. He's a mystery. Silent and brooding, impossible to read. Yet I feel like there's so much of him to discover. He's held back on me, but now that my time on earth is limited, I want to get to know him . . . the real him.

Holding his stare, I finally start to relax. My body sinks back against Zade's, and sensing the change, he loosens his hand over my mouth. Unable to help myself, I reach up and grip his wrist, my fingers curling around it and clutching onto him, needing the closeness and security he can offer while his words replay on a loop in my mind.

We're not alone.

As if on cue, two men appear out of the darkness, and I suck in a deep breath. My eyes widen as I watch them slowly saunter toward us, completely oblivious to the monsters camouflaged by the dark walls of the tunnels.

The silence is killing me, and the heavy thump of my heart sounds like roaring thunder in my ears. Unshed tears burn my eyes as I think about the fate these men will suffer for simply being in the wrong place at the wrong time. A single tear falls from my lashes and sails down my cheek, landing on Zade's wrist. I feel the way his body stiffens behind me. It's as though someone has just stabbed a blade right through his cold, black heart, and he's realized that this person he's been so hell-bent on killing is actually just a broken woman with very real emotions.

With the men so much closer now, Zade doesn't risk moving or saying a damn word, just simply stands there as I fall to pieces in his strong arms. With every step the men take toward us, my heart races faster, and I grip Zade's wrist, my nails digging into his skin.

They move right in front of us and my eyes remain locked on Easton's, willing myself to melt deeper into Zade, terrified they'll notice us. I hold my breath as they take another step, and despite only a few seconds passing, it feels like an eternity. They move past us and I swallow hard, relief pounding through my veins.

Only one of them stops and turns back, his brows furrowed as he tries to search for whatever made him pause in the darkness. My eyes widen, terror claiming me as the other stops with him, looking back to try and figure out what's caught his companion's attention.

Easton's eyes remain locked on mine and he cringes, knowing exactly what he has to do. He doesn't strike me as the type who would usually hesitate, and it has me wondering if his cringe is purely for my benefit—not wanting me to have to see what he's about to do.

I feel Dalton's arm flex beside me, preparing for a fight and I can't help but remember how he gets off on the violence. Both he and Easton step out from the walls, barely giving the men a second to realize what's going on. They don't even get a chance to react when Dalton and Easton step in behind them, grip their heads from behind, and give a devastating twist.

The violent cracks of their spines have bile rising in my throat, but before I can scream or whimper, they each drop heavily to the ground.

"Come on," Zade says, not giving a second thought for the two men who were killed for walking by. His hand falls to my waist, pushing me back out into the center of the corridor as his other hand drops away from my mouth, allowing me to take a proper breath.

I go to look over my shoulder, but Easton steps in behind me, blocking my view of the dead bodies. "Just run," he tells me, shaking his head, regret heavy in his eyes.

Zade doesn't allow me a chance to respond before he's pulling me along, tugging hard on my wrist just as he was before. My body goes numb and I just run, not yet immune to death the same way the guys are.

Sawyer and Dalton run up ahead of us, checking the tunnels are clear, and I realize we must be getting closer to populated areas. I've been down in the tunnels once before, and it didn't take nearly this long to get where I was going. The thought leaves me wondering just how many tunnels there are.

We run for fifteen uninterrupted minutes beneath the beautiful town of Faders Bay—the place I had hoped to call home once again. Now, I can't get away fast enough.

Another gate appears ahead just before Zade pulls me up next to him, and we settle into a brisk walk, the boys crowding me as if to obstruct me from view. Sawyer pushes through the gate and we walk into an open area with a few random men lingering around, sipping on their expensive whiskey while watching a girl up on a stage. The room is similar to the main bar I'd walked into the night I decided it was a good idea to follow the boys here, only this one seems . . . darker. As if the girl up on stage knows that her performance isn't going to finish there, that these men will have her any way they see fit. One at a time or all together. Passing her around like a used toy. And yet, judging by the excitement in her eyes, she seems more than okay with it.

We get a few curious stares, and Zade receives the occasional head nod, but no one looks deeper. No one sees the escaped prisoner hidden between them with all their attention focused on the dancing girl.

With no one the wiser, we slip through the exit and into another tunnel, this one taking us up to street level until we're pushing through a heavy door and walking out into a back alley behind some dirty bar.

It takes me a moment to catch my bearings, and I tug my wrist out of Zade's death grip, surprised when he actually releases it. The boys all turn to look at me—as if waiting for me to explode or have some kind of meltdown. "Just . . . just give me a second," I tell them, bracing my hands against my thighs and doubling over, fighting back tears as the wild emotions rock through my body. Anger, fury, betrayal, fear, relief. I don't know what to focus on or how to feel. All that matters is Zade DeVil. This is all on him.

Dalton creeps in closer and tries to reach for me, but I flinch away from his touch. The fresh air makes it easier to process everything that's happened. "Come on, Firefly. You're not safe yet. We need to get you back to Zade's penthouse."

My head snaps up and I straighten out, fixing Dalton with a

haunting stare. "You're fucked in the head if you think for even a second that I'm going anywhere with you assholes. Thanks, but no thanks. You did me a solid getting me out of there, but I'm done."

Without sparing them another glance, I turn on my heel and go to stalk out of the alley, only getting a step before Zade's strong hand curls around the back of my neck, pulling me back to him and whipping me around to meet his venomous stare. "You're not going anywhere," he growls, his tone so low and deep that I feel its vibrations through my chest.

My hands come up and shove him hard, exhaustion quickly creeping up on me. Zade falls back a step, his death grip on my neck released. "Screw you," I spit, clutching the small, weathered note and shoving it into his chest, watching as he takes it and doesn't even bother looking over it, though something tells me he's known what was written on that note all along. "You really are fucked in the head, aren't you? You think I'm just going to lay down and let you take my life for some bullshit ritual? Let you tear my chest open and go digging around inside? Fuck you, Zade. Anyone in their right mind would run from you, and I'm no fucking different. I'm not going to allow this to happen."

Zade scoffs. "You really think you have a choice in the matter?" he questions, not denying it. "You're my sacrifice, my one road to power. I'm not about to let you slip through my fingers again. There is no way out for you. You don't get to just walk away. Your heart is my fate and you better fucking believe that I'm going to grip it with both hands and tear it right out of your fucking chest."

I back up a step, my heart racing with fear, feeling as though my back is up against the wall. Desperation pounds through me, and my hands shake with the realization of just how brutal this is going to be. The only way out for me is a slow, violent death. Only, it doesn't have to be that way . . .

With a disturbing desperation pulsing through my veins, my hand whips out and clutches the gun at Sawyer's back, my hand curling around the cool metal as I hastily back up a few steps. My eyes go wide, and I lock my haunted stare on Zade's as I lift the gun to my temple. "You'll never fucking have me," I tell him, a tear rolling down my cheek. "If my choices are being brutally slaughtered by you or killing myself in a humane way, then I choose me. Every damn time."

Dalton springs toward me, fear in his eyes. "No, no, no, no," he panics, as Sawyer lunges. But I squeeze the trigger before they can get to me, more than ready to end it all.

The gun clicks, and my eyes spring open just as Sawyer's hand wraps around mine and takes the gun away, guilt heavy in his eyes as if knowing I would have done exactly that.

"What—"

"So fucking predictable," Zade says, striding toward me as the tears flow freely down my cheeks. "The second I realized you knew about the ritual, I knew you would try to take yourself out. I knew you would try to steal this away from me, but I hoped you wouldn't be that fucking stupid. Getting away from me isn't going to be that easy, Oakley."

He steps right up to me, his fingers brushing up my arm and

across my collarbone before curling around the base of my throat. He uses his thumb to force my chin up, meeting my horrified stare. "I'm not ready to die."

"I know," he tells me. "But you will."

I shake my head, not ready to come to terms with this as he releases his hold on my throat, confident that I'm not about to run. I have to fight, have to find a way to survive. "So I'm just supposed to go with you and accept that my life is over? Succumb to this ritual and give my life for you? What's in it for me?" I cry. "I'm not even twenty-one. I haven't lived yet."

Glancing around the boys, I see regret in Easton's stare, devastation in Dalton's, and guilt in Sawyer's, but Zade . . . he's stone cold—the cruel, callous leader he was always meant to be.

"Firefly," Dalton murmurs, stepping into me, ready to feed me whatever bullshit he tells himself to try and make this all okay.

"Don't," I spit, flinching away from him as he tries to reach for me. "Don't fucking touch me."

His hand falls away, and I look back at Zade. "How long do I have?"

"Twenty-eight days."

I crumble, my knees falling into the dirty pavement as I barely catch myself. Twenty-eight days to live. Twenty-eight days to survive. Twenty-eight days to take everything Zade DeVil holds dear and burn it to the fucking ground.

Easton kneels down beside me, hesitating just a moment before placing his hand over my thigh, right where he marked my skin with his cross. "Come on, Oakley," he murmurs, coaxing me to get back up. "We have to get you out of here. It won't be long until they sound the alarm and come searching."

I shake my head, refusing to stand, so he scoops me up in his strong arms instead, pulling me into his chest as I try to figure out how the hell I'm supposed to fit a whole lifetime into the space of twenty-eight days. Hell, I've never even fallen in love.

"I don't want to die," I tell him, my head nuzzled into the curve of his neck.

"I know," he tells me. "Believe me, if there were another way, we would have done it. I'd do anything to spare your life."

My heart shatters, every passing second only making me realize just how fucking trapped I am. There's no way out of this. No freedom for me, no life to be lived. I'll never escape Zade and his crew. I'll never find peace, solitude, or happiness. I'll never be free.

For the next twenty-eight days, I'm a caged bird waiting for execution by the hand of the man who has stolen the life I was supposed to lead.

Easton carries me out of the back alley, the boys close at his back, and as the exhaustion and mental overload begins to catch up to me, I glance back over Easton's shoulder and meet Zade's cruel stare. "You better hope you kill me because, if you don't, I will come for you, and I will burn your whole fucking world to ashes."

Zade nods, accepting what will be. "You have the blood pulsing through your veins. You're the true heir, Oakley. You'll never beat me. You can't, but I'd be disappointed if you didn't at least try." And with that, Easton deposits me in the back of an Escalade, more than ready to take me back to my penthouse prison.

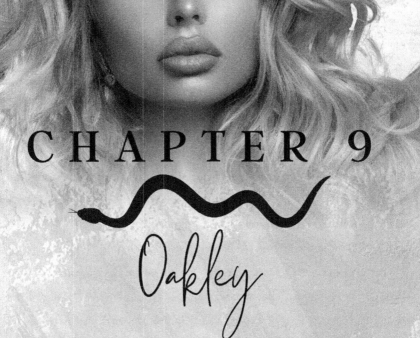

CHAPTER 9

Oakley

I don't recall the car ride back to Zade's hotel. One minute, Easton was putting me in the back, the next, I was opening my eyes to find Sawyer reaching for me through the open car door. Barely a minute later, the elevator opened to Zade's penthouse, and I was forced back into the luxurious apartment.

It's almost eerie standing here in the penthouse now. Don't get me wrong, I hated being here before. I hated the thought of being held prisoner by these guys, but they promised me protection. They made me believe that the safest place for me was under their watchful eyes. Which I suppose to some extent is true. But now, knowing they're only protecting me from these attacks in order to be the ones who get to slaughter me . . . I don't fucking like it. It has me questioning every fucking step I've ever made.

Ignoring the boys. I make my way to my bedroom when Zade's scoff pulls me up short. I turn on my heel and fix him with a scathing stare. "What now, your majesty?" I spit, the words like poison on my tongue. "Did I forget to kiss your feet, or shall I help you sharpen the knife you'll use to slice through my chest?"

He narrows his stare but thankfully remains where he is across the room. "You really think I'm about to let you out of my sight after you ran from me?" he questions. "You lost the privilege of having a bedroom. You'll sleep in my room, right beside me."

I gape at the asshole. "Absolutely not," I tell him. "I'd rather gouge my eyes out with a rusty fork than have to sleep beside you."

"Be my guest," he says, waving toward the kitchen. "They're not rusty, but they'll do the job. I can help you if you'd like. After all, it's not your eyes I need."

I scowl at the prick, my hands shaking at my sides as red-hot rage crashes through my body like a tsunami. "You're such a fucking asshole."

"You're just working this out now?" he questions, leaning back against the dining room table. "You've got two fucking choices. Either accept that you're sleeping in my room, or don't, and I can chain you up in my cell again. Take your pick."

My heart starts to race at the idea of being locked up again, and as he stares back at me, I realize just how quickly he'd do it. Not wanting to take any more risks than I already have, I clench my jaw and spin on my heel before stalking toward his stupid bedroom, knowing damn well if I even tried to go to mine, I would be dragged out by the ankles. Every step I take is like having a fire poker stabbed through my back, knowing just how much satisfaction he gets from my misery. He gets off on power and loves the thrill of forcing someone into submission.

But he made a mistake.

Inviting me into his room is one thing, but having me right beside him while he's at his most vulnerable . . . Well, that's nothing more than a gift. I hope the bastard likes to sleep with one eye open, because I fully intend to take him out. The question is, will I get to his heart before he can get to mine?

Stepping into his bedroom, the exhaustion hits me like a freight train, and without even sparing a moment to snoop through all of his shit, I collapse onto his bed. His pillow smells just like him, and I get a sick sense of satisfaction knowing just how filthy I am after being in those cells. If he's going to demand that I sleep in here with him, I'll be sure to make it as uncomfortable as humanly possible. Zade DeVil will regret the moment he decided to invite me into his bed.

Before even getting a chance to pull the blankets up over my body, I fall into a deep, fretful sleep, and by the time I'm waking, the afternoon sun is streaming through the floor-to-ceiling windows. I clamber out of bed and smirk at the dirty footprints smeared across Zade's blankets, knowing damn well when I come to bed next time, I'll be taking the clean side.

Needing to feel human again, I saunter out into the hallway and make my way into what used to be my bedroom to find a fresh change of clothes and clean underwear, only my room has been stripped bare.

No bed. No rug on the floor. No fucking clean clothes.

"Assholes," I grunt, slamming the walk-in closet door before storming back to Zade's room, slamming that door just as hard. I move into his closet, searching through his drawers for something to wear, and considering he's twice my size, there's not a lot of options.

Finding a pair of sweatpants and a white shirt, I figure I can make it work before moving into his private bathroom. Pulling off my dirty clothes, I throw them across the bathroom before thinking better of it and dumping them in the bottom of the shower. If these are the only clothes I've got that fit me, I'm not about to let them out of my sight. Even if they're filthy and all but torn to shreds.

My feet ache from the hours of pacing through my cell and running through the cold tunnels, and I almost consider drawing a bath, but I simply don't have the patience. Getting in the shower, I turn on the taps and almost gag at the grime coming off the bottom of my feet. I've never felt so dirty. It's disgusting.

I slather myself in soap, scrubbing every inch of my body before rinsing it off and starting over. I shampoo and condition my hair and even trudge across Zade's bathroom soaking wet to search for a razor to shave my legs and everywhere else.

After feeling somewhat human again, I scrub my old clothes the best I can before wringing them out. Stepping out of the shower, I hook my soaking clothes over the side of the bathtub to dry, being sure to leave a growing puddle of water below them, and hoping like fuck Zade doesn't see it and slips through here like an ice skater on crack.

Grabbing a towel, I quickly dry off before stepping into his oversized sweatpants and rolling them at my hips to keep them up. The shirt is next, and as it falls to my knees, I do what I can to roll up the sleeves and tie it off at my waist, feeling like some kind of *Honey, I Shrunk the Kids* failed experiment.

Just to be a petty asshole, I trudge out into the penthouse, bypassing Dalton and Sawyer in the living room, who each give me curious stares, before heading right through to Zade's home office and searching for what I need.

After finding everything, plus my charcoal and drawing pad, I head back to Zade's bedroom and get busy, starting with his closet. If I only get the clothes I walked in here with, then so does he.

Grabbing the scissors, I start cutting nipple holes in every single shirt he owns before turning all his pants into ribbons. His boxers get a dick hole cut out of them for extra easy access, and I slice his socks straight down the middle, so his feet will look like a peeled banana if he tries to put them on. But it's the designer suits that really get me hard.

I send a silent prayer of forgiveness to the Armani and Hugo Boss gods before hacking away at every last suit Zade owns. Once I'm done, I simply close the door, hoping to whoever exists above that I'm here to witness the look on his stupid face when he comes in here looking for a change of clothes.

I consider going to town on his bed with the scissors before realizing just how much that would affect me too. So instead, I grab the sharpie and start jotting down every insult I can possibly think of in big bold letters across his walls and furniture.

Asshole. Prick. Murderer. Bastard. Raging cunt. Jackoff. Pussy. Assbag. Douchebag. Shit slinger.

The list goes on and on until every name under the sun decorates his room and my wrist begins to ache. Only then do I crawl back into bed with my drawing pad and charcoal to let off steam with my art.

My mind jumps between two drawings, the two things that have haunted my mind for the last few days—the dirty cell, and the brutal image of Zade's hand plunging through my chest.

I work on them for hours, getting charcoal everywhere, all over my hands and legs and smudged across my face. I'm just about to start on the detail of Zade's hand clutching my beating heart when a soft knock sounds at the door.

My body freezes and my head snaps up as the door slowly opens. I hate how on edge these assholes have me. Sawyer's face appears in the doorway, and I let out a silent breath of relief, trying to mask it as best I can.

"We got takeou—Oooooh, shit," he says, cutting himself off as he glances around Zade's room at the new and improved wall designs. He steps deeper into the room, making sure to glance over every wall, really taking it in. "Fuck, this is going to get under Zade's skin in the worst way. He likes his home in order and this . . ."

"This is fucking great."

"Hell yeah, it is," Sawyer commends. "You know, I really like how you've switched fonts with every insult. It really keeps it interesting."

"Why, thank you," I say, grabbing Zade's pillow and using it to rub the charcoal off my fingers before getting up, my stomach grumbling at the mention of takeout. "Tomorrow I'm printing off pictures of men's hairy assholes, but only ones with little bits of shit flakes caught in the ass pubes, and I'll redecorate the walls in the home gym."

"No," Sawyer breathes, his eyes wide. "Anywhere but the home gym. I can't be looking at hairy assholes while I'm working up a sweat. That's just not right."

"Take it up with Zade," I tell him, walking to the door. "He wanted to be petty, so I'm giving him petty. This is all on him. Besides, I've only got twenty-eight days to live, remember? Shouldn't I be allowed to live what little time I have left in the way I want? Or do you assholes plan on taking my happiness too?"

Sawyer lets out a heavy sigh before reaching out and gripping my elbow, pulling me back to him in the quiet hallway. He steps into me, pressing my back up against the wall before tilting my chin to meet my heavy stare. "Surely you know if there were a way to save you, I would."

"How could I possibly know that?" I question, pressing my hand to his wide chest and forcing him back a step. "The four of you have lied to me at every turn. You've worked your way into my life and between my legs with nothing but putrid lies, and because of that, I can't believe a word that comes out of your mouth. You've broken me, Sawyer. All of you have. But that's beside the point. Down in that cell, I called in my favors. I asked you to save me, and you told me you were a man of your word."

His face falls, and it's clear when I asked him to save me, he thought I was referring to saving me from Empire's prison, not saving me from becoming Zade's sacrificial lamb. Don't get me wrong, I'm grateful the guys got me out of that cell, but I wouldn't waste my favors on something that was already guaranteed. Besides, why would Zade offer me a favor if he didn't want me to try and save myself?

Not giving him a chance to respond, I walk away, heading down the hallway and following the smell of Chinese food coming from the kitchen. The rest of the guys linger around the kitchen, digging in, and the second I appear across the room, they each look up with curious stares, their sharp gazes sailing over me.

Swallowing my pride, I stride over to the kitchen, and as I move in beside Dalton, I take the plate from his outstretched hand. "Thank you," I mutter, refusing to look up as I feel Zade's stare still lingering on my face.

Going about my business, I load my plate with Chinese food before making myself comfortable on the couch, knowing how Zade hates people eating on the couch. He always made me eat at the kitchen counter or the dining table—but fuck him. The asshole can afford a new couch. Besides, I don't really understand his problem. It's a leather couch. Any spills can be easily wiped up. Not that there should be an issue with spills anyway because, unlike the guys, I don't eat like a filthy pig.

Curling up on the very edge of the couch, I watch out the panoramic windows at the impressive view of Faders Bay below. The sun is only just beginning to set, sending beautiful orange rays across the city with gorgeous hues of purples and pinks as the perfect backdrop.

Despite the bossman's objections, the boys come and join me

in the living room, casually dropping onto the couches around me while still giving me space to breathe, leaving Zade across the room at the table by himself. "You know," Sawyer says in a non-committal tone, digging into his dinner as he keeps his gaze focused on his plate. "The first time I used anal beads on a chick, I didn't realize they were supposed to be removed slowly. I yanked on those things like I was firing up a chainsaw with a pull-start motor. Man, I've never heard a bitch scream like that in my life."

I choke on my dinner, having to beat at my chest to dislodge the food caught in my throat. My jaw drops, and I gape at Sawyer as Dalton and Easton do the same. "What the fuck, bro?" Dalton mutters.

Sawyer shrugs his shoulders. "Oakley says she can't trust us. So I'm hitting her with a little raw honesty," he says, his soft gaze shifting back to mine. I hold his stare a moment when I realize this is more than just trying to be honest. He's trying to cheer me up, trying to keep my mind off my impending doom, and I can't fault him for that. Hell, I might even appreciate it, but I'm not ready to admit that out loud.

"Alright," Dalton says, pursing his lips together as he nods. "You want to go all out with the honesty? Then we'll go all out."

Sawyer smirks at Dalton and lifts his chin. "Bring it."

"I see your anal beads, and I raise you one overly sensitive gag reflex."

"Ahh, shit," Easton says, leaning back on the couch and glancing up at Dalton. The slight movement adjusts the way his shirt collar sits around his neck, and Venom makes an appearance to see what's going on. "I've gotta hear this."

Dalton lets out a heavy breath and rubs a hand down his face. "I've gone years without having to tell this," he says, shaking his head. "This chick was going to town on my cock, and she'd warned me that she had a sensitive gag reflex, but I was getting into it and she was taking me pretty deep. I figured she was exaggerating, so I thought I'd help her out, you know? I put my hand on the back of her head so I could really fuck her mouth, and next thing I know, the bitch was blowing chunks all over my cock."

Sawyer booms with laughter as Easton shakes his head, unable to hide his smirk, but Zade just watches us from across the room, his face still a cold and emotionless mask.

"You're fucking with me," Sawyer laughs.

"Hand on heart, man. I've never scrubbed my dick so hard," he says. "She was too embarrassed and kicked me out before I even got a chance to shower. I had to walk the whole way home before I could clean that shit up."

The boys laugh, and I realize too late that there's a wide smile tearing across my face. I quickly school my features and try to remind myself just how pissed I am with these assholes when Sawyer turns his attention on Easton. "Hit us with it, Cross," Sawyer says. "What's your sex story?"

Easton scoffs. "This isn't junior high," he says. "I don't have to whip out my dick just because you fuckers did."

Dalton laughs and smirks at the big guy. "That bad, huh?"

Easton stands with his empty plate, and I gape at it, wondering how he annihilated that so quickly when I've barely managed two bites.

"I don't have a sex story," he tells us, his eyes sparkling. His gaze shifts to me, roaming over my body with hunger before returning to the boys. "Unlike you children, I know how to fuck."

A soft groan escapes my lips before I even know I've made a sound. My eyes widen, and I curse myself for being so damn obvious. But damn, the man is right. He certainly knows how to fuck. Just the memory of how he fills me has me breathless. "Fuck."

Easton smirks, his eyes filled with a cocky confidence that has me wanting to smack him. "Case in point." With that, he turns on his heel and beelines back to the kitchen and starts loading up his plate again.

Irritation burns through me. It's one thing for me to fall victim to his wicked charm—but using that as a way to put his friends down doesn't sit well with me. "Don't get ahead of yourself, Cross," I say. "You might be able to get me off, but that doesn't mean you're some kind of sex god."

Easton whips around, his sharp gaze locking on mine. "Cross?" he spits, the word like poison in his mouth. "Since when do you call me Cross? It's Easton to you."

"I called you Easton when I thought I saw something in you. When I thought there was some kind of connection between us, something real. But you led me on, just like Sawyer and Dalton did, and now I can't trust any of you," I tell him. I'm not sure if I'm only calling him Cross out of spite, but there's no denying that Easton feels so right on my lips. "As fucked up as it is, Zade is the only one who's been honest with me from the get-go . . . Well, as honest as he could be without actually telling me what was going on. But you three . . . all you wanted was to get your dicks wet, and I know that I'm not innocent in this either. I was more than happy to spread my legs for you. But the difference was that I thought I was screwing three guys who had promised to protect me from Empire's attacks. I played your fucking game, and you got me hook, line, and sinker. You three made me out to be a fool."

Easton narrows his gaze and puts his plate down on the kitchen counter before striding toward me. I feel the guilt radiating off Dalton, but I can't look at him, my gaze held captive by the raw fury in Easton's stare.

He steps right up to me, reaches down, and grabs me by the top of my arms. Easton hoists me up, and I barely have a moment to place my plate down on the couch cushion before I'm pulled to my feet. Easton's strong body presses right up against mine. "I get it, Pretty. You're hurting, and I've been trying to give you space today, but this is where I draw the fucking line," he rumbles, his big knee pushing between my legs until his strong thigh is grinding against my pussy. I grip onto his arms simply to keep myself on my feet, knowing damn well if he pushes this, I'll crumble to the floor.

I suck in a breath, captivated by those dark eyes, and he reaches down, grips my thigh, and pulls it up to circle around his hip. His fingers linger on my thigh, his thumb brushing over the top of it, right where his cross lingers beneath the fabric of Zade's sweatpants. "This fucking means something," he tells me. "I didn't mark you with a cross because I get off on making you bleed. I staked a fucking claim to you, Oakley. I gave you my mark because this is fucking real to me. I might not be over here drooling at your feet like these assholes, but that doesn't make this any less real. So don't you fucking dare dismiss me as a callous liar. I've been honest with you everywhere I could."

Easton grips my chin and holds my gaze, and just when I think he's about to crush his lips to mine, he releases me, dropping his hold and walking away. There's no way in hell I'm about to let him go without saying my piece. "If this is so fucking real," I say to his back, watching as he stiffens and pauses across the living room, "then why are you so quick to send me to my grave and be rid of me?"

Easton turns back, his eyes flaming with a strange mix of unease and caution. He holds my stare and I glare right back, neither one of us relenting. But not having the balls to answer me truthfully, he turns and walks away, leaving me crumbling to the ground, gasping for air.

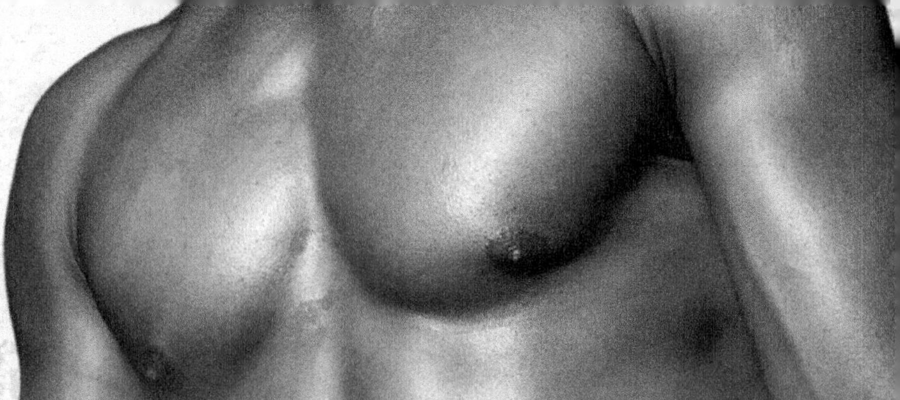

CHAPTER 10

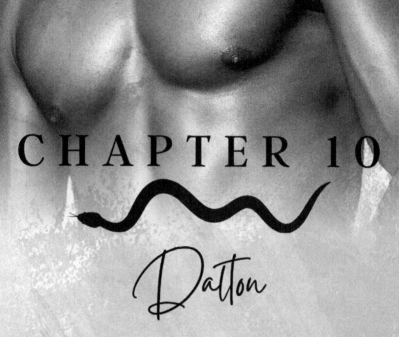

Dalton

After jamming the leftover Chinese take-out containers into the fridge, I turn around to find Sawyer, Cross, and Zade all hovering around the kitchen, staring at me as though I'm about to get my ass handed to me.

My brows furrow, and I look back at the guys in confusion before glancing over Sawyer's shoulder at Oakley sitting out in the den. The second she finished her dinner, she took off to be alone, and I've been itching to get in there and make things right ever since. But something tells me I'm signing up for an impossible fight. I know I haven't known her for long, but I feel as though I know her well enough to tell that this is not going to be easy. She's going to make me work for it, make me walk over hot coals before even considering letting me back into her good graces.

I can't blame her though. I'd be pissed if I found out the chick I was screwing around with was actually part of a secret society that wanted me dead, and yet she wasn't doing anything to try and stop it. Oakley has valid points, but surely she must understand that this isn't what I want. I mean, sure, at first, it didn't matter to me. She was no one, just a random name, but now . . . Now she's so much more. If there were a way for me to change this, to give her the freedom she so desperately craves, I'd give it to her in a heartbeat.

"What's up?" I ask, trying to figure out what the fuck I've done to deserve an intervention.

Cross shakes his head. "No fucking clue," he says, nodding toward Sawyer. "He's running this show."

"Yeah," Sawyer says with unease and nervousness in his deep tone. "I fucked up."

"The fuck are you talking about?" Zade questions, bracing his hands against the kitchen counter, glaring at Sawyer, only that's not well received by Sawyer who's still itching to beat the shit out of him all over again. The tension between them has only gotten worse and Cross and I are constantly on edge, waiting for the moment one of them breaks. Sawyer though, he's not usually one to fuck up. He's careful and calculated, just like the rest of us. But he's only human, and the few times he has fucked up in the past have always been big ones.

"Down in the cells," Sawyer starts. "The first time I found her in there, she asked me if I was a man of my word. I said yes, and then she called in her favors."

"We know this," Zade says, prompting him to get to the point.

Sawyer lets out a heavy sigh. "She asked me to save her, and I assumed she was asking us to free her from Empire's prison. But that's not what she was asking me. She wants us to save her," he says, giving Zade a pointed stare, "from you. And I gave her my word."

"Fuck," Cross says, dragging his hand over his face. He turns around and paces the length of the kitchen. "That favor was too fucking easy. I should have known. She wouldn't waste a favor from each of us on something she knew was already coming."

Dread fills my veins, practically reading Zade's thoughts before the words have even fallen from his fucking mouth. "What's the problem?" he grunts. "Go back on your word. It's not like you haven't already lied to her. What's the fucking difference at this point? You heard her. We haven't exactly given her the impression that we're trustworthy people. Besides, she didn't specify what she meant when asking you to save her, and as far as I'm concerned, we saved her from the cells. We've upheld our end of the bargain."

Sawyer scoffs. "You can try that shit on her all you want, but we both know that's not gonna fly. She's going to hold us to it. You included."

"What does it even matter when she's going to be dead in twenty-eight days?"

I shake my head, swallowing over the lump in my throat. "It fucking matters," I tell Zade. "Now that the truth is out there, I'm not fucking lying to her anymore. She deserves more than that. Besides, you're about to take her life for your own fucking gain. The least you could do is show her enough respect by being honest with her."

Zade clenches his jaw before dropping his head, hanging it low between his shoulders as he braces himself against the counter. "Being honest with her means admitting just how fucking much of a monster I've allowed myself to become for this."

Cross lets out a breath, his gaze lingering on Oakley through the den. "We all have, man. We all have."

I shake my head. None of this sits right with me. "I'm gonna go talk with her."

"And say what?" Sawyer questions.

I shrug my shoulders, just as lost as these assholes. "I don't know, but right now, she feels it's us against her, and I don't want her pushing me away any more than she already has. She needs to know that we're on her side. We might not be able to save her, but I can't deal with her thinking I don't have her back."

Zade lifts his gaze back to mine. "I told you not to get attached, man."

"Too fucking late for that," I tell him. "Look around you, Zade. One way or another, we're all fucking attached—even you. You just don't know it yet."

He scoffs. "That's fucking bullshit and you know it. Unlike you assholes, I've kept my distance, not allowed myself to fall into her trap because I know what's coming. If you were all smart, you'd pull back from her."

"Right. Keep telling yourself that," I mutter, moving around the kitchen counter. "But I don't recall hearing a good fucking reason to have her sleeping in your bed where you can watch her all fucking night long. Her bedroom is fucking bomb-proof, Zade. Once that door is locked, she couldn't escape even if she had a fucking tank. It's one of the safest rooms in this penthouse, and yet you want her in your bed."

Sawyer smirks, not willing to admit out loud that he agrees, but Cross has no issue with it. "She's under your skin, Zade. Just as she is ours. I saw the way you were clutching onto her hand while we were running through those tunnels. The way you held her against your body. Deny it all you want, but the truth is right there in your actions. And I'd bet everything I have that if we can see it, she can see it too."

Zade clenches his jaw, and deciding he's had enough of this conversation, he turns on his heel and stalks out of sight, probably to go work it out in the gym. Cross, Sawyer, and I briefly glance at one another. None of us need to say a word to know what the others are thinking—Zade is full of shit.

Not having any kind of solution to the whole favors thing, I bail too, my gaze already cast on Oakley. Striding through the living room and into the den, I lean against the wall, watching her as she stares out the window at the dark, busy streets below.

I've got to give it to Zade, he's got the best view in town. During the day, with the sun streaming against the high-rise building, glistening and ricocheting off the glass windows, it's incredible. But at night when Faders Bay lights up with activity, it's simply breathtaking.

Not wanting to startle Oakley, I gently rap against the wall and wait until her soft gaze lifts to meet mine. "Am I going to get castrated if I come in and join you?"

She shrugs her shoulders, those gorgeous, bright blue eyes sparkling with mirth. "Apparently you like to take risks," she says. "Why don't you come closer and find out?"

A smirk pulls at the corner of my lips, and I push off the wall before moving across the den and dropping onto the couch beside her, making sure to leave space between us. I don't want to push my limits yet. "I know you don't want to hear this, but I don't want you to hate me, Firefly."

She shakes her head, a barely audible scoff slipping through her lips. "That's like asking the sun to shine during the darkest night. Impossible."

"Then let's move to Antarctica," I say, a stupid grin on my face.

Oakley glances at me, her brows furrowed and her lips pursed with irritation. "What the fuck are you talking about?"

"You know," I say with just enough awkwardness to make me feel like the biggest fucktard who ever walked the planet. "Because of the tilt of the earth's axis, the sun doesn't set for months on end in Antarctica. So technically, you don't have to hate me."

"Really?" she deadpans. "You came in here to give me a geography lesson?"

I let out a heavy sigh and fix her with a hard stare. "Don't act dumb with me, Firefly. You know exactly what I was trying to do. I hate seeing you so fucking broken like this."

"Then tell me how I'm supposed to feel right now," she begs me. "Because I have no fucking idea. One minute I'm telling myself that I can find a way to escape this and free myself, and the next, I'm in a fucking ball on the ground, terrified of what he's going to do to me."

Something aches in my chest, and as tears well in her eyes, I reach out for her, gripping her waist, and pull her into my chest. Her face nuzzles into my neck as she scrambles into my lap, her overwhelming need to hate me overshadowed by her fear. "I don't wanna die," she murmurs, her arms circling my neck, holding me tight.

"I know," I whisper, knowing without a doubt that I would trade my life for hers if it meant she got to live just one more day. My hand roams over her back as my other lays flat against her thigh, holding her to me. "If there was something I could do, anything, Firefly, I would have done it. I've been going through the old by-laws trying to find some kind of loophole, something that could offer even just a little bit of doubt to save us some time, but there's nothing. I come up blank every fucking time."

"Don't bother," Oakley scoffs. "Down in the cells, Sawyer's dad told me there was a loophole way back in the day, but Zade's grandfather had it scrubbed clean. He thought that if he had to sacrifice someone he loved, everyone following him should have to suffer the same fate."

"Fuck."

She pulls back and meets my stare, her watery eyes killing me. "I appreciate you looking though."

I nod. "Do me a favor and don't mention this to Zade. He wouldn't like me searching through all of his father's old shit. But I knew the second I saw you that I couldn't stand the thought of you being offered up as Zade's sacrifice. He warned me not to get too close to you. He knew you'd break me, and now look at me, ready to turn my back on it all just to see the light return to your eyes."

Oakley's gaze drops, the heaviness between us almost too intense to handle. "This can't be it for me," she says. "It's not like I had my life planned out or knew where I would be in thirty years, but this isn't it. There were so many things I wanted to do and see, so many things I wanted to try. I'm not ready to give up. I won't."

Reaching up, I brush the soft strands of golden hair off her face, hating how her wet cheeks affect me. "You're so fucking strong. If things were different, you would have made an incredible leader for Empire. You would have risen in power and ruled over it all. Our people would have followed you blindly. But I don't want you getting your hopes up," I tell her. "Please don't take this the wrong way. I commend your determination to fight through this, to push through right to the end and set yourself free, but I know Zade. He is ruthless and cold. He would tear his own fucking heart out if it meant claiming power. He's worked too hard and suffered silently through his father's abuse to get him right where he is today. He's not going to allow you to slip through his fingers again."

"I just . . . I don't get it," she tells me with a heavy sigh, sitting back on my lap. "Why is he like this? It's not normal for a person to be so . . . intense."

I press my lips into a hard line, truly considering her question and wanting to be able to offer her an honest answer. "Zade is . . . he's complicated. He wasn't always the way he is now. He used to be a normal kid before Empire sunk its claws into him . . . into us. We were all just normal kids. We were put through training at a young age, had to see things not even those fighting our wars would have to endure. We were killers before we'd turned thirteen. That kind of shit leaves a mark. But Zade . . . his father pushed him harder. He knew he would take over as Empire's leader one day, but the abuse he laid down on Zade broke something inside of him. He took away what little humanity he had left. Lawson strived to ensure Zade was going to be the kind of leader he could have only dreamed of. He turned Zade into his puppet, but Zade cut the strings and made his own plan."

"He murdered his own father."

"Trust me, if you knew the man, you wouldn't see that as a loss," I explain. "The day Lawson DeVil took his last breath was the day people all over the world celebrated, but not Zade. Even though he had the most to celebrate. He barely took a chance to process what he'd done before moving on. It was nothing but a business transaction to him."

Her tongue rolls out over her bottom lip, another tear slowly trailing down her cheek. "If he can so easily slaughter his father, the man who raised him, I can only imagine how quickly he'd do the same to me."

I'm almost hesitant to agree with her, not wanting her to know just how right she is, but I'm making a point of being honest with her. "It would destroy whatever goodness is left in him. But you're right. He wouldn't even think twice about it. He'd allow himself to become the monster he's always secretly feared."

Oakley sighs, and the helplessness in her eyes destroys me. I reach up and curl my hand around the back of her neck, my thumb stretched out to graze across her jaw. "Come here," I murmur into the darkness.

She folds back into me, her forehead dropping to mine as her body presses in close. "What am I supposed to do?"

I shake my head, knowing I don't have the answer she's hoping for. "You spend the next twenty-eight days in bliss. Have the time of your fucking life, Firefly. But as much as I can't let you walk out those doors, I'd be disappointed if I didn't get to see you try."

Her brows furrow as a twisted smirk pulls at her lips. "That was the most fucked-up thing you've ever said to me."

"I know," I laugh. "It felt so wrong coming out of my mouth, but it was the nicest way I could be honest without sounding like a complete asshole."

"Oh really? After everything you guys have put me through, now you're worried about coming off as an asshole? Need I remind you that you set me up to be kidnapped after giving me some of the best dick of my life? Way to give a woman whiplash."

Grabbing her waist, I throw her down on the couch cushion, hovering above her with her thigh hooked over my hip, my cock grinding against her sweet pussy. "Best dick of your life, huh?"

Her eyes come to life for the first time since coming back to me, and I grow hard. The need to have her rocks through my body, but this isn't about me. If she's not ready or willing to open up to me, then I'll take a backseat, despite how it'll fucking kill me. The last thing I want is to add something else for her to be cautious about.

Oakley tilts her head back, bringing her lips just an inch closer to mine as her leg locks tighter around my hip, pulling me down harder against her. "I mean, yeah. Right after Cross and Sawyer, of course."

It's like a fucking bullet to the chest.

"Don't fucking play with me," I warn her, my dick straining to get inside her. "You know damn well they don't fuck you like I do. Fill you. Stretch you. I see your face when I push inside you, when you come on my cock. It's not the same with them."

"Hmmmm," she groans before meeting my eye. "You need to stop."

I pull back immediately, certain I've pushed her too far, when she shakes her head. "I mean, you need to stop making it so damn hard to hate you. How am I supposed to make your life a living hell when all I want to do is be your desperate little whore?"

Need blasts through my chest, and I don't fucking hesitate, pressing back down against her and grinding my cock over her sweet pussy. My lips drop to her neck, and her head instantly tilts to the side to give me space to work. "Tell me what you want, Firefly."

She sucks in a gasp, her arm locking tight around my neck while her other slides down my back and into my pants, grabbing a fistful of ass. "I want you to fuck me, Dalton," she says firmly. "I want you to spread my thighs and eat my pussy until I come all over your face, and only after you've done that, I want you to bend me over and spank my ass until I scream so loud that Zade thinks I'm already dead. I want my knees to shake, and if I wake up in the morning and can't feel exactly where you've touched me, then you didn't give it to me hard enough. I want to be spent on the fucking floor, Dalton, unable to move. But mostly, I don't want you to stop until you make me forget why the hell

I hate you so much."

I pull back to meet her eye, hunger pulsing through my veins. "Then what the fuck are you waiting for?"

CHAPTER 11

Oakley

Dalton scoops me off the couch, and I gasp, my body more than ready to be dicked down. I cling to him like a fucking bear as he strides across the darkened den, my pussy aching to be thoroughly fucked.

As I told him what I wanted, what I needed, the hunger in his eyes intensified, and his rock-hard cock flinched against my clit, spurring me on. I couldn't hold back. I laid it all out for him like a fucking challenge, one I know he will more than rise to the occasion for.

His eyes darken as he strides across the room, his hand on my ass, gripping tight. He walks us right over to the massive window before lowering me to my feet. "Are you ready for me?" he rumbles, that deep, seductive tone making my knees shake.

That dark god complex emerges in his stare, and without a doubt, I know I'll be calling him Daddy and begging him to spank me before the night is out.

"Yes," I tell him, captivated by his hungry stare.

"Strip."

My pussy weeps, and I slip my thumbs into the waistband of my borrowed sweatpants and allow them to fall to my feet before quickly kicking them away. His heated stare follows every slight movement, and I put on a show as I grip the hem of my shirt and slowly pull it over my head.

Dalton reaches out, his palm cupping the curve of my breast as his tongue rolls over his bottom lip. He gently pinches my nipple and watches the way my body reacts to his touch. I gasp and groan, already putty in his hands. "Turn around, Oakley," he demands, leaving no room for objection.

I do as I'm asked, and he steps right into my back, forcing me forward until my tits are pressed right up against the cold window, my naked body on display for the whole fucking world to see, but I don't give a shit. All that matters is what comes next.

"Make me scream, Dalton," I beg, my tone breathy and desperate.

His hand settles at my waist, slowly curving around my hip before moving down to my cunt. His fingers roam over my clit, and I grind against him, needing so much more. "You'll be fucking patient," he tells me, that raspy, deep tone in my ear.

Dalton grips my tit with his other hand as his fingers continue circling over my clit, making my knees weak. "Do you remember what

I said to you on the rooftop before I fucked you for the first time?"

"You're my god."

"Good girl," he rumbles right as he adjusts his hand and plunges two thick fingers deep inside my throbbing cunt. "Don't you fucking forget."

I cry out, my head tipping back to his shoulder as his fingers move deep inside of me. I grind down, riding his hand as the heel of his palm rubs against my clit. My arm locks around the back of his neck, holding on for dear life.

I love this version of him. When it's just the two of us, he's so raw and has such a filthy mouth, making demands he knows I won't be able to deny. He gets me so fucking hot and worked up. Dalton's only just getting started, and I'm already on edge.

He works my pussy, his fingers massaging my sensitive walls, and I gasp as I feel his breath on my neck. "Spread those pretty thighs for me. I want to fucking smell your arousal."

"Oh God," I groan, shuffling my feet out as my eyes roll to the back of my head. The anticipation builds rapidly within me, making my hands ball into fists as I brace myself against the window.

I feel his smile against my skin, and then everything starts to move down. His hand releases my tit and grips my ass, giving it a firm squeeze when I feel his warm breath against my cunt. He pulls his fingers free from my pussy and I listen intently as he sucks them clean, groaning with the taste of my arousal on his tongue. "Fucking delicious," he rumbles, my pussy clenching at his tone.

Dalton takes my hips and pulls me back from the window, tilting them just an inch and forcing me to arch my lower back. He bites low on my ass, and I jump, a breathy gasp sailing through my lips. Before I can scold him, his tongue swipes through my cunt.

"Oh fuck," I cry, pushing back against him for more. I brace myself against the window and bend over, offering my pussy and ass to his hungry mouth. He takes me greedily, fucking me with his tongue as he uses his fingers to work my clit, rubbing small circles.

I groan, pushing back again, more than ready to suffocate him with my ass if I have to, but he's not nearly done. He sucks, nips, licks, and fucks, his tongue working right up to my ass and teasing me there. His thumb presses against my hole as his tongue swipes over my pussy again, the torturous circles of his fingers over my clit making my knees shake.

"Oh shit, Dalton," I pant. "I'm gonna come."

"Not yet," he rumbles before grabbing my waist and pulling me to my knees, needing to shuffle us past the window. He pushes me right over, my tits flat against the tiles and my ass high in the air.

He uses his strong thigh to push my knees even further apart and doesn't waste another second before diving back in and feasting on my body. He gives it to me harder, his thumb pushing into my ass as I press back, wanting to take him deeper. His tongue works like magic, flicking over my clit until I'm crying out again.

I come hard, my orgasm bursting through me like a rocket, so strong and intense. Dalton doesn't stop, letting me ride it out on his tongue as my high blasts through every nerve, right to my fingers and toes.

Dalton laps up every bit of my arousal like it's a fine wine, and it's not until I come down that he finally releases me from his sweet torture. I collapse against the tiles, rolling over to watch him, only to find that brilliant, hard cock staring back at me.

He grips it in one hand, his piercing promising me a world of blissful devastation, and hunger strikes through me again. He loses his shirt, placing that breathtaking body on full display. The sharp ridges of his abs, his wide, strong chest, those big shoulders . . . Everything about him makes me weak.

"Who am I?" he rumbles, those dark eyes scanning over my body as he slowly strokes his cock, my thighs spreading wide and watching the way his gaze drops to my waiting pussy.

I meet his stare, knowing exactly what he wants to hear. "You're my god."

His cock flinches in his hand, and he reaches forward, scooping his arm around my back and dragging me to him, my legs on either side of his strong thighs as that heavy cock rests against my pelvis. "I said," he rumbles in a deep, booming tone as he lines himself up with my entrance, his free hand roaming up my body and closing around the base of my throat. "Who the fuck am I?"

Dalton slams his thick cock into me, and I cry out with the most intense pleasure as he stretches me wide, that piercing seated deep inside me. "Oh fuck," I gasp, tipping my head back as his grip on my throat tightens, not enough to cut off my oxygen, but more than enough to send a wicked thrill shooting through my veins. "You're my fucking god."

"Damn straight," he growls as his hips draw back only to thrust straight back into me. His body rolls with his movement, making my mouth water, and I can't help but touch him, my nails digging into his ass cheek as he fucks me.

I'm barely holding on when he takes my knee and bends it right down to my ribs, changing the angle of my hips and taking me so much deeper. "Fuck, Firefly," he growls. "So fucking wet for me."

"Oh, God. Yes."

"You love being my nasty little whore, don't you?"

"YES." My eyes roll to the back of my head, teetering on the edge, but I'm not ready for this to be over. "I need you from behind."

Dalton groans low, more than approving of my change of pace, and within seconds, I'm back on my knees, my chest flat against the tiles as he slams into my cunt, his fingers biting into my hip. He takes me so much deeper, cursing as he sucks in a breath through his teeth. My pussy clenches around his glorious cock. "Fuck, Oakley. Such a tight little pussy. I could fuck you like this all day."

I groan, his words like music to my ears, but when I feel his fingers at my entrance, pushing in and stretching me even wider, words escape me. He mixes them with my wetness before dragging them to my ass and as he thrusts that big cock back into me, he pushes two thick fingers into my hole.

"Shit," I hiss, pushing back against him and slipping my hand between my legs, furiously rubbing my clit as my body relaxes around his delicious intrusions. He gives me everything, fucking me like only a queen should be fucked, drawing out every last bit of arousal from my body until it's too much for me to handle.

His fingers dig into my hip, and I know that come tomorrow, the bruises will be the perfect reminder of my night with him, marked across my skin for all to see. He thrusts into me one more time, and I can't hold on any longer. I come hard, detonating like a fucking grenade around his thick cock, my pussy convulsing and spasming as I clench my eyes, the pleasure far too great.

My high blasts through my veins as I come undone, crying out his name. Not a second later, Dalton comes with me, shooting hot spurts of cum deep inside me, his fingers loosening on my hip. His thumb brushes back and forth over my ass cheek as I simply stare out the window, unable to move or barely breathe.

"Holy shit," I murmur as he slowly pulls back, releasing his fingers from my ass and dropping down on the tiles beside me.

"You can say that again," he mutters, his hand coming down in the perfect spank to my ass. "Now, go make Daddy a sandwich."

I groan at the sharp sting, so deliciously addictive as I lift my head to gape at him. "You're kidding, right?" I laugh. "If I'm capable of getting up and walking my ass to the kitchen to make you a sandwich, that can only mean you didn't fuck me right."

Dalton laughs and reaches for me before hauling me onto his waist, his cum slowly leaking out of me. "You told me you wanted your legs to shake, that you want to still feel me tomorrow, and not to stop until you forgot why you hated me so much. And you and I both know I did exactly that. Fuck, forget remembering why you hate me. I bet you can't even remember your own fucking name right now."

A smirk plays on my lips. He's right. Well, apart from the whole remembering my name thing. The moment his fingers sunk into my pussy, all that mattered was chasing that high, feeling the way he worked my body, feeling that addictive stretch. It didn't matter that he's one of the four men responsible for my upcoming death or that he set me up to be kidnapped. All I wanted was to feel something, and he gave me just that.

I roll my eyes, not willing to give him the satisfaction of being right, and collapse onto his chest. His arms circle my waist, holding me to him as our hearts beat as one. Despite everything, this right here is where I feel safest.

I don't know how Dalton has done it. He's led me into his trap over and over again, and each time I fall willingly. There's something about him, a wicked charm that I find irresistible, something I can't possibly walk away from. While this strange relationship of ours is still extremely strained, he will always be my safety net, my security blanket keeping me warm during this insane storm. The thought of pushing him away . . . Fuck. I know he's Team Zade, but if these are my last days on earth, I want to make the most of them. I don't want to spend these twenty-eight days in a blind rage. I want to live, and if that means letting myself fall madly in love with Dalton Eros, then that's what I'm going to allow myself to do. Ritual be damned.

We lay together in a comfortable silence for who knows how long. All I know is that one minute I'm listening to the steady rhythm of his heart beating so calmly in his chest, and the next, he's slipping me into Zade's bed.

"Oh shit," I say with a yawn. "Did I fall asleep?"

"Yeah, it's fine," he tells me. "Go back to sleep, Firefly. I wanted to go through more of those by-laws and see if I can scrounge up another loophole to save your sweet ass."

I give him a small smile, and he presses a gentle kiss to my forehead before turning and smirking at the state of Zade's bedroom. "Hmm," he says, scanning over the far wall. "Turd slinger? Can't say I've heard that one before. Do I even want to know what it means?"

I shrug my shoulders. "Means how it sounds," I tell him, a clear picture of Zade scooping up dog shit and slinging it through a park permanently engraved in my mind. "You can't tell me he's not the type to grab a shit right out of the toilet and start slathering it over the walls."

Dalton gapes at me. "Who the fuck hurt you?"

I shrug my shoulders. "Not my fault Zade gives off dirty gorilla vibes. That's on him," I lie, knowing damn well Zade gives off smoldering, wickedly dangerous billionaire vibes that get me so fucking hot it makes me hate him more.

Dalton laughs and rolls his eyes as he strides out of Zade's room, leaving the door wide open. Rolling over, I try to get comfortable in Zade's bed and find myself staring at the words scrawled across his wall. Every single one of them is still true, but I can't stop thinking about what Dalton said. How Zade is just as broken as the rest of us. How he was made to be this way from his father's influence, and how deep down, he's scared of becoming the monster I already believe him to be.

No amount of kind words could stop me from despising Zade DeVil. But I can't help but feel as though I understand him better now, and that thought scares the shit out of me. There's nothing worse than trying to humanize a monster.

CHAPTER 12

Oakley

Sleep is impossible to find, and it must be at least one in the morning when Zade finally comes striding through his bedroom door. The lights are turned off, and I quickly make a show of being asleep, closing my eyes just enough so that I can still see him making his way through his room. He glances my way, pressing his lips into a hard line before coming to a startled stop, his gaze lifting to the room around him.

His jaw drops as he reads over the words, taking in every last one of them, slowly turning as his hands ball into fists at his side. I do what I can to keep a straight face, but fuck, it's hard. There's just enough light coming from the hallway to showcase every word, and even if there wasn't, something tells me Zade wouldn't have a problem seeing them clearly. Hell, he was able to see through Empire's tunnels perfectly. He saw the men ahead of us way before I did.

Zade DeVil is so much more than just a monster. He's a trained assassin—someone I shouldn't be allowing myself to be comfortable around.

He glances back at me as if thinking about dragging my ass out of bed to scrub his walls, but instead he lets out a heavy breath and leaves it be. If I weren't in the midst of putting on the show of a lifetime right now, I'd be gaping at him in shock. I was certain that he'd pull me out of bed by the ankle and force me to spend hours fixing my mess. Though, I suppose he hasn't seen his closet yet.

I'm not left waiting long when he strides across his room and clutches the door handle to his walk-in closet, and I discreetly pull the blanket up to cover my mouth, knowing damn well I won't be able to keep my composure. He pushes through the door and switches the light on, and as he moves to walk inside, he comes to another abrupt stop right in the doorway.

"Ahh, what the fuck?" he mutters with frustration, dragging his hands over his face before walking deeper into the room to get a good look at the damage. "No," he breathes a moment later. "Not the fucking suits."

The satisfaction in my veins is almost better than the railing I just got from Dalton . . . almost.

Somehow managing to find clothes I must've missed in my rampage, he saunters out of the closet, turns off the light, and pulls the door shut behind him. Heading into his bathroom, he stops in yet another doorway. "Fucking hell," he grumbles, making me snort a laugh. I'd forgotten about the mess I'd left after my shower.

Closing the door behind him, he quickly showers and returns a few minutes later, bringing a shitload of tension with him, making me all too aware of the fact that we're going to be alone together all night, trapped in the same bed.

Zade strides shirtless across the room, his intricate tattoos on full display as he scans over his bed. He lets out a huff as he takes in the mess of charcoal and dirt I left behind, causing his chest to swell and the delicate pattern of his tattoos to dance in the process. He's so devastatingly beautiful, my fingers twitch in the sheets as they ache to touch him.

He throws the blankets back, more than happy to sleep without them before flipping the pillow over to the clean side. Though something tells me he's slept in much worse conditions. I'm sure training to become the most brutal killer in the world didn't come with luxury mattresses and Egyptian cotton sheets.

He drops down beside me, his strong arm braced behind his head, his bicep bulging and making my mouth water. "Quit the act," he mutters into the darkness, barely sparing me a glance. "I know you're awake."

Fuck.

"Zade?"

"What?"

"Can you tell me about Empire?"

His brows furrow and he glances my way, curiosity sparkling

in those dark eyes. Despite there barely being an inch of his skin unmarred by cuts and bruises, his eyes don't show the beating he got from Sawyer. They remain as cold and callous as ever, reminding me that he doesn't deserve my pity. "What do you want to know?"

I shrug my shoulders as I press my lips into a hard line, really considering his question. "I don't really know," I tell him honestly, surprised he's even playing along. "Everything, I suppose. I don't understand how it runs or how you make things happen. Like is there a human resources department? Because if so, I have a few complaints."

He scoffs, and for a second, I could almost swear I see a hint of a smile pulling at the corner of his lips. "There's none of that shit," he tells me. "We run based on a mutual understanding that our members look out for their own. But if there were, trust me, I have a few complaints of my own."

Rolling my eyes, I roll over to face him better. "Considering our current predicament, I'd dare say your complaints have nothing on mine."

"Did you see the state you left my bathroom in?" he questions. "For what it's worth, you're cleaning that shit first thing in the morning."

"Don't you have like . . . a billion staff members in this hotel who were literally hired to clean up after you."

"Yeah," he scoffs. "After me. I'm not paying them to clean up after you."

"Then it seems we have ourselves a little problem," I tell him, letting him hear the bite in my tone. "What did you mean when you said Empire runs on a mutual understanding?"

He glances at me again. "You've got a lot of questions for someone who says they don't want anything to do with it."

"Can you blame me for wanting to know more about the society who wants me dead?" I question. "Besides, they're rightfully mine. If I intend to steal it out from under you, then it only makes sense for me to know what the hell I'm getting myself involved in."

Zade scoffs, and the sound is like a knife right through the back, making it all too clear what he thinks about the possibility of me actually taking him down. "You've got fight in you, Oakley," he says. "I like that. It's in your blood, the fire to be on top. Any rightful leader of Empire should be able to stand tall like that."

"I sense a but coming."

A wicked smirk stretches across his lips, and he rolls to face me before gripping my chin. "You could have all the will and desire in the world to try and take Empire from me, but you'll never succeed. Understand that, Lamb. I applaud your strength and respect you. After all, you are the rightful heir, and it's been drummed into me my whole life that I should hold nothing above those who possess the blood. It kills me to have to spill even one precious drop, but I will spill it all if it means claiming my crown."

"You terrify me, Zade," I whisper, gently pulling my chin out of his grip.

He nods, and there's sadness in his eyes. "I know," he admits. "I terrify myself sometimes, too."

"You don't want to do this?"

He shakes his head. "Of course I don't want to do this. Do you think plunging my hands inside your chest is going to get me hard? No, not even close. But that changes nothing."

Reaching out from beneath the blanket, I let my fingers brush along his arm, my hand shaking as I come in contact with his skin. I can almost sense the complex design of the ink beneath my fingertips, imagining the way the intricate pattern could come to life with my touch.

Electricity shoots through my fingers and right through to my chest as my heart races. I can barely catch my breath, feeling like I've just run a marathon. Zade doesn't move, doesn't try to push me away or touch me back. He simply stares at me as my fingers curl around his wrist, holding onto him like my only lifeline. I swallow over the lump in my throat, and as the seconds pass, my heart starts to calm, finding an odd comfort in his touch.

I don't look away from his stare, feeling as though this is the first time I've ever really had a moment to talk to him with everything laid out on the table. All the lies are dead and buried. Just two people and a shitload of raw honesty.

"You keep changing the topic," I tell him.

"I don't mean to," he says. "I just don't think the day-to-day running of Empire is really that intriguing in comparison to you."

My cheeks flush, and I try to push his comment to the back of my mind, knowing damn well he doesn't mean that in a sexual way. He's not intrigued by my mind or body, but by the blood pulsing through my veins. "Consider me intrigued," I prompt. "Tell me about it."

He lets out a breath, considering how to explain this to me in simple terms. "Empire started as a group of young men with a hunger for power and the drive to protect their own. They were men in high places in the community, both feared and respected. Police, judges, the town mayor, and even the local mafia boss. Anyone who could bring something to the table. You name it, Empire has it covered. They were sworn to secrecy and made vows to put Empire above their own lives and their children's lives."

"That's fucked up."

He nods. "Over the years as these men were married and had families of their own, the organization began to grow, along with it our power and reach. They quickly rose, taking control of the government and international affairs while maintaining their legacy. When some began to get greedy, The Circle was formed, and along with it, the by-laws they enforced. The original founder, my great-great-grandfather, Arterius DeVil, was officially crowned leader of the organization, and his people vowed to follow him blindly. A vow in which each member still follows to this day."

I scoff, a twisted smirk settling over my lips. "You mean my great, great grandfather?"

His face twists, not liking my stab. "Watch yourself, Lamb."

My gaze narrows, this new little nickname of his sending chills down my spine. "Lamb?" I question. "Don't tell me you mean lamb as in *sacrificial lamb?*"

Zade winks. "It's fitting, don't you think?"

"It's sick."

Zade shrugs, not one to shy away from sick or twisted games.

"Moral of the story," he continues. "There's nothing we can't do. If you get arrested, we can have your record wiped clean in seconds. If you need an international wire transfer to an arms dealer, consider it done. You want to run for president, we'll give you the whole fucking White House."

I shake my head, certain he's exaggerating. There's no way some bullshit secret society out here in Faders Bay could have that kind of pull. "That's insane. No one should have that kind of power."

"And yet we do," Zade says. "That is exactly why I can't let you slip through my fingers. If you were able to see it with your own eyes and fully grasp how we work, you would understand why I need to do this. If I fail, Empire will collapse, and we would be at war. A new leader must rise in my wake, and with no other known heir, the fight for power will commence. You will never be safe. If you think your life is in danger now, just wait until word gets out that there's a secret heir who possesses the ability to steal the power right out from under any potential leader. You wouldn't last two minutes. So believe me, my succession is in your favor."

I shake my head. "So either way, I die," I whisper.

"Yes. You will," Zade nods, a sadness in his eyes. "I need to know what you remember from being taken. What happened after Joe put you in that car? Did you meet with anyone before being taken to the cells? We're no closer to finding out who the fuck was behind this."

"What do you mean? Joe was behind it. He was the one who knocked me out."

"No," Zade says. "Joe was put up to it. He was meant to deliver you to someone else, but instead, he hid you in the cells."

I shake my head, not recalling anything. "I don't know. I was out cold for all of it. One minute I was trying to run from your bitch-ass and save myself, and the next thing I knew, I was waking up in the cell," I tell him. "But why not ask Joe? You don't strike me as the type not to be able to get information out of someone."

He clenches his jaw. "Believe me, we tried," he says. "Whoever got to him first . . . let's just say Joe feared them more than he feared me."

My gaze narrows, trying to pull apart everything he just said, and the realization hits me like a wrecking ball. "Let me guess," I murmur, pulling my hand back from his wrist. "Joe never made it home for dinner?"

Zade watches me for a moment, clearly able to see the fear and hesitation in my stare. "Don't ask questions that you're not prepared to know the answers to."

"Shit, Zade," I say, pushing up onto my elbow. "Do you have to kill everyone who even looks at you wrong?"

"You tell me. You're looking at me wrong right now," he mutters. "But no, I kill those who betray me. And Joe . . . he knew what was coming for him the second he put his hands on you."

I swallow hard and drop back down onto the mattress, looking up at the ceiling. I'm not sure I'm capable of meeting his stare right now.

"Lamb?" he questions into the darkness, forcing my stare back to his.

"What?"

"Who was that man in the cells? The one who held down Harrison?

He said something to you."

Fear pounds through my chest, remembering my father's stark demands not to let Zade know who he is. "I . . . I don't know. Just some guy. I don't know his name."

"You're lying to me, Lamb."

"I swear, I don't know who he is," I tell him. "He was just nice to me when I woke up and started freaking out. I barely even saw his face."

Zade's gaze narrows, not trusting me, but I'm not about to throw my father under the bus just to ease Zade's curious mind. He holds my stare for a few moments before finally deciding to release me from his interrogation. "Alright, Oakley. Go to sleep."

Not allowing myself even a moment of hesitation, I roll over while my hands shake, knowing I haven't fooled him even a little bit. He knows I'm lying, so I suppose I should be grateful that he's not pushing me on it right now. But this isn't over. He'll come for me again, and next time, he won't stop until he gets the answers he's looking for.

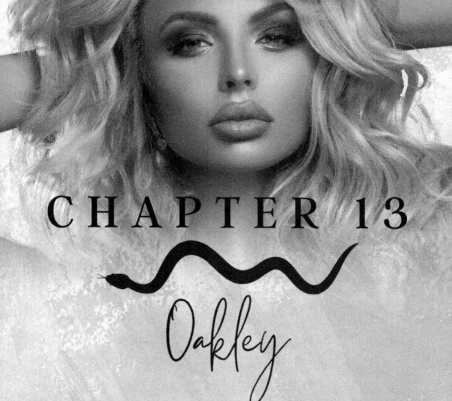

CHAPTER 13

Oakley

The late morning sun shines through Zade's floor-to-ceiling windows, and I squint into the light, not ready to wake. A soft groan pulls from deep in my throat as I make the ugly *just-woke-up* face. I take a deep breath, but the restriction across my chest has my body stiffening. Zade's strong, tattooed arm is locked over me, spooning me from behind, his strong thigh wedged between my legs and his rock-hard cock against my ass.

My God, he's big. I wonder how it would feel . . . No. I can't go there.

As if my slight movement woke him, Zade's body stiffens right along with mine, both of us locked in awkward silence. But there's nothing I love more than an awkward silence. "Wow, Bossman," I say, grinding my ass against his cock. "I didn't know you felt this way about me."

He snatches his arm back so fucking fast it's almost comical, and I watch as he springs out of bed and strides right out the door, adjusting his cock in his pants. I can't help but laugh after him, more than amused. Hell, it almost makes all of this worth it.

The door slams loudly behind him, and for the first time since before dinner last night, I'm finally left alone with my own thoughts to keep me company. I get up to pee, and just because I'm not a complete bitch, I clean up after myself in the bathroom, mopping up the puddle on the floor. With my clothes dry, I get dressed and finally start to feel like myself again, despite the rips and tears throughout my clothes. Until Zade decides to grace me with the return of my things, this will have to do. Though after my rampage through his closet with the scissors yesterday, I might be waiting a little longer than I anticipated.

After brushing my hair and shoving it into a messy bun, I trudge back out to the bedroom, grabbing the two charcoal drawings I was working on yesterday and taking them out to the kitchen counter. Placing them down on the counter, I help myself to breakfast while listening to the rhythmic sounds of Easton and Dalton in the gym.

Sawyer stands out on the balcony, yelling at someone on the phone, and I'm more than ready to eavesdrop on his conversation when Zade strides out of his home office and fixes me with a scathing glare. Apparently, he's a little embarrassed about his need to hold me in his sleep. It's a bit of useful information to store away in a safe place for a later date.

"See something you like, big boy?" I tease, enjoying this way more than I should. He rolls his eyes and ignores me, and I let out a heavy sigh. I can't help but notice how the night's rest did him wonders. His face has already begun to heal, even though there's still a long way to go. "Chill out, Bossman. I'm just having a little fun. Why have you always got such a big stick lodged up your ass? You gotta remove it before it punctures a lung."

He stops by the kitchen counter and braces his hands against it, more than ready to say something about my attitude this morning, when his gaze drops to my drawings. For some reason, it makes me nervous. He studies the image of his hand lodged deep in my chest, and his body stiffens before slowly lifting his stare back to mine. "Is there something you need?"

"Yeah, I um . . ." I swallow, giving myself a moment to try and remember what I was wanting to ask him. "I was hoping I could go sit on the roof to finish these."

"Were you planning on jumping?"

I give him a hard stare. "Only you would think to ask a woman if she plans to jump off the top of your stupid hotel."

"You didn't answer the question, Lamb."

I scowl and roll my eyes. "No, Zade. I'm not planning on plunging to my death today. Besides, if I were going to do it, I'd make it a little more exciting than that. Something that really inconveniences you, you know? Maybe right before your big showdown . . . I'd let you get your hopes up that you're about to get everything you want, and then . . . whoops. Fatal seizure right there on the floor, frothing mouth and everything."

"And you say I'm fucking sick."

"Roof, Zade. Yes or no?"

He lets out a heavy sigh and glances back at my drawings. "Yeah, whatever. But Dalton's going with you. He's probably down to shoot some hoops anyway."

Zade takes off toward the home gym, probably to tell Dalton he's heading up to the roof with me. As he disappears around the corner, I can't help but turn my gaze in the direction of his very empty home office. I bite my bottom lip, wondering what kind of information he's got stored in there.

Dalton mentioned Zade's father kept old books, Empire's by-laws. I know Dalton's been working hard on trying to find another loophole, but I can't help but wonder what other kind of information would be hidden in the depths of those dusty old pages. What I really need are blueprints of the Empire prison system. Hell, the whole underground system would be good. If there's some way I can get back down to my father and save him, I'll take it. We could disappear after that and have the life we were robbed of.

Shit. It's now or never.

I go to slip away when Dalton's tone cuts through the silent room. "Yo, Firefly, you coming or what?"

My head snaps up to find Dalton hovering by the elevator, holding the door open for me, making me wonder just how long I was standing there thinking about searching through Zade's office rather than actually doing it. Fuck, I'm such an idiot.

Grabbing my drawings, I hurry after him and slip into the elevator, suddenly not so excited about wasting another day drawing. I move in beside Dalton, and the door closes us in. He presses the button for the rooftop, and we quickly sail up. "So, umm . . ." I start, suddenly feeling very awkward. "What's Zade's deal?"

Dalton glances down at me, arching a brow as he narrows his eyes, extremely suspicious. "What do you mean?"

Sheepishness sweeps through me, and I can barely maintain eye contact. "You know, like . . . does he have a girlfriend?"

Dalton laughs, a breathy scoff tearing from deep in his throat. "You spend one night with the guy, and you're already fishing for details?"

I purse my lips into a hard line, not liking what he's insinuating, but I can't deny that he's right. My curiosity about my future killer is doing my head in. "You sound jealous."

He shrugs, not denying it. "Not gonna lie, I'm a little curious as to why you're so curious."

I shrug right back, willing the elevator door to open. "I just wanna know what makes him tick."

He scoffs again. "You make him tick."

The elevator dings as the doors finally open, but I suddenly find myself way too intrigued. How could I possibly make him tick? I mean, I know I frustrate the shit out of him. I work extremely hard to make his life a living hell. I mean, why the hell wouldn't I? It's the least I can do for the man who's going to take my life. But I have a feeling that's not exactly what Dalton is referring to. "You didn't answer the question," I remind him, following him over to the basketball court and watching as he scoops up a ball. "What's his deal?"

Dalton shoots, and the ball sails in a perfect arc toward the hoop before dropping straight through it and bouncing back into his waiting hands. "He's got a casual hook-up, just like we all have. Well, at least *had.* I don't know about the guys, but I've only been interested in your sweet little cunt since the second I tasted it."

A strange jealousy pounds through my chest, one I don't quite understand. After all, I don't have the right to feel jealous about the guys having other women in their lives. It's not like our weird little gang-bang relationship is going to go anywhere past day sixty. "Who's this chick Zade's been seeing?" I question, getting back on track, nervous that diving into the other guys' love lives is going to send me flying right over the edge just as Zade feared.

"*Seeing* isn't the right word for it," he tells me, getting chatty as he moves around the court, more than ready to share all of their little secrets. "She's more of a casual fuck, simply out of convenience. Not sure if she'd look at it that way, though." Dalton smirks and glances back at me, his eyes sparkling as the ball comes to a stop in his hands, looking as though he's about to give me the best gossip this world has ever seen. "It's Sawyer's sister."

My mouth drops open, my jaw practically smacking against the court. "Bullshit," I gasp, sucking in a deep breath. "You're shitting me, right? Does Sawyer know?"

Dalton grins. "Yeah. He's not too thrilled about it, but this is Zade we're talking about. If he wants to fuck her, he'll fuck her, no matter how Sawyer feels about it. He'll stop at nothing to get what he wants."

"Yeah. No shit," I mutter, unsure why I still feel this pang of jealousy in my chest. Must be nice being able to get close to a guy like Zade without him wanting to kill you.

Noticing the hesitation in my tone, Dalton glances back at me again. "What's up?" he mutters, a smirk playing on his lips. "You want us all?"

I consider lying, but these guys have a way of seeing right through me, so I give it to him straight. What's the point of holding back details now? "Is that so bad?" I ask. "It's not like I'll be around long enough for it to be an issue. You, Sawyer, and Easton seem to share just fine."

"Something tells me Zade isn't the type to share," he says, giving it to me bluntly. "Plus, isn't there a morality clause when it comes to fucking the dude who's going to end your life?"

I scoff, watching as he continues with the ball, shooting another perfect shot. "I think morality went out the window a long time ago."

Dalton laughs. "Too fucking right."

Abandoning the great idea to come up here to draw, I drop down on the edge of the court and watch as Dalton moves up and down the rooftop. Leaning back on my palms, I kick my feet out in front of me, crossing them at the ankles and settling in for the breathtaking show. "So, like . . . do you guys actually live here with Zade?" I ask, realizing that question had somehow slipped my mind until now.

"Nah," he says with amusement playing in his eyes. "We're just staying while . . . you know."

I roll my eyes. "While you wait for my brutal murder?"

"Yeah," Dalton cringes. "We all have our own apartments in the hotel, but we have other properties too. I've got a place about twenty minutes from here, but I don't usually stay there. Not when all the guys are out here. Besides, there's a rooftop court here. What more could I need?"

"Fair point," I say. "What about Sawyer and Easton?"

Dalton laughs, quickly glancing at me before launching himself into the air and dunking the ball through the hoop. "Shit, you know you really got under his skin when you called him Cross last night? I don't think he was expecting to care so much."

I don't respond, instead holding his stare until he answers my question, but my heart races with his comment. I like that I got under his skin, that something so simple as calling him by a name everyone else uses was enough to throw him over the edge. There's something about him that I can't get enough of. He gives me a thrill, and I love it. He's so mysterious, and every time he touches me, whether it's a subtle brush of his arm as he walks past or when he grips my chin and demands my attention . . . The rush is too much. He's intoxicating.

Dalton finally continues, dragging me out of my thoughts. "Sawyer lives across town in a fucking gated community because he's a bitch like that. But really, I think he likes to be close to his sister since she got all independent and shit. She bought her own place over there and as much as he'll deny it, he hates the thought of something happening to her. But if you ask me, that girl can more than take care of herself."

I nod, wondering if I'll get the chance to meet this mysterious sister before my dreaded twenty-seven days are up. "And Easton?"

Dalton scoffs. "That asshole would happily live in a cardboard box on the street if he had to. Nothing fazes him. He doesn't give a shit as long as his snakes are happy."

"Wait. Snakes? As in plural?"

"Yeah," he says with a soft chuckle. "His place is close by. Cross wanted to be somewhere that was as far away from his father as possible but still within the city. He rarely goes there though. Only when shit goes down and he needs to recoup for a few days."

Dalton goes quiet as he gets into his game. Not wanting to dig too deep into their lives, I scoot over and get comfortable on my stomach, bracing myself on my elbows as I position my drawings in front of me.

Allowing myself to get lost in my thoughts, I get busy working on my vision of the cells, and after a while, I put the finishing touches on it before moving to the other one. I spend ages on it, but no matter how hard I try, I can't seem to get it right. The look in Zade's eyes as he clutches my heart isn't right. I can't seem to capture the same depth in his eyes that I saw in them last night. Originally, I drew them with cruelty, but seeing the strange sadness and determination last night, it all feels wrong.

I get lost in the drawing, focusing way too hard on Zade's eyes and the more I fail to get it right, the harder it becomes to hold back my frustrations. Just as I'm about to crack my charcoal in half and toss the bastard over the edge of the roof, a shadow settles over me, blocking my much-needed sunlight.

My head whips up to find Dalton hovering in front of me, stark naked, those strong thighs leading up to that perfect, pierced cock, and from this angle down on the ground, he looks like a fucking god. My jaw drops, but not because of his mouth-watering body, but because of the perfectly round, pink, sprinkled donut hanging off his dick.

A wide grin stretches across my face, and I scramble to my feet, unable to stop gaping, barely even noticing the box of donuts resting in his hand. "You know," he starts so casually, as though he hasn't even noticed the bright pink donut hanging from his cock. "I've always wondered how many of these bad boys I could fit on my dick."

I can't speak. Only gawk. But damn, I'm so here for this.

Dalton plucks another donut out of the box and hands it to me with a cheeky-as-fuck smirk. "Wanna do the honors?"

"Fuck yeah."

Stepping into him, I take the donut from his hand and, smirking like a fucking idiot, I hook it over his thick cock, wondering where the hell he managed to find donuts with such big holes. Don't get me wrong, it's definitely a snug fit, but the donuts I'm used to can barely fit a finger through them.

"Hmm," Dalton groans. "Still warm."

A snort tears from the back of my throat as I look over my handiwork, knowing damn well I could fit at least another four on that thing. "Aren't you worried about it getting all sticky?"

"Well," he says, glancing down at the donut cock before sending me a panty-dropping wink. "I hope you like strawberry icing and sprinkles."

My tongue rolls over my bottom lip, suddenly extremely hungry. "You know, I think that might just be my new favorite."

Dalton grins before trailing his fingers through the strawberry icing and lifting it to my lips. I open wide, more than happy to play along, and take his finger in my mouth, groaning as my pussy starts to ache.

His eyes become hooded, and I can't help but wonder how a man with two donuts hanging off his cock can manage to look so devilish. Hell, he looks downright dangerous, pink icing and all. He inches toward me when his whole demeanor shifts, his body stiffening, even more than it already is. "Ahh, fuck," he says with a slight cringe.

My brows furrow just as I hear the soft ding of the elevator from across the rooftop. Before I even get a chance to ask how he knew someone was coming before hearing the ding, Sawyer and Easton are stepping out onto the rooftop.

Sawyer gets only one step before getting an eyeful of Dalton's cock and doubles over, clutching his stomach as he howls with uncontrollable laughter. I think it's the first time since his father's imprisonment that I've seen him come alive. Easton, on the other hand, raises his palm to cover Venom's eyes, as if protecting a child from getting an eyeful of their uncle screwing the pumpkin pie on Thanksgiving evening after getting too drunk and assuming everyone had already gone home.

Dalton just stands there and accepts the mockery, not in the least embarrassed about his strawberry-sprinkled donut cock. "Really? You chose right now to come up here?"

"Fuck man," Sawyer says, once he's finally recovered. "I knew you'd go to extreme lengths to steal her attention, but this? Holy fuck."

Dalton grins at his friends. "You can't tell me you've never been curious."

"He's got a point," I tell them. "I think we could get at least half a dozen lined up on this thing."

"Oh, how the mighty have fallen," Easton mutters. "I watched you slit a man's throat without a second thought barely forty-eight hours ago, and now you're fucking donuts. What gives, man?"

"Nah, come on," Dalton says, looking at his friends as though he couldn't possibly be more offended that they aren't stripping down to see who could hold the most. "Don't be like that. It's just a little fun."

Sawyer shakes his head, feigning secondhand embarrassment, but everyone here knows he really doesn't give a shit. He wouldn't possibly miss a chance to screw with his friend though. "Yeah . . . we're gonna go," he says, making sure to sound incredibly awkward about it.

"Come on, guys," Dalton says. "I . . . It's not what it looks like. Really."

The boys walk away while shaking their heads, and I grin back at them before plucking a donut out of the box. "Their loss," I tell Dalton, making sure I'm loud enough for them to hear. I watch as they glance back at me once they reach the elevator, and I scoop my finger through the icing before trailing it over my chest, their sharp gazes zoning in on my movements. "I was just about to see how sticky we could get."

I hear Sawyer's groan from across the rooftop, and he starts to double back, now more than ready to play along, but I shake my head. "No way, grinch," I say, putting my finger in my mouth and sucking off what's left of the icing. "Turn your ass right back around. You don't get any of this cherry pie. But just know, while you're down in your room, madly jerking off, I'll be on my knees taking Dalton's strawberry-covered cock deep in my throat and letting him come all over my face. And to think I could have taken you both at the same time. What a shame."

Sawyer groans, and I make a show of waving goodbye, watching as Easton drags him back into the elevator. As I glance back at Dalton with a wide grin, I find him holding a fist up toward me. My brows furrow, and I stare at it with an odd curiosity, but figure it's not the weirdest thing I've done. And with that, I lean in and sing into his hand microphone.

"The fuck are you doing?" Dalton questions, pulling his microphone back and staring at me as though I'm fucked in the head. Someone needs to remind this guy that he's the one standing naked on a rooftop with two donuts hanging from his Cuntblaster3000.

"What do you mean what am I doing?" I demand. "That's not . . . it's not a microphone, is it?"

"No, you fucking weirdo. It's a fist bump."

My face falls as my cheeks start to flush with embarrassment. "Oh yeah . . . see, that makes more sense," I say, tossing the donut back into the box before letting a grin fly free across my face. "Sooooo, are you going to keep looking at me like I just fell out of the crazy tree and hit every branch on the way down, or are we actually going to see how many donuts we can fit on your dick? Because I gotta admit, I'm actually curious now, and it'd be a shame to get this far and not actually see it through."

"Fuck yeah," he says. "But just so you know, I have every intention of licking strawberry icing off your tits after this, so let's make it fast. Otherwise, these donuts are gonna become glazed, and I'd rather shoot my load all over your face than waste it on something like that."

"Well then," I say, my eyes becoming hooded as my thighs clench to relieve the ache between them. I scoop up another donut, making sure to get my hands all sticky before slowly sliding the donut up his thick shaft. "Let's not waste another second."

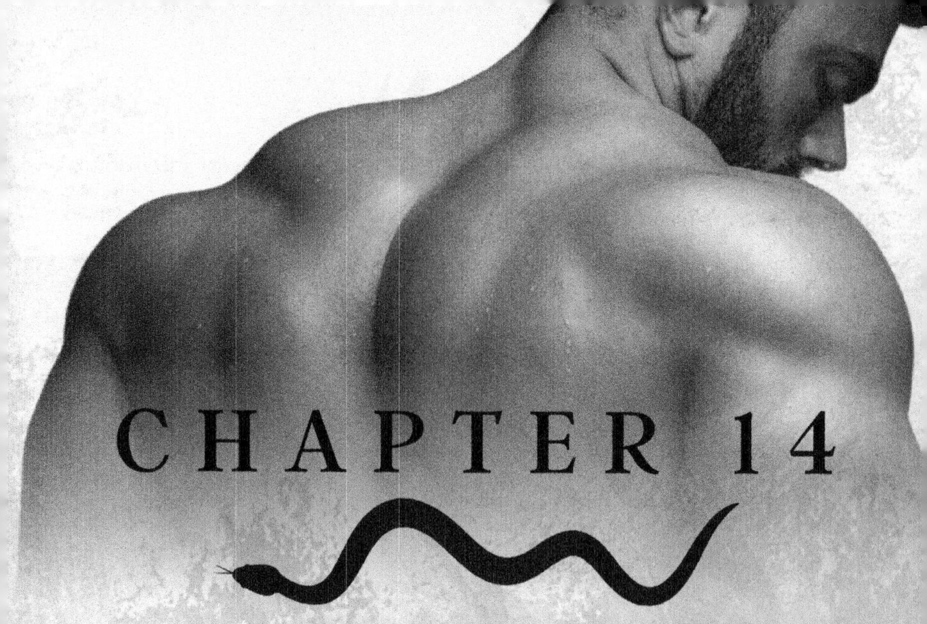

CHAPTER 14

Cross

Wrapped in nothing but a towel, Oakley walks through the penthouse quietly. I can only assume she needed the shower after being fucked on the roof and covered in strawberry icing. Judging by the noise that came from the bathroom earlier, it's fucking clear Dalton wasn't through with her.

My dick's been rock hard since the moment she dragged that icing across her chest, but I had to walk away. It almost kills me to admit I'm envious of the relationship Sawyer and Dalton get to have with her. They're so chill. They get to have fun and make her laugh, but that's not me. I lead a much darker life than they do, and finding peace in humor and playfulness isn't something I'm capable of.

I sit on the couch, watching her reflection through the floor-to-ceiling window, mulling over my reaction to her calling me Cross when her towel parts as she walks, revealing her thigh and hip. She walks slowly as if trying to get the drop on me, but no one gets the drop on me, especially not a little spitfire like Oakley.

"Hey," she rushes out, quickly leaning over the backrest of the couch, startling Venom, and narrowly avoiding getting bitten at the base of her throat. "Woah."

"What's up, Pretty?" I ask as she studies me, unaware of the way I watch her every little move through the window, her eyes shifting to the bullet wound through my shoulder as her lips press into a worrying line. I can't stand her worrying about me, but on the other hand, I fucking love that she does.

"I, umm . . . two things," she says. "I know you're all Team Zade, but tell me you know what he's done with my clothes? The ones I stole from him yesterday are suspiciously missing, and the ones I was wearing before . . . Well, they're gonna need a wash."

I barely hold back a scoff, knowing damn well Zade would have gone out of his way just to make sure she had nothing to wear. After all, he's just as petty as she is. He just likes to think he's above it. With a slight lift of my chin, I indicate toward my bedroom. "Grab something of mine. I'm sure there's a pair of sweatpants you could make work. Otherwise, Benny would probably bring something up for you."

"Ahh, thanks," she says before a cheesy grin stretches across her face. "You wouldn't happen to have a bra hidden in your drawers, would you? Preferably one that's never been used? Maybe some panties too?"

My face scrunches as I finally turn to meet her stare, but as I get a look at the few remaining droplets of water skating down her chest, my throat seizes. What the fuck is wrong with me? I've gotta get a grip.

"The fuck do you think this is?" I say. "If you want decent clothes that fit you, go crawl up Zade's ass."

"Like that will ever happen," she mutters, adjusting the top of her towel, making sure it's secure. "Speaking of Zade," she continues. "I need a favor."

I focus my stare back out the window. "No."

Oakley groans and throws herself right over the back of the couch before sprawling out beside me. She doesn't hesitate climbing onto my lap, straddling me, and instantly making my cock even harder, knowing there's not a damn thing under that towel. Her brow arches as she instinctively grinds down against me, and I can't help but drop my hands to her soft thighs, my fingers brushing over the small cross. My mark will forever live on her skin as a constant reminder that, despite her fucked-up relationships with my friends, a part of her will always belong to me.

Her eyes become hooded as she curls her hand behind my neck, being careful not to disturb Venom. "Do you need me?" she murmurs, seduction deep in her throaty tone.

I nod, watching her closely. "You're not sore after Dalton?"

"I am," she admits. "But I need you too."

Not hesitating, I lock my arm around her waist and lift her just enough to free my cock. I line myself up with her entrance, and as I lower her back down, I fill her to the fucking brim. Oakley gasps as my balls tighten, finally relieving the ache I've had for her all fucking day.

Her eyes roll and she starts to move, slowly riding me, moving up and down on my cock as she circles her hips. I grip her ass beneath her towel as her nails dig into my skin. "Oh, God, Easton," she breathes, letting her towel fall open and teasing me with those perfect tits. "I've missed how you fill me."

"I know, Pretty," I say with a grunt, her pussy clenching around my cock, squeezing me tight as she moves up and down.

"I need a favor."

"No."

She tightens her hold on my cock, all but strangling me with her sweet cunt. "I'm not asking again," she says in warning. "I need a favor."

Letting out a sigh, I play her game, becoming a victim of her pussy. "What is it?"

Oakley groans as she drops down over me, and I lean further back into the couch, adjusting my hips so she goes deeper. "Oh, fuck. I need you to convince Zade to let me work tonight," she says with a breathy groan. "He listens to you."

Fuck. Knowing the likelihood of Zade actually agreeing to that, I take a different approach. "Why the fuck do you want to work? You've got twenty-seven days left, and you want to spend it in a fucking dive bar serving asshole college pricks?"

"I like working," she tells me. "It's mind-numbingly boring, but it's busy, and for those few hours behind the bar, I won't have to think about Empire and the ritual. It allows me to feel normal, assuming Danny will actually let me work. I missed Saturday's shift after I made this whole big speech about not being a flake. Besides, I haven't checked in with Cara in a few days. She probably thinks I'm dead by now. Either that or I've been in a sex-marathon orgy and she's pissed she wasn't invited."

Sounds like Cara.

"Alright, fine," I say with a groan. "If I agree to ask him, would you shut up and fuck me like you mean it?"

Oakley grins wide, her eyes sparkling with wicked hunger, and she adjusts herself on my lap. "Watch me, Easton," she murmurs, taking my hand and pressing it to her body. My gaze immediately drops down between us, watching the way her sweet cunt takes my cock, moving in and out and glistening with her arousal.

My cock flinches with need. What can I say? I'm a visual guy. I like to watch almost as much as I like to participate.

Her hips roll as she bounces up and down on my cock, squeezing and grinding, and I reach between us, gripping the base of my cock with a firm grasp as my thumb reaches up to her sensitive clit, rubbing tight circles and watching how her body responds.

Oakley picks up her pace, and after Dalton probably made her come twice already, she's going to have to work for it. But I know she can do it. Her pussy aches for a release she can only find with me. "Come for me, Pretty. Let me see you."

She takes me harder as Sawyer walks through the living room, stopping to watch her for just a moment before deciding he simply can't resist. He strides toward us and moves around to the front of the couch as Oakley watches him closely. Seeing just how close she is, he doesn't try to get in on the action, simply takes her chin and pulls her head back before dropping his lips to hers and kissing her deeply.

Oakley groans into his mouth as he reaches around her body, gently pinching her nipple and making her gasp. Sawyer moves down to her pussy and takes over her clit, freeing my hand as he rubs tight circles. I lift my fingers to her tits, pinching her nipple again, addicted to the way her body jolts with the touch. She clenches around my cock as Sawyer meets my gaze, knowing exactly how his touch is affecting what she does to me, and there's no denying Sawyer Thorne is one of the best doubles partners I've ever had the pleasure of fucking with. He's intuitive and thinks about the whole fucking scene, and instead of only trying to get himself off, he tries to make it better for everyone involved.

Fierce hunger fires through me, and for a moment, I almost consider inviting him to join, wanting to watch the way he takes her ass. Hell, I might even share and let him stretch that sweet cunt out further if she's down for taking us both, but after fucking Dalton for the past hour, I wouldn't be surprised if she needs a break.

My cock flinches inside her, and she groans into Sawyer's mouth again. He switches out his fingers for his thumb, gently rubbing tight circles over her clit while his fingers dip lower to her entrance, pushing them in beside my cock.

I feel the way Sawyer massages her walls, and fuck, I can't deny it feels good for me too. A breathy moan escapes her lips. I feel myself inching closer to the edge, but I hold onto it, determined to watch her come first, desperate to feel the way her pussy spasms around me.

She's fucking close though, and just the thought has me struggling to hold on.

Pinching her pert nipple again, she gives me exactly what I've been waiting for. She comes hard with a sharp cry into Sawyer's mouth, her tight cunt turning into a spasming mess. "Oh fuck," she grunts, clenching down around me as I finally allow myself to come with her, shooting hot spurts of cum deep inside her pretty cunt.

Sawyer pulls back and smiles against her lips as her orgasm rocks through her. He keeps working her with his fingers and thumb, pulling every last ounce of pleasure out of her as she rides it out. "So fucking gorgeous when you come."

I couldn't agree more. That flush in her cheeks and the way her body moves and jolts . . . I've never seen anything so exquisite.

Coming down from her high, Sawyer kisses her again before finally pulling his hand free. Without another word, he simply walks away, leaving me to stare at this incredible woman who scares the absolute shit out of me.

Oakley reaches down and clutches her towel, pulling it back up around her and takes a second to make sure it's secure. "I don't think I'll ever get used to the way you guys fuck me," she says, leaning forward and brushing her lips over mine, pressing her soft hand to my chest and feeling the way she makes my heart race.

She pulls back with a beaming, satisfied smile, and I don't say a fucking word. If I open my mouth, I know I'll say something neither of us wants to hear—something neither of us are ready for.

As if sensing my need to find composure, she climbs off my lap and gives me another breathtaking smile. "My shift starts at five," she tells me, everything she's refusing to say shining through her dazzling stare. "Make sure Zade knows I'll kick his ass if he makes me jump through hoops for this."

I scoff, knowing exactly how this shit is going to go down, but I'm a man of my word. I told her I'd try, and that's exactly what I'm going to do. "Don't get your hopes up."

With that, Oakley sashays off in the direction of my bedroom, probably to find clothes, and just as she slips around the corner and out of sight, Zade strides in from his home gym, absolutely clueless about the fuck fest that just took place on his favorite seat of his favorite couch.

"What's going on?" he murmurs, seeing the hesitation in my eyes as I try to work out how the fuck to word this. I decide to just rip it off like a Band-Aid and be straight with him.

"Oakley wants to work tonight."

Zade scoffs. "You're fucking kidding, right?" he says, amusement flashing in his eyes.

"I told her you weren't gonna like it, but she insisted I at least ask."

His stare hardens as if reading into the conversation, realizing there's more. "Let me guess, she made some bullshit petty threat to go along with—" he cuts himself off, his brows furrowed as he sniffs the air before giving me a hard stare. "Really man? On my fucking couch?"

I shrug my shoulders. "It's not like I planned it."

"Fucking hell," he mutters. "Ever since you assholes have been spending so much time here with her, there's been DNA spread from one end of my penthouse to the next."

I can't help the satisfied grin that tears across my face. If he knew just how fucking good it is with her, he'd be kicking himself for not taking her sooner. "What do I tell her, man? Her shift starts at five."

"I don't know. You've still got a fucking hole in your shoulder from the last time we were out by those apartments. Not to mention, the last time she was at Danny's Bar, she slipped out the back door. I can't have that shit happening again."

"I doubt she's stupid enough to try it again."

"You clearly haven't been paying attention," he tells me. "Her one goal is to save herself and screw me over in the process. If she sees an opportunity to run, she's gonna fucking take it."

"Then put a tracker on her," I tell him, knowing damn well it's something he's already considered. "Besides, Venom's close to shedding and she's most comfortable in her enclosure back in those shitty apartments. I can take Oakley and wait while she works."

"No. If she really insists on spending her last days working, then we'll all go," he says with a heavy sigh, the very last words I expected to hear from him.

"Yeah?" I question, almost certain I didn't hear him right. The Zade I know would have told her to get fucked and to shove her shift up her ass, and I realize just how right I was last night. Oakley has gotten under Zade's skin. The fucktard is just too blinded by his ritual that he can't see what's right in front of his goddamn face.

Zade looks away, almost as shocked by his response as I am. "Yeah," he tells me, and with that, he walks away, leaving me wondering how the fuck this new dynamic is going to play out.

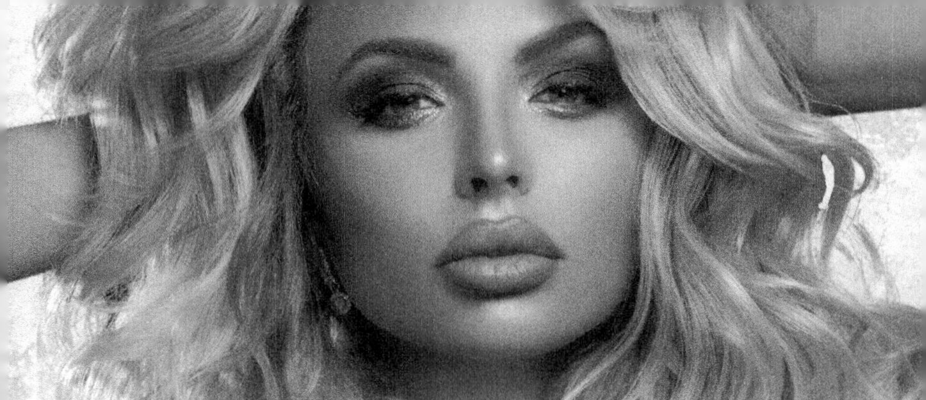

CHAPTER 15

Oakley

My shoulder barges against the door of my small, shitty apartment, and I plow through the doorway to find Cara hovering in the living room, her eyes wide. She looks as though she's about ready to fuck me up, probably assuming I'm some kind of serial killer. But no, that would be the guys at my back, not me.

"Oakley?" she gapes, blinking rapidly as if not believing what she's actually seeing. She races toward me and pulls me into a tight hug, gripping my shoulder before yanking me back to give me a hard stare. "Where the fuck have you been? I've been worried sick about you. I mean, shit, girl. If you're going to go on a week-long bender, the least you could do is invite me to come along."

"Sorry," I laugh. "It's a long story."

"Well luckily for you, I have a lot of free time."

I swallow hard, not sure why I wasn't expecting her to welcome the long explanation. Most people shy away from comments like that, not in the least interested in hearing the ins and outs of other people's lives.

I fumble over what to say when she's distracted by the four brooding assholes pushing their way through our apartment. "Umm . . . What the fuck?" she demands, gaping at the boys making their way down the hall, barging into every room and sweeping them, checking for any assassins who might possibly be hiding under my bed. Her eyes widen further seeing the state of Zade's face, undeniable horror and concern flashing through her eyes before she quickly masks it.

"Hey," she calls after them as I cringe, trying to work out how the hell I'm going to explain this one. They each ignore her, and for a moment, I wonder if they even heard her. "Hey, assholes," she says more firmly. "What the hell do you think you're doing? You can't just barge your way into my apartment uninvited. Fuck off out of here."

Dalton strides past her, and as he catches her eye the awkwardness washes over her, reminding me of the conversation about their weird sexual encounter. I can't blame her for being awkward. I would be too. But I'm sure if she knew about his newfound donut kinks, she wouldn't feel so bad.

Deciding he's done with his part of the sweep, Dalton drops onto the couch and scoops up the TV remote before exiting out of the movie Cara was watching. Though, let's be honest, the movie was probably nothing but background noise. I can almost guarantee that she was reading instead, and just to prove a point, I scan through the living room and find her Kindle lit up on the coffee table.

Smugness tears through my chest but comes crashing back down when I catch her eye. "What the fuck is he doing?" she mouths to me, her eyes wide as she nods toward Dalton, as though the asshole can't sense that she's talking about him. But something tells me he's not the kind to care.

"Like I said," I tell her, not bothering to mask our conversation with ridiculous whispers that he can hear anyway. "Long story."

"Then get started," she says.

"Wish I could," I say, grabbing her hand and dragging her down to my room. "But I've got a shift starting in twenty minutes."

We pass Zade on the way to my room, and I make sure to fix him with a hard stare, but as he passes by and I pull Cara into my room, I catch a strange look in her eye . . . desire, maybe something a little more.

My brows furrow as Zade looks back at her with nothing but an intense boredom that seems to break her heart, which doesn't make sense. Cara doesn't even know him. She barely knew his name up until a little while ago, and since then, it's not like he's been hanging out here. He's been too busy keeping me prisoner in his ivory tower.

Shrugging it off, Cara and I step into my room, and I get busy stripping off my clothes and searching for my black tank and jeans. Hell, maybe even some clean underwear too.

"Okay, girl. Spill. Why the fuck are our four stalker neighbors currently rampaging through our apartment?" she questions. "I don't know if maybe you've forgotten, but you shouldn't be hanging out with those assholes. They kidnapped you, Oakley. Locked you up in a cell for twenty-four hours, then knocked you out." She steps into me and grabs my wrists, flipping them over to see the scars left from the cuffs the boys fastened around my wrists. "Tell me I didn't imagine this."

I groan, frustrated for having dug myself a hole that I have no idea how to get out of. "I just . . . they're not that bad."

"Okay, let me repeat myself," she says, clearing her throat as I attempt to pull my tank top over my head. "THEY KIDNAPPED YOU, YOU FUCKING TWAT! This isn't a fucking book, babe. This shit doesn't have a happy ending for you. This is real life. You can't just disappear for days on end to hang out with your kidnappers."

"Do you trust me?"

She gapes at me as though I've clearly lost my mind. "Umm, no."

Rolling my eyes, I let out a heavy sigh. I walked right into that one. "Look, I . . . I don't know how to explain it or even where to start, but just know that while these guys really are assholes at heart, they're kinda alright, and for the most part, they're trying to look out for me. They just have a really fucked-up way of showing it."

Cara watches me a moment longer, her gaze narrowing before her mouth finally pops open. "Holy shit. You're fucking them all."

"No," I rush out. "Well, kinda. Not all of them."

Her jaw drops further, and I see at least a million questions flashing in her eyes as she drops onto the edge of my bed. "But like . . . What? Which ones?" she breathes, looking dumbfounded, and honestly, for someone who reads about this shit every single night, I thought she'd be a little more enthusiastic. "And how? Like, all together, or at different times?"

Stepping into my jeans, I jump a few times to get them up and quickly button them before running my fingers through my hair, trying to tame my loose curls. "I mean, sometimes it's together, and sometimes it's just one on one."

Her eyes widen as if finally registering what's going on. "Which ones?"

"Dalton, Sawyer, and Easton."

"Easton?" she questions. "I thought the other guy's name was Cross?"

"It is," I confirm. "It's his last name, but I kinda like Easton, so I call him that."

"Right, okay, so . . . You're not screwing the scary one?" she questions with a strange reluctance in her tone that puts me on edge. "You know, ummm . . . What's his name? Zane, is it?"

"It's Zade," I tell her, noticing how she seems to be holding her breath as she waits for my response. "But no. He's too intense for me. Besides, the others are keeping me more than busy." I add, unsure why I feel hesitant to tell her that I've started to consider what being with Zade would be like.

Cara lets out a breath and glances away as if to compose herself, and my brows furrow, unsure what the hell is going on with her, but when I glance at the time, her odd behavior is the furthest thing from my mind. "Oh, shit. I have to go."

"What?" she rushes out. "Oh, hell no. You can't drop a bomb like that and then leave without giving me any of the juicy details. What the hell am I supposed to do until you get back?"

I shrug my shoulders as I race around my room, hoping like fuck Zade lets me come back here after my shift to grab some of my clothes before shipping me back off to my penthouse prison. "I don't know," I say with a smirk, "go find your vibrator and let off a bit of steam." I laugh as I run away from her scathing glare, shooting back out my door and slamming face-first into Sawyer's chest. "Ahh, fuck." I mutter, rubbing my head, positive that's going to leave a red mark. His pecs are so fucking solid, it's like running into a brick wall.

"You good?" he questions, briefly glancing over my head at Cara who follows me out.

"Yeah, I'm fine," I say. "But I'm gonna be late for work. We need to go."

Zade lets out a heavy sigh from the living room as he watches out the window, scanning every inch of the darkness. "Not too late to pull out," he suggests.

A grin stretches across my face as I meet Easton's stare across the room. "Oh, it's way too late to pull out now," I murmur under my breath, recalling the exact moment he didn't do that.

Zade looks back at me, his face scrunched with distaste, but thankfully he doesn't say a word. I can only imagine the vile bullshit that would pour out of his mouth, leaving me wondering where the man I spent an hour talking with in bed last night has disappeared to. Hell, he's left me almost giddy to do it all over again tonight. Assuming we end up back at his penthouse, of course.

Cutting it way too close, I get my ass out the door with the boys following my every step, and before I know it, I'm barging through the door of Danny's Bar, a nervous anxiety sitting heavily in my gut. Heather works the busy bar, yet she clocks me the second I appear in the doorway, her face falling and quickly morphing into an irritated scowl.

"Ahh, shit," I mutter as Sawyer steps in behind me, his hands on my hips.

"You'll be fine," he tells me. "It's too fucking busy for her to deny you anyway."

Not gonna lie, he's got a good point, and it instantly eases me. Not wanting to waste any more precious time, I slip into the crowd and make my way to the bar, grabbing an apron as I pass the small opening to get behind the bar, not even bothering to clock in. Hell, what does it matter anyway? I'll be dead soon enough, and if by some miracle I'm not, then I'll be on the run, racing against the clock for my life.

"I—"

"No," Heather says, cutting me off. "No way in hell. You skipped out on your shift Saturday night without even a text after you gave me this whole big spiel about how I could count on you. The bar was packed, and I was left alone to do it by myself. Danny had to come in, and believe me, he's pissed."

"Shit," I say with a heavy sigh, knowing there's no excuse under the sun she would ever accept, not even the cold hard truth. "You know I wouldn't skip out on my shift without a word unless it was really important. Come on, Heather. I've never given you reason to doubt me. I'm not the type to just not be bothered showing up or deciding some bullshit party is a better use of my time. I'm a good worker."

She presses her lips into a hard line, really not wanting to give me another chance, but in this packed bar, what choice does she really have? "Danny's not going to like it," she warns me. "When he comes in to raid the till, he's gonna have something to say about it."

Thank fuck.

"I know," I say, sucking in a sharp breath through my teeth and cringing. "I can handle it."

"Good, now hurry up and get to work. I wanna get on top of this crowd before the 9 p.m. rush comes through."

With that, I get busy, and just as I had hoped, the rush of customers keeps me occupied with mind-numbing work. At least until Danny shows up. Just as Heather had predicted, he drags me to the quietest part of the bar and bitches me out until all four of the guys are beginning to creep toward me. Which naturally brings on another spout of bitching for breaking his cardinal rule of not bringing one's bullshit into his bar.

Realizing that wasting time reaming me is only making the line at the bar longer and stressing out Heather, he huffs away and leaves me to get back to my work. By nine thirty, everything has finally started to calm enough that I can actually catch my breath.

The guys chill out in their favorite dark corner as I go about the bar, quickly cleaning up where I can. I straighten up the bottles and wipe over the bar as Hannah, our other bartender, starts washing up some of the schooner glasses.

A guy approaches the bar, and being the closest, I step up in front of him and give him a beaming smile, knowing damn well he's been handing out tips like candy all night. "What can I get ya?" I ask, already reaching for a glass.

His eyes sparkle, roaming over my face as he braces himself against the bar, and I can't help but notice how attractive he is. He's almost a clone of Dalton with his messy dark hair and blazing eyes. Hell, I wouldn't be surprised if he gets around on a Harley, too. But in comparison to Dalton, he's almost dull.

His lips lift into a subtle smirk, his eyes dancing with all that cheesy goodness that gets my blood pumping. "How about a date?"

My brow arches, not having expected that, but honestly, I should have. I get asked out multiple times during my shifts, and it's usually by drunken idiots who are only looking for someone to take home and screw. Only this guy certainly isn't drunk, and judging by the way Dalton and Sawyer are scowling at his back, I might just take him up on it. After all, I've only got twenty-seven days to live. Why not make the most of it?

"What's your name?" I ask with a flirty smile, pouring him a beer despite not having asked for one.

"Harley," he says, making me laugh.

"Of course it is," I say, handing him the drink as I notice Zade getting to his feet. I offer him my hand, making sure to turn the charm right up. "I'm Oakley."

"Oakley and Harley, huh?" he murmurs, holding onto my hand

a moment longer. "We already sound like the world's cutest couple."

A real laugh tears from my throat, and I'm surprised. I flirt with customers all the time, though that's generally for the sake of raking in tips. None of them have made me laugh for real. Hell, the fact that it seems to be getting under all the guys' skin only makes it better. "Indeed we do," I tell him, more than prepared to take this all the way, despite a real lack of interest in the guy. I mean, he's cute and all, and he can probably fuck like a king, but I already have more than I can handle.

"So, what do you say?" he questions as Zade and Dalton stride across the bar, more than ready to warn this guy away by any means necessary, even if it means beating him to a pulp in the alley behind the bar.

"You know what?" I say, just as Zade and Dalton get close enough to overhear our conversation. Just to prove a point, I ramp up the flirting. "I'd love to go on a date with you."

"Tonight?" he questions with a hopeful spark in his dazzling stare, completely oblivious to the storm brewing at his back.

I laugh. "Wow, you're eager," I say, knowing he'd probably end up dead if I agreed to that, and considering I'm not a cold-blooded killer like my new friends, I swiftly decline. "I'm working late tonight, but let me give you my number and we can figure something out."

"Alright, sweet," he says, digging into his pocket and handing me his phone. I quickly swipe my thumb across the screen, unlocking it and adding my number to his contacts, not even sure I know where my phone is. After all, I haven't seen it in a few days. It's not like I have anyone to call anyway, apart from my apparent not-aunt when she sends the occasional check-in text. But I suppose that's all an act to cover her tracks. I doubt she even cares about me at all.

Handing his phone back, I arch my brow. "You know, a man who doesn't use a passcode to unlock his phone makes me nervous," I tell him. "In my experience, that means he's usually too confident for his own good."

His lips kick up into a wicked smirk, his eyes dancing with hunger. "And what if I am?"

"Then it sounds like we're more than compatible. But I must warn you, anything you wanna throw at me, I'll give back twice as hard."

Harley laughs, slipping his phone back into his pocket. "I'll see you around, Oakley," he says, that confidence shining through his stare. I nod and watch as he scoops up his beer and walks away, shouldering past Zade and Dalton, oblivious to their rage.

My gaze shifts to the boys, more than pleased with myself. But it's not like I'm actually going to go out with the guy, something Zade clearly hasn't figured out. "Out back. Now."

Ooft. Bossman is cranky. I wonder if he'll spank me.

Without waiting to see if I'll follow him, he strides to the back of the bar, and as Dalton goes to follow him, he meets my stare, and a wild smirk cuts across my face. "What?" I question, as innocently as ever.

Dalton rolls his eyes and continues to follow Zade as I turn to Heather. "Give me two minutes."

She nods and goes about her duties as I scurry after the guys. Not seeing which way they went after stepping through to the back, I walk through the door and past the kitchen to look for them. When I round the corner to the back of the bar, a hand snakes out like lightning, gripping the front of my shirt and throwing me up against the wall.

Zade moves into me, his hard body pressed right up against mine, fury in his cold stare. "What the fuck do you think you're doing?" he rumbles.

"Ooooh," I say, hunger bursting through my veins, forcing my knee between his thighs and pushing up just enough to grind against him, knowing damn well that my response isn't at all what he's looking for. But I'm starting to learn with Zade just how easily I can frustrate him, and it's the best fun I've ever had. "Bringing me back here to throw me around, huh? Wow, Bossman. I knew there was something a little kinky about you. Tell me, does Sawyer's sister like it when you throw her around, too?"

Zade clenches his jaw, the fury in his eyes turning to red-hot rage. He glances at Dalton with an accusatory stare, but Dalton just presses his lips into a hard line and shakes his head as though he had nothing to do with allowing that little piece of information to slip.

Zade's stare turns back to me, and a second passes as I wait for him to release me. When it becomes obvious that he doesn't plan to, my lips twist into a wicked smirk before letting out an ear-shattering scream. "HELP ME! PLEASE, HELP ME!"

Zade's eyes bulge out of his head and he shoves harder into me, his hand slamming down over my mouth as Dalton hastily looks around, making sure no one is about to come running to my aid. "What the fuck is wrong with you?" Zade hisses, his stare cold and lethal.

He pulls back just an inch to allow me to speak. "Wait. You're not trying to kill me?" I question, giving him a blank stare.

"You know damn well I'm not about to kill you. Not yet, at least."

"Ahh, my bad," I say, giving him a hard shove, pushing him off me and forcing his hands off my body. "In that case, asshole, you have no fucking reason to put your hands on me like that. I mean, shit. Who the fuck do you think you are ordering me around in the middle of my shift? I'm trying to work."

Frustration burns through his stare, and I watch the way his hands ball into fists at his side, clearly itching to grab me again. "You're not fucking working. You're too busy trying to work out how to fuck your customers."

I grin at him. "What's the matter, Zade? Jealous I'm not trying to fuck you?"

He scoffs. "Wake up," he tells me. "Not every fucking man who walks this planet wants a piece of your over-used, communal pussy."

"No, they certainly don't," I agree with him, stepping into him and raising my chin, my lips barely a whisper away as my tits brush against his wide chest. "But *you* do, don't you, Zade? You could barely control yourself this morning, that rock-hard cock pressed against my ass. Did it feel good?" I whisper. "Did you pleasure yourself while thinking about me?"

Dalton groans from behind Zade, his hands running through his hair as he starts to pace, knowing damn well I'm under his skin.

"You're not going out with that guy," Zade tells me, avoiding my question.

I laugh and step back, needing the space between us. "I had no intention of actually going out with him. But now that I know just how badly you don't want me to, I think I just might."

"Like hell."

An ugly scoff tears from the back of my throat as anger pulses through my veins like poison. "Is it not enough that you're taking my life in twenty-seven days?" I hiss. "You have to take my freedom too? If my days are numbered, then you bet your ass I'm going to live them well. And if that means going out with some random guy I met in a bar, who probably only wants to see if he can fuck me, then goddamn, you better believe I'm going out with that guy."

"No. I—"

"What the hell is going on back here?" Danny's booming tone cuts through the tension, his sharp gaze raking over the guys before coming to me. "What did I tell you about bringing your bullshit into my bar?"

"I know. I'm sorry. They were just leaving."

"Like hell we were," Zade says as Dalton's hands flinch at his sides, ready to throw down like the fucked-up little violence addict he is.

My heart races, the irritation in Zade's eyes making me nervous. I don't know Danny very well, but I've seen him effortlessly throw assholes out of his bar, and I don't doubt that he's about to try it on Zade and Dalton. Only, I can guarantee that this will end a little differently than what Danny is used to.

Danny strides toward us, and as his stare hardens, I notice Zade reaching around to his back, no doubt going for his gun.

Panic tears at me, and before I even think about what I'm doing, I cut in front of Danny, blocking him from Zade as I meet his ferocious gaze. "Leave," I tell him with a pointed stare, knowing damn well this isn't going to go down well. I subtly shake my head, silently begging him not to do anything stupid. "My shift ends in twenty minutes. Cross and Sawyer can walk me back. Please, just . . . go."

I feel Dalton's stare flicking between us, but I don't dare take my eyes off Zade until I see his hand finally relax back by his side and a wave of relief crashes through me. He takes a step toward me, gripping my chin. "Don't try anything, Lamb," he warns me, his words like bullets right to the chest.

He holds my stare for a moment longer before finally releasing my chin and stepping around both me and Danny and striding out through the back door. I let out a heavy breath and meet Dalton's gaze. Unease flashes in his eyes, and he gives me a small smile before following Zade, leaving me with Danny.

"You in some kind of trouble?" Danny questions, his gaze narrowed as he watches after the guys.

"Nothing I can't handle," I promise him before forcing an encouraging smile across my face and hoping like fuck he doesn't try anything stupid. Before he gets a chance to question me, I scurry away, heading back out into the bar to finish my shift. Zade is definitely going to have something to say about this when I get back home.

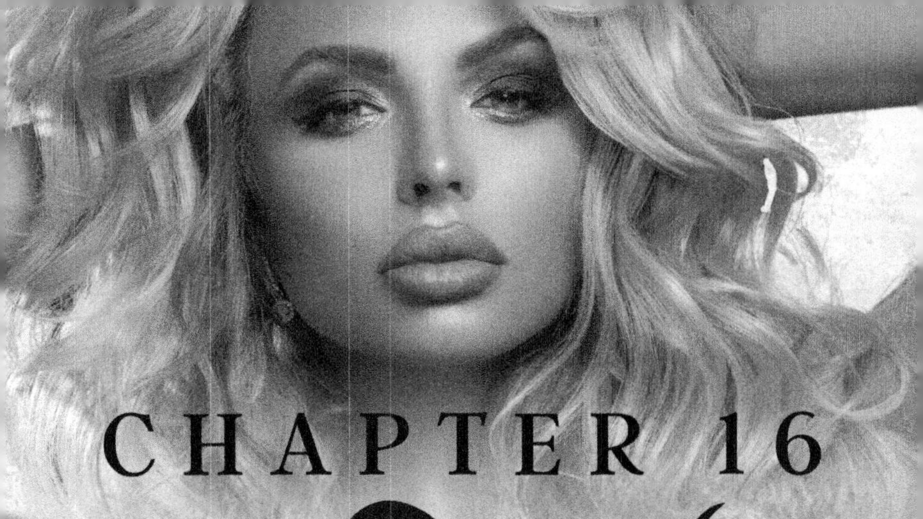

CHAPTER 16

Oakley

My feet drag along the pavement with Easton on one side and Sawyer on my other. Dalton and Zade walked out of Danny's Bar twenty minutes ago, and the pumping adrenaline made me feel wide awake, but now that it's burned out, I'm more than ready to crash.

"You shouldn't stir Zade like that," Easton warns as we walk away from Danny's Bar, a strange sadness growing in the pit of my stomach. I'm certain that Zade isn't about to let me go back there. Not after how everything just went down.

"I can't help it," I tell him honestly as Sawyer scoffs, a breathy chuckle vibrating through his chest. "He makes all these bullshit demands of me, throws me around like a fucking ragdoll, and just expects me to accept it. I get that he had a screwed-up life and dealt with who knows how much abuse from his father over the years, but that doesn't give him the right to treat me the way he does. I'm getting whiplash from his mood swings. I mean, if the guy is determined to take my life, then the least he can do is put up with every bit of bullshit I throw his way."

Sawyer looks over my head and fixes Easton with a pointed stare. "She's got a point, man."

"I know she does," he mutters. "But the more she gets under his skin, the more he gets under mine. He's like a fucking child. I've never seen him this irritable before."

A pang of satisfaction settles into the pit of my gut, only hanging around for a moment before vanishing again. Getting under Zade's skin was great those first few times. Watching how quickly I could make him squirm was getting me off, but I'm starting to learn that satisfaction never lasts. At the end of the day, it doesn't change the fact that he's still going to kill me.

Letting out a heavy sigh, I look up at Sawyer, my fingers brushing past his as he walks by my side. "I don't think I ever said thank you for getting me out of those cells."

"Sure you did," he says. "Kind of."

I give him a hard stare. "You know damn well that I didn't," I tell him. "I was so worked up and pissed at you all for lying to me that I never stopped to consider just how dangerous that was. And even though there will come the day that you march me into Empire's sacred tomb and take my life, I'm still grateful that you came and got me out of there. Those cells were . . . It's just not somewhere I was willing to spend another second. So thank you."

Easton simply nods as Sawyer gives me a tight smile. "Does this mean you forgive me?"

I scoff, a loud, barking grunt pulling from the back of my throat. "Hell no," I say with a laugh. "But it does mean that I can be civilized with you guys. You know, apart from Zade."

Sawyer grins, his eyes sparkling, and I know exactly what's going through his mind. "Civilized, huh?" he questions, almost sounding disappointed. "I prefer it when you're animalistic. Wild and raw. You taste best that way."

Hunger burns through his stare, and I realize I've caught my breath. Forcing myself to inhale, I attempt to shake it off. What is it about these guys? With nothing more than a single sentence and a pointed, heated stare, I'm putty in their hands. Perhaps it's the danger, or I've just become a sex-crazed whore over the past few weeks. Either way, if these guys asked me to get on my knees right here in the middle of the deserted street and play doubles, I would in a heartbeat.

Noticing my body's reaction to his intensity, he smirks at me as though I just played right into his hands. Sawyer stops in the street and curls his hand around the back of my neck, pulling me to a stop. "What's wrong, Doll? You need something from me?"

The softest moan slips from between my lips as I nod, captivated by his stare. I feel Easton step in behind me, and my heart starts to race. His hands come to my hips before circling around to the front of my jeans, and I suck in a breath, feeling as he pops the button and pushes them down my hips.

Sawyer's hold on the back of my neck tightens, and he pulls me in closer, tipping my head back. Before the thrill has even sailed the whole way through my body, his lips crush down on mine, and his tongue plunges into my mouth.

I groan into his kiss and step out of my jeans, not giving a shit that I'm half-naked in the middle of the street. Easton's fingers find my clit, slowly massaging, rubbing tight circles, and making my knees shake with anticipation. "This is going to be hard and fast," he tells me, just moments before his lips come down on the sensitive skin below my ear, the two of them already sending me into pure, blissful satisfaction.

I feel Easton grinding against my ass as I reach down between me and Sawyer, freeing that delicious monster from the confines of his pants. As his cock springs free, I grip it tightly, his velvety skin so welcome in the palm of my hand. My thumb rolls over his tip, collecting the small bead of moisture, and as I pull back from his kiss, I hold his stare and suck my thumb clean.

His gaze burns with hunger, his cock flinching in my hand, and without a second of hesitation, Sawyer reaches down and grasps my thigh, hooking his arm beneath my knee and pulling it up as high as it'll go, opening me wide.

Sawyer lines himself up with my entrance as Easton continues rubbing torturously slow circles over my clit, making me growl low. Sawyer pushes inside me, and my walls stretch so deliciously around him, his satisfied grunt like music to my ears.

He starts to fuck me, the chill of the late evening brushing upon my skin, yet I've never been so fucking hot.

My arm curls up around the back of Easton's neck, holding him close as his lips work their way down to the base of my neck, his heavy cock now free against my lower back. He reaches below me with his free hand, mixing his fingers with my wetness and feeling the way Sawyer enters me, fucking me like a damn god.

Easton drags my wetness back to my ass, and my eyes roll as he pushes two fingers inside me, slowly stretching me. I try to push back against him, but with my knee hooked high over Sawyer's strong arm, I can't move. I'm completely at their mercy.

Easton pushes his fingers deeper into my ass, and I turn my head while hooking my arm around Sawyer's neck, trying to hold on. Easton's eyes lock right onto mine, barely a breath away. "Take me," I tell him, so fucking ready for this.

His lips latch onto mine, and I feel his deep growl vibrating through his chest and against my back. He wastes no time sliding his thick cock between my folds, mixing with that wetness, and my brows furrow, realizing he's not releasing his fingers from my ass.

I feel him at my entrance, right there with Sawyer, and I suck in a gasp, my eyes widening. "You can take it," Easton tells me in an encouraging tone as Sawyer slows his movements, pulling out just enough to make room for Easton. Nervousness crashes through my veins, and then as one, they both push into me, and a loud groan rumbles through my chest.

"Holy fuck," I breathe, never having stretched so far in my life.

They take me slow at first, letting me get used to it, and as Easton's other hand returns to my clit and starts rubbing those tight circles I love so much, my body relaxes. The boys find a rhythm that has my eyes rolling to the back of my head, and as my nails dig into Sawyer's shoulders, that familiar, intense feeling builds within me.

My pussy clenches down around them, and Sawyer's sharp inhale has shivers sailing over my skin. Easton's fingers slowly move in and out of my ass, encouraging the orgasm slowly building within me. I've never had two guys inside of me like this, but the thought of their thick cocks rubbing together like that . . . goddamn.

"Fuck, I'm gonna come," I pant, barely able to get the words out as we hear Sawyer's phone beeping, each of us studiously ignoring it, way too occupied to be thinking about something like that.

Easton's fingers keep working my clit and ass as they both fuck me like a goddamn queen, and I dig my nails even deeper into Sawyer's shoulder as my world explodes around me. I see stars behind my eyes as my pussy shatters around their cocks. I clench down around them, my high blasting through my body with such intensity Sawyer has to hold me up. A sharp cry tears from my throat, and as my orgasm takes me higher, Sawyer and Easton come right along with me, filling me to the brim with hot spurts of cum as their pleasured grunts echo through the deserted street.

Sawyer's phone beeps again, and it's like a bucket of ice water being tipped over my head. I quickly come down from my high, all too aware of the fact I'm being wickedly fucked in the middle of the street for anybody to see. Hell, I wouldn't be surprised if Cara has been watching from her bedroom window with her phone in hand, recording every second of it on the off chance that I feel like watching the replay later.

My head falls against Sawyer's chest, and he gently releases my knee, letting me find my balance before he moves. Easton lets go of me, slowly pulling out, fingers and all, as Sawyer meets my stare. "You good?" he murmurs into the night, watching me cringe as he pulls out of me too.

"Sore," I admit, "but nothing a cool bath can't fix."

He nods and steps back to give me space to dress as Easton hands me my jeans, his pants already done up. Sawyer quickly folds himself back into his pants and checks his phone as he waits for me, only his soft curse has me glancing up again. "I gotta run," he says, his gaze falling on Easton and giving him a purposeful stare. I can't help but feel as though I'm missing something. "It's my sister. Apparently, Mom's having a bad night."

My heart breaks for his family. I couldn't imagine what his mom is feeling right now, knowing that in only a handful of days, her husband, the man she's had by her side for who knows how long, and the man who gave her children, is going to be executed. Don't get me wrong, Nikolai is a piece of shit . . . kinda. He's very clearly a caring man who loves his family, despite the way he treats Sawyer, but he's also the asshole who knocked me out cold and tried to kill me in some filthy murder dungeon for the sole purpose of trying to take Empire as his own.

Before Easton gets a chance to respond, Sawyer is taking off around the corner of my apartment complex toward the parking lot, and I'm left with one hell of a broody, yet deeply satisfied man. "Come on," he says, nodding toward the main door of the apartment complex—the very spot where I first met Dalton.

I trail along with him, and he quickly unlocks the door before holding it open for me. The door closes with a heavy thud behind us, and we make our way down toward our apartments, both of us more than aware of Zade hovering in his open doorway, his hands jammed deep in his pockets as he watches me intently.

Easton stops at his door, shoving the key into the lock, and as I continue down the hall to my apartment, I hesitate. "What's up?" Easton asks, his door swinging open before him.

"I, um . . . I kinda don't want to go down there," I say with a cringe, feeling like the world's shittiest friend. "The second I get into my apartment, Cara's going to jump deeper down my throat than you've ever been. I accidentally mentioned something about this weird little . . . thing we're all doing and then bailed before she could force the details out of me. Now I'm really not in the mood to delve into all of that."

"Then come in here and chill with me," he says, stepping over the threshold of his apartment and holding the door open for me. "I've just gotta sort out Venom and then we'll be heading back to the DeVil Hotel anyway. You don't need to go back in there if you're not feeling it."

Without another thought, I follow Easton into his apartment, glancing over my shoulder and watching Zade as I go. He narrows his hard stare on me, but soon enough, Easton's door closes, blocking him out.

Easton's apartment is completely void of all the normal comforts you would expect in a home. There are no photos or decorations, no dishes left on the counters, and in place of a TV on the living room wall, there's an enormous snake enclosure. I can't say I'm surprised, though.

He heads straight to Venom's tank, and I follow behind him, intrigued by his love for his snake. I spy Venom in the corner of the enclosure, all curled up and looking pretty chill for a snake. "Shit," he says with a heavy sigh. "I thought she would have shed by now."

Worry dances through my stomach, and I watch the snake a little closer. Clearly my assumption was wrong. "Is she okay?" I question, not knowing a damn thing about snakes. But I know I don't like Easton's tone.

"She'll be fine," he says, opening the enclosure and reaching for the snake. "She's always struggled with shedding. The whole process makes her uneasy."

"Oh, really?" I ask, leaning in a little closer and gazing at her face to see her top layer starting to lift around her mouth. "Can you just . . . pull it off?"

Easton shakes his head before making his way into the kitchen and grabbing a clear plastic tub from below the sink. He puts it up on the counter before quickly filling it with an inch of warm water. "She just needs to soak in a warm bath for a minute and that should help. If it won't come off naturally, then I'll intervene, but it's better if she can do it herself."

I watch with wide eyes as he lowers Venom into the water and she just sits there so casually, chilling in the bath as though she's had a big day and needs a few minutes to unwind with a glass of red wine and a good book.

Easton leaves her for a minute and moves about his kitchen, pulling out a frozen baby mouse from the freezer and placing it down in an old take-out container, making my skin crawl. "Are you . . ." I start, needing to swallow back a gag. "Are you defrosting a dead mouse on the kitchen counter?"

Easton glances at me as if only now just realizing how socially unacceptable that is before shrugging his shoulders and deciding he doesn't give a shit. "The snake's gotta eat," he says. "Besides, it's not like anyone actually eats off this counter."

I suppose he has a fair point. But for future reference, if I happen to wander down to Easton's real apartment in the DeVil Hotel, I'll be sure not to eat off the counter.

Venom chills in her makeshift bath for twenty minutes, and as we wait, I hurry to the bathroom, trying to mop up the mess of cum leaking out of me. It's no use, though. These panties were destroyed long before Easton even finished unlocking the main entrance to the apartment complex.

Returning to the kitchen, I hover by Venom's dead mouse as nerves pulse through my veins. "I feel like I don't really know anything about you," I tell him, watching as he gazes over his snake.

He lifts his intense stare to meet mine. "I could say the same for you."

I scoff, sure that he's fucking with me. "That's bullshit, and you know it," I tell him. "I'd bet everything I have that you and the boys have files upon files overflowing with information on me. The second Empire gave Zade my name, you would have done your homework. I bet you even know my first boyfriend's name."

His lips kick up at the corners. "You mean Adrian? Lasted six months, and as far as I could tell, you broke up with him because you walked in on him jerking off over his stepmom."

My jaw drops. "Holy shit," I breathe, gaping at him. "That's fucked up. You know that, right?"

Easton just smirks and lets the conversation fall away, but I'm still no closer to knowing a damn thing about him—apart from the killer computer-hacking skills he must have.

After getting Venom settled back in her enclosure, I watch with fascination as Easton feeds her and makes sure she has everything she needs before closing the lid. He presses his lips into a hard line as I meet his stare. "What's wrong?"

He shrugs his shoulders before moving back across the room toward the front door. I follow him out into the hall, and he ducks back inside the door to turn out the lights. "I just don't like leaving her, but she'll be more comfortable to shed alone. She likes this enclosure best."

"Oh really?" I ask, feeling as though I'm learning so much about what it means to be a snake dad. "Does it take long?"

"No, it shouldn't," he says, closing the door behind him and making sure to lock the deadbolt—something he probably wouldn't bother doing if he planned to stay the night. It's a little sweet the way he tries to protect Venom while she's here alone. "I'll swing by in the morning and check on her. She should be good."

A smile pulls at the corners of my lips, and as if sensing us in the hallway, Zade and Dalton appear, ready to get their asses out of here. Without another word, we stride back out of the old, worn apartment complex and pile into Zade's SUV, every passing second leaving me more and more convinced that Easton isn't the monster I originally thought him to be.

He's broody and probably the hardest to get a word out of, but today felt different with him. He was honest with me, and while he wasn't telling me anything particularly important, that doesn't change the fact that he was opening that line of communication, allowing me the chance to get closer to him. And shit, I think I liked it.

It's one thing letting him rail me, but now, just like with Dalton, I'm getting confused. I think I like him, but liking him gives him the power to hurt me, and the idea alone is scary as fuck.

My heart races, and I find myself watching him as he sits up front beside Zade in the driver's seat. As we make our way back to the DeVil Hotel, I find my hand resting against my thigh, Easton's cross right below my palm.

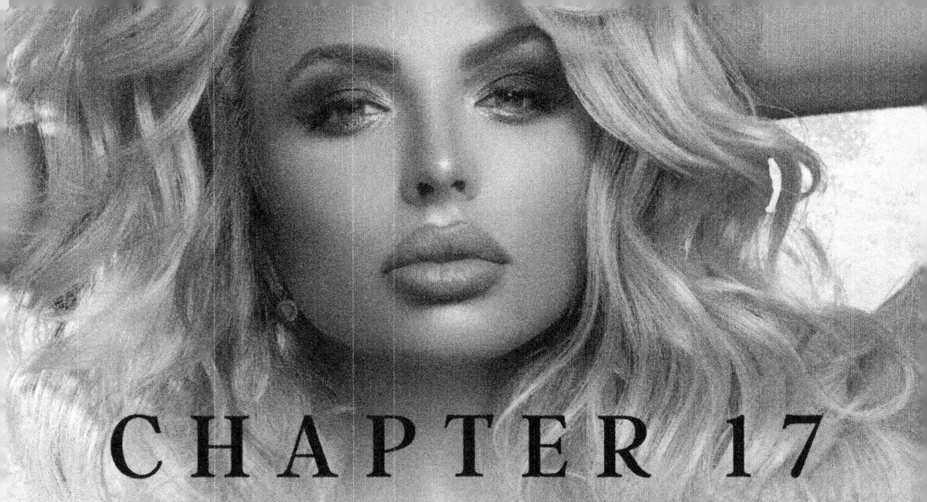

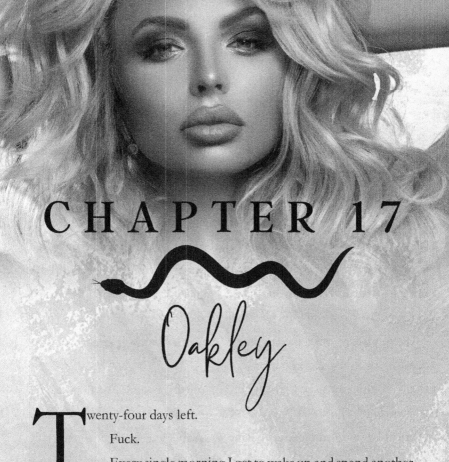

CHAPTER 17

Oakley

Twenty-four days left.

Fuck.

Every single morning I get to wake up and spend another day surviving is a blessing, but when that little clock goes off inside my mind, I'm reminded just how much time I don't have.

In the grand scheme of things, twenty-four days is quite a lot. I could do plenty of things in that time, like somehow escape these guys I've been slowly falling for and find a way to save my dad. But it's been days since I got out of that prison, and I'm not even an inch closer to saving myself. Though having said that, it's also been days since Joe shoved my unconscious body into the back of a car, and the boys aren't any closer to finding out who was behind that, either.

It's just after ten when I finally roll my ass out of bed and make my way into the bathroom. Zade got up and left ages ago, something I'm starting to notice has become routine for him. It's not as though he's going to come right out and say it, but it's pretty damn obvious it's his way of avoiding me.

I've left him alone these past few days, not pushing him too much in the hopes he might loosen the reins a little. While the whole living situation has become calmer, he's not stupid. If anything, he's tightened the metaphorical collar around my throat. He comes to bed now and just stares at the ceiling, not daring to fall asleep before I do. I haven't pried for any more information like I did that first night, and he hasn't attempted to offer me anything either. It's like two perfect strangers sleeping in the same bed.

Lifting my gaze to the bathroom mirror, I wipe away the tear that sits on my cheek. It's the same every morning. Every time another day ticks by, and I find myself having to scrub a line from the mental tally that haunts me, the tears start to flow. Most of the time, I can pull myself together and put on a brave face for the guys, but I know they see my pain—especially Easton. He's so observant. Dalton and Sawyer can see it too, but I don't think they really grasp just how much it's weighing down on my shoulders.

I'm running out of time, and my desperation is starting to suffocate me.

After quickly brushing my teeth, I glance over Dalton's shirt hanging low around my knees, making sure it's clean enough to spend another day in. Zade still hasn't returned my clothes.

Grabbing the brush, I start working on my hair and realize just how bad it is. My soft blonde curls are messy and dry, and considering I haven't slathered bleach through them since leaving Missouri, my roots are a hot mess.

Realizing there's not a lot I can do about it now, I make my way out to the main part of the penthouse, hearing the familiar sound of weights in the home gym. Dalton stands by the elevator, looking as though he plans on spending his morning shooting some hoops. I consider heading up there too, but I need coffee and food before I can even think about facing the day.

"Goddamn, you look good in my shirt."

A rush pulses through me, and I try to find a little composure before I end up screwing him right there in front of the elevator. "All the guys working out?" I ask, already certain of his answer but needing to make sure.

"Yep."

"Zade and Sawyer still tiptoeing around each other and making it awkward as fuck for everyone else?"

He gives me a stupid smirk, his brows bouncing. "Wouldn't have it any other way," he says, just as the elevator dings its arrival and the doors open before him. He strides in then turns around to meet my stare, holding his arms out on either side of the door, keeping it open. "You coming up?"

"Maybe," I say, the perfect opportunity to snoop through Zade's office staring me in the face. "I need to eat first, though. After the workout you and Sawyer gave me last night, I'm starving. I need to replenish that energy."

"Damn straight," he says with a wink before stepping back to allow the doors to close. The second I'm alone, I make a break for it, silently rushing through Zade's home, doing everything I can not to make a sound.

I make my way to his home office and hold my breath as I gently close the door behind me, hoping like fuck it isn't one of those doors that click when closing into place. The boys tend to check on me every few minutes, whether it be a discreet glance in my direction or a blatant shove through the door to make sure I haven't drowned myself in the bathtub. So sooner rather than later, one of them will come looking for me. When that happens, I don't want to get caught in here.

Making it quick, I tear open drawers and thumb through papers, finding a whole bunch of stuff that doesn't mean shit to me. There are names and black calling cards scattered through the drawers, probably the files of people Empire has sent Zade to kill in the past.

Finding nothing that's going to help me, I move through the office and scan over the bookshelves. Noticing the framing on one shelf is slightly different from the rest, I furrow my brows and give it a small shove, certain that the stupid thing is probably going to fall and squish me. Though knowing my luck, it would only break a few bones, maybe paralyze me. Not quite enough to kill me though.

The whole shelf slides back and opens up into a hidden storage room, and my jaw drops. This is so much cooler than I ever imagined. It's like straight out of a spy novel. I've always loved shit like this in the movies, though this one doesn't quite seem like a secret room. The framing is a little too obvious for that. My guess is Zade just wanted his office to look good without having an ugly storeroom door in the middle of it.

Making myself at home, I traipse into the storage room and stare at the huge array of boxes and files. The room is just as big as the office itself, and it's filled with rows upon rows of shelving, each of them full to the brim. Hell, I can only imagine what kind of crap I'd find in Zade's father's home office. Though from what I've learned of Zade, he strikes me as the type to be on the ball with that kind of stuff. Zade probably has three hard copies and two digital ones of every piece of information Lawson DeVil ever possessed—one copy for everyday use and the other stored on a secret backup server. Hence why I'm so confident that there will be Empire blueprints in here somewhere. Finding them is the biggest challenge.

I have to give it to Zade, he likes his organization and has this storeroom perfectly set up. The files are separated into groups: members, The Circle, leadership, by-laws, finances, and events. Hell, there's even a section for their most beloved weapons dealers and lists of dirt that could be used to blackmail every single one of Empire's members.

Each section has also been organized in alphabetical order, and after realizing this, I take a shot in the dark and head over to the files labeled *EMPIRE ESTATE*. More than aware of just how quickly time is passing, I pull the big box off the shelf and pry open the lid, doing what I can not to sneeze at the dust collected on top of the box.

It's packed full of documents, and I start thumbing through them, not really sure what I'm looking for, but I'll know when I find it. Coming up with nothing, I shove the box back onto the shelf before pulling out the next one, and right on top is a large tube. My eyes light up like Christmas morning, and I grab the tube before flipping it up to reach the top. I pry off the little circular lid and tip up the contents, watching as rolled-up papers fall out.

Blueprints.

Bingo.

Rolling them out across the ground, I feel like a fucking genius when I realize that not a damn thing has been labeled. There are at least twenty poster-sized blueprints in here, none of them detailing which part of Empire they showcase. It's like trying to complete one of those puzzles where all the little pieces are the same color. I don't doubt it was created this way on purpose. Empire is extremely secretive, and I'm sure they wanted to cover all their bases on the off chance these blueprints were to get in the wrong hands—like mine for example.

It's impossible to tell what's a walkway or corridor opposed to one of the entrance tunnels. What's a prison cell or an open entertainment area. This is fucking bullshit. It's going to take me ages to figure this shit out, time I simply don't have.

I try to arrange the papers across the ground when I hear a soft buzzing sound coming from out in the office. My back stiffens, positive that I've been caught. I sit extremely still, holding my breath as I listen out, but nothing comes.

My brows furrow, and I slowly get to my feet, tiptoe across the storage room, and crane my neck to see out into the office. Finding the room empty with the door still closed, I let out a relieved breath. Then the same buzzing starts again.

What the fuck is that?

Moving through the room, I try to follow where it's coming from, searching through the bookshelves on the opposite side of the room. I move things out of the way, positive that I won't be able to put everything back where it belongs. It will be a dead giveaway for Zade, but hell, what's he going to do? Kill me? Well shit. That's nothing new.

Reaching up, I brush my hand along the top shelf, hoping there's nothing sharp up there. Just before giving up my search, my hand curls around a phone. My brow arches, and I pull it down, a wide grin stretching across my face. It's not just any phone. It's *my* phone. I haven't seen this thing since before Joe decided to take me for a joy ride to the pits of hell.

Unlocking my phone, I find a slew of texts from Cara, some missed calls, a shitload of emails, and about a thousand social media notifications. There are a bunch of other things, but it would take me too long to search through all of that now. All too aware that my time is quickly running out, I dart back into the storage room and drop to my knees in front of the blueprints. That's when I realize I'm going to be here all day trying to sort them out. Shit!

Wanting to get out of here, I settle for taking a quick photo of each of the papers on my phone before quickly storing them in a secure folder. Though something tells me if Zade really wants to know what I'm doing on my phone, he could very easily figure it out.

Deciding that I have enough information to sort through for now,

I hastily roll the blueprints up and shove them back inside the tube before capping it and placing it right back where I found it. Double checking I haven't missed anything, I put the box back on the shelf and silently slip out of the storeroom, trying to work out how to close the secret door.

My phone feels like hot coals in my hand as I silently open the office door and peek out into the penthouse, listening to the familiar sounds of clanking weights in the home gym. It doesn't necessarily mean that they're all in there, but it's a pretty clear indicator they're not searching for me yet.

Certain the coast is clear, I hurry out into the kitchen before rushing through the living room and toward my old bedroom. Despite the room being nothing but an empty shell, I need privacy.

Barging through the door, I lock it behind me and fall back against it, sliding to the ground. Swiping my thumb across the screen, I enter my code and unlock it with every intention of going over the blueprints. Only my curiosity is far too great, and I open my text messages instead, reading the very latest from Cara.

Cara - Dude. What the fuck? You never came home! Don't tell me you're too caught up in your raunchy fuck fest that you forgot I've been dying for those juicy details? GET YOUR BITCH ASS BACK HERE AND TELL ME ALL ABOUT IT!!!!!!!!!

A smile pulls at my lips, and I can't help but laugh. I freaking love her—most of the time. She's a lot to handle, and I'm sure had we been given more time together, she would have made an incredible long-term bestie.

I quickly respond.

Oakley - Girl, these dudes are full on. If I can get back there to tell you all the juicy details, I will!

Cara - BOO! WHORE! But remember, if you're going to have three guys finger bang you, make sure they trim their nails. No one wants to be finger banged by Freddy Krueger, sis!

I snort a laugh, so loud I swear I hear a slight pause in the boys' reps coming from the gym.

Oakley - Why do I feel as though I'm going to regret telling you about it?

Cara - No regrets, girl. Embrace it.

All too aware of my father rotting in a cell while I'm laughing at bullshit texts about being finger banged by Freddy Krueger, I exit my texts before opening the secure folder and trying to piece together this impossible blueprint puzzle.

I must spend at least twenty minutes on it before hearing Sawyer yelling through the penthouse. "Doll, where the fuck are ya?"

Knowing he'll come barging through this door without hesitation, I roll my eyes as I call back, more than prepared to humiliate myself if it means getting just a few more precious moments of privacy. "I'm taking a shit. Leave me alone."

A moment of silence follows before I hear Sawyer's footsteps heading toward my room. My eyes bulge out of my head, and I scramble across the empty room before diving into the private bathroom and hastily dropping my phone into the toilet roll holder. I make a show of flushing the toilet, knowing damn well that asshole would be listening through the door just to make sure I'm not lying to him, and then I go as far as to turn on the taps to wash my hands.

I'm busy drying them against Dalton's shirt because Zade couldn't even leave a hand towel in here when I hear another buzz from my phone. Hearing Sawyer's footsteps walking away from the door, I quickly check it again only to find a new text from an unknown number.

Unknown - Babe, it's Harley. I met you at Danny's. What do you say about that date? Dinner Saturday night?

A scoff pulls from deep in my chest, and I nearly delete the text before reconsidering. A date could be fun. I'm not exactly interested in dating Harley, but he seemed like a really cool guy. Plus, I wouldn't mind getting out of this penthouse, even if it's just to sit in a restaurant and listen to some guy try to work his way into my pants. The boys would never go for it, though. Especially Dalton. He's happy sharing me with his friends, but I don't know how he'd feel about me seeking out another man's attention.

Well, kind of. It's not like I'm going to let the guy take me home, and I can guarantee the boys will be sitting right across the restaurant. The fact that it'll frustrate the shit out of Zade is even better.

The only question is, how do I get the boys to agree to this?

Thinking it through, I realize the only way for this to work is with a little bit of manipulation, my most prized party trick. And with that settled, I text him right back.

Oakley - It's a date.

CHAPTER 18

Oakley

Striding out of my useless bedroom, I find Easton and Zade making their way out of the home gym. Both of them are shirtless, showing off those perfectly sculpted bodies, their tattoos only making it that much better. Sawyer's already in the kitchen, standing in the open fridge, last night's takeout busily being inhaled. A smirk pulls at my lips. The guy didn't even bother to heat it up first.

Zade collapses into the chair at the head of the dining table, lounging back into the seat with his legs stretched out. Easton drops onto the couch, his elbows braced against his knees, all three of them looking as though they've pushed each other to the limit.

Striding into the kitchen, I reach up to grab myself a coffee mug when Easton's voice cuts out across the penthouse. "You only just getting up now?" he questions, his gaze discreetly flicking toward the clock.

"Something like that," I murmur, not really wanting to go into the details of what I've been doing for the past hour. Plucking a spoon out of the cutlery drawer, I give my coffee a stir before picking up the mug and lifting the rim to my lips. Taking a quick sip, I groan as the sweet goodness makes its way down my throat. "So, umm . . ." I start, nervousness beginning to pulse through my veins, unsure how this is going to go down. "Do we have any plans for the day?"

I feel Zade's stare like two lasers hitting the side of my face, and I make a point not to look his way, knowing he'll be able to see right through me.

Sawyer shrugs before finally deciding to get himself a plate. "Nah, we're just chilling," he says, his way of grazing over the fact that they'll be spending the day trying to scrounge up possible suspects of who could be behind the attacks on me.

Walking around the kitchen counter, I go to join Easton on the couch, dropping down beside him and crossing my legs as I sip my coffee. "Why?" comes Zade's accusatory tone from the dining table, not one to trust that I could simply be asking an innocent question. He'd be right, though. I'm not.

"I, umm . . . I was wondering if it would be such a big deal to get my hair done today," I say with a slight cringe.

Easton glances at me, his brows furrowed. "Don't get me wrong here," he starts, making my blood pulse just a little bit faster through my body. "But what's the point?"

Glancing away, I let my gaze fall to my mug and let out a shaky breath, putting on the show of a lifetime. Hell, my eyes even well with tears, and when I blink, they fall down my cheeks for maximum effect. "Because it's important to me," I tell him in a small voice, letting him hear the vulnerability in my tone. "I don't want to die not looking my best, you know what I mean? If I'm going out, then I want to go out looking fabulous, and maybe that's incredibly vain of me and it'll all be for nothing, but it means something to me."

Zade scoffs from across the room, not buying my bullshit for even a second. "No, absolutely not," he says. "You'll be dead, Oakley. Your hair doesn't matter."

I purse my lips and meet his stare from across the room. "Do you believe in the afterlife?" I ask him.

He shakes his head. "No."

"Well, I do," I lie, not really sure what I believe in when it comes to what happens to us after we die. I have to have hope that there's something more out there—for my sanity's sake. "It's a firm belief of mine that we go into our afterlife the same way we died. You're robbing me of my heart, Zade. And if I don't get to take my heart into the afterlife, then the least I can do is make sure I look like a fucking queen."

Zade gives me a blank stare. "You don't really believe that shit, do you?"

"Do you have any kind of proof to suggest I'm wrong?" I throw back at him.

"No," he says. "It just sounds ridiculous. Once we're dead, we're dead. It's not like there's some magic portal waiting to push us through the birth canal of a new life."

I scoff and roll my eyes, sipping my coffee again. "I suppose it's easy for someone like you to reject the idea when you don't have a soul to protect." Zade rolls his eyes, but I continue, feeling as though I'm barely scraping by on this one. "Okay, consider this," I say. "I'll be dead in twenty-four days, and I'm out here trying to live life to the fullest with what little time I have left. Getting my hair done is something I enjoy, so why the hell not? It's not like I'm asking to go and sit in a salon for hours. We could get a mobile stylist to come here. I don't even need to leave this little prison you've got here."

"I don't fucking like it," Zade says.

"Yeah, no shit," I scoff. "You've made that perfectly clear."

"What's the problem?" Sawyer says, taking his plate to the dining table and sitting down a few places away from Zade. "She just wants her hair done. It's not a big deal, and it's not like we're going anywhere today. Call Benny, he'll organize for someone to come up."

Hope starts to blossom through my chest when Easton nods. "Yeah, sorry man. I'm with Sawyer on this one. It's a little bit of bleach in her hair."

Zade clenches his jaw, clearly not liking his friends not having his back on this one. But they're right, it's not a big deal. I mean, considering the bullshit excuses I gave him, it sounds innocent enough. Now if he knew I wanted this so I could go out on a date on Saturday night and look hot as hell, that's a different story. "Fine," he finally says. "But I don't want some hairdresser up here for hours."

"It'll be quick," I promise him. "I just need to touch up my roots, and maybe put a treatment through my hair. It's looking a little dry."

Zade lets out a huff, and I jump up from the couch and skip across the room to grab the phone. "Oh, while we're at it," I say, the phone wedged between my ear and shoulder as my fingers hover over the buttons to dial Benny. "What's the ETA on the whole clothes situation? When am I getting those back?"

"You're fucking kidding, right?" he questions. "You destroyed all of my clothes."

I scoff and shrug my shoulders, more than happy to gaslight him into thinking he's exaggerating. "It was a few shirts and some underwear. What's the problem? You're a billionaire . . . at least, I think you are. Wait," I say, my eyes widening as I gape at Zade. "Is it rude to ask people if they're billionaires?"

He just stares at me. "It was a shitload more than just a few shirts and underwear. You tore through over a million dollars of designer suits."

I stare at him in horror. "You're lying," I breathe. "Like that was a couple thousand dollars at most, right? Spare change to you."

He arches a brow, his silence speaking volumes, and suddenly the idea of getting my hair done seems so trivial. I cut up over a million dollars of suits. What the fuck is wrong with me? I should have googled that shit before going ass to the wall with the scissors.

My stomach clenches, feeling sick about it, but considering he hasn't torn me a new asshole about it, perhaps a million dollars is only spare change to him. Perhaps I'm looking at this the wrong way.

Zade doesn't push me on it, and before I can talk myself out of this, I press the button on the receiver for the hotel concierge.

"Holla," Benny calls down the line, all too thrilled about being able to serve Zade. "What do you need, Mr. DeVil."

"Hey, Benny. It's Oakley," I say, something brightening within me. There's something about Benny that just makes me feel alive. His sunshine is contagious.

He lets out a playful sigh. "Oh, Miss Oakley. Hungry again? Perhaps I need to get you the direct number for the kitchen."

I laugh, knowing that would be more than helpful. "Thanks, but I actually need something else," I tell him, not really sure how all of this works. Before becoming Zade's hostage in his fancy penthouse, I'd never even visited a hotel before, let alone stayed in one. "I'm wondering if you happened to have a good hair stylist on speed dial? A mobile one who could come up here this morning and do my hair?"

"Of course," Benny says. "I'll make a few calls and have someone come up shortly. Shall I charge it to Mr. DeVil's credit card?"

A wide smile stretches across my face, and I meet Zade's stare across the room. "Yes, Mr. DeVil's credit card would be great."

Benny ends the call with a promise to order a burger for my lunch and have it sent up later, making sure to add an extra serving of fries and my favorite diet soda.

An hour later, there's a knock at the door, and Easton, who's freshly showered and making my mouth water, crosses to the door and welcomes the hairdresser. He shows her to the dining table where she quickly sets up, her eyes widening as she catches sight of Dalton and

Zade across the room.

I make my way over and take a seat at the table before telling her what I want, and she quickly gets to work. "So, like . . . You just live here with all of these hot guys?" the hairdresser questions.

I bark a sharp laugh, getting a side eye from Zade. "Yeah, something like that," I tell her, scooting a little lower in my chair and gazing out the window at the impressive view below.

We fall into mindless chatter just like every time I visit the hairdresser, and within only a few minutes, the boys are scurrying away, already bored out of their minds. They head into Zade's home office, and I don't miss the way they leave the door wide open, not trusting me not to try and make a break for it. But I don't know what they're expecting to happen. Do they think I'll shrink-wrap myself and threaten the hairdresser to shove me in her bag and take me out of here?

After twenty minutes, I've learned my hairdresser's name is Sarah, and she's been working at the salon across the street for seven years with hopes of opening her own salon one day. She has a boyfriend who has commitment issues and a dog who struggles to control his bowels when he gets nervous.

I smile and chat along, answering her questions as best I can while keeping it all very vague, knowing the boys won't approve of me so casually sharing details about my life right now. If anything, Zade needs me to fade away and become invisible. The fewer people looking for me after the dreaded sixtieth moon, the better.

Sarah finishes applying the product and sets the bowls of bleach aside. "Alright, girl," she says, making a show of cleaning up her things. "Give it half an hour and we'll check your process."

I smile before getting up from the chair. "Perfect, I'll be back in two seconds," I tell her, more than aware of just how useful the next thirty minutes could be when trying to figure out the blueprint puzzle. But it's a risk. If the boys were to walk out, they'll see my phone. I'll have to be discreet. If anything, I can place it on the table by Sarah's things, letting them think it's hers.

Scooping my phone out of the toilet roll holder in my private bathroom, I head back out to the dining table, being careful not to move around too much. Zade would tear me a new asshole if I accidentally got bleach all over his fancy penthouse. Though I'm starting to wonder if he really cares as much as he lets on. After all, I didn't get my ass handed to me for the whole designer suits fiasco like I should have. Hell, this guy is going to kill me. Why should I care so much about destroying his suits? What the fuck is wrong with me?

Dropping back down at the table, I prop my feet up on the chair beside me and frown as I glance out the window, taking in the heavy storm clouds rolling in over Faders Bay. "Shit. Looks like it's gonna be a nasty one," I mutter while unlocking my phone, noticing how the dark clouds make it easier to see the penthouse's reflection through the floor-to-ceiling windows.

Not thinking much of it, I drop my attention to my phone and get busy scanning over the twenty images of the blueprints, wishing I were somehow able to print them off and lay them out like a puzzle. It would make this so much easier.

After fifteen minutes, Sarah steps behind me and glances over my hair, checking on its progress. I watch her through the window, and she nods to herself, liking what she's seeing. "Maybe another ten minutes and we'll be good to start rinsing," she tells me.

A smile pulls at the corners of my lips, feeling like I'm somehow claiming a piece of myself back. I don't have a lot of control at the moment. Hell, I have none at all, so being able to do this has helped to restore just a bit of that. It's the small things in life.

Sarah steps back toward her things, and as I go to drop my gaze back to my phone, something catches in the light. My brows furrow, and I watch her more closely as she picks something up from her kit. Is that . . . is that a fucking blade? No, it can't be. Surely I just imagined it.

Darkness spreads over her face, and she quickly moves in behind me. Fast as lightning, she grips my hair and rips my head back, exposing my throat as her hand whips around in a shallow arc toward my throat.

Oh, hell no.

Panic tears through me, and I throw myself to the ground, a sharp blood-curdling scream tearing from the back of my throat. Sarah comes down on me, the blade slashing toward me as I hear the boys making a break for it, but they're not going to reach me in time. I'm on my own here.

With not many options, I slam my elbow into her tit and she screams out in agony, falling back, and I fly for her, the blade still flailing around. Overwhelming fear blasts through my veins, and realizing it's either her or me, I catch her wrist. Without even a moment to consider what I'm doing, I turn the blade on her and drop my weight down.

"NO, DON'T FUCKING KILL—"

Too fucking late.

The blade plunges through the base of her throat as I let out a raw scream of horror, my eyes wide and filled with fear. Sarah's body jerks and spasms, and there's a gurgling in her throat as blood pools around her.

Zade races in, dropping down beside Sarah, his hand pressing against her chest as if to keep her pinned, but it's not like the bitch is going anywhere. "Who fucking sent you?" he spits, rage tearing from him as I scramble away, not stopping until my back slams against the floor-to-ceiling window. My hands shake as thunder rocks through the sky, the whole fucking hotel vibrating from its force.

What the hell have I done?

My whole body convulses as bile rises in my throat. I'm no better than the guys.

Dalton drops down in front of me, clutching my chin and forcing me to meet his stare, but I look around him, trying to look at the girl as Zade desperately attempts to get some kind of information out of her. But there's no use in trying; she can't talk like that.

Her body stops jolting and the gurgles turn to silence. She's dead. I'm a killer.

"Oakley," Dalton grunts, demanding my attention, but my body shakes so violently, I can barely focus on his face.

I'm a killer.

Zade curses and gets to his feet. His hands are covered in Sarah's blood, yet he doesn't even seem to notice as he paces the length of the dining table. "FUCK," he roars, shoving his hands against Easton's chest as he stops in front of him. "I fucking knew this wasn't a good idea, but you fuckers insisted I was overreacting, and now look. We invited this bitch right in here, and now she's dead on my floor, and we're no closer to figuring out who's behind this."

Fuck. Fuck. Fuck. How could something as innocent as getting my hair done turn into something like this?

Dalton shakes my shoulders, and I'm finally able to focus on his face and hear his words. "Fuck, Firefly," he rumbles. "Did she say anything? Who is she?"

I shake my head. "Thirty minutes," I mutter. "She said my hair would be processed in thirty minutes."

"Shit," Sawyer says. "She's in shock."

Easton says something under his breath before striding toward me and crouching down, his hand dropping to my shoulder. "Are you good, Pretty?"

"I . . . I, umm . . . my hair is burning. The bleach, it's . . ."

"Fuck," he grumbles, glancing at Zade as he tries to figure out a game plan before turning his stare back on Dalton. "Put her in the shower and get that shit out of her hair while we clean this up. We'll regroup after that and try to figure out what the fuck just happened."

Dalton nods, and without a moment of hesitation, he scoops me up off the floor and carries me to his private bathroom. He deposits me on the edge of the vanity before pulling his old, worn shirt over my head and reaching around me to unclasp my bra. "You're going to be okay," he offers, seeing the torment in my eyes.

I shake my head. "I killed her."

"It's a game of survival, Firefly. You did the right thing. It was kill or be killed."

Deep down, I know he's right, but that doesn't take away from the fact I just took someone's life.

Dalton puts me through a shower, scrubbing the bleach from my hair as I barely manage to stand. Ten minutes later, I'm standing in the living room, staring at the spot where Sarah's body used to be.

My hair is soaking wet, dripping down my body as I wear nothing but one of Dalton's clean shirts. There's still blood marking the floor, bleach and toner strewn across the room, and my phone half hidden under the table, still unnoticed by the guys.

I swallow hard as I stride forward and try to help put the room back together, collecting the toner she would have used on me had she not ended up dead on the dining room floor. Discreetly scooping the phone up from the ground, I put it with a few of the things I'll need to finish my hair later before grabbing the cleaning products and scrubbing blood from the floor. Tears linger in my eyes, falling to the floor as I work.

The cold, hard truth resides in my chest and darkens my soul. I'm a killer—a brutal, stone-cold killer. And in this very moment, I come to terms with my fate. For the first time, I truly believe that when Zade tears my heart from my chest, I will deserve nothing less.

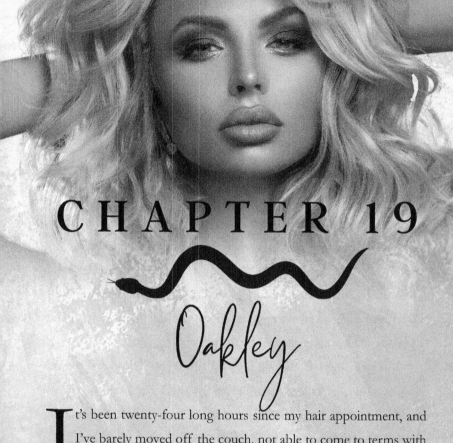

CHAPTER 19

Oakley

It's been twenty-four long hours since my hair appointment, and I've barely moved off the couch, not able to come to terms with what I've done. I don't know how the boys do it. They're so casual about taking a life, and yet here I am, barely able to function.

It pisses me off. I've wasted precious time, stuck in the torment of my own mind rather than trying to push it aside and figuring out a way to save myself and my father.

"Come on," Zade says from across the penthouse. "We're leaving."

My head snaps up to notice the four boys hovering in the kitchen, weapons spread out over the counter. My brows furrow as I take it all in. Each of them are packing, weapons loaded over every available space on their body. They don't even try to conceal them. "Where are we going?" I question, my heart heavy as I rise from the couch.

"There's a meeting tonight," Zade explains. "I'm expected to attend, and I figured, why waste a good opportunity."

There's a strange tone in his voice, and as I hold his dark stare, understanding dawns. "You're going to use me as bait to lure out the attackers."

"Damn straight," he says before glancing at the time on his phone. "That gives you about thirty seconds to get dressed and ready, otherwise you're going in that."

My gaze drops to Dalton's old shirt, and I let out a heavy sigh, all too aware of the fact that I haven't showered today. Hell, the top of my head is still yellow after Dalton washed out the bleach. I never got around to toning my hair.

Hastily making my way to my old bedroom, I burst through the door and storm right into my walk-in closet, finding all of my clothes right back where they belong. I suppose Zade felt like shit after everything went down yesterday, and the least he could do for allowing an attack like that to slip past him again was to offer me my clothes back. Though that offer didn't also come with the bedroom. I'm still stuck sleeping in Zade's bed, but if I'm honest with myself, I've found it quite comforting. I sleep peacefully beside him. I'll never admit it to him, but I think he knows. Surely, he must know.

Seeing as the guys weren't particularly dressed up, I figure this must be a casual thing, and I grab a pair of short workout leggings and find the matching crop before pairing it with an oversized hoodie. I step into a pair of runners before twisting my hair up into a messy bun, not daring to look at myself in the mirror, knowing I'll see nothing but a mess of yellow, splotchy hair.

Hurrying out to the guys, I meet them just as the elevator opens and I step in with them, my heart racing. I'm not thrilled about the prospect of being used as bait to draw out an attacker, but nothing is going to happen to me—the boys simply won't allow it.

We get down into Zade's Escalade, and I don't miss the way Dalton looks longingly toward his Harley. Candice is his baby, and the fact that he hasn't been able to ride her much lately is probably weighing on him. But honestly, I think we have bigger things to worry about than that.

The Escalade peels out of the underground parking lot, and we drive for ten minutes before Zade captures my stare through the rearview mirror. "You hungry?" he questions, something the boys have asked me non-stop since my hair appointment, though I suppose that's what happens when a woman loses her appetite around a bunch of over-the-top alpha assholes. "It could be a while before you get the chance to eat again."

My stomach rumbles, but I narrow my gaze, not trusting him one bit. Had it been Dalton, Easton, or Sawyer who had asked, then perhaps I'd be happy to go along and see where this line of questions will take me, but with Zade, I can never really trust his intentions.

"I could eat," I tell him, glancing out the window and realizing we're in a deserted street, not a restaurant or fast-food chain in sight.

"Okay, good," Zade says. "Then how about a plate of harden the fuck up? You've been moping around non-stop over that dead bitch.

You're the blood heir. Things like this should be bouncing off you. We're about to walk into a room with some of the most dangerous people in the country, and you're acting like a little bitch. Pull yourself together."

Yanking the knife from Dalton's hip, I throw myself out of my seat and up against the back of Zade's, my arm flinging around him as I press the tip of the blade against his throat. I expect him to panic, to swerve a little, or at the very least slam the brakes, but not a single one of the assholes even flinches.

Zade just keeps his eyes on the road, cool as a fucking cucumber. "There's the fucking fighter I know you are," he says with such nonchalance that it blows me the fuck away. "Go right ahead, Lamb. Take me out. Save yourself. But open your fucking eyes, there's one of you and four of us. True, you could slit my throat before any of the boys get their hands on you, but what happens to you then? You won't be able to escape them. You might be fucking them and opening those pretty legs like their greedy whore, letting them live out their wildest fantasies, but when it comes down to it, will they have your back or will they execute you without hesitation?"

I swallow hard, hating how fucking right he is, and despite the blade in my hand, I've never felt so out of control.

I press the tip to his skin harder, getting the sweetest satisfaction out of the drop of blood that trails down his throat, but he still doesn't flinch, allowing me to push the boundaries. My hands start to shake, and I get flashbacks of the knife plunging into Sarah's throat. The horrific images burned into my brain make me gasp, dropping the blade to his lap.

I fall back into my seat, tears welling in my eyes, hating how fucking weak I feel. Now on top of that, I'm painfully aware of just how hungry I am, though something tells me I'll be waiting until I get back to my prison before being able to eat.

Fifteen minutes later, we pull up at an abandoned warehouse on the outskirts of Faders Bay. There's not a person in sight, but I'm not foolish enough to assume there aren't people hiding in the shadows.

Zade steps out of the Escalade before coming to my door and opening it. He grips my arm and pulls me to my feet as the boys discreetly get out of the car and slip into the darkness, fading from sight, not a single one of them bothering with a glance in my direction.

Zade turns me and pulls my wrists behind my back, quickly binding them with thick rope. "In that warehouse, you're my prisoner, and you'll fucking act like it. Don't speak, don't look at anyone, just exist. Is that clear?"

I swallow hard and nod, not sure what kind of hostile environment he's about to drag me into, but judging by the way his eyes bounce around the darkness, I'd dare say he's not comfortable bringing me here. After all, one stray bullet could end it all.

With Zade gently pushing me along, we walk through the parking lot, and I let the numbness claim me, accepting what will be.

We make our way through the opening of the old, dirty warehouse, and I nervously glance around as we enter. I don't see a single person in here, but I feel their stares, and my skin prickles with goosebumps.

"Zade," I whisper, wishing he would step closer, needing the security he can offer. I feel too vulnerable, too open, and I don't like it one bit.

"Just keep walking," he murmurs, his tone so low that I have to strain to hear it, his hand shifting to my wrist as his thumb gently moves back and forth to keep me calm.

He pushes me along, deeper into the warehouse, and one by one, they step out from the darkness, at least twenty of them. Men from all walks of life stare back at me. Old, young, scrawny, and jacked up. Some look like they could be international arms dealers, while others look like acne-riddled computer hackers that live in their mom's basement.

Zade stops, pulling back on my wrist to keep me from taking another step.

"Bold move bringing her here, Zade DeVil," an older man in a designer suit says, making a show of removing his jacket as if to prepare for some kind of showdown. He glances around, his gaze scanning the room before pointedly searching outside the door we just came through. "And without your boys at that."

Zade simply scoffs, not a word spoken, and yet his confidence comes out loud and proud. They don't need to know that the boys are outside this very warehouse, taking out the backup that each of these assholes probably brought along. Besides, I've seen just how lethal Zade is. He doesn't need his boys to be able to run this show. He could take out every man in this room with barely a flick of his wrist.

"One of you has information I need," he says, his gaze shifting around the room, taking in the men before him. While he hasn't specifically introduced them to me, there's no doubt in my mind who these people are. They're the ones you don't want to meet in a dark alley, the callous murderers Empire has trained to handle their dirty business. They're the men you hire when you need a ghost, someone who's not afraid to get their hands dirty.

A voice rings out from across the warehouse, and my head whips around to follow the sound. A younger guy, maybe in his late twenties, stands near the exit. He's well put together and deliciously handsome, but there's something feral in his eyes, something wicked. "You don't rule over Empire yet, DeVil. We don't owe you shit."

"You don't want to make an enemy out of me, Rust," Zade tells him, watching the guy closely as he pushes off the wall and strides toward us. "Tell me what I need to know and I'll ensure your honesty is rewarded. There will be great benefits for those who show their support for my rule."

Rust strides right up to us, his gaze locked on my face, his boldness encouraging the rest of the dangerous crowd to creep in closer. Zade's hand tightens on my wrist, more than ready to pull me away at a moment's notice. Rust nods to the old man in the suit before focusing back on me, his gaze like acid on my skin. "He's right. Bold move bringing Empire's long-lost princess here," he rumbles, making my eyes widen, realizing that my DNA isn't as much of a secret as I'd thought. Rust slowly circles us, and he meets Zade's stare. "Any smart man would take you out of the picture and take the bitch for himself. Why would I fall to your feet for empty promises when I could put a baby in her and sire an heir of my own?"

I swallow hard, unease rocking through me. I know I don't have a great deal with Zade, but something tells me he's the lesser of the two evils. The idea of being taken by this man terrifies me, and I find my hand twisting around in my binds, gripping onto Zade's with everything I've got.

Another man from the opposite direction steps forward. "Fuck that," he growls. "I say we take them both out while we've got the chance. The rest of us can fight it out for leadership."

Zade grunts his disapproval, still as fucking cool as a cucumber, as though this meeting is about as relaxing as a warm bubble bath on a cold winter's night. "Need I remind you of the likelihood of any one of you surviving such a poor, desperate attempt like that? Say you did manage to kill me, what then? I can guarantee that not a damn one of you would survive the callous nature of The Circle. Without me claiming leadership, the world you know would crumble."

Rust scoffs, now behind me. "I'm willing to take that chance."

Without a second of warning, Rust lunges for me, and in the same instant, Zade throws me to the ground. With my hands bound behind my back, I have no way to save myself, and I crash to the dirty floor, my tits taking the brunt of the brutal fall.

Rust's momentum throws him forward, and Zade uses that to his advantage, his hand shooting out and gripping the back of his head. He throws him down beside me with an incredible show of strength. The guy's face slams into the filthy concrete, and a scream tears from my throat as I scramble away.

The other men start to move in, but when Zade pulls a gun on

Rust, they slow their movements, not completely backing down. "I didn't want to make an example of you, Rust. You've been good to me over the years. But then you went and tried to put your hands on what's mine. You disrespected me, Rust."

Terror blasts through my veins, and knowing what's coming, I glance up at the men around us, not wanting to see Rust's brains splatter across the warehouse. But something tells me, the second Zade pulls that trigger, this fucked-up little game will take a turn for the worst.

The men look ready. Their hands flinch at their sides, prepared to draw their weapons, half of their wicked stares locked on Zade, the other half looking at me.

I swallow hard. I know Zade is as lethal as they come, but there are at least twenty other men in this room. There's only so much ego can do before reality comes crashing in.

Where the fuck are the boys?

BANG!

Rust's blood splatters across my face as a gasping squeal tears from my throat. It's fucking on.

The old warehouse quickly becomes a flurry of action, and gunshots are heard from all around. I hastily try to get to my feet, my bound wrists making it much harder than it ought to be. Men race toward Zade, and before I can even make sense of the mess, another two men are dead.

My eyes flick from left to right, my heart racing with fear, terrified someone is going to break through Zade's hold to get to me. Men turn on one another as if settling old scores, and if they're not shooting, it's a fucking brawl. Blood drenches the floor, and men fall down all around me as others flee, realizing this bullshit isn't worth their life.

I hear commotion and fighting coming from outside and realize what's keeping the boys busy. There's no way that Zade can hold these assholes off for long, so I pull against my binds trying to free myself.

Almost dislocating my thumb, I pull one of my hands free, and the rope falls to the ground behind me. Without a moment of hesitation, I lunge forward and grab the knife at Zade's hip, tearing it from the holster. "Don't do anything stupid," he roars at me.

"You're the one doing something stupid," I spit back at him, knowing damn well there's not a thing I'll be able to do to help defend myself against these trained assassins, but the feel of the knife in my hands makes it just a little easier to breathe. "I'm just trying to even the field a little."

Zade scoffs, clearly deciding that my need to help is going to do nothing but slow him down, but he doesn't have time to argue his point as another asshole comes hurtling toward us, his ferocious gaze locked on me.

My heart pounds, but when I hear a window smash across the warehouse, I catch the slightest glimpse of Dalton's face before Zade steps in front of me, blocking the asshole's path. I feel Dalton's intense stare as he tries to cut through the warehouse, past the brawls, and through a spray of stray bullets. Each echoing BANG makes my body jolt with fear.

Dalton gets stuck across the warehouse, and Zade grunts with irritation as the asshole reaches him, swinging wide with a pair of brass knuckles toward Zade's face. He avoids the hit like a pro, but the guy is relentless and keeps coming for him. Even I can tell he's poorly trained, but he's got brute strength on his side. The guy is a fucking monster.

He pushes Zade back, and I hastily scramble away when someone grabs me from behind. I scream, and without even taking a second to look, I swing hard with my knife, clutching it tightly in my palm. The blade sinks into the guy's ribs, and he roars out in pain, his grip somehow tightening on my body.

Panic like I've never known claims me, and my fight-or-flight instincts kick in. I try to stab him again, but he's ready for me now. His arm locks around my chest, pinning me against his body. With his free hand, he catches my fist and squeezes it so fucking hard that the knife clatters against the blood-stained concrete—a sound that will forever stay with me.

Zade grunts. His back is turned to me, but I'm sure he's aware of what's going on. When he quickly snaps the asshole's neck like a fucking twig, he spins to find me, his stare wild and raw.

"ZADE," I scream, everything happening all too fast.

His hand flinches at his side, moving like lightning, and my eyes widen with horror as he raises a gun, his finger already braced against the trigger. "DOWN," he roars, blindly trusting me to do as I'm told, and fuck, who the hell am I to argue with him now?

I attempt to throw myself down, but with the guy's arm braced against my chest, there's not far I can go. I only have one chance to get this right, and I didn't come this far to die like this.

Taking no chances, Zade pulls the trigger, and I feel the whoosh of the bullet flying over my ducked head and blasting right through the guy's skull. His arm falls free of my chest, and my momentum sends me stumbling forward.

Zade grabs me as two guys come for us, one on each side, and he quickly throws me down. My knees graze the concrete beside Rust's lifeless body, his dead eyes staring right at me. But with the guys now on us and Zade fighting right over my head, I have no choice but to stay where I am or risk my world being quite literally shredded to pieces by their sharp daggers.

I use the moment to find Dalton, making sure he's doing alright. He's got three guys on him, but I see Sawyer jumping through the broken window like a fucking cat, springing right into the action.

He jumps in to help Dalton, but Dalton lets out a grunted refusal. "Get Oakley out of here," he roars over the fight and gunshots. "I'll hold them off."

My stare is wild as Sawyer's gaze connects with mine. He immediately makes his way for me, and I find myself wondering what the fuck happened to Easton. God, I hope he's okay.

Dalton holds the three guys off with ease, and I watch him in awe. I knew he was good, but fuck, I didn't realize just how well-trained these guys are. Dalton's like a fucking ninja, quickly eliminating his targets, and before I can even suck in a breath, his three targets are down to one.

Sawyer gets stuck trying to dodge and weave the madness breaking out around him, narrowly avoiding multiple fights in order to get to me. He and I both know every second counts.

I keep my stare locked on his face as he makes his way across the darkened room, wishing that someone had thought to turn on the lights in this place, or at the very least, turned their high beams on to give us something to work with. Sawyer gets halfway across the room, having no choice but to stop and slit someone's throat. Blood gushes out all over his shirt. He pushes the bleeding guy away, and as his body falls to the ground, one of the two assholes hovering over my head drops heavily to the ground as well, splashing blood all around me.

The guy stares at me, not quite dead yet, and it's the most fucked-up thing I've ever seen.

Zade continues to fight the other guy, quickly gaining on him now that it's just one on one. As the boys work from either side of the warehouse, they quickly start thinning out their enemies.

Sawyer is just about to me when my head whips around the room, trying to figure out our best way out of here. I see the old man in the suit across the warehouse at the same time Dalton does. His hand is held high, his gun aimed right at Zade's head, and despite the distance, something tells me the asshole never misses.

"OAKLEY, NO," I hear Dalton's panicked roar across the warehouse at the same time I let out a terrified scream, not even sure of the words that come bursting out. Zade's eyes widen, hearing the raw fear in Dalton's tone, but it's too fucking late. I throw myself to my feet with every ounce of strength I possess and launch myself at Zade like some kind of fucking linebacker, at the same moment the old fucker pulls the trigger.

The loud BANG echoes through my mind as the force of my body slamming into Zade makes us stumble to the side, a sharp, agonizing sting slicing through my arm. We careen right into the guy Zade's fighting, his knife slashing right across my chest in his efforts to take Zade down. Zade tries to catch me in one hand as I scream in pain while fending off his target with his other. But then Sawyer is right there, gripping onto the back of the asshole's head and violently twisting before he even knows what's going on.

I fall awkwardly into Zade's arms, and he quickly catches me, lowering me to the dirty ground. His eyes are wild as he quickly scans over me, trying to figure out if the blood spreading over my chest is going to be fatal.

"Fuck, what were you thinking?" he rushes out as Sawyer turns to defend us, watching our backs. "You could have fucking killed yourself."

"My arm," I say with a clenched jaw, more than ready to ignore his ranting. "It hurts."

Zade grips my elbow and raises my arm to get a better look. "Yeah, I fucking bet it does," he says, a strange emotion flashing in his eyes, something I can't quite decipher. "You got shot."

"Fuck," I say with tears in my eyes, watching Dalton race through the warehouse, hopefully on his way to find the asshole who put a bullet through my arm.

"You'll live," Zade tells me, gripping the bottom of his shirt and tearing it over his head. He rips it into ribbons before tying it around my arm to control the bleeding, and I cry out again. "Just a flesh wound. As for your chest though," he adds, glancing over the gash before pressing what's left of his shirt to my chest. "That's gonna scar."

I scoff. "No worse than what you're gonna do to me."

Zade clenches his jaw just as Easton races in, clearly disheveled from the shit he's been dealing with outside. But considering he's in here and not out there, I'd dare say there's nothing but dead bodies lining the surrounding woods.

"Fuck. What happened?" he rushes out, dropping to his knees at my side as Sawyer fends off the last of our enemies, making me realize that despite all the shit that just went down here, we still didn't get any of the answers we were looking for.

I go to respond, but Zade beats me to it. "The fucking idiot jumped in front of a bullet to save me."

Easton's eyes go wide as Zade's arm slides beneath me, scooping me back to my feet and holding my weight. "You did what?" Easton rushes out, a mix of awe and rage in his eyes, as if he doesn't know how to feel about it, and honestly, neither do I.

"Yeah, pretty fucking stupid, huh? If I'd just let that dickhead take Zade out, I would have been a free woman. Instead, I saved the guy who has absolutely no intention of saving me. Call me a sucker for punishment."

Zade's arm tightens around my waist as he leads me out of the warehouse, suddenly at a loss for words. "You jumped in front of a bullet," Easton reiterates. "What the fuck is wrong with you?"

I shrug my shoulders and instantly regret the movement. "I didn't jump in front of a bullet, I was trying to shove him out of the way,"

I mutter, knowing the boys aren't going to see this from my point of view. "Besides, if Zade dies, that doesn't leave me with good options. Better the devil you know, right?"

The boys get me into the Escalade, and my body starts to shake, feeling cold and unable to calm myself. "We'll get you home and fix you up," Easton promises, scooting in beside me despite usually being the one to travel up front with Zade. "Nothing a hit of morphine can't handle. It'll put you right out."

I swallow hard and nod. The other door opens and Sawyer climbs in, glancing over me with a scowl, but a yawn is all I can manage. I'm suddenly very tired. "Hey Zade," I murmur, noticing he still hasn't said a word since walking out of the warehouse.

"What?"

"I've got some bad news."

His gaze narrows on me through the rearview mirror before thinking better of it and turning right around to fix me with a hard stare. "What?" he demands, his accusatory tone barking through the stationary car as we wait for Dalton.

Deciding I have no reason to hold back, I force a smile across my face, but it doesn't get far. "I snooped through your office and found my phone," I start, watching the way his gaze darkens with anger, but I go on before he starts to think that's all there is to it. "You remember that dude who asked me out at Danny's Bar last week?"

Zade doesn't respond, but his lethal stare is confirmation enough. "He asked me out, and I'm meeting him for dinner tomorrow night."

"Like fuck you are," Zade spits as a strange look flickers through

Sawyer's eyes. Jealousy maybe. Apprehension?

"Considering I just saved your stupid ass from getting a bullet right between the eyes, you really have no leg to stand on. So this is how it's going to go," I tell him. "You're going to drive me back to your place and pump me full of painkillers and bandage me up. Then I'm going to go to bed and probably sleep right up until the late afternoon. I'll get up and get myself dressed, and I might even put a little extra effort into my hair and makeup. And then the four of you overbearing assholes are going to accompany me on my date. You're going to sit way across the restaurant and pretend you don't even know me. You're not going to interrupt or send me scathing looks, you're going to sit and enjoy a meal with your friends. I'm going to laugh at the guy's jokes and try to enjoy myself while getting to do normal things with normal people who don't get off on the thought of tearing my heart out of my chest. I'm going to let him pay for my dinner, and then I'll kiss him on the cheek and let him think there might be something between us. He'll offer to drive me home and hope that I'm going to spread my legs for him, but I'll kindly let him down and play the whole, *I don't sleep with guys on the first date* angle. He'll leave, and I'll wave goodbye knowing that I will never see him again."

Sawyer leans around Easton, catching my stare. "So, you're not interested in this guy?"

"Not in the least."

"Then why go out with him?"

I shrug my shoulders as I see Dalton appearing out of the woods, his lips pressed into a hard line, clearly not happy. "Because I have every intention of having a normal, fulfilling life over the next twenty-three days, and if that means going on the equivalent of a Tinder date, then that's what I'm going to do."

Zade clenches his jaw, clearly not liking this. He shakes his head, muttering under his breath until he finally comes out with a barely audible, "No."

"Zade, disrespectfully, fuck you," I tell him as Dalton clambers into the Escalade with a huff and Zade hits the gas, not down with hanging out here a moment longer than necessary. "You brought me out here to use as bait, and you failed. You didn't get what you needed and nearly lost your life in the process. If it weren't for me, you'd be dead on the warehouse floor. So, you're going to accept that I'm going on a date tomorrow night. You don't have to like it, but you have to respect it. Otherwise, I'll be the one putting a bullet through your head, and this time, I won't hesitate."

Zade lets out a huff and focuses on the road, going awfully quiet as Dalton whips around. "Tell me you're not going on a date with that fucktard who asked you out from Danny's Bar? You know he won't be able to fuck you like I can."

"Oh, believe me," I say with a laugh before cringing as the subtle movements make my body scream for sweet relief. "Nobody can fuck me like you can."

Pride surges in his eyes but as he glances back at Zade, the pride falls away, replaced with something much more sinister. Dalton's lips press into a hard line, already knowing what he's about to hear.

"You didn't get him, did you?"

"I've told you a million times before," Dalton murmurs darkly. "Santos is a fucking ghost. Not even you could have gotten him tonight."

"Fuck."

My brows furrow, and I turn to meet Sawyer's stare. "Who's Santos?"

Sawyer shifts his gaze to the gaping bullet wound in my arm before glancing back up again. "The fucker who gave you that," he says as his gaze darkens, venom pooling in his wicked stare. "But don't worry, Doll. Not even a ghost is safe from us."

And with that, he settles back into his seat, my gut screaming that this is only the beginning. We've only hit the tip of the iceberg, and sooner or later, this sinking ship is going to be nothing but a horrendous wreck at the bottom of the deepest ocean.

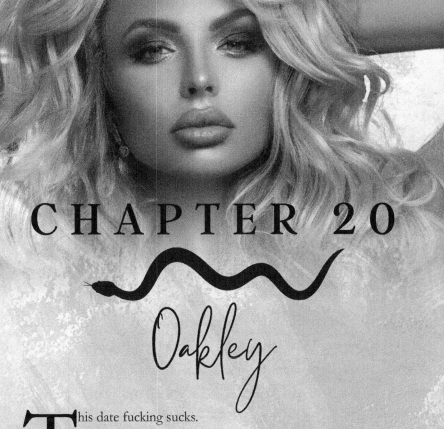

CHAPTER 20

Oakley

This date fucking sucks.

I did my hair, even put the toner through it, and spent time on my makeup before stepping into a sexy little outfit, all for this guy to stare at me like he's about to shit his pants.

What gives? He was so confident at the bar. If I knew he would be the nervous type, I wouldn't have bothered. Hell, it's not even worth using him as bait to get under Zade's skin. He's been telling me about his ex-girlfriend and how she would be furious if she knew he was out on a date tonight, and honestly, what the actual fuck? This is not the kind of bullshit I signed up for. I was looking for a good night, a little bit of fun. My last shot at being wined and dined, because fuck knows the guys aren't about to do it.

They sit across the restaurant, all four of their stares locked on me. I've avoided looking over there for the fear of what I might see in their eyes—straight-up amusement. All four of them tried to talk me out of this, and I should have listened, but I was far too caught up with proving some kind of point.

Hell, after the night I had, I should be home in bed, nursing the massive bullet hole that's currently residing in my arm. Well . . . okay, it's not massive. More like a really nasty graze. The bullet tore through a bit of flesh, and I spent the night bent over the dining table while Easton stitched it up. Not gonna lie, it hurt like a bitch. But he was right, a good dose of morphine made it so much better. I don't even remember him stitching up the gash across my chest.

The waitress comes by our table and gives Harley a flirty smile, and he lays on the charm for her, something he very clearly hasn't been doing for me tonight. But considering the way he came onto me in the bar, he seemed so into me. Maybe I read it wrong. But then he wouldn't have asked me out or even bothered to come along. If he's not feeling it, then what the hell are we doing? Perhaps that makes me a bitch. I came into this with the full intention of using him for a good time, despite the three fuckboys I have who are more than happy to throw me around like a ragdoll and take me at a moment's notice.

Harley and I put in our orders, and the waitress quickly scurries off with a bounce in her step, her hips swaying from side to side. I pour myself a glass of ice water and lift the straw to my lips as Harley watches me a little too closely. "So, ummm," he starts as a sheer layer of sweat starts to form over his forehead. He pointedly stares at the bandages peeking out of the top of my shirt. "You good? What happened?"

Letting out a sigh, I place my water back on the table. "Would you believe me if I said I got into a shootout with twenty assassins and got my ass handed to me by some asshole's knife?"

His eyes widen, real fear flashing in his gaze, but he quickly blinks it away before swallowing hard and grabbing his water. He hastily takes a sip and tries to laugh it off. "You're such a joker," he says, his eyes nervously flashing around the room before connecting to a table by the bar.

I follow his stare before connecting with Zade's, and suddenly it all makes sense. Frustration burns through me, and I curse myself for not being firmer with the guys. I gave them my rundown of how I expected this to all go, what I wanted, and what I didn't, but not once did I tell them they couldn't get to Harley before I could. They found a loophole and exploited it just like good little criminals should, and that's on me. Next time, I'll know better.

Clenching my jaw, I take a deep breath before slowly exhaling and counting to three. When I open my eyes, I fix my hard stare on Harley, my hands braced against the table. "What did they say to you?"

His eyes widen again, the sweat starting to turn into puddles on his forehead. "Ahh, what?" he asks in a panic, nervously flicking his gaze between me and the boys. "I don't know what you're talking about."

Standing up, I brace my hands against the table and slowly lean toward him, holding him captive with my menacing stare. "I'm not asking you again, Harley," I growl, the anger pounding through my veins, my tone filled with venom. "What did they say to you?"

"That . . . that," his eyes widen with embarrassment. "Fuck."

My brows furrow as his hands dive under the table, and I can't help from stepping back and glancing down at the puddle forming under his seat. "Did you just piss yourself?"

"Uh-huh," he mutters, as still as a statue, barely meeting my stare.

My stomach twists with disgust, and I let out a breath, trying to keep myself from gagging. "What did they say to you?"

Harley swallows hard. "The one with the dark hair," he says, finally getting somewhere as he flicks his gaze back toward the boys' table. "He said he'd kill me if I even looked at you wrong, and . . ."

"And what?" I spit, clenching my jaw, more than ready to shove a ten-foot pole straight up Zade's ass.

"And . . . and I believe him," he says, his hands starting to shake. "I don't know what kind of fucked-up shit you're into, but I didn't sign up for this."

Letting out a heavy sigh, I can't help but notice as the piss puddle starts to run across the ground, moving toward the next table. "Leave," I tell him.

Harley hastily stands, not wasting a single second. He goes to bail when I shake my head. "Not so fast." He turns back, devastation in his eyes, the thought of having to sit here with me a moment longer weighing down on him. "This was a date, was it not? What kind of gentleman doesn't pay for his date's meal?"

His eyes widen, and without hesitation, his hand plunges deep into his pocket, yanking out his wallet. He throws a few hundred dollars down on the table, not stopping to check how much he's paying before dropping the whole wallet along with it, his hands so fucking shaky it's embarrassing. Then without even raising his gaze to mine, he bolts for the door, leaving a trail of piss behind him.

I shake my head, almost humiliated for simply having to claim I was on a date with the guy. The waitress strides past, and I call out to her as I scoop the money off the table and shove it into my bra. "Sorry, my date kinda had an accident," I tell her, indicating to the puddle slowly making its way across the restaurant. Her eyes widen in horror. "But listen, I'm still hungry, and I didn't get my ass all dressed up for nothing. So if you wouldn't mind, have both of our meals delivered to that table over there," I say, indicating the only other empty table in the restaurant. "And be sure to charge my meals to them." I point toward the boys' table. "And while you're at it, give yourself a good tip."

Her brows furrow, and she reluctantly nods, probably one of the strangest conversations she's had within the walls of her workplace. Then without wasting another moment, I lift my iced water off the table and stride across the restaurant, making myself comfortable at my new table. I slouch down in my chair, kick my feet up on the chair directly opposite me, and settle my stare on the boys, letting them see the darkness swirling within my gaze.

Both mine and Harley's meals are delivered to my table ten minutes later, and I make a show of taking my damn time, eating them both. Though I have to play this smart and leave the fries for last, otherwise, I won't have enough room for the good shit.

The boys stare back at me, and I'm sure the second Harley left they expected me to drag my ass back to them, but if they want to fuck with my night, then I'll happily fuck with theirs. A waitress comes past with a Diet Coke and places it down on my table with a smile. "What time does the restaurant close?" I ask before she gets a chance to scurry off.

"2 a.m."

A grin stretches across my face as I glance at the boys. It's barely nine, but if I have to sit here for five hours, enjoying nothing but my own company while the boys are forced to sit there and wait, then that's exactly what I'm going to do. I look up at her with a beaming smile. "Perfect."

The waitress is called to the next table and she quickly moves along as I lift my Diet Coke to my lips, wondering what the restaurant's dessert menu looks like. I take my time, slowly working through the two meals, but damn it, those fries. They're going to be my downfall.

An hour passes, and I watch as the boys get antsy, starting to figure out my plan. Sawyer goes to get up, probably to come and tell me to hurry up, but Zade calls him back, making him sit down. I can't hear what's muttered between them, but when all four of their sharp gazes come back to mine at the same time, I can only imagine what bullshit has been said. Though coming from Zade, I'm sure their plan is to wait me out, assuming I'll break before they do. And they're probably right. They've been trained to endure the worst conditions, but I've been preparing to take on two meals like this my whole life.

Another twenty minutes pass when my stomach starts to ache and my phone buzzes on the table. I quickly scoop it up and find a new text from Heather. My stomach sinks.

Heather - Wow. And to think I almost believed you when you said bailing on your shift last week was a once off. You missed your shift last night and now tonight! Don't bother coming back. You're fired.

FUCK! Work didn't even cross my mind.

Soaring guilt storms through my veins and drops heavily into my gut. Working in a bar wasn't exactly my dream job, but it was fun and meant something to me, and now . . . I hate that I've left a bad taste in Heather's mouth and let her down. This isn't who I am as a person, but with everything going on right now with random shootouts and murdering hairdressers, work has been the furthest thing from my mind.

Suddenly not so hungry, I push the two plates aside and slouch back into my seat, feeling like shit. The waitress comes by and gives me a strange smile, her eyes hard and too focused. "All finished?" she asks, her tone not matching the strange look in her eyes.

I sit back up out of sheer politeness and nod. "Umm, yeah," I say. "Thanks."

She reaches forward to take the plate, but her hands linger as she inches closer to me, blocking the boys' view of me. A slip of paper falls out of her hand, right into my lap, and I catch it with wide eyes, quickly burying it deep in my pocket. Then as if nothing happened, she picks up both plates and scurries away with a fake smile.

The note burns in my pocket, and despite the need to sit here all night and waste the boys' time, I push up from my chair, grab my things off the table, and make my way to the bathroom. There's no way I can open this note while the boys are watching.

I don't dare look back at them, but I sense their stares on my back, knowing without a doubt one of them will be standing right outside the bathroom door as I pee.

Pushing through to the bathroom, I head into a stall and quickly lock the door behind me before tearing the note out of my pocket, only having a few moments before I'll be bombarded by an alphahole. Having no idea what this could be about, I go into this with an open mind, hoping like fuck this is some kind of weird way for the waitress to slip me her number rather than anything sinister like everything else seems to be these days.

The note is like a dead weight in my hand, and I quickly unfold it before glancing over the small letters, my heart sinking with every new word.

You were supposed to run. You promised you would run.

What are you doing? Going on dates and messing around with DeVil's crew.

Don't be foolish, daughter. Get your ass out of there. Save yourself before it's too late.

Time is running out.

Dad.

What the fuck?

My heart races, and I drop down on the toilet, unable to hold my weight. I look over the note again, reading the words over and over, my hands shaking violently.

How the hell did he get this to me? How did he know I was on a date?

So many fucking questions race through my mind, but one thing is for sure—my father has a bigger pull than I could have ever known. He would have to know people out here watching over me and tracking my every step. But how? He's supposed to be a dead man, supposed to be some kind of nomad locked in Empire's prison system. How the hell does he have people working for him when no one is supposed to know he's even alive?

A wave of guilt crashes through me, and I whip around, throwing myself off the toilet before violently throwing up my two dinners straight into it. I've been out here fucking around, concentrating on living my best life for the little time I have left, when I should be finding a way into the darkest pits of Empire to free my father and save both of us before it's too late.

Fucking hell. I've been so stupid. It's been a week, and all I've managed to do is find some bullshit blueprints that are absolutely no use to me.

I hear someone outside my stall and groan, knowing it's one of the boys. "You good?" I hear Easton on the other side of the door, and honestly, I'm surprised he hasn't broken the door right off the hinges to check on me.

"Fine," I lie, trying to calm myself. "Just over-ate."

He scoffs, and the amusement in his tone makes me want to smack him. "Yeah, no shit. I know grown-ass men who couldn't put food back the way you just did."

The thought of stuffing any more food down my throat has me wanting to throw up all over again, but I quickly find a little bit of control and try to compose myself, knowing the second I open this small door, Easton will be able to see right through me. He's just that good.

"Could you grab me some paper towels or something like that?" I ask.

I hear him moving around the bathroom, and I quickly shove the note back into my pocket. Barely a moment later, he shoves a handful of paper towels over the top of the stall, and I take them greedily, wiping over my face and starting to feel better.

Confident there aren't chunks all over myself, I make my way out of the stall and run straight into Easton's chest, his gaze locked on my face. He doesn't say anything, just watches me, and just like that, he becomes suspicious. He allows me space to step around him and I move to the sink to wash my hands and rinse the taste of vomit out of my mouth.

He doesn't take his eyes off me, and I'm grateful when he allows me to walk out of the bathroom without questioning me. Not in the mood to keep playing this bullshit waiting game with the boys, I stride right up to their table and avoid Zade's gaze like the plague. "I'm ready to go," I tell them, watching as relief flickers through Dalton and Sawyer's eyes.

"Done fucking with my night, I see," Dalton says, standing from the table. "Why the sudden change of heart?"

I glance away, not able to handle the intensity in his stare, but thankfully, Easton chimes in, a smirk stretching across his lips. "She over-ate. I caught her blowing chunks in the bathroom."

Humiliation washes over me as the boys laugh, and not wanting to listen to their shit, I turn on my heel and stalk out of the restaurant, more determined than ever to get my ass back down in those cells and break my father free.

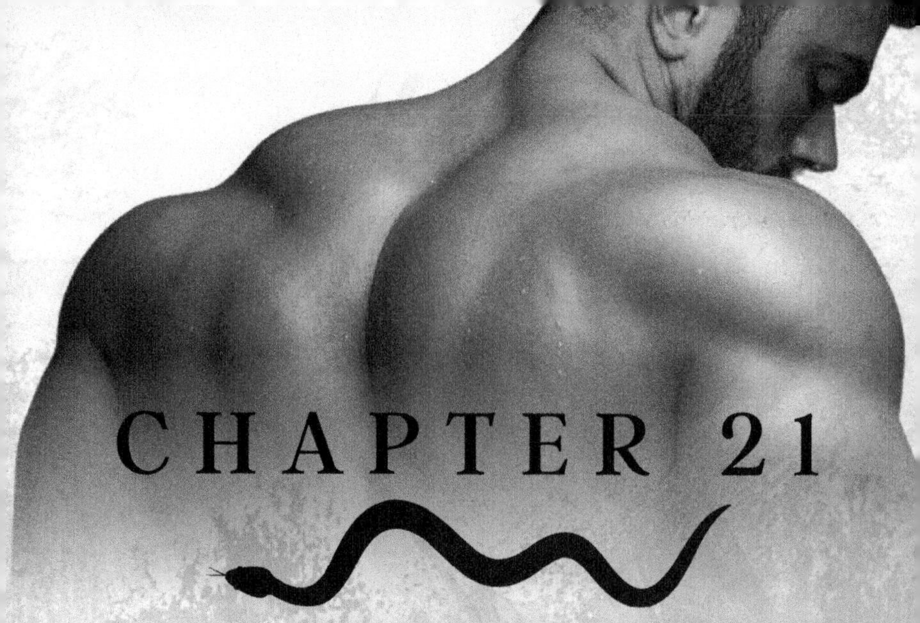

CHAPTER 21

Cross

Mmm, so fucking gorgeous.

I stand in Zade's bedroom, watching as Oakley sleeps, just as I've done most nights after getting her back from the cells. Not gonna lie, the first night Zade questioned it, but quickly came to the realization that it's best just to let it go. I only need a few hours and then I'm good to move on.

I'm a people watcher. I don't read them by the words that come out of their mouths, but by the way their body responds, and Oakley Quinn . . . her body fucking screams to be heard. Which is exactly why I'm here now.

My Pretty is a pretty little liar, and I'm going to find out why.

After walking out of the restaurant bathroom stall, I could see it all over her face. She wasn't sick because she over-ate. Something happened to fuck her up and cause such a violent reaction, and it's something big.

As she sat at her table being the little spitfire that she is, she was fine. She held a stubbornness in her eyes that got my dick hard under the table, and if we weren't in the middle of a restaurant, I would have had no choice but to go to town on myself. But after the waitress took her plates away, that stubbornness was replaced with burning curiosity. She got up immediately, walking too fast for her normal stride, and I was out of my seat in seconds, waving Dalton off when he attempted to go after her first.

Oakley Quinn was delivered a note by that waitress, and I wanna know what the fuck it said.

Moving through Zade's bedroom, I drop down beside Oakley and slowly pull open the bedside drawer, keeping my eye on her to make sure she doesn't wake. Scanning through the drawer, I find nothing before trailing my fingers beneath the edge of the mattress and under the floor rug, trying to figure out where the hell she would have put it.

It occurs to me that she could have flushed it in the restaurant bathroom, but she's not the type to dispose of things. When she was locked up in the prison, she held onto the note Joe sent her like it was her only security blanket, so there's no way she would throw this away.

When she came home, she showered and went straight to bed, grabbing one of Zade's shirts from his closet, not bothering to walk down to her room and find something comfortable of her own. And with that, I make a point to search through Zade's closet before moving through to his private bathroom. All that's in here is the dirty clothes hamper and I search through it, plucking out the tight jeans that made her ass look fucking edible.

My fingers slip into the pockets and my body freezes as I find a folded-up piece of paper inside. I should have fucking known she wouldn't bother hiding it. She's too cocky, too confident in her actions to think for even a second that we would question her sudden trip to the restaurant bathroom.

She thinks she's gotten away with it, but she can't fool me.

Dropping the jeans back into the hamper, I hold the note and quickly unfold it as I listen to the sound of her soft breathing in the other room, her body locked in Zade's arms, just as they sleep every night.

My gaze shifts over the note, expecting to find some bullshit from one of The Circle members or a threat from whoever sent Joe to attack her outside the DeVil Hotel, but this . . . fuck. I wasn't expecting this.

You were supposed to run. You promised you would run.
What are you doing? Going on dates and messing around with DeVil's crew.
Don't be foolish, daughter. Get your ass out of there. Save yourself before it's too late.
Time is running out.
Dad.

Matthias Quinn is alive, and not only that, but he must also have the pull and skill of an army to be watching our every move without alerting us to their existence. I would bet my fucking life that he's the man who stood across from Oakley in those cells. Hidden in plain sight. Bound and broken by Empire's prison system. But not anymore. His days are officially numbered.

Stepping out of the bathroom, I slip the note into my pocket before walking back around to Oakley's side of the bed. I stand over her, not even disappointed to find she betrayed us. She knew her father was alive, and she didn't say a damn word. She knows Zade would slaughter him like cattle. Keeping it from us is in her best interests, but as much as it kills me, I'm not here to cater to her best interests.

Reaching down, my fingers trail over her arm, brushing over her fair skin, down over the subtle curve of her hip, and back up to her throat. My fingers curl around it and gently squeeze until her eyes spring open with fear. I clamp my other hand over her mouth.

Mmmm, that fear is intoxicating.

My knee presses into the mattress, and as her eyes adjust to the darkness and she sees it's only me, her body begins to relax. Confident she's not about to scream, I lift my hand from her mouth and clamp my fingers over her hip, gently pulling her away from Zade.

She remains silent, just as I knew she would, watching me intently and allowing me to roll her onto her stomach. She hitches her knee up, knowing what's coming, but I pull her hips up instead, needing to see her wide open for me. I fucking love her like this, her ass up and chest down, that needy cunt begging me to take it.

Slipping Zade's oversized shirt up over her ass and down her back, I pull her panties to the side, my cock already straining for her. She's already so aroused, and I push my fingers deep into her cunt, loving the way she pushes back against me, the softest moan slipping from her lips.

Not here for the fucking foreplay, I position myself behind her while freeing my heavy cock. With her panties pulled to the side, I free my fingers and line myself up with my pretty little liar as I take her hips, my fingers digging into her soft skin.

Oakley's hands bunch into the sheets in anticipation, and as I slowly push into her sweet cunt, I meet Zade's stare, having woken up the second I touched her. He watches intently, taking her in just as I knew he would. Hell, this fucker wants her just as much as I do, but for now, he'll settle with the smell of her arousal in the air.

Oakley groans, trying to keep quiet, and I reach down, curling my hand around her thick hair, holding her face against the mattress as I start to fuck her the way she likes, being cautious not to disturb her injuries. Then with her head locked toward the window, I slip my other hand into my pocket, feeling the note between my fingers before handing it to Zade. And as I fuck her harder, Zade reads the note from her father, his eyes darkening with pure rage, yet another obstacle in his way to the top.

Zade meets my stare and nods, both of us on the same wavelength—Matthias Quinn must die. His tongue rolls over his bottom lip as his gaze shifts back to Oakley, watching the way she pushes back against me, learning the way she likes it, memorizing the sounds of her soft groans, the need she has for my cock.

She comes hard and fast, her fingers tightening in the sheets. She stays as quiet as possible, clearly not realizing that Zade is already awake beside her. Her pussy convulses around my cock, and it's all I need to fall right over the fucking edge. I spill my load into her sweet cunt, clenching my jaw as the overwhelming satisfaction tears through me.

Oakley pushes her leg out, collapsing her hips back to the mattress as I pull out of her and straighten her panties, releasing the hold on her hair. She snuggles deeper into her pillow as I step off the bed and fold my cock back into my pants, her eyes glued to my face. "Go to sleep, Pretty," I murmur through the dark room, her betrayal making something tighten in my chest.

And with that, I walk straight out as the sound of Zade moving across the bed fills the room. He pulls her back into his arms, and not a moment later, she's falling back into a deep sleep as though nothing even happened, my cum spreading between those pretty thighs.

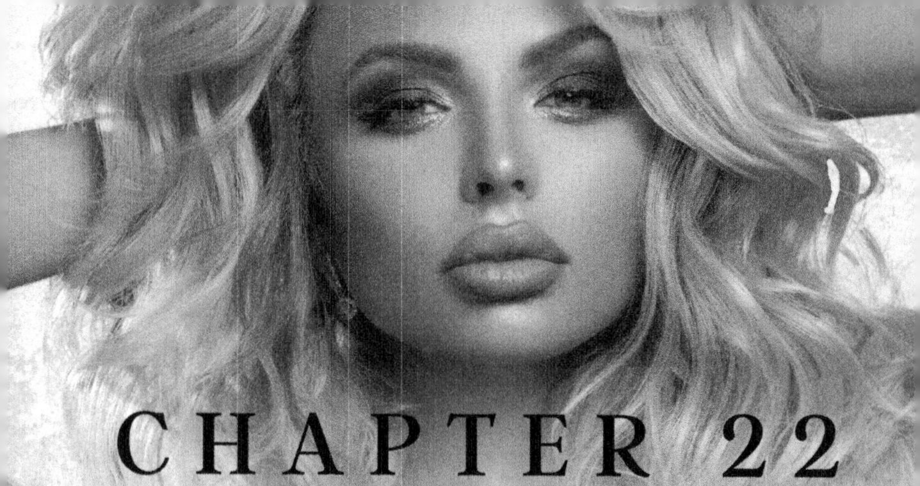

CHAPTER 22

Oakley

A throat clears at the opening of Zade's storeroom in his office, and my head whips up, finding Zade leaning against the secret bookshelf door, watching me with an arched brow.

Ahh, fuck.

Sprung.

"The fuck do you think you're doing?" he asks, finding me spread out on the floor, at least five of the ancient by-law books spread out around me and a highlighter in my hand.

"I, ummm . . ." I start nervously, wondering how best to explain why I've just defaced all of these antique books with a highlighter, and hell, maybe even dog-eared a few of the pages. But when it comes to

Zade, it's best just to give it to him straight. At least, mostly straight. "I'm trying to find a way to rise up in power and steal it all out from beneath you."

He scoffs as if the idea is preposterous to him. "Alright then," he mutters, his brows slightly bouncing. "Carry on then."

He turns his back and stalks into his office before heading for the door, and I stare at the empty doorway, almost offended that he doesn't believe I could actually find what I'm looking for. "Hold up a second," I call, scrambling to my feet and hurrying after him. I catch up only a second later and trail behind him, infuriated by the way he doesn't bother to stop and look back at me. "Why aren't you bitching my ass out like you usually do?"

"Because there's no point," he says, striding through the penthouse and out to the living room where Dalton and Sawyer are throwing a football back and forth, making a disapproving scowl stretch across Zade's face. "I've spent years going through those by-laws, trying to figure out a way to take it from my father. If there were a way, I would have done it already."

Fuck.

"You mean, apart from murdering him in cold blood and stealing it from his cold, dead hands."

Zade finally graces me with a smile, and shit, it's fucking dazzling. Butterflies swirl through my stomach at the mere sight of it. "Exactly," he says, his eyes darkening with the reminder. "But let's be real. You don't have the fucking balls to take me out, and even if you did, you couldn't beat me. It's over for you, Oakley. I commend you for trying.

But no matter how hard you try, you're no match for me."

I swallow hard. His words aren't harsh, just stating the truth. And while I appreciate him being honest with me instead of insulting me with lies, it feels like a bucket of ice water being tipped over my head. No matter how close I get with these guys, their resolve never fades. They will follow through, even if it means killing themselves in the process.

"You know," I murmur as he continues on his way. "I really like how you underestimate me."

His lips kick up at the sides of his mouth, and I'm about to start gawking at the thought of me actually making him almost smile when Sawyer throws the ball just a little too hard. Dalton's stare is locked on my tits, and as he goes to lift his hands to catch the ball, it flies straight past his fingers, crashing into Venom's small enclosure behind his head.

Glass shatters as the ball slams against the back wall and comes spiraling back out, Venom flying out with it. The snake drops to the ground and quickly slithers beneath a cabinet, terrified, and before Sawyer and Dalton's heads can even whip around to find Easton, his gun is drawn and bullets are whizzing through the air.

A blood-curdling scream tears from the back of my throat, and I drop to the ground as the boys haul ass, running for their fucking lives. Easton has impeccable aim, so the fact that the boys aren't already dead on the ground tells me this isn't about ending them. This is pure punishment. You fuck with his snake; he fucks with you.

My hands circle over my head, certain I'm about to get one of the stray bullets right to the chest as Zade lets out a heavy sigh and strides toward his couch, barely even noticing the bullets whizzing past his face. He takes a seat and leans back, getting comfortable as he waits for Easton to run out of ammunition.

Each loud *BANG* makes my body jolt with fear, and I find myself commando crawling across the floor until my body is pressed right up against Zade's legs, hating myself for how desperately I need his security. Despite knowing there's no way in hell Easton would allow a bullet to come anywhere near me, I can't shake the fear.

The second he's out of bullets, Sawyer stops running and braces his hands against his knees as Dalton slams into the back of the couch, both of them trying to catch their breath. Easton just shakes his head, more than pissed off, before storming across the penthouse, getting down onto his hands and knees, and trying to coax Venom out from under the cabinet. Hell, I wouldn't be surprised if he tears the cabinet apart to get to her.

Getting up off the ground, I spare a glance toward Sawyer and notice a trail of blood down his arm and then another low on his calf, and I suck in a breath before whipping around to look over Dalton, finding the same. Two fresh bloody grazes. "He actually shot you."

Easton scoffs from across the penthouse. "You really think I'd let those assholes get away unscathed?" he questions, and he's right. I honestly should have known better. "We're going to have to go and get Venom's enclosure from the college apartment."

"What?" Zade says with a sigh. "What's wrong with the one in your place downstairs?"

"Venom prefers the other one," Easton grunts, fixing Zade with a hard stare, a clear warning of what will happen if he dares to push him on this. He turns his stare on the boys before pointing at the shattered glass. "Clean this shit up."

Dalton and Sawyer don't dare argue about it, quickly getting to work as Easton finally lures Venom out from under the cabinet. He places her up around his neck, and she instantly slithers beneath the neckline of his dark shirt, finding comfort hidden within. Not gonna lie—I'm pretty fucking comfortable when wrapped around him too. The snake's got good taste.

Within the span of an hour, the boys are stitched up, the old enclosure has been thrown in the trash, and we're pushing through the main door of the college apartment complex. As we stride down the long corridor toward Easton's door, I can't help but think about the day I moved here. I so desperately wanted this place to be my new home. Only now, Zade's penthouse is starting to feel more like where I belong. Not that it really matters. To the guys, I'm only there out of convenience. I'm sure if I weren't Zade's sacrifice, I wouldn't be welcome to take up space in his home.

The boys stop by Easton's door, but I keep on going, striding further down the hall. "Where the fuck are you going?" Easton mutters, his hands pausing as he unlocks his door.

I turn around to find all four of them staring after me. "Ummm, I was going to say hi to Cara," I say, a little unsure how they couldn't have pieced this together themselves. "I mean, should I have put in a written request forty-eight hours ago and waited for formal approval?"

"Damn right you should have," Zade says, though I can't really tell if he's being serious or not.

I arch a brow, more than ready to throw down over this. What's the big deal? It's not like they were expecting me to be the one to haul the big enclosure out on my back. Besides, I'll probably be back before they've even worked out how to get the stupid thing through the door. I mean, that's what I'll tell them if they were to ask, but we all know I'm lying.

With no hint of a refusal, I give the boys a smug grin before spinning around and soaring back up the hallway before Zade decides to change his mind. I can only imagine what's going through his head right now. I don't doubt he's thinking the worst, assuming the second I'm out of sight, someone's going to jump out from under my bed and slaughter me. I suppose my track record isn't the best, so he'd be right to constantly assume the worst, but I appreciate him giving me the benefit of the doubt.

Reaching the door of my apartment, I take it slow, gripping the handle and giving it a turn before silently slipping inside the apartment. Cara is nowhere in sight, but I can hear her in her room.

A smile pulls at my lips as I creep toward her open door, holding my breath and feeling like a fucking elephant trying to make my way across the creaky floorboards. Her voice flows out the door, and I realize she must either have someone in there with her or she's on the phone, and before I scare the shit out of her, I figure I better get a feel for what I'm about to walk in on.

Pressing my back up against the wall by her door, I listen in, feeling like the worst kind of creeper. But honestly, this shit is tame compared to what I've been dealing with. Besides, I'd really prefer not to rush into her room only to find her in the midst of shooting an orgy gang bang and being cream-pied by five guys.

"I don't know," she hisses, and judging by the lack of response, I can only assume she's on the phone. There's a pause, and the way she lets out a frustrated sigh has me wondering who the fuck could have her reacting like this. "You don't think I've been trying? They're keeping her away."

Shit. Whatever this is, it doesn't sound like a conversation she would want me overhearing. I go to leave, but her words come out fiercer now, and I couldn't ignore them even if I tried.

"I can't do that. They'll know," she says. Another pause. "Oh, sure. I'll just send Zade a text, asking him where the fuck they're stashing her, shall I? What the fuck is wrong with you?"

What the fuck? Zade?

My blood runs cold. Cara told me she barely knew the guy.

"No. No, no, no," she rushes out, fear in her tone. "Please don't hurt him. I'll . . . I'll try harder. I'll find her, but she hasn't been back here in days. I can't give you a location if I don't know where the hell she is. Please, just give me some time."

My heart races, and suddenly pieces of the puzzle begin to fall into place.

Cara is the one who's been giving up my location. She's the one responsible for the attacks. But why?

Tears well in my eyes, and I desperately try to hold them at bay.

I consider running straight back out the door and telling Zade, but I can't do that without at least confronting her first.

Anger, fear, and betrayal pulse violently through my veins, and I storm through the opening of her door, my hands clenched into tight fists at my side. I meet her stare, watching her eyes widen as she realizes what I know. "Shit," she breathes through the phone. "She's here."

The phone falls from her fingers, and all I can do is stare at her. "It was you. All this time. It's been you."

"No. No, Oakley," she rushes out, stepping toward me only for me to quickly back up. "It's not what you think. Please, I had no choice."

I shake my head, not trusting her for a second. Her betrayal somehow cuts so much deeper than the guys'. "I've been running for my life," I mutter, the lump growing in my throat and making it hard to breathe. "Attack after attack. I've come home to men in my bedroom, snipers, assassins. I was fucking drugged and put in Empire's prison, and it's all because of you. You betrayed me. You *keep* betraying me."

"Oakley, please. I'm sorry. I—"

"No," I say, shaking my head as I back up more. "No, this isn't okay. No excuse could ever make up for what you've done. You lied to me. You made me believe you knew nothing about Empire. You said you didn't know the boys, and you let me foolishly believe you were my friend."

"I am your friend," she insists. "Please, just let me—"

I scoff in disbelief. "You think I'm going to believe you now? You've lied to me since the beginning. Do the boys even know who you are?"

Her brows furrow, confused by my questions. "Yes, of course they know who I am."

Why am I not surprised? Empire set me up here; Nikolai told me himself in the cells. I should have put that together earlier, but I suppose I had hoped that Cara was just an innocent bystander in all of this. I stare at her, dumbfounded. "And do they know you're the very reason for my location being compromised?" I question, certain if they thought for one second that she would betray their trust, she'd never have been placed here to watch over me.

"NO," she panics, racing forward and gripping my shoulders. "No, please. You can't tell them. If Zade ever found out. If Sawyer—fuck. No. Please, I swear, I'll do anything. He'll kill me. Zade will kill me."

I laugh, unable to believe this woman as I shove her off me, watching as she stumbles back a few steps. "Oh, I get it. So it's my life over yours."

Tears form in her eyes, and she looks at me with regret. "Zade is going to kill you anyway. I just—"

"Thought you'd beat him to it," I finish for her.

"No, that's not it at all. I had no choice."

"You always have a choice," I tell her, my heart truly breaking. I honestly thought we were friends. I know things were a little strained and that I didn't know her as well as I had wanted, but this . . . no. This is tearing me apart in a way I wasn't expecting. "And I choose me. Forgive me."

And with that, I let out a blood-curdling scream.

Cara's eyes go wide, terror rocking through her stare, and it's like all her nightmares have just manifested right in front of her. But nothing should scare her more than me—not after what she's done. It's one thing being a shitty friend, but this . . . I'm not about to let this fly.

Knowing what's coming her way, Cara frets and races toward the living room window that overlooks the parking lot and grips the handle before throwing the window wide. But it's too late. The boys are already bursting through the door.

Cara looks back over her shoulder, absolute fear in her eyes. I expect her to lock onto Zade, knowing he's the biggest threat, but she looks at Sawyer instead, guilt like I've never seen flashing in her haunted stare.

The boys come to a startling halt, taking in the scene around them, and I can guarantee that this isn't anything at all what they thought they were gonna bust in here to find. "What?" Dalton rushes out, hurrying to my side and looking over me, checking me from head to toe.

Sawyer, Easton, and Zade creep forward with suspicion, knowing I wouldn't have screamed for nothing. I nod toward Cara, half hanging through the window, and Sawyer storms ahead, grabbing her waist and hoisting her back into the kitchen, gripping her arm tightly as he looks back at me. "Someone better tell me what the fuck is going on right now," Sawyer roars, his other hand flinching at his side.

I don't hesitate, more than ready to put my life before hers. After all, she didn't feel the need to protect mine. "I overheard her on the phone. She's the one who's been giving up my location."

"What?" Sawyer grunts, his brows furrowed as he glances at Cara.

Zade and Dalton narrow their stares.

"No," Cara breathes, unable to steal her gaze away from Sawyer's furious stare. "She's got it wrong. I swear. I . . . I—"

Sawyer's gaze hardens even more, and he tugs her arm hard, dragging her across the small apartment as her feet struggle to keep up with his long strides. He takes her right over to the couch before shoving her down into it, all four of the boys crowding around. "Start talking."

Cara swallows hard, flinching with every slight move the boys make, and it becomes even more clear that she knows exactly what these guys are capable of. She nervously glances toward Zade, that same guilt flashing in her eyes as he gives her nothing but a dead stare. "I had no choice," she finally says, her stare locked on Sawyer's again. "They said it was either her or you. They were going to kill you, Sawyer. I couldn't let that happen."

What. The. Fuck.

My eyes flick between them like some kind of ping-pong match, trying to figure out what the connection is there. Why the hell would she care about what happens to Sawyer? Were they together in another life? Has she been in love with him for years?

I look a little closer, taking in the betrayal in Sawyer's eyes and the guilt in hers—eyes that I'm starting to notice look all too similar. Those same blazing blue eyes, the same blonde hair. Mannerisms. Temper. Smile.

"Holy shit," I breathe, backing up a step as if physically taking a blow to the chest. I meet Sawyer's stare, and he looks back at me as if knowing exactly what's about to come out of my mouth. "She's your sister."

He clenches his jaw, his gaze softening. He talks about his sister every now and then. Down in the cells with his father, after beating the shit out of Zade, hell, even Dalton mentioned her. But not once did they actually use her name.

Holy fuck. How could I have been so naive?

But if she's his sister, then Zade and Cara . . . fuck. Why does that make me want to claw her eyes out?

A betrayal so much worse than Cara's tears through my chest, and I shake my head, my gaze flicking from each of their stares. "All of you lied to me."

Zade clenches his jaw. "We can deal with that later," he grunts, fixing his attention back on Cara. "Who the fuck are you reporting to?"

She shakes her head, refusing to say a word, and Zade takes a step closer, her face breaking with fear. "I'm not going to ask again."

Sawyer's hand flies up against Zade's chest, pulling him up short. "Watch it, man. That's still my fucking sister you're talking to."

"What's with your family?" Zade mutters. "Not a damn one of them knows what's good for them."

Sawyer clenches his jaw, Zade's comments only making the tension between them rise. "You don't want to go there right now, Zade," Sawyer warns. "Fucking question Cara and that's it. But if you put a fucking hand on her, I will end you. You hear me?"

Zade holds his stare for a moment before turning back to Cara, her hands violently shaking in her lap. "Do you have any idea just how fucking lucky you are right now? If it weren't for your brother being here—you'd already be dead. So before you decide to hold back from me, keep that in mind. Now, tell me what the fuck I need to know."

"Hartley Scott," she says, tears running down her face. "I report to Hartley."

"FUCK," Sawyer spits, his hands at his temples. He walks up and down the length of the couch before coming back to the center and looking at his sister. "How could you be so fucking stupid?"

Cara throws herself to her feet. "Stupid?" she screeches, shoving her brother hard. "He was going to kill you if I didn't give her up. He had the fucking live feed with the sniper right on your goddamn chest. What the fuck was I supposed to do? I'm not losing you for this bitch."

"You lie," Zade growls. "You fucking lie to save your brother, and then you call me."

Cara scoffs, falling back to the couch. "Right, because calling you has always worked out so well for me in the past. Check my phone, asshole. I've tried calling you at least five times just this fucking week. Have you answered any of my calls or even attempted to call me back? I don't think so."

Frustration burns through me, and I watch as she crosses her arms over her chest as though she's the one who's been wronged here. "Uhh, I don't want to alarm anyone," I say. "But do we need to be going?"

All five of them look up at me in confusion, and I let out a heavy sigh. "She was on the phone with Hartley when I got here. He knows I'm here."

Dalton grunts in frustration. "Fucking hell, Cara. Is it really so goddamn hard to keep your mouth closed?"

Sawyer inches toward his sister. "Lay off," he tells Dalton. "She told us what we needed to know."

"And what?" Dalton argues. "You think that's it? That she gets to just walk away because she cooperated? Fuck that, man. You know that's not how it works."

"Alright," Zade says a moment later, realizing this is only going to get ugly from here on out. He turns to Cara, not looking pleased about any of this. "Grab your shit. You're coming with us."

She stiffens on the couch, her eyes wide as she looks up at him. "To your penthouse?" she questions nervously. "You've never invited me back there."

"Don't fucking mistake this," he growls. "I'm not inviting you to stay with me. You'll be locked in my cell until I figure out what the fuck to do with you."

She throws herself to her feet again, her hands flying out. "No. Absolutely not. I'm not some bitch you can just order around."

"Yeah," Zade scoffs. "You are."

Sawyer shakes his head, looking at his sister. "Just get your shit, Cara. Fighting it is only going to make this worse."

She looks up at her brother, hitting him with a big doe-eyed stare. "Don't do this to me," she whispers. "Not when our family is already falling apart. We'll never be able to come back from this."

"Now, Cara," he says, something breaking in his tone. "Don't force my hand."

Cara holds his stare for a moment, realizing she won't be able to get herself out of this one, and with that, she turns on her heel and storms off toward her room, Dalton and Zade following behind.

Easton, Sawyer, and I make our way out of the small apartment, and as the door closes behind me, I know that I will never return here again. A heaviness spreads through my chest, but I push it aside, not wanting to get caught up on things that simply don't matter.

After getting Venom's enclosure loaded into the back of the Escalade, we pile into the car, and within moments, Zade and Sawyer are there with Cara, breaking into my piece of shit car. I shake my head, watching the sight. "They could have just asked for the keys."

Easton scoffs. "You ever known Zade to do things the easy way?"

"I guess not," I say, and with that, Easton hits the gas, and we sail back through the city toward the DeVil Hotel.

The moment we return to the hotel and walk into Zade's penthouse, Sawyer grips Cara's elbow and leads her right through to the fucked-up little cell the guys kept me in the first time they decided to kidnap me. My heart aches as I watch him have to push his sister through the door, but I don't miss the way he discreetly slips her Kindle through with her. I can only imagine the bullshit going through his mind. His father first and now his twin sister.

Zade was right; Sawyer's family doesn't know what's good for them.

Cara screams for forgiveness, but the sound cuts off a second later as the door seals shut, and with that, Sawyer turns back to face us and lets out a heavy breath. "I need a fucking drink."

CHAPTER 23

Zade

Oakley sleeps soundly in my arms, her tight body pressed right up against mine, and it's the most confusing thing I've ever had to deal with. I fucking hate having her in my bed because every damn night it gets harder to resist her, especially when she's whispering my name in her sleep. It's starting to fuck with my head, and I can't allow that to happen.

There are only nineteen days left. I need to hold it together. The boys have all fallen victim to her charm, and I won't lie, I understand why. I'd do anything just to get a taste. But this right here is as far as it'll ever go.

Oakley fucking Quinn is going to be the death of me.

She mumbles something in her sleep, and I pull away from her before slipping out of bed. I stare down at this little she-devil who insists on making my life a living hell, and I can't help but hate myself for what I have to do to her. Keeping her at arm's length is fucking killing me.

Knowing Cross is bound to sneak in here at some point during the night and will stay until I return, I grab my things and make my way out of my room. I pass Sawyer in the living room, sitting in the same spot he's been since we arrived home—his elbows braced against his knees, staring toward the hidden door of my cell, feeling sick to his stomach over what his sister has done.

"You good, man?" I murmur, crossing the penthouse toward the elevator.

Sawyer just grunts, not wanting to look up at me, and I get it. If Sawyer had his way, he would have given Cara a slap on the wrist and sent her on her way. He's protective of her, and in his eyes, she can do no wrong. With his father on the chopping block, Sawyer has an overwhelming need to step up and be the man of the family—the one his father could never quite be, and I can't help but wonder how much weight is coming down on his shoulders.

He wants to blame me, but at the end of the day, I'm not the one who betrayed Empire. With the tension already riding high between us, I don't know how well we'll come through the other side. But there's no doubt in my mind, Cara Thorne needs to be held accountable for her actions. Hell, I understand she had a gun to the back of her head at first. She was a puppet with her strings pulled, and considering her choices, I don't blame her for giving up Oakley's location. But what about the second time? The third or fourth?

Cara Thorne betrayed me as her future leader, and I won't allow that to slide.

Knowing Sawyer is going to sit out here all night, I push the button for the elevator without another word. It arrives immediately, the doors sliding back and welcoming me in. I arrive in my private garage barely a moment later and scoop up the keys for my black Bugatti.

The engine roars to life as I fly out onto the city streets of Faders Bay. Driving out through the suburbs and through the surrounding gated communities of the rich and famous, I pull up outside the Scott residence.

I haven't been here since I was a kid, and there's good reason for that—Hartley Scott is a fucking twat. If he could remove a few of his ribs to suck his own dick, he would.

Since the moment his name came flying out of Cara's mouth, I knew I would end up here. I can't let this slide, but something doesn't sit right with me. Hartley Scott is a coward. He's always been bigger than his boots, wanting to be the guy in charge but not having the backbone to follow through. Someone else is definitely pulling his strings, and I want to know who.

Stepping out of my Bugatti, I scale the gate, hauling myself over with ease. I drop down onto the manicured lawn before making my way toward the main residence. My gaze shifts across the property, noticing the security system and taking note of the cameras. Hartley has gone hard with his security, and because of that, I won't be killing him here tonight. But when the time is right, I will take my dagger and slam it deep into his stomach before twisting the knife just right. It'll be fucking delicious. I can't wait to hear the pain in his cries.

Knowing the alarm will go off when I try to get through the door, I don't bother being discreet. Making my way around the side of the property, I find myself standing outside Hartley's office. My elbow goes straight through the glass before I reach in and unlock it. I open it just enough to pull myself up and through the small gap, dropping down inside his home.

I slowly walk around his office, scanning over his papers as I listen, waiting for him to come down here, gun in hand, trying to bust whoever had the audacity to break into his home. But nothing ever comes. He must not have heard me.

Taking another minute to go through the files on his desk, I find all the usual documents I should expect from a member of The Circle—member files, blackmail, proof of money laundering, but nothing that tells me who the fuck is pulling his strings. I disregard it all and, knowing he's the type to take it to the grave, I realize there's only one way to do this.

Striding out of his office, I make my way up the stairs and into his bedroom, finding him sound asleep beside his wife. They don't touch one another, and a smirk pulls at my lips. Even in sleep, she can't fucking stand him.

Making my way around to her side, I take my knife and use it to slowly lift the covers, peeling them back so softly she doesn't even stir. She's wearing an eye mask and a silk tank and shorts, and I've got to give it to Hartley, she's fine. Definitely the kind of woman I would probably end up with. Someone to stand at my side during Empire events and bear me an heir, but she probably wouldn't be able to stand me. She'd sleep in another room, and that would be fine with me. As long as she smiles in public. So tell me why the fuck I only see Oakley's face when I think of what I want for my future?

Shit.

Hartley though, he probably bought this one. Promised her the world if she were to marry him, and probably never followed through. They're both still quite young. In their mid-thirties, and as far as I'm aware, they don't have any children.

The tip of my blade settles onto her porcelain skin, and I slowly trail it up and down her waist like a soft caress. As if finally sensing a presence, Hartley's eyes spring open, and his hand flies across to his bedside table for the gun that rests there. He turns it on me, but I barely pay it any attention. The man is so easy to read. Instead, I keep my gaze locked on his sleeping wife. "She's pretty," I murmur into the darkness, keeping my voice low so I don't wake her.

Hartley sucks in a breath as his eyes adjust to the darkness, taking me in and noticing just how much danger his wife is in. "Get away from her," he spits, his gaze flicking between me, his wife, and the knife in my hand.

"Wouldn't it be a shame if you were to lose the one thing that means the most to you?" I mutter, the knife slowly making its way back up over her ribs and reflecting against the soft moonlight streaming through the window. "One puncture is all it would take."

The gun flinches in his hand. "I'll fucking kill you."

I laugh. "You've been trying to kill Oakley for weeks. You've had every opportunity under the sun to take her out, but you fail every damn time. You think you could even touch me?"

Hartley clenches his jaw, his hands shaking. "I . . . I don't know what you're talking about," he says. "I would never betray the blood."

Well, shit. This motherfucker is giving me whiplash. "Which one is it? You'll kill me if I touch your wife, or you would never betray the blood? You can't have both. So I suggest you choose wisely."

Hartley swallows hard, not knowing how to respond, but I don't need him to. It's clear as day this asshole is nothing but a spineless cockroach, clinging onto anything he thinks could give him a shred of power. "Just how far would you go for the blood?"

He meets my stare, not liking my line of questioning. "I'd do anything."

"Mmmm," I say, studiously dropping my gaze back to his wife, making a show of enjoying her curves. "And just how much are you willing to lose?" A smirk rests across my lips, and I let my question sink in. "A woman like this requires a real man. I bet she despises you. Cries herself to sleep every night after you fuck her. I bet you've never made her scream."

Hartley finally grows some balls and slides out of bed, standing opposite me as he holds the gun firmly in his hand. "Touch her and you die."

Again with the whiplash.

My gaze lifts to his, and I slip my dagger back into my belt. "I know what you're doing, Hartley," I tell him, striding back around the bed and putting myself right in front of him. "I know you're behind these attacks, and I know you've been using Cara Thorne to do it." I pause, letting each of my words truly sink in. "Do not fool me, Hartley. I will destroy you. I will take your pathetic life in my hands and tear you to shreds until there's not a damn thing left, but not before I slaughter every last person you're working for, and as you watch them perish, the weight of their deaths will fall on your shoulders."

And with that, I walk out of his bedroom, knowing without a doubt the motherfucker took the bait.

Making my way back out to my car, I turn the key and listen to the sweet sound of the engine roaring through the quiet streets. I take off, making a show of cutting across the front of his driveway as he watches me leave through his bedroom window.

The Bugatti flies through the streets, but I don't get far, discreetly pulling into a neighboring property and cutting the lights. My eyes remain locked on the street, and sure enough, Hartley's Aston Martin shoots past me two hours later.

Hook, line, and fucking sinker.

Waiting for him to get far enough ahead, I slip out into the streets, keeping my lights off as I follow him through the city and out to the countryside. We drive for well over an hour before I watch Hartley pull into the drive of a huge estate, something my father could have only dreamed about owning.

I come to a stop behind a row of tall bushes and park, silently sliding out of my Bugatti and sticking to the shadows as I creep closer. Hartley's Aston Martin rolls up next to the giant house at the end of the long driveway—his idea of being discreet.

He gets out of his car and quickly glances around before slipping through a side entrance of the massive home. Not wanting to risk going in straight after him, I move around the property before breaking through the lock on the back door.

I move like lightning through the dark home, trying to get a feel for who could live here. A brief thought flashes through my mind that I'm about to walk in to find Matthias Quinn, but that's not possible. The guy is locked up in Empire's prison, and while he makes the most sense, there's no way he could pull it off. Getting notes around is one thing, but being here tonight . . . no. He couldn't. Besides, his note was instructing Oakley to run, not to help him pull off the greatest heist of all time.

Hell, a part of me had kinda hoped it was Matthias. At least that way it would be easy. All I'd have to do is go down to those cells and put him down. I'd barely have to lift a finger to wipe out the true blood heir that could challenge my rein, and in nineteen short days, I'll take out his dazzling daughter too.

"What could possibly be so important that you had to drag me out of bed at this time?" a feminine voice says, the conviction in the tone telling me without a doubt that this woman is the one pulling his strings.

"It's Zade DeVil," I hear Hartley respond, prompting me to follow their voices through the home. "He knows."

"He knows?" she responds, a slight hint of panic creeping into her tone. "That's . . . no. That's not possible."

"He was just at my home, holding a dagger to my sleeping wife," Hartley spits. "Believe me, he fucking knows."

"Shit," she says. "And you came straight here? How foolish could you be?"

"Relax. I waited before leaving. He drove off and I wasn't followed."

Fucking idiot. I certainly kept my distance at first, but after the first half hour, it became abundantly clear that he wasn't checking his surroundings.

Creeping closer toward what must be a formal dining room, I hear the subtle hint of pacing across the polished marble tiles. "What did he say to you?"

"He said I'm a fucking dead man, that's what," Hartley growls. "You promised me if I stood by you, you'd have my back. You'd protect me and my wife."

"That I did," she responds. "But how can I protect you when you're so foolish as to bring the Thorne girl into the mix? She's a liability, and you should have put a bullet through her head when I told you to. What else did Zade say? Does he know who you work for?"

"No," Hartley says. "I don't believe so."

"Right. Of course," she responds. "Had he known, he would have killed you right there in your home."

Damn fucking straight. It sounds like this woman is the only one who thinks clearly around here.

Moving through the manor, I reach the opening of the formal dining room, and as I peer in, I see Hartley across the room. His back is to me as he converses with the woman, both admiring her and cowering from her. She stands at the window, peering out into the night, and judging by the way her hands grip the window frame, she's not particularly having a great night.

She turns around and my world crumbles, that familiar face that's haunted my dreams since I was a boy staring straight back at me.

"Well. Hello, son," she says, fondness in her eyes. "I was wondering when you might be joining us." With that, she lifts a gun, aiming right between my eyes, and pulls the trigger.

CHAPTER 24

Zade

My father always said my mother was a cold-hearted bitch, but fuck, I could never have imagined that. Hell, I hadn't imagined anything because since I was a boy, I knew she was dead. Nikolai even confirmed it for me the night I spoke my vows and gave my intent to rise to power. He told me that my father had sacrificed her, that he had plunged his hand inside her ribcage, and that he stole that cold, black heart right out of her chest. But seeing as though she's right here staring down the barrel of a gun, I'm inclined to believe there was another woman on the chopping board that night.

The bullet hurtles toward me, and I fly out of there like a fucking bat out of hell, a million questions storming through my head. She wasn't taken from me, she fucking abandoned me, and now she wants my throne for herself.

I hear her enraged scream as the bullet plunges into the wall behind my head, but I'm too fucking fast. Now that she's missed, she'll never catch me, and something tells me she already knows. Hell, I wouldn't be surprised if she's watched over me my whole fucking life, learning my weaknesses, figuring out what makes me tick. I bet she saw this coming a mile away. She's fucking cold and calculating, just like me.

I always knew I was nothing like my father, but this right here. This is exactly what I would have done. Hell, I did. I slit my father's throat the first chance I had and took his crown for myself. Now my mother wants a piece of the pie, a piece I'm sure she truly believes that she deserves.

Fuck, it only makes me miss her more. But my mother died a long time ago, and that's exactly how she's going to stay.

My hand hovers over my gun, but I can't bring myself to actually grab it, knowing there are so many questions I need answered before I put her in the ground. If I were to end her now, I might never know how this came to be, and that's going to eat at me until my dying days.

Flying straight back out the way I came, I race toward my Bugatti as bullets rain down around me. I've never run from gunfire in my life, and to do so now feels so fucking wrong. Reaching my car, I dive through the door and shoot back down the street in seconds. In the rearview mirror, I see the moment she gives up the fight, knowing damn well she won't catch me.

I sit with my thoughts, unable to wrap my head around everything that just went down. Everything I knew to be true was nothing but complete bullshit. The woman I loved, who birthed me, just tried to kill me, and I don't doubt that this has everything to do with my father.

Everybody within Empire has their dark secrets, and this right here was my dad's. He never deserved to stand at the head of Empire. Hell, he didn't even complete his ritual.

I'm just outside the city limits when my hand dives for my phone. I've been contemplating going straight back to the penthouse and trying to forget that any of this happened, but I need answers, and I need them now. I'll never be able to relax without them.

The phone rings once before the call is answered. "You with Oakley?" I ask Cross.

"Describe *with?*" he questions.

I shake my head, knowing exactly what the asshole is doing. She's sleeping and he's creeping on her again, but I suppose it's not the worst thing he could do. I mean, fuck. He could be responsible for tearing her heart out of her goddamn chest. "You're fucked in the head, bro," I tell him. "Bring her down to Empire. I need to meet with Nikolai and it's the perfect time to test her loyalty to her father."

"Alright," he says. "Give me fifteen."

The phone goes dead, and I toss it over to the passenger seat as I fly right into the city and out the other end, following the old train lines until I pull up at an abandoned parking lot. It's barely been ten minutes, and Cross hasn't arrived yet, but he won't be long. There are multiple entrances to Empire throughout the city, many of them even well outside of the city limits and into neighboring towns, but Cross knows this is where I need him to meet me.

My mind is a fucking mess as I pace outside my Bugatti. I can barely think straight.

This bullshit with my mother has fucked with me in a way I wasn't prepared for. It makes me feel weak, pathetic. It makes me feel as though I'm not fucking ready to take the reins of this society, but it's all in my head. I've been ready for this for years, and the fact that I'm questioning myself only pisses me off.

Cross pulls up just a moment later, his matte black Lamborghini shooting through the parking lot and making my jaw clench. That Lamborghini is fucking beautiful, and once upon a time, it used to be mine, until I lost it in a fucking bet and had to hand him the keys. Who fucking knew that Cross had such big balls? I'll never play Russian Roulette with the bastard again.

Cross pulls up right beside me, his window down as he stares out at me with apprehension. "You good?" he questions, reading me like a fucking book.

I shake my head. "We'll talk when I get back."

Cross nods and with that, Oakley bails out of the Lamborghini before Cross takes off like fucking lightning, leaving me staring at the girl who's been sending my world into chaos. Only now, meeting her pissed-off stare, the cloudiness begins to fade from my mind and suddenly everything comes back into perspective, making it easier to breathe again.

Oakley stares back at me, her brow arched as her hands fly out wide, clearly not too pleased to be here. "What the fuck, Zade? I was sleeping."

My lips press into a hard line. As hard as her attitude usually gets me, I'm not in the mood for it tonight. "Let's go."

I start walking toward the entrance of the train tunnel, and with her only other choice to remain out here in the dark by herself, Oakley scurries after me, huffing and puffing with every fucking step. "What the hell is going on?" she questions as we approach the external door, and I pull the big brass key from my pocket.

"I need to speak with Nikolai, and I figured what better opportunity to spend some quality time with you, too."

She gives me a blank stare, clearly not appreciating my bullshit quite as much as I do. "The only thing you like to spend quality time with is your hand," she throws back at me, and I can't lie, she's not wrong. The number of mornings I've woken up with wood after having her ass grinding back against me through the night is messed up. But I'm not about to admit that.

Opening the big, metal door, I go to walk through, only to notice Oakley hesitating out in the cold tunnel. "What?"

"The last time I walked in there willingly, I got knocked out and tied up by the very man you're here to see," she explains, a real fear hidden behind her eyes. "The next time I was in there, I was locked in a prison cell and thought I was going to die down there."

"And both times I've been there to save your ass, Lamb," I remind her, heavily focusing on those blazing blue eyes, only to scold myself for paying so much attention. "Do you really think I'd get this far just to let something happen to you now?"

She lets out a heavy breath before finally stepping in after me, though I can tell she's not comfortable here. She sticks right to me, her hand snaking out in the dark and latching onto my belt loops as if being close will save her. "Do you get just how fucked up it is to say things like *I'll never let anything happen to you* while knowing you'll be the one responsible for killing me?"

"Trust me," I mutter darkly, "the irony isn't lost on me."

We reach the next gate, and I stop to put in my security code. Oakley's hands start to shake and my fingers flinch at my side. The need to reach out and hold her pulses strongly through my veins, but I don't dare. The wires are already getting too crossed between us. I can't afford to muddy the waters more than they already are.

We get through the main entrance and to the bar, and I pause in the entryway, quickly scanning the crowd around us, making sure there's no one here who's going to try and put a bullet between Oakley's eyes. With the coast clear, we push through the bar and slip into the twisted world of Empire, trailing through the long tunnels and winding our way toward the lonely prison at the bottom.

The further we get, the closer Oakley stands to me, her whole body cold and shaking, proving just how badly this fucked-up place has already messed with her. Shit, she was barely down here for twelve hours. "Zade?"

"What?"

"You're going to have to distract me before I end up shitting my pants in the middle of this tunnel."

My brow arches and I glance back at her to see just how serious she is. I let out a heavy sigh and let her have it, determined to not have to be the one to deal with that. "Tonight I followed Hartley Scott out to the countryside and he led me right to the person who's been behind all of this shit."

"What?" she breathes, stopping in the middle of the tunnel and tugging on my belt loop to bring me to a stop. I look back at her, those wide eyes staring straight into mine. "This is huge. Why haven't you said anything?"

Looking into her stare, I find I simply can't lie to her anymore. "It was my mother."

Her face falls, horror flashing in her wild stare. "What?"

Pressing my lips into a hard line, I nod and continue down the tunnel, not able to have this conversation while she's staring so intently into my eyes. "My mother died a long time ago. I was only a kid, but she was the one good thing I had. My father had already started his training to mold me in his image, and my mother was my escape. She advocated for me when I couldn't do it for myself, and sometimes it worked, but other times, she'd end up black and blue on the bathroom floor. When she died, I died right along with her and became this . . . this ghost of the person I once was."

"I don't understand," Oakley whispers. "If she's dead, then who did you see?"

Her question is like taking a bullet straight to the chest. "The night I made my vow to rise as the next leader of Empire and was made aware of what I would have to sacrifice, Nikolai told me that my father had gone through the same thing. That he had sacrificed my mother for the ritual. However, that couldn't be true when I just saw her out in the countryside, living it up in a fucking mansion."

Oakley gapes at me. "So who the hell did your father sacrifice?"

"That's a good fucking question."

Oakley falls silent, lost in her thoughts as we make our way right down to the bottom of the tunnels—the main entrance to Empire's prison system. I hold my breath, waiting to find Harrison, knowing damn well he's not about to let me pass for a second time. Especially not after how the last time went down. Only, he's nowhere to be found.

Pulling out my master key, I unlock the heavy gate and cringe as the loud squeal of the hinges echoes right back up through the long tunnels, and no doubt the prison cells ahead. "You good?" I murmur, needing Oakley to not pass out right now.

"Fine."

With that, we make our way down the old, rickety stairs, and I lead her through the maze of cells before finally approaching who I believe to be her father. I stop and turn back to Oakley, making a point not to glance at Matthias's cell as to not give anything away. "Just wait here," I tell her. "I need to speak with Nikolai in private."

Her eyes widen as if terrified of being left alone, but she doesn't hesitate to agree, studiously keeping her eyes locked on mine as if forcing herself to refrain from glancing at her father. I nod and turn back around, following the dark hallway until I finally find Nikolai, looking disheveled and broken in his stiff, dirty bed.

I step right up to his cell as I spare a glance back at Oakley, watching how she makes a show of ignoring her father, though even in this darkness, I can see his hands gripping the bars, trying to get as close to her as possible.

Knowing there's not a damn thing he can say to her right now that will change the outcome of her fate, I turn my attention to the cell before me. "Nik," I say, trying to keep a level tone to not startle him from his sleep.

His eyes peel open, and he peers at me through the darkness. "That you, DeVil?"

"Yes."

Nikolai clambers out of bed, sitting up and putting his feet on the cold ground, needing a moment to find his bearings before pushing up to his feet. "How's my boy?"

"It's not your boy you need to worry about," I tell him. "Cara's lucky she's not in here sharing your cell. She's been working with Hartley Scott to move against me."

"What?" Nikolai spits, his eyes wide. "No, that couldn't be right. Cara would never."

"I suppose the apple never falls far from the tree," I tell him. "We caught her red-handed."

"Shit," he mutters, starting to pace his cell, suddenly not so tired. "What has Sawyer been doing? I told him to look out for her, and now she's gone and gotten herself into trouble. What's going to happen to her?"

I shake my head, not having an answer for him. "She seems remorseful. It started out of necessity. She was given an impossible choice and she chose family over friendship. You should be proud."

He narrows his gaze at me. "Why do I sense a *but* coming along?"

"She's foolish, Nik. You raised her to be your pretty little princess, giving her the impression that this world can't hurt her because you would always have her back. But what now? She directly betrayed the blood, and then she continued to do so after the threat had passed. I have no immediate plans to deal with her, but she will not escape this unpunished. There's still so much else that requires my attention. However, despite how Sawyer feels about me right now, he's one of my closest friends, and I can't take his sister from him. Especially so soon after losing you. They will have each other to get them through this, but Cara needs to check herself. One wrong move and I won't hesitate to eliminate her."

Nikolai nods. "Thank you, Zade. I do not know how to repay you. Please speak with Sawyer. Make sure he knows to keep his sister in line."

"I will," I say, quickly glancing up at Oakley to see that she's inched forward toward her father's cell, her gaze locked on his, failing my test. "However, that is not the reason for my visit."

"Oh?" Nikolai says, his brows furrowed.

I nod. "The night of my initiation, after I spoke my vows, you mentioned that at the time of my father's ritual, he had sacrificed my mother."

"Yes, I remember."

"And you are certain about that?"

He looks at me as though I've lost my mind before gripping the bars and moving in closer. "What the hell is going on, Zade?" he demands, not liking being left in the dark.

"My father did not sacrifice my mother," I inform him. "Because only two hours ago, she stood right before me with her gun trained between my eyes."

Nikolai's eyes go wide, falling back a step and releasing the bars. "No," he breathes in horror. "No, that can't be true. I saw it with my own eyes. I felt her fear as she screamed for mercy. She died right before my eyes, Zade."

I shake my head. "Then my father fooled you."

He stares at me in disbelief, falling back another step until he's sitting on the edge of his dirty bed. "Sitting down here in this cell day in and day out, I've had a lot of time to think. The more I go over it, the more I realize what a fraud your father was. He didn't just fool us, boy. He was fooling himself."

Clenching my jaw, I nod, never having agreed more. "I don't wish to rule like my father, Nikolai. I know you believe me to be too young and inexperienced. However, I can assure you I am ready."

"I see that now, Zade. And I hope that one day, you will be able to find it within yourself to forgive my sins, against both you and Oakley Quinn."

"Do you truly wish for me to rise in power?" I ask, my gaze shifting back up the corridor to where Oakley now stands almost directly in front of her father's cell.

Nikolai nods and meets my heavy stare. "Of course I do."

I shoot a pointed stare up toward Matthias's cell before locking my stare back to Nikolai's, my brow arching with accusation. Moving closer, I lower my tone, making sure I won't be overheard. "Then perhaps it just slipped your mind to tell me that Matthias Quinn is still very much alive."

His eyes widen just a fraction and he flies back to his feet, bracing his hands against the bars and locking onto my stare. "No, Zade. Surely you must know that had I known, I would have shared it with you. I am still trying to work out why your father would have spared him instead of burying him ten feet under. Matthias might have the blood and be the natural heir, but he is no leader. I didn't know he lived until I was thrown in here myself."

I hold his stare a moment longer before seeing the agonizing truth within his eyes. "Okay, Nik. I believe you," I tell him, "and I'll be sure to note your willingness to help during your trial."

He shakes his head. "No, don't try to give me false hope. I will be executed. Just please . . . make sure my boy knows I love him. I never told him that enough."

I give Nik a tight smile, knowing this may very well be the last time I see him before he's executed. "He knows," I tell him. "Cara too."

CHAPTER 25

Oakley

Standing across from my father and not being able to save him or even throw my arms around him is the most excruciating thing I've ever lived through, but I can't risk letting Zade know who he is. If he knew that my father still lived, he wouldn't hesitate to kill him, and he might very well be my only way out.

Even after all these years, my father still considers himself the rightful leader of Empire, and even if I'm somehow able to save him, I don't doubt that he would try to challenge Zade for it. But that can't happen. Zade is a brutal monster. He's callous and cold and would slaughter him with ease. On the other hand, if my father were able to rise in power, then Zade would forfeit his claim and my life . . . fuck, I'd be free.

Unable to resist, I inch toward my father, my innocent childhood heart still so desperate to have him hold me. Those horrid twelve hours in the cell across from him weren't nearly enough, but goddamn, they helped to revive something deep within me. His face gave me hope, and now I want to help restore that same hope within him.

"What the hell were you thinking coming down here?" my father berates, his tone so low I can barely hear it. "With him of all people. I told you to run."

"I'm not a child anymore, Father," I hiss, keeping my eye on Zade, making sure he can't overhear our conversation as he speaks privately with Nikolai. "I make my own decisions, and I am not running from this. I'm not going to let you suffer down here. I'm working on a plan. I just need some time. I'm going to get you out of here."

"Don't be a fool, Oakley. You can't save me. Just get out of here and run. Empire will slaughter you, and if that were to happen . . ."

He searches for the words, but I see it right there in his eyes. I'm his whole world. His little girl. He's spent years loving me from inside this filthy cell while I have lived a happy life, far away from this sinister world, and now my time has come to make it right. "I'm not going to abandon you," I promise him just as Zade turns around and starts making his way back toward me, his eyes locked heavily on mine. "Shit, he's coming."

My father immediately falls back into his cell, hidden within the darkness as Zade strides toward me. "Did you say something?"

"No," I say, shaking my head and trying to hide the thick emotion in my tone. "Did you get everything you needed?"

Zade's lips kick up into a wicked grin as he reaches me. "I sure did," he says, his gaze shifting to my father's cell and peering in. He meets his broken stare, and the tension in the prison grows, sending waves of shivers sailing over my skin. Zade doesn't look away, just lets his silence speak volumes as fear rocks through my veins.

What did Nikolai tell him? Does he know?

Panic tears at me when Zade looks back at me. "What are you waiting for? Let's go."

Without a second of hesitation, I turn on my heel, my gaze flashing to my father's for just a moment before I hastily hurry back up toward the old, rickety steps. Zade walks behind me, his long strides pushing me faster as the tension quickly builds between us.

We hit the stairs, and I hurry up them before slipping through the gate at the top. Zade doesn't bother to stop and lock up, just keeps pushing me along, not wanting to spend another moment down here than what's necessary.

"This way," he says when we reach a fork in the tunnel, guiding me toward the left, the old lanterns becoming more spaced out and making it nearly impossible to see. We pass by the place Dalton and Easton snapped those men's necks, and a shiver sails down my spine, unease blasting through me.

The tunnels start inching up on an incline, and it gets a little easier to breathe when Zade's arm brushes past mine, the electricity burning between us. The tension is like nothing I've ever known as I wait for him to tear me apart, to tell me he knows I lied, and when he grabs my hand and pulls me back, shoving me up against the wall of the tunnel,

I prepare for the worst.

Zade clenches his teeth, his hand locking around my jaw as he steps in, fury burning in his eyes. Then just as I wait for the onslaught of threats, his lips come crushing down on mine in a bruising kiss. My body turns to liquid, melting in his strong arms, my eyes closing with pure satisfaction. His tongue plunges into my mouth, and I kiss him back, bracing my arms around his neck. When he tears away from me, gasping for air, all I can do is stare at him.

"FUCK," he roars, pacing up and down before me, his eyes flicking between me and the dirty ground, his hands at his temple.

Seconds pass and the silence becomes too much. I step out from the wall, forcing myself right in front of him, knowing damn well I won't be able to get his attention otherwise. My hands come up and shove hard against his chest, forcing him to stop pacing. "What the hell was that?" I demand, his lips still burning against mine, the taste so fucking delicious.

He shakes his head, anger pulsing through his stare. "I don't fucking know."

"You can't do that," I hiss. "You can't just kiss me and shrug it off with no explanation. You're going to kill me, Zade. Literally. You're going to literally kill me." I shove him hard in the chest again, feeling hot tears pooling in my eyes, the overwhelming emotion too much for me to handle. "You're confusing me. I don't want to be with you. I don't want to fall for you, but every fucking night you hold me against your chest with your arms around me, it feels so damn good. You're so fucking hard to resist. The only thing keeping me from wanting you is the fact that you despise me. I need you to despise me, Zade. You can't want me like this."

He clenches his jaw, so fucking angry with himself, but he doesn't dare move. He just stares back at me, his hands balled into tight fists at his side as if to keep himself from reaching out for me again.

I shake my head, seeing a fierce desire starting to overshadow the anger. "You can't do this, Zade. Don't make me fall for you because I won't survive this. You're going to fuck this all up, and then you're going to break me."

He inches toward me, and I take a hasty step back, the overwhelming need to throw myself at him quickly fading. He steps toward me again, but this time, I don't move. I'm so captivated by his deadly stare. I need him. I need every damn part of him.

His hand shoots up, clutching the back of my neck before pushing me up against the wall again, his body pressed firmly against mine. "Too fucking late." And with that, his lips slam back to mine, devouring every inch of me and claiming my mouth as his own.

My legs circle his hips, and he presses into me, grinding that thick cock against my pussy as my arms twine around his neck, holding on so fucking tight, desperate to keep him closer.

His tongue sweeps through my mouth, his hands roaming over my body as though he can't get enough. It's a torturous game, our lips fighting for dominance, but where Zade DeVil is concerned, there's only ever been one boss.

He kisses me like I'll never be kissed again, and my eyes flutter, wishing he would strip me bare and take me right here in this filthy tunnel. Then just like the first time, he pulls away, leaving us both gasping for air. Only he stays right here, his body up against mine as his forehead tips forward, both of us trying to work out what the fuck is happening here.

My hands slowly fall from around his neck, sliding down over his shoulders and finding purchase against his chest, feeling just how quickly his heart beats beneath my palm. "You can't do that again," I breathe, terrified of what happens from here, and hating myself for liking that so much. "I don't want you."

His tongue rolls over his bottom lip, and my eyes gently roll, having such a small taste and knowing it can only get better. "You're a liar, Oakley," he rumbles. "You want me more than you know. You just wish you didn't."

And with that, he pulls back, releasing his delicious hold and turning away. He starts walking up the long tunnel, and all I can do is gape at his back, my heart racing wildly in my chest.

CHAPTER 26

Oakley

Giddiness blooms through my chest as I sneak across the penthouse, my gaze locked on Sawyer as Dalton's remains locked on my ass. I have eighteen days to live, and Dalton has made it his mission to ensure I enjoy every last one of them.

Easton's busy in the kitchen while Zade is doing everything in his power to pretend he didn't give me the most breathtaking kiss I've ever received in my life, and I'm damn sure he's trying to pretend he didn't like it either. But if he's happy to ignore it, then hell, so am I. The last thing I need is for things to get complicated between me and Zade.

Where he's concerned, I need there to be a big, solid line between us—something that's so big it's impossible to cross. I thought there was, and yet Zade fucking DeVil found a way to tear it down. The bastard practically shit all over my line. He's killing me in eighteen days. Butchering me. I can't fall for him. I need to hate him, need to spend my night dreaming about how good it would feel to take a knife and slit his throat to earn my freedom. Except for last night, I was dreaming about how good it would feel to ride his cock like a fucking cowgirl. But then that quickly turned to me wondering how good it would be if all four of the guys took me at once. Naturally, that's when Dalton came storming in and woke me up. I could have murdered the bastard.

Zade didn't talk to me the whole drive back to the penthouse, and he sure as fuck didn't say a word as we were locked into the tension-filled elevator. When we got into bed, he made a point not to hold me, and I came to the conclusion that Zade DeVil and I can never be left alone again.

Putting it to the back of my mind, I keep sneaking through the big apartment, trying to keep quiet as I lock Sawyer in my sight. My back slides along the wall, and I'm all too aware of just how loud I am. Hell, I can practically feel Dalton rolling his eyes.

"Whatever the fuck you're trying to do," Sawyer says from the couch. "I can see you. You're like a fucking elephant trying to tiptoe across a frozen pond, only the ice is breaking under your feet, and you are scrambling to keep your head above water."

My jaw drops, and I step away from the wall, gaping at Sawyer. "You did not just call me a fucking elephant."

He shakes his head. "You're right. I called you a clueless, scrambling elephant."

"You're an ass," I tell him, hating how down he's been since his sister was caught and shoved into Zade's fucked-up little prison cell yesterday. "But you're lucky you're cute."

Sawyer rolls his eyes as my gaze cuts to Dalton. A grin tears across his face, and he subtly nods, more than ready to put my training into practice. "So, ummm . . . Dalton taught me a magic trick," I tell him, waving my hands around like some kind of magician. "Wanna see?"

Sawyer's gaze cuts across to Dalton, his brows furrowing as he tries to work out what the hell we're up to. "Alright," he says slowly, turning his stare back to me, the suspicion in his eyes so deep it's almost off-putting. "I'll bite. What's your trick?"

A sly grin stretches across my lips. "I can make you fall asleep."

Easton scoffs from the kitchen, Venom circling his fingers. "This I'd like to see," he mutters, clearly thinking I don't have a chance in hell to pull this off. As usual, these guys have become accustomed to underestimating me.

Sawyer grins back at me, opening his arms out wide, inviting me to give it my best shot. "Have at it, Doll."

"Okay, but solid warning," I say, more than playing it up. "Just because I know how to make you go to sleep, doesn't mean I can wake you up. So, I might very well be condemning you to a comatose life."

Sawyer scoffs. "I think I'll take the risk."

I wink. "Good choice."

With that, I hold out my hand. "Right this way, good sir," I say, getting a thrill as he places his hand in mine. He lets me pull him up off the couch, and I lead him across the room to the dining table, pulling out a chair for him and asking him to sit his mouth-watering ass down.

As he takes his seat, I catch Dalton's gaze again, and the sly grin across his face has me desperately looking away, knowing damn well I'll give it away before getting to have my fun. "Alright," I say, catching Sawyer's eyes. "Keep looking straight ahead and listen to the sound of my voice."

He gives the slightest chin lift, acknowledging my instructions while gracefully refraining from rolling his eyes at my bullshit. I start walking around him, clicking my fingers, and waving my arms like some kind of magician before finally coming to a stop right behind him.

I place my fingers against his face and gently drum them against his temple. "Okay, Sawyer. You need to relax your mind. Take a deep breath in and then out. Are you relaxed?"

"Mmhmm," he rumbles, sounding bored.

Then without warning, my arm locks around the base of his throat and I pull hard, blocking off his airway as I use my other hand to hold my arm in place and pull tighter, his stupid muscly throat making it almost impossible. "Abracadabra, motherfucker!" I call as Dalton howls with laughter, shouting encouragement to pull harder and put my fucking back into it.

I give it my all, but Sawyer just sits there as though I'm not even touching him. "Really?" he mutters, clearly not impressed.

"Go to sleep," I grunt, almost out of breath. "I'm gonna make you my bitch."

Sawyer gives me another few seconds before letting out a heavy sigh and gripping my arm, then before I know what the fuck is happening, he stands up and flips me right over his shoulder. A loud shriek tears from the back of my throat before my back slams against the ground with Sawyer coming down over me, keeping me pinned with his big body. Both my wrists are locked in just one of his hands and braced above my head. His knee is jammed between my legs, shoved right up against my pussy, but it's his face right there in front of mine that has me gasping for air.

Sawyer holds my stare as my eyes widen, still trying to process how the fuck that just happened. I could have sworn I had that one in the bag. "Next time you let Dalton teach you something like that, make sure it's not so fucking predictable. Or at least do a few push-ups first. Doll, you need some muscle before you go and try to choke someone out."

I give him a blank stare before a grin pulls at my lips. "Made you smile though, right?"

Sawyer holds my stare, not a smile in sight, but the longer he looks at me, the harder he fights against it. And sure enough, a smile starts pulling at the corners of his lips before turning into a full-blown grin. He rolls his eyes and shakes his head but refuses to release me. "You're a fucking idiot."

I shrug my shoulders as a brilliant warmth spreads through my chest. "Maybe," I whisper, raising my chin just enough to let my lips gently brush over his. "But I'm an idiot who can't stand to see you looking so down."

Something softens in his eyes before he dips his head lower, kissing me properly. I melt into him as his other hand brushes down my body and grabs a handful of ass.

His kiss becomes hungrier, desperate, and I match his urgency, more than ready to take him right here on the ground. If any of his friends feel the need to join, then I'm down for that too.

"Wow," Zade grunts, his tone the biggest mood killer known to man. "You're really gonna fuck her right there while your sister is held prisoner twenty feet away. Fuck, Sawyer. I knew you were a savage, but I had no idea you were this cold."

Sawyer's head pulls up, leaving me high and dry, and he lets out a heavy sigh. He gets to his feet before pulling me up with him and fixing a heavy stare on Zade. "She's not a fucking prisoner," he reminds him, something he's been saying since the moment she got here. "She's just chilling out in there, staying away from the bullshit until the ritual passes."

"Right," Zade says, playing on his guilt. "You've been locked in that cell a time or two. Tell me, did it feel like you were just chilling out?"

A chill sails over my body, remembering the time I was held hostage in that room, and while Cara isn't being detained in the same way I was—drugged and bound—it's still not somewhere I'd like to spend multiple hours at a time.

"Fuck off, man," Sawyer grunts, dropping back onto the couch, his gaze locked on the cell's hidden door. "She's only here so we can keep an eye on her, make sure she's not mixing with the wrong crowd again. Besides, she's got her Kindle in there. She'll be okay."

I scoff. "Right, because her Kindle battery life is really going to last that long."

Sawyer glances up at me with his brows furrowed as if he did not even consider that, and honestly, I'm surprised. He usually thinks everything through.

Letting out a soft sigh, I drop down on the coffee table, meeting Sawyer's guilt-ridden stare, hating how broken he is. "It's alright not to be okay with this. Cara fucked up, and she needs to be held accountable for that," I say before turning my gaze on the ultimate cock blocker. "But . . . is she really a prisoner, though? Does she have to be locked in there?"

Zade's brows furrow. "What are you getting at?"

"I just mean, if she's not technically a prisoner and you only have her here to keep an eye on her, then why can't you shove her in one of your spare bedrooms? You have about a million of them. Does she really need to be locked up like that? Like you were saying, it's not particularly comfortable in there. You could just put her in a spare bedroom and install a lock on the outside of the door so she can't slip out while you're not watching. That way she'll at least have a bed and a bathroom and will be able to feel somewhat human over the next eighteen days." I explain, feeling as though I need to justify myself. "Don't get me wrong, I'm furious with her. I should be the last person trying to advocate for her right now, but that's a long time to keep her locked up like that. Especially when you're not going to kill her."

All eyes fall on Zade, and I watch as his face scrunches, clearly not having considered the comfort of his hostages. Everyone seems to hold their breath, waiting for his response when he finally shrugs his shoulders. "I guess that'll be alright," he says as Sawyer springs off the couch. "Just don't put her anywhere near my room. I don't wanna hear her banging on the door and screaming about how much she fucking hates me for hours on end."

Sawyer gets a few steps away, a newfound liveliness flashing in his eyes before flipping back around and rushing into me, gripping my shoulders and crushing his lips to mine. "You're fucking amazing," he tells me, his eyes beaming with happiness as he takes off at a sprint across the penthouse, through the kitchen, and opens the hidden door.

He quickly hashes in the code before moving through to the steel door that goes directly into the cell. Easton and Dalton trail down the hallway, probably to go get a room set up for Cara—all sharp objects removed and the door lockable from the outside.

I can't help but watch through the open cell door as Sawyer walks in and lets Cara know what's going on. She starts to cry, begging him to let her go, and it only gets worse when he grips her arm and starts leading her out of the cells. Her gaze falls to mine, guilt soaring through her eyes before turning her stare on Zade. There's heartbreak there, but also a lot of anger. On the other hand, Zade just looks at her like a piece of gum stuck to the bottom of his shoe.

It's all too much. I have to look away.

As Sawyer leads her down the hallway and toward her new luxury prison cell, I find myself staring at the empty couch beside Zade's.

"You shouldn't do that," he murmurs when we're finally left alone.

My brows furrow, and I glance up to meet his stare. "Do what?"

"You're allowing them to get too close," he says. "You should do them a kindness and keep them at arm's length. They're all getting attached, and when you . . . ya know, it's gonna kill them."

My brow arches. "That's rich coming from the guy who threw me up against the wall of the tunnels last night."

"We're not talking about you and me. This is about them."

"Sounds like you're trying to find a reason to keep me all to yourself."

Zade scoffs. "You think too highly of yourself," he says. "I couldn't give a shit who you fuck, but you're allowing them to get emotionally involved. It's no longer just physical, and that poses a problem."

"For you maybe," I tell him. "I enjoy their company, and I know this is a strange concept for you, but I like them, and it's not just because they know how to get me off just right. They're amazing guys, and I have a connection with each of them that I haven't felt with anyone before. I'm not going to stop getting to know them. I don't *want* to stop. Besides, you're the one who's taking my life, so really, it sounds like a *you* problem. I'll be dead and gone, and that leaves only you to deal with the fallout of your own actions. That's not on me, Zade."

"Come on, Lamb," he says, leaning forward and bracing his elbows against his knees. "You can't think about it that way. Yes, I will have fallout from each of them when you're gone, and that's something I'm going to have to deal with, but what about them? It's the same as what you said to me yesterday. You asked me not to kiss you because you didn't want to fall for me, and that's valid. But you're doing to them, exactly what you asked me not to do to you. If you allow them to fall for you, they're going to be the ones left broken and picking up the pieces."

A heaviness settles into my chest, and I realize just how right he is. I've been so busy considering how I feel about this, that I haven't considered what I'll be leaving behind. My brows furrow, and I glance up at Zade, meeting his haunted stare. "Does it make me a monster if I want them to love me?" I ask in a small voice.

He shakes his head, something I'm not quite sure of flashing in his eyes. "I think that makes you human."

Something shatters in my chest, and despite everything that's happened since moving back to Faders Bay, I've never felt so broken. Not when I was locked up in Zade's cell, not when I was running for my life, and not even when I was thrown in Empire's prison. The thought of breaking their hearts destroys me, but that's exactly what's going to happen.

I can't keep away from them. Not now. I'm in too deep. Perhaps I'm selfish. Perhaps I am a monster—forgive me if I'm wrong here—but Zade was the one who put these men in my life. Zade is the one who's taking me away from them. Not to mention they all know what's going down in eighteen days, yet they've each allowed themselves to get close.

This isn't on me, and Zade DeVil does not get to make me feel guilty over the fact that he's ending my life for his own sick ambitions. It's not as though I'm being taken from them by some fucked-up incurable disease. Zade is physically taking my life, so he doesn't get to put the weight on my shoulders. This is his burden to bear.

Besides, the way I see it, he told me last night that his mother never perished during the ritual. She got to live a long and—maybe—happy life, while Zade's father got everything he wanted. So why the hell isn't Zade getting off his ass and figuring out how the fuck his father did it? Hell, as for the boys, as far as I'm aware, Dalton is the only one who's actively trying to find a way to save me. Perhaps Sawyer and Easton deserve to get their hearts torn to shreds.

Standing up, I stride across to Zade, shoving my hand into his shoulder and forcing his back against the couch. My knee presses down against the cushion, and I lower myself to straddle his lap. Those dark, venomous eyes cloud with apprehension, but I ignore them as I circle my arms around his neck.

I suck in a breath, my chest rising to press against his, and despite his resolve, his hands fall to my waist. Leaning in, my lips hover just a breath before his, and I lower my tone to the softest whisper. "You're a small, broken man, Zade DeVil," I tell him. "Even your father, as shallow and weak as he was, could find a way to spare your mother's life, and yet day in and day out, you sit here with the resolve to follow through with this bullshit ritual. You're a sheep falling in line and following orders like a good little boy, and yet I thought you wanted to be a leader." I pause a second, watching as he swallows hard, soaking in every word like a fucking sponge. "You don't get to put your guilt on my shoulders. You're taking my life for your own benefit and have the audacity to sit here across from me and tell me that it's my fault the boys will end up with broken hearts. Absolutely not. If they're going to stand by and twiddle their thumbs while their best friend kills the woman they're falling for, then how the hell is that my fault?"

I push off him and stand in front of the couch, staring down at him to see nothing but a hollow brokenness in his eyes. "Be the fucking man I know you can be, Zade. Be a true leader and put an end to this bullshit. Hell, just be a good goddamn friend. The ball is in your court, but remember, what you do with it defines the kind of man and the kind of leader you will be. Right now, all I see is a weak little boy."

And with that, I walk away, hoping that just this once, he feels as small as what he makes me feel.

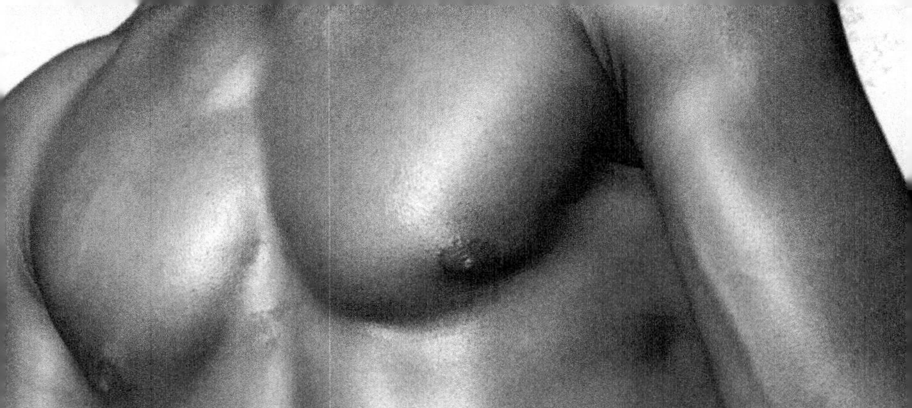

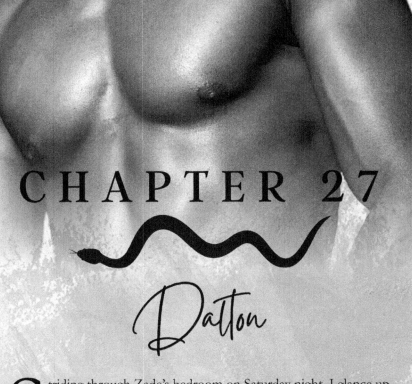

CHAPTER 27

Dalton

Striding through Zade's bedroom on Saturday night, I glance up at his freshly painted walls to the new tally Oakley's been using to keep track of her remaining days. Every time I see it or watch as she removes another strike, a part of me dies.

Fifteen days to go.

Zade was right. I should never have allowed myself to get so fucking attached to her. He warned me, and I shrugged it off. I didn't know that she would capture me so completely. This was supposed to be a little fun before Zade took her away, but it's become so much more than that. And now the thought of what's going to happen to her, the brutality of it all … fuck. It makes me want to tear Zade's heart right out of his fucking chest, but how could I when he's never possessed one?

Shit. That's not fair. This isn't on him. This is on The Circle. They knew exactly what they were doing when they offered up Oakley's name, and up until now, I've never had a reason to question them. I've always been taught to follow blindly, but now that it's my girl on the chopping block, I can't be their perfect little soldier.

Making my way over to the bathroom door, I prop my shoulder against the frame and peer in at Oakley as she goes step by step through her skincare routine, smiling at me through the mirror when she finally notices me. "What the hell are you doing? Why do you need so many things?" I ask, stepping through the open door just a little and glancing over the array of products she asked Benny to track down for her today.

A smirk plays on her lips, and I prepare myself for whatever bullshit is about to come flying out of that enticing mouth. "I'm a walking thirst trap, Dalton," she says, stating it as though it's a cold, hard fact. She's not wrong, though. "This shit doesn't come naturally."

Bullshit. Every ounce of her beauty is all natural.

She leans closer to the mirror, making a face as she massages the lotion into her skin, but all I can think about is how much it looks like cum. Fuck, that's got my thoughts stuck on giving her one hell of a pearl necklace.

"Men drool when they see me," she continues, not noticing my brief moment of distraction. "You know why, Dalton? Because my skin is so hydrated. It reminds them that they're thirsty."

A wide grin stretches across my face and I can't help but laugh, even more so when she meets my gaze through the mirror and her resolve breaks. Her straight face cracks into the most breathtaking smile as she laughs right along with me.

Fuck, how could anyone harm her?

"Alright, my little walking thirst trap," I say. "Do you wanna get out of here for a few hours?"

Her brow arches and her smile quickly falls away as she gapes at me. "Huh?" she grunts. "What do you mean *get out of here for a few hours?* Has this been cleared by Bossman, or are we making a break for it?" She pauses just a moment as her eyes widen with excitement. "Please, God, tell me we're making a break for it."

"Chill out, Houdini," I laugh. "We're just going for a ride. And yes, before you get ahead of yourself, I got the all-clear from Zade. He knows exactly where you'll be at all times."

Her face falls again. "Fine," she says, almost breaking my heart at the thought of there not being some elaborate escape in her near future, but it's not as though she's about to deny a chance to get out of here. She glances down at Easton's oversized shirt that hangs down to her knees. "Maybe I should change."

I go to agree before thinking better of it. "Nah, no point. Just come like that."

She arches a brow, confused about where I could possibly take her where she won't need to get dressed. But it's just going to be the two of us, riding through the streets of Faders Bay with the wind in her hair, free as a fucking bird. All she needs is herself . . . and possibly a helmet.

After she finishes up in the bathroom, she grabs a pair of runners and pulls on a leather jacket. Her hand falls into mine, and without wasting another moment, we break free of this penthouse prison. Once we hit the private garage, we find Candice, my Harley, waiting patiently for the ride of her life.

Not a single word comes out of my mouth, but Oakley must see it in my stare. "Fuck, if you're about to cum in your pants, give a girl a little warning."

Rolling my eyes, I spank her ass as she passes me and nods toward my bike. "Get on before I make you room with Cara tonight."

Her eyes go wide as she gapes at me in horror, her hand braced against the seat of my bike as she goes to fling her leg over it, pausing mid-air. "You wouldn't," she breathes, having the misfortune of looking like a dog about to piss on a fire hydrant in that position. "She'd kill me in my sleep."

"I'm about to kill you if you don't stop trying to mount my fucking bike," I laugh. "For fuck's sake, and you're the one telling me that I'm about to cum in my pants."

"Yeah, well unlike you, I'm not wearing any pants."

A wide grin stretches across my face, and my cock flinches, coming alive and reminding me that I haven't buried it into her sweet pussy since this morning.

Rolling her eyes, she climbs on the back of my bike and balances herself, her tiptoes barely touching the ground as I reach for the helmet, but she shakes her head. "Do you plan on having an accident tonight?"

"No," I say, "But—"

"Then I'm not wearing it."

"Don't be stupid."

"I'm not sure if you've noticed," she says. "But I don't have great options in life, and if I can somehow manage to take myself out in a more humane way than having my heart ripped out of my chest, then I will."

I shake my head and shove the helmet over her head as she sighs. "Not on my watch." Then just to rub salt in the wound, I make a show of bopping the top of her head before straddling my bike.

Oakley's hands immediately fall to my waist as the Harley roars to life, the loud engine rumbling through the underground garage. I hit the gas and break out onto the roads of Faders Bay with Oakley's arms circled around me, her body pressed right up against my back.

The wind whips back through her hair, and I feel as her body truly starts to relax for the first time in weeks, leaving all the bullshit back inside the penthouse.

I weave through the backstreets of the city for over an hour, going out past the city limits and right back across town. She doesn't say a word, just rides with me, taking in the scenery and getting lost in her thoughts.

We pull up at a red light, and I reach back, my fingers brushing over her bare thigh. "What's up?"

Her lips press into a hard line as sadness creeps into her eyes. "I don't want you to fall for me, Dalton," she murmurs, her voice barely audible over the sound of the roaring engine. "You're too good. And when Zade . . . it's going to break you."

A heaviness settles into my chest, and I reach back, gripping her waist before pulling her around me, settling her over my thighs. Gripping the helmet, I pull it off her head so I can see her properly, desperately needing those blue eyes on mine. "It's too fucking late for that," I tell her. "The moment you looked at me that first night outside the college apartment complex, I was a fucking goner. I could have pulled away from you then. I knew the consequences of getting involved with you, but I did it anyway."

Oakley lets out a heavy sigh, her eyes roaming over my face, tears welling in her eyes. "Don't say it, Dalton."

I shake my head, not understanding how I possibly couldn't. "I'm in love with you, Oakley. Every fucking piece of me belongs to you."

The tears fall from her eyes and she looks at me so fucking broken. "You can't," she breathes, her voice breaking. "I'm going to die. He's going to tear my heart right out of my chest and you'll be left with nothing."

I shake my head, my hands gripping her waist and holding her tighter. "Not if I can help it," I tell her. "Some way, somehow, I'm going to save you from that ritual, Firefly. Whether it's a loophole or if I have to physically stand against Zade. I'm not going to allow your heart to stop beating."

"You can't stand against Zade," she whispers. "No one can stand against him."

"I can and I fucking will," I tell her, "and if I go down trying, then we go down together."

Her tears fall more forcefully, and she locks her arm around my neck, her lips barely a breath away. "I'm not ready to die."

My lips crush against hers, kissing her deeply as her words rock through my body, shattering what little soul I possess. Her kiss becomes hungry and desperate, and I give her exactly what she needs, even when she reaches down between us and frees my cock from the confines of my pants.

I'm already fucking hard, my cock straining for her touch, and as she moves her fist up and down in the dark, deserted street, I have to have her, and I don't have a fucking second to waste.

My arm locks around her waist, lifting her just enough to guide my cock to her entrance, more than happy for her decision to walk out of the penthouse without any fucking underwear. Lowering her down onto me, she groans into my mouth as my cock stretches her sweet little pussy. I take her deep, and as usual, she waits just a moment, getting used to my intrusion before finally moving up and down, bracing her arms around my neck to give her leverage.

She grinds and moves, not bothered by the fact that the red light has turned green and we're stopped in the middle of the street, the loud rumble of the bike probably drawing attention from all around. All that matters at this moment is being one.

Oakley clenches around me, and my eyes flutter, the satisfaction so fucking strong. I go to grip her ass, more than ready to take this to the next level, when she gasps, her eyes going wide over my shoulder. "Oh, shit," she breathes. "Someone's coming."

Sparing a glance in my side mirror, I see a black SUV slowly coming this way and I sigh, hating to disrupt our moment. Oakley braces against my shoulder and tries to pull away, but I hold onto her tighter, refusing to let her move. "Don't even think about it," I tell her, reaching around her with my other arm to take hold of the throttle. "Hold on."

I take off and she squeals, gripping onto me with everything she's got as we leave the black SUV behind. She laughs and grins at me, hair flying around her face, but she doesn't dare stop riding me. "Holy shit," she beams, yelling over the rumble of the bike. "This is insane."

Fucking amazing is what it is. Just the thought of her fucking me while riding is making my cock strain painfully inside her, so fucking close to the edge.

She grinds against me, her pussy squeezing around my cock as she carefully leans to the side, not blocking my view of the road. She starts taking me harder and faster when I notice the black SUV follow us around the bend.

I watch it closely, not wanting to alarm Oakley. Running into other vehicles on the road is expected. Having them possibly make the same turn is a coincidence, but having them follow you when you have the most wanted chick in the city riding your cock . . . well, that just won't do.

Maintaining my speed, I take a left and then another, doubling back in the direction we just came while desperately trying not to come as I wait to see what the SUV does. Anyone minding their own business would continue on, but someone trying to tail us would follow me right around the bend.

"Oh God," my little Firefly moans, her face dropping into the crook of my neck as she rides my cock like a fucking queen, my whole body becoming putty in her hands.

She's so fucking wet for me, loving the extra thrill just as much as I do. Behind us, the SUV takes the left, and I fear that this is about to take a turn for the worst. "Firefly," I grunt, clenching my jaw as my cock jolts inside her.

Her head lifts from my neck, her eyes glassy with pure satisfaction, but meeting my eyes, she stops moving. "What is it?" she calls over the sound of the engine, whipping her head to the side to try and keep her hair from flying around her face.

"I need you not to panic and reach into my pocket." Her brows furrow, and I spare a glance into my side mirror, watching as the SUV's headlights appear through the darkness. "Get my phone and call Zade. Tell him we're being followed."

"WHAT?" Her eyes widen, looking over my shoulder to see the same SUV from the red light. Her whole body clenches, including her pussy, and I swear, she almost cuts off the circulation to my cock.

"Do it now, Firefly. And when you're done, I'm going to need you to reach for my gun."

"Fuck. Okay."

Oakley slips her hand into my pocket and quickly grabs my phone, but trying to unlock it with one hand isn't easy while flying through the streets with my cock still buried deep inside her. Her hair flies around both of our faces, obstructing my view of the road, but it's nothing I can't handle.

She finally gets the phone unlocked and hastily finds Zade's contact before shoving it against her ear as I take a right turn, sending us back in the direction of the penthouse. She shakes her head, her panicked stare flashing to mine. "I can't hear anything," she calls over the rumble of the bike.

"He'll answer," I promise.

She waits just a moment before her eyes widen a little further. "Zade?" she calls, her brows furrowed, not sure if she's actually hearing him. "Zade? Can you hear me?" She looks at me in a panic. "FUCK," she grunts before continuing anyway. "We're being followed by a black SUV."

Oakley pauses, straining to hear when we fly over a bump and the phone falls straight out of her hand, smashing into a million pieces on the road. "SHIT!"

"Don't worry," I tell her. "He's coming. Now, grab my gun. It's down by my right leg. There's a small compartment. You'll have to open the latch."

"Jesus fucking Christ," she mutters, gripping onto me with everything she's got as she claws her way down my body, her pussy twisting over my cock. I try to hold onto her as best I can, more than aware of what could happen if her hair were to get caught in the engine.

Oakley's fingers work the small latch, and before I know it, she's climbing her way back up with the gun in her hand. "Now what?" she says, wide-eyed.

"Your call," I tell her with a grin, enjoying this far more than I should. "Either you're shooting that thing or I am. But fair warning, if you start shooting while riding my cock, I will come before you and I can't have that."

Her eyes widen again and realizing she's way out of her realm of expertise, she shoves the gun into my chest, and I take it from her while keeping my other hand on the throttle. "Alright, Firefly. Hold the fuck on."

Quickly glancing back over my shoulder, I ease up on the throttle, letting them get a little closer when Oakley starts riding my cock again, getting off on the wicked thrill like my feisty little she-devil should.

"Oh, fuck," I groan, my balls tightening. This is the best goddamn thing that has ever happened to me. Riding my bike while my girl rides me in the middle of a fucking shootout. Holy fuck. I will die a happy man.

We fly down the main straight of Faders Bay, only a few minutes away from the DeVil Hotel when two other SUVs pull out to join the first, clearly realizing their cover has been blown. Without wanting them to be able to gain on us, I aim right for the driver of the original car.

BANG!

The bullet ricochets off the glass and I curse. "What's wrong?" Oakley questions, peering over my shoulder to watch the show, her pussy working me right to the darkest pits of hell.

"Bulletproof glass," I tell her, quickly glancing at the road ahead before focusing back on the SUV and lowering the gun to the front tire. Only before I can take another shot, guns appear out the windows of the three SUVs, making my cock flinch with excitement.

Oakley's pussy clenches around me, and as I take my shot, blowing out the front right tire of the first SUV, she cries out, reaching her limit and coming hard. Her fingers dig into my shoulders as the SUV violently swerves and hits the curb, sending them into a death roll behind us, but all that matters is the way her walls start convulsing around me.

"Oh, fuck. Firefly," I groan into her ear, my own release spiraling out of control and blasting through my body. I come hard, shooting hot spurts of cum deep inside her sweet cunt as bullets from the two remaining SUVs start whizzing past our heads, only making me come that much harder.

She squeals as her high rocks through her, trying to duck her head down in front of me, more than prepared to use my body as a human shield, but I wouldn't have it any other way. I would stand in front of every one of these fucking bullets if it meant saving her.

We fly around the small bend and find a familiar Escalade hurtling toward us, and a breath of relief flies through my lips. "Is that Zade?" Oakley rushes out.

"Yeah."

Her body seems to relax against me, and as the Escalade storms past us, I meet Zade's stare through the tinted windows. Then he's gone, soaring past me and cutting the Escalade around in a narrow arc, coming to a screeching halt in the middle of the road. Right between us and the SUVs.

Sawyer and Cross fire back as Zade pulls himself out the driver's side window and shoots over the top of the Escalade. I come to a stop, the Escalade offering protection from the bullets, as Oakley watches with wide eyes, our view mostly blocked. I free myself from Oakley, settling her down on the back of my bike before stuffing my cock back into my pants as though stuffing a Thanksgiving turkey. I stand before her, ready to take one of the boys' places if it comes down to it, but it won't. My boys are just that fucking good.

In the space of four seconds, one of Zade's bullets penetrates the gas tank on one of the SUVs, and a loud explosion rocks through the city center, taking them all out. The heat from the blast has Oakley shrinking back, throwing her hands up to protect her face. Before the sound has even finished echoing through Faders Bay, Zade looks back toward me as he slides back into his Escalade. "Get her back to the penthouse. Now." Without a second glance, he takes off like a bat out of hell, my bike sailing closely behind.

CHAPTER 28

Oakley

My hands shake as I stand in my closet, trying to figure out what the hell I'm supposed to wear to an execution. Nikolai's trial is today, and I can only assume it would be much like sitting through a court case, only the sentencing is going to be a tad harsher than anything I've seen on *Judge Judy*.

So many questions about today have been circling my mind, seeing as I have no idea how this is going to play out. Am I going to be questioned and brought forward to speak in front of The Circle? Is it going to be my statement that ensures a bullet is put between Nikolai's eyes? Or will they dismiss me because I'm simply a nobody? Despite being the true heir, I have no standing within their ranks, but it's not like that information is widely known—at least I don't think it is. I'm starting to wonder just how many people actually know about my existence.

"What's taking so long?" Easton's voice booms through my room, startling me as he appears in my closet doorway. "Wait. You're not dressed yet?"

I look back at him with a scowl. "Well, excuse me, but I haven't exactly been to an execution before. I don't know what's appropriate to wear."

Easton rolls his eyes and strides deeper into my closet, grabbing my usual jeans and crop. "We're going to a private trial," he explains, "not a fucking grand ball. It's only going to be immediate family and those who have been personally invited to attend. The Circle wants to limit how many people are in there due to the likelihood of your lineage being exposed."

"And in turn, Zade's," I finish for him.

"Exactly."

Easton gives me a tight smile before walking out of my closet with instructions to hurry my bitch-ass up. Knowing just how serious today is for the guys—but mostly Sawyer—I make it quick.

All the guys are waiting for me in the living room when I finish getting dressed. Zade and Dalton's eyes fall on me first, both of them checking me from head to toe—one of them with fondness and the other with apprehension. Easton's gaze lands on me next, quickly putting Venom away in her enclosure before looking back at me. "You ready?"

I nod as my gaze shifts to Sawyer. He sits on the couch looking miserable, his stare trained on the floor in front of his feet. My heart breaks for him. All morning he's been trying to be strong, trying to act unbothered, but now that it's time to go, it's finally starting to sink in.

He's not going to be able to save his father.

"Yo," Dalton says, stepping closer to him to gain his attention. "Do you wanna get Cara, or should I?"

Sawyer lifts his head, looking around as though only just realizing there are people in the room. He shakes his head and lets out a heavy breath before getting to his feet and running a hand through his hair. "Nah, man. It's fine. I'll get her."

He disappears back into the penthouse as Zade meets my stare and nods toward the elevator. "Let's go." Before Sawyer returns with his sister, the rest of us make our way to the private garage, and just as we're about ready to hit the road, Sawyer strides out of the elevator with his sister in tow.

They drop down into Easton's Lamborghini, and we wait for them to take off first. Zade follows closely behind as if expecting the twins to pull off some stupid escape plan to try and free Cara, but Sawyer wouldn't dare. He drives straight out to the boys' favorite entrance into their little fucked-up world, following the old train lines until he pulls to a stop into the familiar, abandoned parking lot.

My hands shake as we make our way through the long tunnel toward the entrance, having no idea what to expect. But in this awkward silence, I don't dare ask. As we approach the big, heavy door, it doesn't escape me how Zade creeps in closer to me, as if expecting another attack. Hell, I shouldn't be surprised. At this point, I should learn to expect them, too.

We make our way through the main entrance and deeper into the underground world. As usual, the long, cold tunnels send shivers sailing across my skin, but I hold myself together, sparing cautious glances toward Sawyer and Cara. They both look like shit, but it's not as though I expected them to be jumping off the walls. They're not fooling themselves. They know the likelihood of their father actually pulling through this.

It's a long walk, passing through the main bar and deeper into Empire. We take paths I've never walked before, and the further we get, the more intricate I realize this place is. The tunnels turn into properly lit walkways with wide access and painted walls as the rooms we pass become fit for a king. "Holy shit," I whisper, taking it all in, the once dark and gloomy underground world is now a stunning, modern facility.

It's another ten minutes before the boys slow and Zade leads us toward a door. He glances back, his jaw clenched as if not sure how he wants to play this. Without a word, he opens the door, and we stride into a private room that's been set up like some kind of courtroom.

There are a few people already lingering, and they all glance back at us as Zade discreetly steps in front of me, blocking their view. The boys continue on with Cara as Zade turns to face me, gripping my upper arm in his tight clutches. "This way," he murmurs.

He leads me across the back of the room and through a side exit before depositing me into a small room. "You'll be here during the trial," he explains. "I can't have you out there. If you need anything, forget about it. This could take anywhere from twenty minutes to twenty fucking days. You do not move from this room. At some point, The Circle may request your version of what went down that day, but I will attempt to steer them away."

I nod, swallowing hard, hoping like fuck that I don't have to go in there and be the reason for this execution to go ahead.

Zade points up toward a small panel on the wall. "If you're bored, open that slider. You'll see and hear straight into the trial. However, you will not be able to communicate through it. Think of it as the glass police use in their interrogation rooms."

Zade looks over me one last time as if he's terrified about the prospect of leaving me alone in here. But what exactly can happen? Anyone would have to get through the courtroom to be able to reach me, and I doubt anything like that is gonna slip past Zade and the boys.

Pulling the door closed behind him, I immediately move across the room and open the slider to get a good look into the courtroom. It quickly begins filling with people, and I watch with wide eyes as everyone takes their seats.

Zade, Easton, and Dalton sit toward the back, getting the perfect view of the whole room while Sawyer and Cara sit on the opposite side with an older woman who's the spitting image of them. Other men in suits pour into the room, and I watch as nearly every seat is taken. Some of the men walk around with an air about them, acting as though they're important. I can't help but wonder if these are some of The Circle members. Yet, no matter how self-important they are, they all seem to watch Zade, waiting for and wanting his approval.

There's too much chatter in the room to be able to focus on one individual conversation, so instead, I just watch. I only wait a few minutes before the door opens and Nikolai strides in with Harrison at his back. All eyes fall to them as Sawyer's mom leaps out of her seat and races across to her husband, throwing her arms around him as she sobs. Something shatters in my chest as I watch Sawyer go after her, trying to pull her away as Harrison pushes Nikolai forward, forcing him to the front of the room.

His wrists are cuffed at his back, and as Harrison forces him into a chair, he locks the cuffs around the armrests of the chair.

Someone stands and calls attention to the room, getting the proceedings started, and it doesn't go unnoticed how both Cara and Zade stare at this man with disdain. I can't help but wonder if this is the infamous Hartley Scott. And in that case, I should be applauding Zade for his ability to remain seated so calmly instead of flying across the room to put a bullet through his head.

The trial gets underway with oaths murmured throughout the whole room, and as they start going through a long list of charges, I drop my ass to the chair, suddenly not feeling it. Zade said it could take twenty minutes or twenty days, and I'm starting to think my execution will come before Nikolai's.

After the first hour, my ass starts to get numb, and after the second, I'm pacing through the room, groaning and trying to think of anything other than my need to pee. They take a short break, and I couldn't be more grateful when Dalton appears in my little doorway and shows me to the bathroom. Hell, he even finds me some snacks while muttering about how this thing is taking so much longer than he thought.

Hearing the trial starting to commence again, he scurries out into the main room, and I find myself watching again when it occurs to me; if Harrison is here watching over Nikolai, then who's down in the cells watching over my father?

I grow antsy in my little room. The more I think about it, the quicker I pace, circling the small space before glancing through the one-way window and starting the process over. It becomes a twisted cycle, and after another half hour, I almost make myself sick. Especially after noticing the keys hanging off the side of Harrison's belt.

The voices in my head start whispering, telling me to make moves that I'm simply not ready for, but when might I get another chance like this? Both The Circle and the guys are occupied, while my father is just waiting down there to be set free.

Fuck. This is stupid.

This is going to get me killed.

I rub my hands over my face as if that could somehow scrub the thoughts from my mind, but it only brings me a new resolve. Without another second of hesitation, I move right to the door of my small room and settle my shaky hand over the handle.

Taking a breath, I push down and grin to myself as the door silently swings open, like a sign sent from the heavens above. The only good thing to happen to me since moving back to Faders Bay. You know, apart from the exquisite dick I've been getting along the way.

Creeping out into the small hallway, I slowly walk around to the courtroom and peer inside. People are up in arms, some desperately trying to defend Nikolai's actions, when the asshole running this thing suggests that he's a callous, selfish man who's only interested in his own gain, calling Nikolai an enemy to the brotherhood of The Circle.

Sawyer stands and defends his father, insisting how he's dedicated his whole adult life to The Circle, a loyal servant of Empire, and how one moment of weakness shouldn't be held against him. Cara gets up beside him, arguing right along with her brother as Nikolai watches them both with fondness in his eyes. My heart almost breaks, only the moment is gone when the guy running the show calls Cara out for speaking out of place. Because of course they wouldn't allow a woman to have an opinion in the court.

Nikolai's wife throws herself to her feet with a gun in hand, and just like that, it's all on.

Everyone is out of their seats, and I take it as a sign from the sex gods above—it's go time.

Throwing myself down, I scurry across the back of the room, terrified I'm about to be caught. I make it to the edge of the back row of chairs to where Harrison stands, his hand hovering over the gun at his side, but as the room starts to find a little bit of control, I realize it's now or never.

Reaching up, I unhook the keys from his belt, and as I start to bolt for the door, my gaze comes to a startling stop on Dalton's. He watches my every step, and I prepare for the worst. Only, I see heartbreak flash in his eyes, and he gives me a small smile, silently telling me it's okay to run.

I hold back tears, not having the time to get emotional, but I find myself mouthing those words I never thought I'd say. "I love you."

He simply tips his head, not wanting to give me away, and without a backward glance, I fly out the door and race back down the hallway. My heart pounds, unable to believe I just did that. Zade's going to kill me when he finds out. I'll be locked away, tortured, and tormented—assuming he catches me, of course.

Seconds pass, but it feels like a lifetime. I'm moving too slowly.

The modern facility starts morphing back into the old, rustic underground bullshit I'm used to, and I find myself pulling to a stop, glancing left and right. One way leads me to my freedom, taking me back out into the train tunnels, and the other way leads down to the prison cells.

I could get out of here—free myself and run as far as my feet can take me. I could board a plane and get my ass halfway across the world, somewhere Zade won't be able to find me. But where the hell could I go? Could I even get through airport security without him finding me?

Knowing the likelihood of me surviving on my own, I take the road less traveled and drag my ass down to the cells. It's bad enough coming down here with the guys, but doing it by myself has me wanting to double over and blow chunks across the dimly lit tunnels.

The further I get, the more my footsteps seem to echo. I sound like a fucking elephant racing through here. If Zade hasn't realized I'm gone yet, then he will soon. Hell, all he'd have to do is follow the sound of the stampede racing through the tunnels.

Reaching the end, I slow my steps, not having considered that Harrison could have had someone step in for him while he attended the trial, but I find the gate left wide open with not a soul in sight.

My hands shake, and I can barely hear myself think over the heavy beating of my pulse in my ear. This is fucking insane. If I live through this, I'll have to buy myself a big juicy burger as a reward. Maybe even a milkshake to wash it down.

Fuck, what the hell is wrong with me? *Concentrate, Oakley.*

Holding my breath, I slip through the gate, feeling as though this is some kind of trap, but I don't have the luxury to work it out right now. Time is not on my side.

Reaching the old, rickety stairs, I grip the railing and hurry down them, wishing Empire had bothered to spend a little bit of that blood money to upgrade their prison system. Hell, would some more lighting go astray? Perhaps a set of concrete stairs?

My feet hit the ground and everything else fades away. All that matters is getting to my father.

Hurrying through the long corridors, I try to remember just how far down I need to go, my gaze locked on the left, desperately searching for that one familiar face. "Dad?" I hiss through the darkness. "Dad?"

Someone grips the bars further down, throwing themselves up against them. My eyes widen, and my heart threatens to jump right out of my chest. "Oakley? Is that you?"

Relief pounds through my veins, and I race toward my father, my hands fumbling with the keys. "Yes," I breathe, tears streaming down my face. "I'm here. I'm here. I'm getting you out of here."

"Oakley, no," my father panics, gripping the bars tighter. "You stupid, beautiful child. I told you to run. You have to get out of here.

It's too dangerous. If Harrison—"

"He won't. He's at the trial with Nikolai, but I can't leave you. I won't. I won't survive out there on my own," I tell him, so fucking scared and riddled with anxiety that I can't get my hands to work. The keys shake so violently against the lock that I can't get it in. "I need you. We can get out of here together."

"Oakley, no. I . . . fuck."

Resolve flashes in his eyes and realizing that this could be his only chance, he stops fighting it. My father reaches through the bars and grips the keys, taking them from my hands and hastily jamming them into the lock. He goes to turn the key when something grabs me from behind, yanking me away from my father's cell and throwing me up against the bent bars of the cell that used to belong to me.

A throaty, terrified scream tears through me as Harrison's face appears out of the darkness, bearing down on me as his hold tightens around my throat. The pressure of the bars against my back is too much, and I feel as though just a little more pressure could have my ribs snapping right around them, but none of that will matter if I'm dead.

"Don't fucking touch her," my father growls, hastily trying to unlock his cell, searching frantically through the array of keys.

"You," Harrison spits at me as if not even noticing my father's escape attempt behind him. "The second you showed up in my cells, I knew you were going to be more trouble than you were worth."

Without giving me a second to try and fight my way out of this, Harrison draws his gun and presses the cold barrel to my temple. My whole fucking life flashes before my eyes, and I watch as darkness flashes in his stare. No hesitation. No regret. Just an overwhelming dark need to watch my brain splatter across the back of my old cell.

I see it, the very second he goes to pull the trigger.

"NO!" My father screams out, raw and broken, and I meet his haunted stare over Harrison's shoulder, knowing this is it.

BANG!

Harrison crumbles, blood splattering across my face as unbelievable horror blasts through my chest. He falls away with a heavy thud against the dirty ground, and I stumble forward, the moment of being released almost taking me right down with him.

My eyes widen, my heart racing with fear, and I whip around, finding Zade staring right back at me, fury pulsing from his venomous stare. He strides toward me, not saying a damn word, and I've never been so fucking scared in my life.

I shake my head. There's no telling what he might do. "Zade . . . Zade, no," I breathe as he reaches for me, gripping me by the hair and yanking me into him, the hot barrel of his gun pressed against my head as he looks back at my father.

"Hand over the keys," he tells him, my father's eyes flashing between me and Zade, realizing he's unhinged enough to actually do it.

My father swallows and holds my terrified stare. "I'm sorry," he tells me before reaching through the bars and dropping the keys right into the center of Zade's palm, then without a moment of hesitation, Zade lets the gun fall away, shoving it into the back of his pants and pushing me ahead with a brutal hold.

He gives me a hard jab in the back. "Move," he rumbles, his tone so thick and filled with betrayal, his demands leaving absolutely no space for argument.

I hastily move back through the cells, hot tears streaming down my cheeks, knowing without a doubt I have failed. Not just today, but altogether. I will never find another chance to be free of this. I had one shot and I blew it. Forever destined to suffer at the hands of Zade DeVil.

He leads me back up through the tunnels and into the modern walkways. Every step feels as though I'm drowning, and my knees threaten to give out from beneath me. It's not long before we're walking back through the door of the courtroom, Zade's hand now securely locked around my arm.

I expect to find things much like I left them, somewhat controlled . . . apart from that brief moment where I'm sure Sawyer's mom's life flashed before her eyes. But as we stride back in, I find Cara latching onto her father while Sawyer desperately tries to pull her away, her loud, desperate screams darkening something deep inside my soul.

Dalton's eyes flick to mine, horror rocking across his features when he sees the blood splattered across my face. He didn't expect to see me again—and certainly not like this. But before I even get a chance to process everything that's going down, Hartley Scott raises his gun and puts a single bullet between Nikolai's eyes, right here in front of his wife and children.

CHAPTER 29

Sawyer

The ice clinks in the bottom of my glass, and I throw back what's left of my whiskey before reaching over and replacing it with the bottle.

Today my father was executed. I could have handled it. I was prepared for it. Hell, I thought Cara was prepared for it. But the way she broke, the way she threw herself at him, desperate to save him—it fucking killed me.

She's my twin sister. We shared a womb. It's my job to protect her from the hardships of life and shelter her from this messed-up world we belong to. I promised my father that I would watch over her. I made a solemn vow to myself. But today, I failed.

It's well past two in the morning, and I've sat here on Zade's couch for three long hours, staring at the bottom of my glass. Following the execution, I went home with Mom and Cara. Zade gave her a day to grieve before he'll inevitably lock her back in his spare room.

A part of me wishes I didn't go. I should have just come straight back here afterward. The way Mom and Cara clung to me, burdening me with their grief. It was the right thing to do, but it was too much. I'd give up everything in a heartbeat if it meant taking their pain, so I sat there and took it all, letting it weigh down on me.

I'm the man of the family now. It's my duty to protect them, even if it means protecting them from themselves.

Mom tried to keep herself composed. She's been preparing for this since the second Dad was thrown in the cells. She knew it was coming, but Cara was a fucking mess. She hoped and prayed and dreamed that this was all a misunderstanding. She believes in the sanctity of The Circle and had faith that they would let him go. But that bullet . . . fuck.

I don't know what killed me more—the sound of the bullet penetrating my father's skull or the agonized scream that tore from my twin sister's mouth.

Mom got drunk and then, despite the dangers, took a few sleeping pills and went to bed. But Cara, she sobbed for hours on end, every last cry darkening my already black soul and leaving a stain on my heart. I'll never forget the sound of her cries. It'll fuel my need for change. Hell, it'll fuel my need to get sweet vengeance.

My father should not have died today.

Despite everything he did, despite the long-standing traditions of Empire, my father's loyalty to the cause and the brotherhood of

The Circle should have been valued. He should have been spared. But fucking Hartley Scott—he was far too eager to pull the trigger. He ran the show and created a narrative, painting my father as a callous, selfish man. While we have certainly had our differences over the years, he was a good father.

Lifting the bottle of whiskey to my lips, I take a deep pull, desperately needing the alcohol to dull my senses. As I slam it back to the coffee table, I notice Oakley standing across the penthouse, her broken stare locked on me.

I look away, unable to handle it. "I don't want your pity," I warn her.

She pushes off the wall and strides toward me, her eyes locked so heavily on mine that it makes me want to fucking scream. She's too much, too good for this world, and the closer we get to the ritual, the closer I come to losing the last shred of humanity left inside me.

Oakley walks right into me, her knee pressing against the couch cushion before climbing onto my lap and straddling me, Easton's old shirt bunching around her waist. She rests her hand against my shoulder before reaching back for the whiskey and taking a pull of her own. "Do you think I'm the type of woman to insult you with pity?"

I press my lips together, knowing she's damn right.

My hands fall to her hips, my fingers digging into her creamy skin, desperate to feel something. "You should have run faster," I tell her before shaking my head, replaying what Zade told me after my father was executed, the words only now coming back to me. "What were you even doing down in those cells? You could have saved yourself."

Her gaze falls from mine, and I realize that we're all missing something here—everyone apart from Zade that is. After all, he knew to go looking for her in the cells. Had it been anyone else, we would have searched for her out on the street.

"I was trying to help somebody," she tells me, glossing over the details, and if I weren't so fucked in the head right now, I might even push for more. "But I don't think he ever really wanted my help."

"People usually don't," I tell her, recalling the day I busted her out of those very cells and tried to save my father. He didn't want my help either. It killed me then, just as much as it kills me now.

"You're going to be okay, Sawyer," she tells me, lifting her hand to the side of my face. "You're one of the strongest guys I know. And while I know it sucks right now, it'll eventually get easier to breathe."

I shake my head as her hand falls away, clutching the front of my shirt. "Don't pretend that you know what I'm feeling," I tell her. "You were only a kid when your father was killed. You still had a fucking life ahead of you. You got to be a carefree child whose main concern was what you were going to wear to school. We're in very different situations, Oakley. My father's execution means the weight he held is now mine to bear. I'm going to be initiated into The Circle and maybe next time, I'll be the one pulling the fucking trigger."

"You won't," she tells me, with such conviction that I almost believe her. "You're going to be the change that Empire needs, just as your father had hoped for you. And I know you're not the sentimental type, but you're going to take on his legacy and ensure that he's going to be proud of the man you'll be."

"I think you underestimate Empire's traditions. They're bound by oaths and vows. Making change isn't going to be as easy as you think it is. We hold thousands of members, each of them bound by the same vows. Making change means standing against every last one of them."

She shrugs her shoulders. "I have faith in you, Sawyer. With you and Zade at the top, I don't think there's a lot that can stop you."

I shake my head, my hand curling around the back of her neck as my thumb stretches out across her jaw, her skin so soft beneath my touch. It's almost hard to believe just how strong she is under her fragile skin. "You terrify me, Oakley," I tell her with raw honesty. "You shouldn't believe in me the way you do."

She leans toward me, the tilt of her hips grinding her pussy against my dick. "Try and stop me," she murmurs before her lips brush over mine.

My hand tightens at the back of her neck, and I hold her to me, my cock coming alive in my pants, straining against the fly. A desperation rocks through me, and I take her by the waist and throw her down on the couch before pushing between her thighs and hovering over her. "I don't like the thought of someone owning a piece of my heart," I tell her. "You can't have it."

Oakley scoffs, her hand bunching into the front of my shirt and pulling me down to her. "Then stop trying to take a piece of mine." And with that, I crush my lips down to hers, more than ready to lose myself in her sweet body, desperate to feel something other than this gut-wrenching pain.

A deep hunger blasts through me, and my hands can't work fast enough, reaching down between us and bunching Easton's shirt up before gripping her lace panties. I tear them right from her body, the fierce desperation like nothing I've ever known.

Oakley groans into my mouth as her body jolts and grinds, silently screaming for me to take her. "Fuck, Sawyer," she grunts just as I push two thick fingers deep inside her soaking cunt. She throws her head back, groaning loudly, and I drop my lips to her exposed throat. "Oh, God. Fucking take me."

Oakley's head rolls to the side as my lips move against her sensitive skin. She reaches down between us, hastily undoing my pants and shoving them down my hips. My cock springs free, dropping heavily against her hip, and she wastes no time curling her small hand around me. She squeezes tight and gives it to me hard, knowing I'm not here to fuck around.

This isn't about getting off and feeling our bodies move together as one. This is raw. Hard and fast. Fucking animalistic. This is about losing myself in her body as she gives it to me, allowing me to use her as a way to manage my overwhelming grief.

Her hand moves up and down three times before I grip her thigh and hook it high over my hip, opening her wide for me. I smell her arousal, and it's fucking on. Neither of us is here for the bullshit foreplay—not tonight.

Meeting her hungry stare, I guide my cock to her entrance. She clenches her jaw and digs her nails into my back. "Fucking take me, Sawyer. Now," she demands, letting me know just how ready she is.

Before she can take another breath, I slam my cock deep inside her and she cries out, gasping as her nails dig in deeper. My eyes flutter, her tight cunt squeezing around me. "Fuck," I grunt, pulling back as I slip my arm beneath her body, lifting her hips.

I slam deep inside her again and she groans, her whole body jolting as the fire burns through us both. "Fuck. Right there, Sawyer. Again."

And just like that, I go for fucking gold.

I fuck her hard and fast as she clings to me, desperately trying to hold on. It's wild and animalistic, and I devour her body in a cruel and meaningless way, simply using her for what she can offer, and fuck, she lets me take everything I need.

The way her pussy spasms and jolts around my cock tells me she's more than on board with this, even more so when she pushes me off her, flips over onto her knees on the couch, and shoves her tits down against the cushion, her sweet cunt on display and desperate to be fucked.

Taking her hips, I dig my fingers into her skin and give it to her hard as she slips her hand beneath her, vigorously rubbing tight circles over her clit. I drop my gaze to her pussy, watching the way my cock stretches her, slamming balls deep inside her, and I groan as her walls tighten around me. She's close, so fucking close.

My balls tighten, swelling and throbbing as I feel myself teetering on the edge, but I'm unable to let go and force myself over. Oakley pushes back against me, taking as much from me as I'm taking from her.

Oakley's hand fists into the cushion, and as I slam back inside of her, she comes hard, crying out with undeniable pleasure. Her high rocks through her body, her walls spasming around me, convulsing and squeezing the fucking life out of my cock. It's just what I need to launch me right over the fucking edge.

I detonate, coming hard with a loud, agonizing roar, and my eyes close as I pour hot spurts of cum deep inside her. The overwhelming satisfaction blasts through my veins, and I collapse against the couch, struggling to catch my breath.

My heart races, certain she must be sore, and if she is, she doesn't say a damn word about it. She simply crawls back onto my lap and takes another swig from the bottle of whiskey. Her lips part with a sharp hiss as she reaches out and refills my discarded glass on the coffee table. "Who knew you could fuck so hard?"

A stupid grin stretches across my face, and my hand comes down in a perfect, sharp spank against her ass, the sound echoing through the big penthouse. She yelps and laughs, and fuck, it feels good to see her like this. Even on the darkest night, she shines brighter than a supernova.

Her eyes fill with a seriousness as she lets out a heavy breath and relaxes against me, dropping her hand to my chest and resting her palm over my racing heart. "I take it you're not about to call it a night and go to bed?" I shake my head and she presses her lips into a hard line. "Do you want me to sit with you?"

I consider it a moment, knowing having her right here in my lap could have me at peace within moments, but the fact that she can do that has me fucking terrified. That's not something I'm willing to explore tonight.

"No," I finally tell her. "I think I need to be alone a while. Besides, you've had a big day too. Go to bed and call it a night."

"You sure?" she questions, climbing off my lap and glancing down at me. I give her a tight smile and nod, not wanting her to see just how much the grief is tearing me apart. Though I can't lie, that moment with her helped me in a way I wasn't prepared for. It opened me to be able to start processing, put the anger aside, and accept the fact that my father is gone.

Oakley gives me a warm smile before walking around the couch, and as I lift the glass to my lips, she leans over the back of the couch and presses a kiss to my temple. "You're gonna be alright, Sawyer," she tells me. "Don't stay up too late."

And with that, she's gone, leaving me to find the bottom of this bottle.

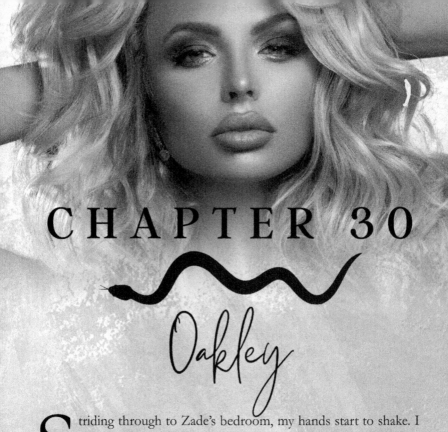

CHAPTER 30

Oakley

Striding through to Zade's bedroom, my hands start to shake. I haven't spoken a word to him since he caught me down in those cells, and to be completely honest, I really don't know how to feel about it. On one hand, I want to thank him for saving my life and for having my back. He got to me just in time. But on the other hand, a part of me wonders if he only did it for his own benefit.

Was there any part of him that wanted to save me just because he wanted to? I don't think I'll ever get the chance to know.

He was furious. I've seen him mad plenty of times. Big mad. But this was different. He looked at me as though I'd betrayed his trust, that my attempt to leave had hurt something inside of him, something he hadn't realized he was capable of. I don't know. This could all be in my head, but I know it's not. At least, I don't think so. I feel it with Zade. There's a connection between us, and it terrifies me.

How can I want the man who's going to kill me? More so, why can't I just be satisfied with the three I've already got? Well, who could say if I've really got them. Dalton maybe, but the other two? I can't help but wonder if this is all about convenience for them. I know I feel something, but it's impossible to read them. Hell, I think I'm better off kept in the dark.

Stepping through the threshold of Zade's bedroom, I find him standing by his window, staring out at the vast city. It must be around two in the morning, and a part of me had hoped that I'd walk in here to find him already asleep in bed. But I should have known better. He's never gone to sleep before I have, so I don't know why I would have thought tonight would be different.

Feeling Sawyer's cum starting to spread between my thighs, I keep my head down and move across Zade's bedroom, feeling his gaze locked on me through the floor-to-ceiling window. Pushing through to the bathroom, I quickly clean myself up before splashing water over my face and noticing the few hickeys Sawyer's left branded across the base of my throat.

I roll my eyes and prepare to face the firing squad, not sure how any of this is going to go down. Though I don't doubt he has one burning question—who the fuck was I trying to save?

Making my way out of the bathroom, I creep across the room, hoping like fuck he can let this go for tonight. Reaching the bed, I peel the blankets back and slip under the sheets before realizing I've been holding my breath. I have no idea why I'm trying to sneak through the room or even why I'm trying to be discreet about it. He can see me clearly through the reflection in the window, and Zade DeVil does not miss a damn thing. Like how the hell he knew to come after me in the cells. I haven't told a soul about my father being down there. There's no way he could know. Though he questioned me about the man who helped us during my prison escape, and I know he didn't buy the bullshit response I gave him, but surely that wasn't enough for him to figure it out.

As far as Zade is aware, my father is dead, and that's the way it's going to stay.

A few seconds pass, and for just a brief moment, I wonder if he really is going to let this go for tonight, when he finally turns to face me. His fiery stare locks right onto mine, and I watch as he walks through his room, over to the armchair and takes a seat, leaning forward and bracing his elbows on his knees, clearly very deep in thought.

I swallow hard, knowing it's coming.

"I'm going to give you one chance, Oakley," he tells me, his venomous tone sending chills spreading through my body, turning my blood to ice. "Who was he?"

I pull the sheets up higher, covering most of my face as though it could somehow save me from Zade's wrath. "I don't know who you're talking about."

Rage burns through his stare, and I watch as he visibly takes calming breaths, keeping himself from tearing me to pieces. "Don't pretend like you don't know what the fuck I'm talking about," he spits.

"You're embarrassing yourself. Tell me who the fuck he is. Otherwise, I will go down there and find out for myself."

Fear slams through my chest, and I come to a crossroads, not knowing my next move. If I tell him, Zade will go down there and kill him. If I don't, Zade will still go down there and kill him. There's nothing I can do to prevent this.

Tears well in my eyes, and I desperately try to blink them back, wondering if he knows what kind of impossible situation he's putting me in. "I can't," I breathe. "Please, don't push this. I gave my word. I won't break it."

Zade watches me a moment before standing and striding toward me, a heaviness in his dark eyes. He reaches the side of the bed and turns before sitting on the edge, looking back out at the view. Though something tells me this time he's not seeing it.

He holds his hand out to me, and horror blasts through my chest as I find a familiar piece of paper resting in the palm of his hand. I close my eyes, allowing the fear to sail right through my body before letting out a shaky breath and reaching for my father's note.

I don't say a word. I don't think I need to. It's clear he knows.

Zade isn't looking for a confession out of me. He's testing my loyalty.

"You should have come to me with this," he tells me, not daring to meet my eye, both of us staring toward the window. "The second you knew, you should have told me."

I scoff, shaking my head. "So you could murder the only real family I have? So you could take him away from me again, just like your father did all those years ago? Hell no, Zade. You're fucked in the head if you truly think I would have ever come to you with this. I might be sleeping in your bed every damn night, curled in your arms, and falling for every last one of you, but don't mistake that for loyalty. I am not on your side."

He leans forward onto his knees again, letting out a long, shallow breath as he lets my words really sink in. But as my gaze rests on his reflection in the window, I see nothing but deep conflict in his eyes, and realize he's just as messed up over this as I am. His whole life, it's been instilled in him to always remain loyal to his cause and his people, and lately, all of that has been coming into question. It clearly doesn't sit well with him.

There's no doubt in my mind that he still plans to follow through with the ritual—no matter what parts of his soul he has to sacrifice. But if there's a chance there might be a small part of him that doesn't want to do this, just a little piece of humanity left inside his heart, then I'm going to find and exploit it to save my ass. Even if it means falling in love with my monster.

Desperately needing him to hold onto this, I push the sheets back and clamber across the bed before climbing over his lap and straddling him, both of us slightly awkward with the intimacy of it, but he knows this is nothing sexual.

Unable to help himself, his hands fall to my waist, and he meets my eyes, waiting to hear what I have to say. "Look," I murmur, the silence beginning to weigh me down. "There's no denying that you're going to make an incredible leader, despite how much you still have to learn about yourself. And God, I wish there were some way for you to figure out how to have everything you've ever wanted without having to take my life in the process. But when it comes to having to choose between your future or mine, I'll pick me every damn time. If having the future you've dreamed of your whole life means that I have to forfeit mine, I'm not ready to die."

He lets out a heavy breath, his hand coming up and curling around the back of my neck, his thumb stretching across my jaw. "Believe me, Lamb," he murmurs, his tone thick and raw. "If I could have it all, I would."

A tear falls down my cheek, and I hate myself for being so weak and broken. "Are you going to kill my father?"

"Yes," he tells me, not sugarcoating it or gloating, just giving me the cold, hard facts out of sheer respect. "However, his death is not of importance to me right now. I don't know how many of Empire's members are aware of who he is, but that doesn't matter. He's locked in a cell, and until he figures out a way to break out of there, he is no threat to me. So, yes, I will eventually kill him, but I will not make you live through the pain of losing your father again."

I drop my forehead to his, my arm looping around his neck. "Are you angry with me?"

"I was," he says. "You've messed with my head. I don't like that you want to get away from me, but I understand why. If I were in your position, I'd be trying to run too. Though you were foolish to try and save your father first. The blind cannot lead the blind. In order to free someone, you must first know how to free yourself."

"Shit, Zade," I breathe, a soft smile kicking up the corner of my lips. "That was way too deep for two in the morning."

"Just giving it to you straight."

A heaviness rests on my shoulders, and I give him another small smile before climbing back into bed and pulling the sheets up to my shoulders. Zade gets up and moves around to his side of the bed, and my gaze follows him as he peels up his shirt, shrugs out of it, and drops it to the ground, putting that magnificent body on display. But the heaviness is too much, and I can't even take a moment to appreciate it.

Zade slips under the covers and immediately pulls me into his arms, rolling me in the process so that my back is tight up against his chest. "Go to sleep, Lamb," he murmurs through the night, his arms offering me the sweetest serenity, despite being the ones I should fear most.

I close my eyes, but sleep doesn't find me as thoughts of Nikolai Thorne and my time in Empire's prison roll through my mind. "What is it?" Zade questions, able to sense my internal struggle.

"Nikolai said something to me when I was in the cell," I tell him, "and it's just not sitting well with me."

"What'd he say?"

Pressing my lips into a hard line, I roll in his warm arms and lift my gaze to meet his. "He told me how those who are sacrificed during the leadership ritual are not permitted a proper burial in order to keep people from asking too many questions. They're buried away from the general population, deep in Empire's tombs where no one will ever find them. But I don't want that," I whisper, that heaviness returning. "Promise me, Zade. After you kill me, give me a nice burial. Somewhere the boys can come visit me, where I won't be left alone to rot in the ground. If you can't free me now, then at least free me in death."

Zade dips his head, his lips brushing over mine in the softest kiss, and it breaks my heart.

"I promise."

CHAPTER 31

Oakley

My knees bounce as we drive through the streets of Faders Bay, and I'm not going to lie, with Cara sitting right beside me in the back of Zade's brand-new Escalade, things are a little awkward. And the fact that the boys are dead silent isn't helping.

It's Sawyer's initiation day, and apparently, it's a big deal. Big enough that Zade felt the need to break out the new Escalade after the old one had a little incident with a shower of bullets. Who would have known being a billionaire meant you could order a car and have it show up in the valet parking of your big fucking hotel within ten minutes? But that's not what's important. It's their need to torture me with this awkwardness.

There are a lot of things I can handle in life. Hell, apparently being the target of multiple hitmen is one of them, but awkward silence certainly isn't. It's been four days since Nikolai's execution, and I can't exactly say that things have gotten better for Cara. She's been holed up in her room since she was brought back. The original deal was to lock her in Zade's spare bedroom, but she's had full access to the penthouse—not that she's taken advantage of it. I never even see her eat. I almost feel bad for her, but then I remind myself how she got herself locked up here in the first place, and that guilty conscience of mine just fades away.

Dalton's bike rumbles through the street as he overtakes the Escalade, and I roll my eyes, knowing just how desperately he craves the thrill of driving like a fucking idiot on that thing. The speed, the freedom, the engine between his legs. He loves it. I just wish I was on there with him, but my backless black satin gown and strappy heels don't make riding on the back of a Harley very practical.

I still don't understand why I have to wear this stupid outfit. Don't get me wrong, the plunging neckline and high slit in the side is a girl's version of a wet dream . . . Actually, that gets me thinking. What is a girl's version of a wet dream? Is it a soggy fantasy? A moist delusion? Clammy hallucination?

Easton spent the morning explaining the importance of today's initiation. How it's a grand event, something that should be celebrated among their people. This is a new era, a new member welcomed into the brotherhood of The Circle, though judging by the look in Sawyer's eyes, he doesn't see it that way, and I simply can't bring myself to celebrate something he's being forced into simply because of the blood that runs through his veins. He'll do it though, because that's just who he is. Besides, I don't think anyone actually knows what would happen if he were to deny the role. Hell, I don't think denying it is actually an option.

There's nothing about today's initiation that's normal. It's the first time Empire will accept a new member into The Circle without a current ruling leader, and they've asked Zade to step in to perform all the culty bullshit that goes along with it. There's no telling if Zade's actually into it, but I don't think so. He's so hard to read, but he agreed out of duty, and I'm not going to lie, a thrill shot through me when I realized I was going to be able to watch him do his thing.

All this time it's been clear to me that I would die in order for Zade to rise in power. I'll never get to see him lead, never get to see him actually claim what he worked so hard to achieve. Maybe that's a bit morbid of me, but there's no denying Zade is just the kind of man who belongs at the top.

Ahhh, fuck it. Who am I kidding? I only get a thrill in watching him because he's dressed in a goddamn five-piece suit and looks like a fucking snack. I mean, damnnnn. I know Zade and I haven't crossed over to a sexual relationship, but what I wouldn't give for that man to bend me over and spank my ass.

We drive for another ten minutes, and I watch out the window, staring at the scenery because it's better than trying to hold any kind of conversation in this awkward silence. We arrive at an old, run-down church, and as I step out of the Escalade and straighten my gown, I stare up at the incredible building. It's clear this place used to be the star of the city back in its prime. All it needs is a little elbow grease, and I'm sure it'll sparkle.

Cara steps out of the Escalade behind me with apprehension in her eyes. Her gaze briefly flickers to mine as we meet each other's stare and hastily look away, more than ready to pretend that didn't just happen.

Dalton sits back on his bike, waiting for us to get closer before finally stepping off and making my mouth water. Hell, just remembering the way I rode him on that thing the other night has me ready to demand the guys hold guns on me so I can do it all over again and recreate the thrill and adrenaline that pulsed through my veins.

As we stride closer to the church, a strange nervousness settles into my chest. I don't think doing Empire-related things, especially things that call for The Circle and the hundreds of members to be in attendance, is really in my best interests. They're so unforgiving, relentless, and unpredictable. By this stage, I know the boys will protect me no matter what, but I hate walking into a room and not knowing what I will be met with.

"You'll be fine," Easton murmurs, sensing my fear as Dalton moves in closer to Cara, placing his hand on the small of her back. To anyone walking by, it would look as innocent as escorting a date into an event, but we all know he's there to ensure she doesn't make a break for it.

I give Easton a small smile before focusing back on the path ahead, and soon enough, we're making our way up the grand stairs of one of the most architecturally pleasing buildings I've ever stepped into.

There's something a little gothic about it, and it sends a thrill shooting wildly through my veins.

There are a few people lingering throughout the church, some I recognize from Nikolai's trial, but I zone them out, focusing on the high ceilings and beautiful stained-glass windows. I can't say I'm the type who's ever enjoyed being in a church. I always thought they would have burned down the moment I stepped foot inside, but that doesn't mean that I can't appreciate the beauty.

Easton leads me right to the top of the aisle before pushing me along to the very end of the first pew, the very easiest position to bail out of if need be. Not to mention, from here, the rest of today's guests will only see the back of my head and have absolutely no idea who I am.

Zade stands in the front with a few of The Circle members, talking privately as people fill the church, and when Sawyer's mother walks in wearing an extravagant black gown with dark glasses, all eyes fall on her. She's fucking stunning, like a slightly older version of Cara, and as she makes her way right down the aisle to sit front and center to watch her son's big day, both Cara and Sawyer stand. They shuffle along the pew and sit down beside her, and I don't miss the way Cara clutches her mother's hand. It fucking kills me. I've never seen such a haunted family.

Minutes tick by, and as I'm left alone with nothing but my own thoughts, I can't help but wonder how it's all going to go down for me. It won't be a grand occasion like this. I won't get the fancy church and expansive crowd. I'll be the dark stain on Empire's reputation.

There are only ten days until Zade's hand will plunge into my chest, and the very thought has tears springing to my eyes. Mostly I've been doing okay, but as the days continue to count down, it gets harder to make it through. Today, in particular, I've been a mess.

Every now and then, the overwhelming fear cripples me. Fear for what will happen during Zade's ritual, fear for the life I won't be able to live, fear for my father who'll never be free, fear for the boys whose hearts will break.

It's too much.

The rush of emotions is paralyzing. I go from grieving the life I've never lived, to desperately needing to spend every waking minute living life to the fullest. The whiplash of emotion is exhausting, and a part of me just wants it over. If it's going to happen, I need to be through with this countdown. The anticipation is going to kill me long before Zade gets the chance to.

Dalton glances at me, his brows furrowed as he takes in the tears welling in my eyes, and I watch as something breaks inside of him. This has been our routine these past few days. This man feels so deeply that it's inspiring.

"You know," he starts, making me hold my breath. I never know what might come out of his mouth in situations like this, but when he wants to cheer me up, I've learned to come prepared for the worst. "I was using your phone the other day, and I just happened to scroll through your search history . . ."

My eyes widen with horror, and I suck in a breath, knowing exactly what he would have found. "I swear, I was searching for a pianist and that just came up."

Dalton arches a brow. "Right. So you meant to search for big pierced pianists jerking off?"

My cheeks flush, and I bury my face in my hands, embarrassment washing through me, but there's no denying that Dalton succeeded in his mission to get my mind off the ritual. I barely have a chance to recover from my mortification when Zade moves across the front of the church and takes his position behind the dais.

He looks out over the sea of extravagant gowns and suits, and I can't help but notice how fucking nervous he looks. Hell, it's more than that. He looks like he's about to be sick to his stomach. My brows furrow as I watch him closer, and judging by the way Easton and Dalton stiffen beside me, they notice it too.

I don't think I've ever seen Zade look nervous. He's always so put together, always so calm and calculated. He knows every move that's going to happen long before it does, and the fact that today is different puts me on edge.

Zade's gaze shifts to Sawyer before looking over his family. Then in a flash, resolve and determination force their way through his stare, and the Zade I've come to know is back.

He holds his hands out wide. *"In life, we prosper,"* he says, the captive audience living for every word from their future leader. *"But in death, we rise."*

A chill sails down my spine, hating how fucking culty this bullshit is.

"We gather here today, not to mourn the death of our brother,

Nikolai Thorne, but to rejoice in his sacrifice. As his blood runs dry, we open the pathway for our future to rise in power. A new generation of servitude, bound to the brotherhood by oath, bound to our Empire, bound to you."

Zade's gaze sails across the congregation, like a god looking down on his servants, and I can't help but notice the excitement bubbling through the crowd. This moment is truly something they value—a regal event within their society.

"Let us not wait a moment longer to initiate the firstborn heir of the Thorne legacy into our ranks," Zade says as Sawyer stands, fixing his suit jacket, more than ready to put on a show for his people. He goes to take a step as Zade continues, welcoming him before the eager crowd. Only, Zade's gaze falls away to someone else in the crowd. "Put your hands together as we welcome his heir to take the sacrificial oath of servitude to our people, Miss Cara Maisie Thorne."

My jaw drops, my gaze swiveling to Cara to see nothing but horror in her stare as she clutches her mother, looking around as though there's been some kind of terrible mistake. She shakes her head violently as gasps sound through the old church, both Dalton and Easton muttering under their breath beside me.

"The fuck?" Sawyer demands as the other members of The Circle get to their feet in outrage. Sawyer pushes ahead, moving toward Zade and looking at him with venom. "What the hell are you doing? *I'm* the heir. I'm my father's firstborn child. Besides, she's a woman. She can't move into a position of leadership, even if she was the heir."

The whole fucking church is up in arms, people standing within their pews yelling obscenities toward Zade, clearly not approving of the idea of welcoming a female into their ranks—especially into a position of power.

Zade clenches his jaw. "I have no choice," he spits, clearly uncomfortable with this too. "I must follow through on our laws. Cara Thorne is Nikolai's firstborn child. She is his heir."

"No," Sawyer spits. "Check the fucking records. I am. My father trained me for this. It is written within his vows, in his legacy, that I am to inherit his position within The Circle. He's prepared me my whole fucking life. I won't allow you to do this. Don't ruin her life."

Zade lets out a heavy breath, and it's clear just how much weight he holds on his shoulders. "Sawyer," he murmurs, lowering his voice. "I'm sorry, brother. I don't want this any more than you do, but your father lied to you. Cara is the firstborn. He told me when I visited him in his cell. He had hoped to find a way to change the laws to make you his heir, but he ran out of time. Cara was always the one who was fated to rise in our ranks. Not you."

"No," he says, shaking his head, refusing to believe it as people in the crowd start yelling out, demanding to see the by-laws. Sawyer glances back at Cara, desperately trying to figure out a way to save her from this hellish life, desperation pulsing through him. His stare turns to his mother's, his eyes widening just a fraction as he throws himself at her feet, clutching her hands. "Please, tell me this is wrong. Cara can't be thrown into the brotherhood. They'll slaughter her at the first chance."

His mom breaks, tears filling her eyes as she grasps both of her children's hands. "It's true," she cries. "Cara was delivered first. She is my firstborn child and fated to inherit your father's role. I'm sorry, Sawyer. We should have told you, but we had hoped . . . thought we had more time. Thought your father could find a way to save her."

Sawyer throws himself back to his feet and runs his hands through his hair as Cara desperately tries to pull out of her mother's grasp, more than ready to bolt out of here in overwhelming panic. "I . . . I can't . . . No. This isn't right. This isn't . . . Sawyer was meant to inherit it, not me. I can't. They'll kill me."

"Come. Now," Zade says, rich authority in his tone that demands a captive audience.

Cara swallows hard as Sawyer watches on in disbelief. My heart aches for him, knowing he can't save his sister just as much as he can't save me. Cara stands on shaky legs and makes her way toward Zade. Her eyes flick between her mom, her brother, the enraged crowd, and Zade.

Sawyer falls to his knees, his lifelong training from his father making him one of the only people in this room who would know exactly what Cara is about to face once her oath has been made.

She stands shakily at the front of the church as Zade looks out at his people. "I know this is unexpected. Unheard of, in fact. However, Cara is the rightful heir to inherit her father's role. She is the eldest-born child and will be initiated into our ranks."

"No," she panics. "The by-laws state that anyone in leadership, whether that be The Circle or higher, must be male." The crowd erupts in agreement, more than happy to have Cara's back if it means getting her out of there.

"That's not exactly what it says," Zade says, giving me a pointed stare and making my back stiffen. "I have personally scoured through the by-laws, and it states that The Circle was created on the shoulders of a brotherhood, and in death, a new heir shall reign. It does not specify gender, just that they will enter into a brotherhood."

Zade pauses, allowing that to sink in, and my mind starts to spin. Is this specifically for The Circle, or is this for leadership in general? Because if it is, that could mean that I do have the right to claim leadership. I could stand up here right now and tell every last one of these ruthless assholes exactly who I am and save myself. It might be frowned upon, but not an illegal move in this fucked-up game.

"It has been assumed for years that The Circle must be built on the backs of our men," Zade continues, "passed down from father to son, and until now, that has never been put into question. Our by-laws are generations old, not created with the sharp eye for detail we are used to in today's world. Therefore, in order to maintain the sanctity of our sacred laws, Cara Thorne must be initiated as the newest member of The Circle."

Sawyer shakes his head, looking up at Zade, more broken now than when he watched his father's execution. Cara stares back at her brother, fear in her eyes, silently pleading for him to save her, to do something to make this all go away.

One of The Circle members stands with a gun in his hand. "She's only the heir if she's the oldest *living* child," he says. "I say we put a bullet through her head and finish this now."

Without hesitation, Zade lifts his hand, and I barely see the flash of his gun before the bullet is flying from the chamber, the loud *BANG* reverberating through my chest. The bullet slams into The Circle member's shoulder and the asshole goes down with an agonized roar, blood seeping between his fingers as he clutches his wound.

"Anybody else feel like questioning me?" Zade asks, his voice booming through the church as my hands shake. The overwhelming need to stand and declare myself takes over my every need and desire.

My knees bounce, desperation pounding through my veins, fueling my every thought.

Go, Oakley. Tell the world who you are. Put an end to this. Save yourself.

Zade meets my stare, his eyes widening with just a hint of fear, and it's as though he has a window straight through to my thoughts. He subtly shakes his head, warning me not to do a damn thing, but I have to do it. I have to give myself a fighting chance—even if it means taking away every last one of Zade's hopes and dreams.

I have to do it.

Swallowing hard, I throw myself to my feet, my head raised high, and without a second to even figure out how this is going to go down, I push forward, hastily making my way toward the dais. My heart pounds, fear and determination blasting through my body.

Just one more step. One more breath, and I'll give myself the freedom to live another day.

Eyes begin to turn toward me as I hold Zade's stare, taking in his raw fury, but not even he can stop me now. I'm seeing this through. I'm telling my truth, and I'm claiming back what's rightfully mine.

I am the rightful blood heir, and I'm going to steal it back in the same way it was stolen from me.

Check-fucking-mate, Zade DeVil.

Power rocks through my veins, and as I go to position myself in front of the church, ready to face the people who will be mine one day, a strong hand locks around my arm, yanking me back against a hard chest.

I go to let out a squeal when Easton's hand clamps down over my mouth, dragging me back before a single word can even come out of my mouth. "Don't be fucking stupid," he growls in my ear, dragging me to the very edge of the church as Zade meets Easton's stare, giving him a firm nod. No matter what bullshit comes out of their mouths, they will always value Empire's fucked-up laws and rituals over my very life.

My chest aches with hopelessness, feeling my only chance slipping through my fingers as Easton pulls me back behind a velvet curtain, masking us from the men and women of Empire.

I claw at his hand, seeing a side exit that Easton leads me to when I hear Zade's booming tone on the other side of the curtain. "Let us commence," he says, his tone lowering again. "Repeat after me. I, Cara Maisie Thorne, stand before you with the blessing of the brotherhood to make the sacrificial oath of servitude to our people."

There's a short pause as we reach the side exit. "I, Cara Maisie Thorne," she cries as Easton drags me kicking and screaming through the side exit, "stand before you with the blessing of the brotherhood to make the sacrificial oath—"

Her words cut off when Easton slams the door closed between us, and without a moment of hesitation, he drags me back out to the Escalade, throws me in across the backseat, and slams the door behind him as rage blasts through my veins.

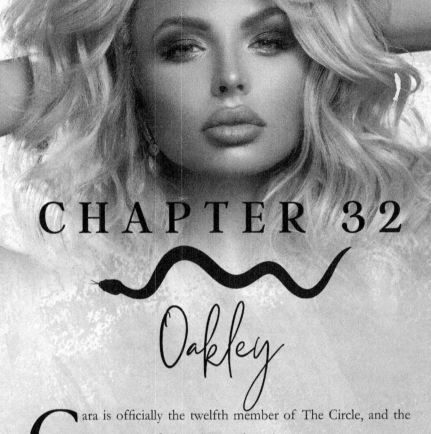

CHAPTER 32

Oakley

Cara is officially the twelfth member of The Circle, and the twins are not fucking happy about it.

We stand in the same storeroom I'd been in during Empire's annual ball all those weeks ago, the first time I'd let Easton and Sawyer touch me. Fuck, I'd give anything to go back to that—to a time when I thought a few strange guys in a secret society was as bad as life was going to get.

A huge celebration rages just outside the doors, and despite the booming music and noise coming from the eager partiers, all I seem to hear is the arrogant, brutal argument tearing through the storeroom. And fuck, you better believe I'm getting in on the action.

My hands shove violently against Zade's chest as I get right in his face. "YOU FUCKING ASSHOLE," I roar, tears stinging my eyes.

His jaw clenches, coming right back at me, but Sawyer cuts in, his fist flying toward Zade's jaw just as Dalton's arm locks around my waist and hauls me out of the way, shoving me back behind them as a brawl breaks out. "You've known for four fucking days, and you didn't say a goddamn word, you fucking bastard," Sawyer booms as Cara squeals, desperately trying to grab Sawyer and haul him back.

Easton rushes in, trying to get between the boys, but this isn't like last time when Zade just stood there and took Sawyer's anger. This time, he fights back. I suppose he's met his quota of bullshit he's willing to shoulder for one day. "And what the fuck would you have done?" Zade throws back at him, returning with a devastating blow that rocks Sawyer back and pushes him straight into his sister. "The only way out for her is death. Abrahms was right. Would you prefer I put a fucking bullet through her head instead so you can come in pretending to be some fucking gallant knight to protect her? I did what I had to do."

I throw myself right back into it. "No, you did what benefits you best," I spit at him. "Like always. You don't give a shit about anyone but yourself. As long as Zade DeVil still gets to wear a fucking crown on his head, then nothing else matters."

"You don't know what the fuck you're talking about."

"Oh, don't I?" I argue, shoving him again as Easton still tries to hold back Sawyer. Dalton comes for me, trying to grasp my arm only for me to evade him. "You should have told him. She could have had a chance to run, but you don't give a shit, do you? You don't give a shit about Sawyer or his family, and you sure as fuck don't give a shit about the heart beating inside my fucking chest. As long as you get to tear it out at the end of the day, right?"

Zade comes at me, his hand snapping toward my throat as his eyes flame with venomous rage, but Sawyer breaks through Easton's hold and he goes flying back, knocking into Dalton as Cara screams again. But it's the fucking Sawyer show now. He comes bursting through, slamming into Zade like a fucking freight train, taking him to the ground, his fists flying wild and free.

Dalton is quick in on the action, but there's no way to tell if he's actually trying to help or if he's in there just to throw a few punches like the deranged psychopath he is. Easton tries to pull Sawyer off Zade and gets an elbow to the face, which only pisses him off, and in a matter of seconds, all four of them are scuffling on the ground.

All I can do is stare, my mind a fucking whirlwind. How the hell has it come to this?

Cara throws herself on top of the pile, aiming for Zade's throat as I try to calm my racing heart, only there's no fucking use. I've never been so worked up. I'm a means to an end for Zade, and despite everything, he'll still throw me under the bus, just as he did Cara.

I shake my head, my hands balling into fists as a raw desperation fires through me, and my survival instincts kick in. If I stay here, playing the role of the boys' perfect little whorish pet, I will be sacrificed. No doubt about it.

But if I run . . . Fuck. What other choice do I have?

They will never stop coming for me, and I will never find my freedom, but it's better than staying here and handing myself over to Zade's blade. Staying here means giving up, and that's not me. My daddy didn't raise a quitter.

Fuck Dalton, Sawyer, and Easton. I don't even know what it is I have with them, but it's over now. It has to be. I choose me.

As the boys fight it out on the ground, my heart kicks into gear, my hands instantly growing clammy as I whip back to the door. It's been left open after the boys came storming in here, dragging me along with them.

All I would have to do is run.

Glancing back at them, I realize just how quickly time is running out. This fight isn't going to last forever. I have maybe a few seconds to gain some ground on them, so if I'm going to do this, I need to do it now.

A whimper sails through my lips, fear of what's to come threatening to cripple me, but I have to put myself first. I will not give my life for this.

And with that, I turn on my heel and sprint for the door, fear rocking through my chest.

I don't look back as I race through the door and out into the party, coming face to face with the thick crowd. I push my way through the bodies, certain the boys have already realized I'm gone and are coming for me. The ballroom is packed, loud music blasting through my ears as strobe lights flash through the crowd, making it so much harder to navigate.

"MOVE," I roar, desperately trying to get through the crowd, tears streaming down my cheeks. The main door is so far away, and I stare up toward it, knowing there's no way I'll make it in time. They'll find me way before then.

Standing in the middle of the dance floor, I frantically search for a way out before breaking to the right and squeezing past the eager partiers. I catch an accidental elbow to the ribs, but I push through it, ignoring the pain before finally reaching the small door that leads out to the busy kitchen.

Barging through it, I race into the kitchen, my gaze shooting from left to right, searching for a way out. "Miss," one of the chefs calls after me. "You can't be back here."

I search around, frantic and desperate. "Help," I rush out. "Please. I need help."

One of the waitresses stops and grabs my shoulders, looking into my eyes and seeing the pure fear within them. "What's wrong?"

"I need to get out of here. A . . . a window or a back door. Please."

She immediately steps out of my path before pointing further down the kitchen and into the back. "There's a break room through there. It has a window out onto the street."

Racing past her, I don't even stop to say thank you, just push on ahead, my strappy heels slamming down against the dirty kitchen tiles. I push past a small bathroom before running straight into the break room and gripping the blinds. I open them wide, my hands shaking so violently I can barely clutch the window latch.

The window is old, and I have to shove it hard before pushing the table right up against the wall and climbing up onto it. Then gripping the window frame, I let out a shaky breath and haul myself up through it. I have to brace my ass against it, sliding one leg out at a time.

My dress gets caught and rips, but it's the least of my problems as I stare down at the ground below. I'm going to have to jump.

Finding my nerve, I go to push out when I hear a loud roar coming from behind me. "OAKLEY, NO!" I look back, my heart racing with fear, finding Zade and Dalton racing through the kitchen, Sawyer and Easton flying around the corner behind them.

Terror grips me, and knowing this is my only shot to save my life, I jump, hurtling toward the ground as my heart breaks, knowing I have to leave Dalton, Sawyer, and Easton behind.

I fall heavily to the ground, my strappy heels snapping against the concrete as my arms and knees are viciously grazed. Adrenaline pulses through my body and I scramble to my feet, not allowing the pain to affect me.

One foot slams down in front of the other, and I race out onto the road just as Zade's face appears in the open window. "OAKLEY," he roars after me, but I don't dare stop, sprinting ahead.

I get another few feet, knowing they're coming for me when my body is thrown into the air, a loud explosion rocking through the city behind me. A blood-curdling scream tears from my throat as my body slams against a parked car and quickly drops to the ground.

My head spins, and my ears pound from the blast. I'm disoriented and unsure. I can't see through the debris raining down around me, and the fire and smoke cause havoc across the city. I crawl along the ground, unable to find my footing when I rock back, falling onto my ass.

The heat is unbearable as the fire casts an orange glow across Faders Bay, and as my senses finally start to adjust, I look back at the extravagant ballroom to find nothing but an empty shell. The kitchen workers. The partiers. Cara . . . the boys.

Gone.

All gone.

Crippling heartbreak tears through my chest, and I heave for oxygen only to choke on the thick smoke. As tears stream down my dirty face, I hold onto a lamp post and pull myself to my feet, my knees shaking beneath me. Then without a backward glance, I run. Never to return here again.

THANKS FOR READING

If you enjoyed reading this book as much as I enjoyed writing it, please consider leaving an Amazon review to let me know.
https://www.amazon.com/dp/B0BP2D3M4D

EMPIRE EXTRAS

Empire Pinterest Board
https://pin.it/6DZLmZN

Cara's Smut_XPERT Bookstagram
https://www.instagram.com/smut_xpert/

Playlist
https://open.spotify.com/playlist/1NBPuMI15YFObcqC-716Qf0?si=fcb9db9b46084fa1

STALK ME!

Join me online with the rest of the stalkers!!
I swear, I don't bite. Not unless you say please!

Facebook Reader Group
www.facebook.com/SheridansBookishBabes

Facebook Page
www.facebook.com/sheridan.anne.author1

Instagram
www.instagram.com/Sheridan.Anne.Author

TikTok
www.tiktok.com/@Sheridan.Anne.Author

Subscribe to my Newsletter
https://landing.mailerlite.com/webforms/landing/a8q0y0

MORE BY SHERIDAN ANNE

www.amazon.com/Sheridan-Anne/e/B079TLXN6K

YOUNG ADULT / NEW ADULT DARK ROMANCE

Broken Hill High | Haven Falls | Broken Hill Boys
Aston Creek High | Rejects Paradise | Boys of Winter
Depraved Sinners | Bradford Bastard | Empire

NEW ADULT SPORTS ROMANCE

Kings of Denver | Denver Royalty | Rebels Advocate

CONTEMPORARY ROMANCE (standalones)

Play With Fire | Until Autumn (Happily Eva Alpha World)

PARANORMAL ROMANCE

Slayer Academy [Pen name - Cassidy Summers]

Printed in Great Britain
by Amazon

22659407R00214